Lynne Graham

Brides *of* L'Amour

MILLS & BOON

BRIDES OF L'AMOUR © 2024 by Harlequin Books S.A.

THE FRENCHMAN'S LOVE-CHILD
© 2003 by Lynne Graham
Australian Copyright 2003
New Zealand Copyright 2003

First Published 2003
Fourth Australian Paperback Edition 2024
ISBN 978 1 038 90590 1

THE ITALIAN BOSS'S MISTRESS
© 2003 by Lynne Graham
Australian Copyright 2003
New Zealand Copyright 2003

First Published 2003
Fourth Australian Paperback Edition 2024
ISBN 978 1 038 90590 1

THE BANKER'S CONVENIENT WIFE
© 2004 by Lynne Graham
Australian Copyright 2004
New Zealand Copyright 2004

First Published 2004
Third Australian Paperback Edition 2024
ISBN 978 1 038 90590 1

Published by
Mills & Boon
An imprint of Harlequin Enterprises (Australia) Pty Limited (ABN 47 001 180 918), a subsidiary of HarperCollins Publishers Australia Pty Limited (ABN 36 009 913 517)
Level 19, 201 Elizabeth Street
SYDNEY NSW 2000
AUSTRALIA

MIX
Paper | Supporting
responsible forestry
FSC
www.fsc.org   FSC® C001695

® and ™ (apart from those relating to FSC®) are trademarks of Harlequin Enterprises (Australia) Pty Limited or its corporate affiliates. Trademarks indicated with ® are registered in Australia, New Zealand and in other countries. Contact admin_legal@Harlequin.ca for details.

Printed and bound in Australia by McPherson's Printing Group

CONTENTS

The Frenchman's Love-Child

Find more of
Lynne Graham's
fabulous books

BRIDES OF L'AMOUR

*The mother, the mistress
and the forgotten wife...*

Tabby, Pippa and Hilary: three friends whose lives
were changed forever in their teens by
a tragic accident. But the wheel of fortune
must turn up as well as down, and these
young women are about to get their share of
blessings...in the shape of three gorgeous men.
Christien, Andreo and Roel are all determined to
woo them and wed them...whatever that takes!

The Frenchman's Love-Child—
Tabby and Christien's story #2355 November 2003

Coming soon

The Italian Boss's Mistress—
Pippa and Andreo's story #2367 January 2004

The Banker's Convenient Wife—
Hilary and Roel's story #2379 March 2004

CHAPTER ONE

A QUESTIONING FROWN in his keen dark eyes, Christien Laroche studied the portrait of his late great-aunt, Solange. A
quiet woman who had never made a wave in her life, Solange
had nonetheless startled her entire family with the contents of
her will.

'Extraordinary!' a cousin commented with fierce disapproval. 'What could Solange have been thinking of?'

'It grieves me to say it but my poor sister's mind must have
weakened towards the end,' an aghast brother of the deceased
lamented.

'*Vraiment!* To leave a piece of the Duvernay estate away from
her own family and favour a foreigner instead…it is unbelievable!' another exclaimed in outrage.

In a more laid-back mood, Christien would have been struggling not to laugh at the genuine horror that his relatives were
exhibiting. Wealth had not lessened their passionate attach-
ment to the family estate for that atavistic link back to the very
land itself still ran deep and strong in every French soul. But
they *were* all overreacting for the bequest was tiny in terms of
monetary worth. The Duvernay estate ran to many thousands

of acres and the property in question was a little cottage on a mere patch of ground. Even so, Christien had also been angered by a bequest that he considered both regrettable and highly inappropriate. Why had his great-aunt left anything at all to a young woman she had only met a few times several years earlier? That was the biggest mystery and one he would have given much to comprehend.

'Indeed, Solange must have been very ill for her will is a terrible insult to my feelings,' his widowed mother, Matilde, complained tearfully. 'That girl's father murdered my husband, yet my own aunt has rewarded her!'

Lean, strong face grim at the speed with which his parent had made that unfortunate connection, Christien remained by the elegant windows that overlooked Duvernay's glorious gardens while the lady who acted as his mother's companion comforted the weeping older woman. Although almost four years had passed since his father's death, Matilde Laroche still lived behind lowered blinds in her huge Paris apartment, wore the dark colours of mourning and rarely went out or entertained. Christien was now challenged to recall that his mother had once been an outgoing personality with a warm sense of humour. Indeed in the radius of her unending grief he felt helpless for neither counselling nor medication had managed to alleviate her suffering to any appreciable degree.

At the same time, it was only fair to acknowledge that Matilde Laroche *had* suffered a devastating loss. His parents had been childhood sweethearts and lifelong best friends and their marriage had been one of unusual intimacy. Furthermore, his father had only been fifty-four when he died. A prominent banker, Henri Laroche had rejoiced in the vigour and health of a man in the very prime of life. However, that had not protected Christien's father from a cruelly premature and pointless death at the hands of a drunk driver.

That drunken driver had been Tabitha Burnside's father, Gerry. In all, five families had been shattered that appalling night by just *one* car accident and Henri Laroche had not been the only casualty. Gerry Burnside had also managed to kill himself, four of his passengers and leave a fifth seriously injured, who later died.

That fatal summer, four English families had been sharing the rambling farmhouse situated just down the hill from the imposing Laroche vacation home in the Dordogne. His late father had remarked that he should have bought the property himself to prevent it being occupied throughout the season by a horde of noisy holiday-makers. Naturally no Laroche would have dreamt of mixing with tourists, whose sole idea of amusement seemed to rest on getting sunburnt, drunk and eating too much. However, his parents had only stayed at their villa on a couple of occasions that summer and most weeks, aside of visits from his friends and initially from his lover at the time, Christien had been left in peace to work.

There had been three Burnsides in the large party staying at the farmhouse: Gerry Burnside, his youthful second wife, Lisa, and his daughter from his first marriage, Tabby. Before Christien had met Tabby, he had only ever seen the two young women at a distance and would not have been able to distinguish one from the other. Both Lisa and Tabby had been shapely blondes and, not only had he initially assumed that they were sisters he had also assumed that they were of a similar age. He had had no idea whatsoever that *one* of them had been still only a schoolgirl...

Of course, even at a distance, Tabby had had promiscuous tramp written all over her, Christien conceded wryly, his wide sensual mouth curling with disdain. Like most young males in the grip of rampant lust, however, he had still been an eager participant in all that had followed. Tabby's nude nightly swimming sessions in the *gîte*'s underwater-lit pool could only have been staged for his benefit. He would not have stayed home specially to watch her, but, on the evenings that he had enjoyed a glass of wine on the villa terrace, her provocative displays of her full breasts and deliciously curved bottom had provided him with considerable entertainment.

He didn't blame himself for enjoying the view. Any guy would have got hot and hard watching her flaunt her charms. Any guy would have decided that, at the first opportunity, he would take immediate advantage of so obvious an invitation. Of course, it had not occurred to Christien then to wonder why Tabby so often stayed at home while the rest of the party dined out every evening. Only with hindsight had he appreciated that she must have been targeting him all along. Of course, she had first seen him in the village and would soon have found out who he was and, perhaps more crucially, what he was worth. Realising that the Laroche villa overlooked the pool at the farmhouse, she had guessed that sooner or later he was certain to catch a glimpse of her bathing naked.

That from the outset Tabby should have set out to entrap him surprised Christien not at all. Even as a teenager, he had learnt that women found his sleek, dark good looks irresistible and were capable of going to extraordinary lengths to attract his attention. But he had never been vain about his phenomenal success with the female sex. He was well aware that sex and money together provided a powerful draw. He had been born very, very rich. He was an only child, born to two wealthy only children and, as an adult, he had become even richer.

Blessed with the Laroche talent for making money and sensational entrepreneurial skills, Christien had dropped out of university at the age of twenty. Within nine months, he had made his first million in business. Five years on from there, sole owner of an international airline that was breaking all profit records, and suffering from a certain amount of burn-out from working a seven-day week, Christien had been getting bored. That summer, he had been ripe for something a little different and Tabby had more than satisfied him in that department.

Tabby had played no games and she had come to him on his terms. He had had her on the first date. Six weeks of the wildest sex he had ever experienced had followed. He had been obsessed with her. Her strange insistence on not staying the night in his bed and keeping their entanglement a secret from her family and their friends had added an illicit thrill to their every encounter. What he would never, ever forget, however, was that after only six weeks of explosive sexual fulfilment he had been ready to propose marriage so that he could have access to that fabulous body of hers at all hours of the day.

Marriage! Christien still shuddered at that degrading recollection. His meteoric IQ rating had not done him much good while the urge to indulge his powerful libido had overruled every other restraint. The shattering discovery that he had been making love to a schoolgirl had blown him away. A schoolgirl of seventeen, who was a compulsive liar!

While Veronique had been agonising over how best he might protect himself from the threat of a horrendous scandal, Christien had still been so lost in lust that he had decided that he could cope with a teenage wife whom he would teach to tell the truth and keep in bed most of the time anyway. But, the next day, he had seen his potential child bride behaving like a slut with a spotty youth on a motorbike and, all rage, disbelief and disgust aside, he had immediately broken free of his obsession...

'If that Burnside girl sets foot on Laroche soil, it will dishonour your father's memory!' Matilde Laroche protested.

Drawn from his brooding recollections with a vengeance, Christien almost winced at the tearful note in his mother's overwrought exclamation. 'There is no question of that happening,' he asserted with soothing conviction. 'She will receive an offer to sell the property back to the estate and she will naturally accept the money.'

'This matter is so unpleasant for you to deal with,' Veronique remarked in a sympathetic and discreet murmur at his side. 'Allow me to take care of it for you.'

'As always you are generous, but in this case there is no need.'

Christien surveyed the beautiful, elegant brunette he planned to marry with open appreciation.

Veronique Giraud was everything a Laroche wife should be. He had known her all his life and their backgrounds were similar. A corporate lawyer, she was an excellent hostess as well as being tolerant of her future mother-in-law's emotional fragility. But neither love nor lust featured in Christien's relationship with his fiancée. Both of them considered mutual respect and honesty of greater importance. Although Veronique was naturally willing to give him children, she had little enthusiasm for physical intimacy and had already made it clear that she would prefer him to satisfy his needs with a mistress.

Christien was quite content with that arrangement. Indeed the knowledge that even marriage would not deprive him of that valuable male freedom to essentially do as he liked, when he liked, had very much increased his willingness to embrace the matrimonial bond.

In little more than a month, he would be over in London on business. He would pay Tabby Burnside a visit and offer to buy the cottage back from her. No doubt she would feel flattered by his personal attention. He wondered what she looked like some years on…faded? At only twenty-one? He almost shrugged. What did it matter to him? But he also smiled.

A house in France, Tabby reflected dreamily, a place of their own in the sun…

'Of course, you'll sell the old lady's cottage for the best price you can get,' Alison Davies assumed on her niece's behalf. 'It'll fetch a healthy sum.'

Fresh, clean country air in exchange for the city traffic fumes that she was convinced had made her toddler son prone to asthma, Tabby thought happily.

'You and Jake will have something to put away for a rainy day.' Her aunt, a slender brunette with sensible grey eyes, nodded with approval at that idea.

Lost in her own thoughts, Tabby was still mulling over the extraordinary fact that Solange Roussel had left her a French property. It was fate, it *had* to be. Of that latter reality, Tabby was convinced. Her son had French blood in his veins and now, by an immense stroke of good fortune and when she least expected it, she had inherited a home for them both on French soil. Of course that was meant to be! Who could possibly doubt it? She looked into the small back garden where Jake was playing. He was an enchanting child with mischievous brown eyes, skin with a warm olive tone and a shock of silky dark curls. His asthma was only mild at present, but who could say how much worse it might get if they remained in London?

The same day that the letter from the French *notaire* had arrived to inform her of her inheritance, Tabby had begun planning a new life for herself and her child in France. After all, the timing could not have been more perfect: Tabby had been desperate to come up with an acceptable excuse for moving out of her aunt's comfortable town house. Alison Davies was only ten years older than her niece. When, in the wake of her father's death, Tabby had been left penniless and pregnant into the bargain, Alison had offered her niece a home. Tabby was very aware of how great a debt of gratitude she owed to the other woman.

But, just a week earlier, Tabby had overheard a heated exchange between Alison and her boyfriend, Edward, which had left her squirming with guilty discomfiture. Edward was going to take a year out from work to travel. Tabby had already known that and she had also been aware that her aunt had decided not to accompany him. What Tabby had not realised, until she accidentally heard the couple arguing, was that Alison Davies might be denying herself her heart's desire sooner than ask her niece to find somewhere else to live.

'You don't need to use up your precious savings! Thanks to your parents you own this house and you could rent it out for a small fortune while we were abroad. That would cover *all* your expenses,' Edward had been pointing out forcefully in the kitchen when Tabby, having returned from her evening job, had been fumbling for her key outside the back door.

'We've been over this before,' Alison had been protesting unhappily. 'I just *can't* ask Tabby to move out so that I can offer this place to strangers. She can't afford decent accommodation—'

'And whose fault is that? She got pregnant at seventeen and now she's paying for her foolish mistake!' Edward had slammed back angrily. 'Does that mean *we* have to pay for it too? Isn't it bad enough that we're rarely alone together and that when we are you're always babysitting her kid?'

Tabby was still terribly hurt and mortified by the memory of that biting censure. But she regarded it as justifiable criticism. She felt that she ought to have seen for herself that she had overstayed her welcome in her aunt's home. She was appalled that Alison should have been prepared to make such a sacrifice on her behalf, for her aunt had already been very generous to her. Indeed, all that Tabby could now think about was moving out as soon as was humanly possible. Only then would Alison feel free to do as she liked with her own life and her own home. At the same time, however, she did not want the other woman to suspect that she might have overheard that revealing dialogue.

'I'm afraid I *still* can't stop wondering why some elderly French lady should have remembered you in her will,' Alison Davies confided with a bemused shake of her head.

Dragged out of her own preoccupied thoughts by the raising of that topic yet again, Tabby screened her expressive green eyes and looped a stray strand of caramel-blonde hair back behind one small ear. Some things were too personal and private to share even with her aunt. 'Solange and I got on very well—'

'But you only met a couple of times...'

'You've got to remember that what she's left me can only be a tiny part of what she owned because she was very well off,' Tabby muttered in an awkward attempt to explain. 'I'm over the

moon that she's left me the cottage but I suppose in her eyes…
it was just a little token.'

Tabby was reluctant to admit that, on each of the occasions
she had met Solange Roussel, she had connected with the older
woman on a very emotional level. The first time she had been
bubbling with happiness and quite unafraid to admit that she
adored Christien. The second time she had been a lot less sure
of herself and she had not been able to hide her fear that Christien was losing interest…and the third and final time?

Months after that fatal French holiday that had torn apart so
many lives, Tabby had travelled back to France alone to attend
the accident enquiry. She had been desperate to see Christien
again. She had believed that the passage of time would have
eased his bitterness and helped him to acknowledge that they
had *both* lost much-loved parents in that horrendous crash. However, she had soon learnt her mistake for, if anything, the intervening months had only made Christien colder and more
derisive. Even Veronique, who had once been so friendly towards her, had become distant and hostile. As Gerry Burnside's
daughter, Tabby had become a pariah to everyone who had lost
a relative or been injured in any way by that car crash.

On the day of that enquiry Tabby had finally grown up and
it had been almost as cruel and life-changing an ordeal for her
as the aftermath of that car accident. Even though the previous
months had been a nightmare struggle for Tabby to get through,
and she had had to borrow money from her aunt just to make
that trip back to France, she had still been full of naive hopes
and dreams of how Christien would react to the news that he
was the father of her newborn baby boy.

But on the day of that official hearing, her dream castles had
crumbled into dust. In the end she had not even got to tell Christien that she had given birth to his son, for she had baulked at
making that announcement in front of an audience and he had
refused her request for a moment's privacy in which to talk.
Devastated by that merciless refusal to accord her even the tini-

est privilege in acknowledgement of their past intimacy, Tabby had fled outside sooner than break down in tears in front of him, his relatives and friends. Out there in the street a hand had closed over hers in a comforting but shy gesture. In disconcertion, Tabby had glanced up to meet the look of pained compassion in Solange Roussel's understanding gaze.

'I'm sorry that the family should have come between you and Christien,' the older woman had sighed with sincere regret. 'It should not be that way.'

Before Tabby had been able to respond and admit that she suspected something rather less presentable than family loyalties might ultimately have led to her having been dumped by Christien, Solange had hurried back into the building where the enquiry was being held. His great-aunt had doubtless been fearful of being seen to show sympathy to the drunk driver's daughter.

'You are planning to sell this French property…*aren't* you?' Alison pressed without warning.

Tabby drew in a deep breath in preparation for breaking news that she knew would surprise the brunette. 'No… I'm hoping to keep it.'

Her aunt frowned. 'But the cottage is on Christien Laroche's Brittany estate…isn't it?'

'Solange said that Christien rarely went to Duvernay because he much prefers the city to the country,' Tabby volunteered stiffly, for even voicing *his* name out loud was a challenge for her. 'She also told me that the estate was absolutely enormous and that her little place was right on the very edge of it. If I keep myself to myself, as I plan to do, he's not even going to know I'm there!'

Alison still looked troubled. 'Are you sure that you aren't secretly hoping to see him again?'

'Of course, I'm not!' Tabby grimaced in embarrassment. 'Why would I want to see him again?'

'To tell him about Jake?'

'I don't want to tell him about Jake now. The time for that has been and gone.' Tabby tilted up her chin for if Christien and his snobby, judgemental family had been affronted even by the sight of *her* at that accident enquiry, her son's very existence would surely only further offend and disgust them. 'Jake's mine and we're managing fine.'

Alison said nothing, for she was not convinced and she knew just how vulnerable Tabby could be with her open heart and trusting nature. She had always felt very protective towards her late sister's only child and she was well aware of the dangerous effect that her niece appeared to have on the opposite sex. Tabby had blonde hair the colour of streaky toffee, green eyes, dimples and an incredible figure that bore a close resemblance to an old-fashioned hourglass. The one quality that Tabby had in super-abundance was the sort of natural sex appeal that caused havoc.

When Tabby walked down the street, men were so busy craning their necks to get a better look at her luscious curves that they had been known to crash their cars. In actuality misfortune *did* seem to follow Tabby around, Alison conceded ruefully, thinking of the amount of bad luck that had shaped her niece's life in recent years. Yet, Tabby would still rush into situations where angels feared to tread and, even though the results were often disastrous, she remained an incurable optimist.

Reminding herself of that fact, Alison rested anxious grey eyes on the young woman seated opposite her. 'I hate to rain on your parade, *but*... I suspect you haven't considered how expensive it would be to maintain a holiday home in another country.'

'Oh, I'm not thinking of the cottage as a holiday home! My goodness, is that what you thought?' Tabby laughed out loud at the very idea. 'I'm talking about a permanent move...about Jake and I making a new life in France—'

Startled by that sudden announcement, her aunt stared at her. 'But you can't do that—'

'Why not? I can do my miniature work anywhere and sell

what I make on the internet. I'm already building up a customer base and what could be more inspiring than the French landscape?' Tabby asked with sunny enthusiasm. 'I know that to start with things will be tight financially, but, because I own the cottage, I won't need much of an income to get by on. Jake's at the perfect age to move abroad and learn a second language as well—'

'For goodness' sake, you're making all these plans and you haven't even *seen* this cottage yet!' Alison exclaimed in reproof.

'I know.' Tabby grinned. 'But I'm planning to go over on the ferry next week to check it out.'

'What if it's uninhabitable?'

Tabby squared her slight shoulders. 'I'll deal with that when I see it.'

'I just don't think that you're being practical,' Alison Davies said more gently. 'Going to live abroad may seem like an exciting proposition, but you have Jake to consider. You'll have no support network to fall back on in France, nobody to help out if you need to work or you fall ill.'

'But I'm looking forward to being independent.'

At that declaration, her companion looked taken aback and then rather hurt.

Steeling herself to press home that point, Tabby swallowed hard for she knew it was the most convincing argument that she could put forward. 'I need to stand on my own feet, Alison... I'm twenty-one now.'

Her cheeks rather flushed, her aunt got up and began clearing away the supper dishes. 'I can understand that but I don't want you to burn your boats here and then find out too late that you've made an awful mistake.'

Tabby sat there and thought about all the mistakes she had made. Jake came running in the back door and ran full tilt into her arms. Breathless, laughing and smelling of fresh air and muddy little boy, he scrambled onto her knee and gave her a boisterous hug. 'I love you, Mum,' he said chirpily.

Her eyes stung and she held him tight. Most people were too polite or kind to say it, but she knew that they all thought Jake was her biggest mistake so far. Yet when Tabby's life had fallen apart only the prospect of the baby she'd carried had given her the strength to keep going and trust that the future would be happier. Christien had been like the sun in her world and it literally *had* felt like eternal darkness and gloom when he had gone from it again.

A frown still pleating her brows, Alison turned from the sink to study the younger woman again. 'Before you moved in here I worked with a guy called Sean Wendell,' she confided. 'He was mad about France and he moved to Brittany and set up an agency managing rental property. I still hear from Sean every Christmas. Why don't I phone him and ask him to give you some support while you're over there?'

As Tabby emerged from her preoccupation to give her aunt a look of surprise the brunette grimaced. 'I know, I *know*... I shouldn't be interfering but, for my sake, let Sean help out. If you don't, I'll be worrying myself sick about you!'

'But exactly what am I going to need support with?' Tabby enquired ruefully.

'Well, for a start you'll have to deal with the *notaire* and there's sure to be a few legalities to sort out. Your French is fairly basic and might not be up to the challenge.'

Tabby knew that her linguistic skills were rusty but was dismayed by the prospect of being saddled with a stranger. In truth, though, at that moment it was hard for Tabby to focus her mind on what was only a minor annoyance because the past had a far stronger hold on her thoughts. As she helped Jake get ready for bed, memories that were both painful and exhilarating were starting to drag her back almost four years in time to that summer that already seemed a lifetime ago...

For all of her childhood that she could remember, the Burnside family and their three closest friends—the Stevensons, the Rosses and the Tarberts—had gone to the Dordogne for their

annual holiday and either rented *gîtes* very close to each other
or found accommodation large enough to share. The Stevensons had had a daughter called Pippa who was the same age
as Tabby and her best friend. The Ross family had had two
daughters, Hilary, who was six months younger and her kid
sister, Emma and the Tarberts had had one daughter, Jen. Way
back when Tabby, Pippa, Hilary and Jen had been toddlers, the
girls had attended the same church playgroup and their mothers
had become friendly. Even though their respective families had
eventually moved to other locations and much had changed in
all their lives, those friendships had endured and the vacations
in France had continued.

But in the autumn of Tabby's sixteenth year, the contented
family life that she had pretty much taken for granted had vanished without any warning whatsoever. Her mother had caught
influenza and had died from a complication. Gerry Burnside
had been devastated by his wife's sudden death but just six short
months later, and without discussing his plans with anybody,
he had remarried. His second wife, Lisa, had been the twenty-
two-year-old blonde receptionist who had worked in his car
sales showroom. Tabby had been as shattered by that startling
development as everybody else had been.

Almost overnight her father had turned into an unfamiliar
stranger, determined to dress like a much younger man and
party and behave like one too. He had no longer had time to
spare for his daughter, because his bride had not only been
jealous of his attention but also prone to throwing screaming
tantrums if she hadn't got it. To please Lisa, he had bought another house and spent a fortune on it. From the start, Lisa had
resented Tabby and had made it clear that her stepdaughter had
been an unwelcome third wheel.

Lisa had certainly not wanted to go on the traditional French
holiday with her husband's friends that summer, but for once
Gerry Burnside had stood his ground. Full of resentment, Lisa
had made no attempt to fit in and had gloried in shocking her

besotted husband's friends with her behaviour. A helpless on-looker suffering from all the supersensitivity of a teenager, Tabby had died a thousand deaths of embarrassment and had avoided being in the adults' company as much as she'd been able.

At the same time, unfortunately, Tabby had also felt like a fish out of water with Pippa, Hilary and Jen. Her friends, with their stable homes and loving parents still safe and intact, had seemed aeons removed from her in their every innocence. In addition she had been too loyal to her father to tell anyone just how dreadfully unhappy and isolated she'd been feeling. And then she had seen Christien and all her own petty anxieties and the rest of the world, and indeed everyone in it, had no longer existed for her.

It had only been the second day of their vacation. Mulling over the humiliation of having been called a 'nasty little bitch' and sworn at by Lisa in front of Pippa's aghast parents at break-fast time, Tabby had been sitting on the wall under the plane trees in the sleepy little village below the farmhouse. A long, low yellow sports car had growled down the hill and round the corner like a snarling beast and had come to a throaty, purring halt a little further down the street.

A very tall, well-built male wearing sunglasses had climbed out and sauntered into the little pavement café. Clad in an off-white shirt with the cuffs carelessly turned back and beige chi-nos of faultless cut, he had sunk down at a table and tossed a note to the owner's son, who had run into the shop next door to fetch him a newspaper. He had been so cool she had been welded to his every move.

The bar owner had greeted him with pronounced respect and had polished his already clean table. The coffee and the ubiqui-tous croissant had been delivered with an understated flourish and a moment later the newspaper. The little scene had been *so* French she had been fascinated. Then Christien had hooked his sunglasses into the pocket of his shirt. She had found herself staring at that lean bronzed face, the black hair flopping over his brow, the stunning dark-as-midnight eyes that seemed to glint gold in the sunlight, and her heart had hammered so fast it had been quite impossible for her to breathe.

For a heartbeat in time, Christien had looked back at her and she had been mesmerised, entrapped, taken by storm. That one look had been all it had taken. *Un coup de foudre*, love like lightning striking fast and hard. He had turned his attention to his newspaper. She had feasted her eyes on him, quite content just to stare and admire and marvel at his lithe bronzed perfection. Eventually he had strolled back across the pavement and swung back into his equally beautiful car and driven off again...slowly, certainly slowly enough to get a good look at her from behind his tinted car windows.

'Who is he?' she had asked the sullen youth who cleaned the pool at the farmhouse.

He had not recognised her enraptured description of Christien, but he had recognised the car she had described. 'Christien Laroche...his family have a villa up the hill. He's richer than a bank.'

'Is he married?'

'You must be joking. He has a string of hot slick chicks. Why? Do you fancy your chances? You'd only be a baby to a bigshot businessman like him!' he had mocked.

On that recollection Tabby forced her thoughts back into the present, but she was annoyed with herself for thinking about Christien. Solange's legacy had tempted her into looking back to events that had no relevance except insofar as they had taught her a few much-needed lessons. She tucked Christien's son into bed and smiled down at him with tender appreciation. Whether she liked it or not, even at three years old Jake was his father in miniature, for his looks and height were pure Laroche and he was much too clever for his own good. But, if Tabby had anything to do with it, Jake would never, ever regard women as numbers to be scored off on some sexual hit list.

The following week, Tabby sold the one valuable item that she still possessed: a diamond hair clip that Christien had once given her. It did not hurt to part with it as she had not worn it since the night he'd given it to her and she did not live a life where diamond hair clips were of any use. She was delighted to discover that the clip was worth a great deal more money than she had ever appreciated. Indeed, with careful handling the proceeds of the sale enabled her to buy an old van to use for transport and left her with enough cash to meet the other expenses entailed in moving across the English Channel. Alison had persuaded her to make her first trip to France alone and Tabby planned to leave her son in her aunt's care over a long weekend. The cottage was certain to need a good clean and clouds of dust would only leave poor Jake coughing and wheezing.

One week before her departure, Tabby had just got back from taking Jake to nursery school and was in the midst of eating her breakfast when the doorbell sounded. A piece of toast in her hand, she went to answer the front door. When she had to tip her head back to get a proper look at the tall dark male in the charcoal-grey business suit poised on the step, her toast fell from her nerveless fingers.

'I would have phoned to tell you that I intended to call, but your aunt's number is unlisted,' Christien murmured, smooth as glass.

The breath feathered in Tabby's constricted throat. His fabulous accent purred down her spine like the tantalising promise of something dark and forbidden. Her senses snapped onto instant alert and she could not drag her bewildered gaze from his lean, dark, exotic features. Without even knowing she was doing it, she backed away, reacting to a subconscious feeling of being under threat. Exciting threat, though, delicious threat, the kind of threat that appealed to all that was weak and wanton in her nature. But he *was* even more irresistible than she remembered and, no matter how much she hated herself for it, her heart was already thumping like a road drill inside her.

Yet she could not really believe that Christien Laroche stood in front of her again, that he should be on the brink of entering Alison's home or that he should even deign to speak to her. How *could* that feel real?

Tabby trembled, dilated eyes green as emeralds pinned to him. At their last meeting, he had regarded her with a derisive distaste that had pierced her like a knife, and there might as well have been poison on that blade for the pain had not ended there. She had hated herself for loving him, loathed herself for the craving she could not suppress and despised her sorry self for striving to trace Christien's features in her son's innocent baby face.

'What are you doing here?' Tabby breathed shakily.

His brilliant dark eyes narrowed and a slight curve that only hinted at a smile softened the line of his wide, firm male mouth as he thrust the door shut in his wake. He dominated the space she was in and shrunk the hall of Alison's house to claustrophobic proportions. He was much taller, broader and more powerfully impressive than she had ever allowed herself to recall. Breathtakingly good-looking too, and very well aware of the fact. He was the type of guy she should have run a mile from. That she had not had the wit to run, that she had to her own everlasting shame ended up in his bed within hours of first meeting him, was a continuing source of deep mortification to her.

'I've come to make you an offer you can't refuse.'

'Oh, I can refuse, all right…there isn't anything you could offer me that I wouldn't refuse!' Tabby launched back at him as wildly as though he were offering her the seven deadly sins all packed together in one handy bag.

Unmoved, watchful, Christien studied her, his attention travelling from the tumbling mane of her caramel-blonde hair to her bright eyes and the freckles scattered across her slanted cheekbones. But his gaze lingered longest on the soft, vulnerable fullness of her mouth. He only had to look at her ripe pink lips to remember how the caress of them had once felt against his skin. As his body betrayed him by hardening in instantaneous response and he recalled that no other woman had since given him that much pleasure, but that she had gone behind his back with some lout on a Harley-Davidson, raw anger seized Christien without warning.

'You want to take a bet on that, *chérie*?' he demanded in his sexy, whiplash drawl.

CHAPTER TWO

'I DON'T BET on a certainty and I didn't ask you to come in!' Beneath the insolent onslaught of Christien's appraisal, Tabby's rounded face was burning like a furnace.

Nobody, but nobody, could do insolence as well as Christien Laroche did. Arrogant dark head high, he could elevate one satiric brow and make people feel about an inch tall. It was a talent that came from being the latest in the line of several hundred years of ancestors, every one of whom had thought of themselves as an exceptional being. Self-assured to a degree that was intimidating, Christien knew himself to be superior to most in intelligence and it could not be said that that knowledge had made him humble.

'But then you were never very good at saying no to me, *ma belle*,' Christien countered with silken sibilance.

Tabby flinched. Her hands snapped into small fists while he continued to look her over as though she were human flesh adorned with a sale board. His bold scrutiny lingered on the firm jut of her full breasts below the faded red T-shirt she wore and Tabby got even tenser. Beneath her bra, her own body was letting her down by reacting to his visual attention. As her tender nipples pinched into straining prominence, Tabby spun round and headed fast into the sitting room.

Already she could barely think straight. Christien had always had that effect on her but she was also feeling humiliated. How could she argue with him? She had never managed to say no to him, had never wanted to. She had been *enslaved*. Even though she had been a virgin when they had met, from somewhere inside her he had somehow brought out a secret slut whom she had never dreamt existed. He was the one male in the world whom she should never have met, for with him she had discovered she was without defence.

Christien would not allow himself to take further note of the effect of that faded red cotton stretching across her lethally bountiful chest. Expelling his breath on a slow, pent-up hiss of annoyance as he found himself wondering how she would react if he just reached for her as he had once done without thought, he planted himself several feet away from temptation. She was not beautiful, he reminded himself. Her nose was a little too large, her mouth a little too wide and she was way too short for elegance. But, for all that, put the whole lot together, throw in the freckles and the dimples that had once laced her glorious smile and he had wanted to veil her like an Arab woman and lock her up in a turret at Duvernay, to be seen, relished and enjoyed solely by himself. Remembering the fierce possessiveness she had once inspired him with, he was gripped by rare discomfiture.

'I would like to buy back the property which my great-aunt left you in her will,' Christien imparted coldly.

Even as he spoke Tabby lost colour. She studied the laminated wood floor, fighting valiantly to overcome a ridiculous sense of hurt and rejection. For what other reason would he have come to see her after so long? He could not even stand for her to own one miserable little piece of what had once been Laroche land and property. Well, that was his bad luck, Tabby thought with sudden anguished bitterness.

'I'm not interested in selling,' Tabby said tightly. 'Obviously, your great-aunt wanted me to have the cottage—'

'*Mais pourquoi*…but why?' Christien asked her. 'That still makes no sense to me.'

Tabby had no intention of telling him that she believed that his great-aunt had felt sorry for her because *he* had broken her heart! Or that, in her opinion, for the older woman to have felt so sympathetic she must once have suffered a similar experience of her own. 'I expect it was just a whim…she was a lovely person,' she framed tautly, for she very much wished that she had had another chance to meet the older woman.

'In France,' Christien drawled in his deep, dark voice, 'it is not the done thing to leave even a small portion of ground to someone outside the family. I am willing to pay well over the market price to ensure that the cottage remains a part of the estate.'

Raging, hurting resentment flared through Tabby, although she was trying very hard to stay calm. Unhappily, discovering the purpose of Christien's visit had only made that an even greater challenge. Three years ago, Christien had icily rejected her pathetic pleas for even a moment alone with him and she did not believe that she would ever forgive him for that. But now the same incredibly wealthy and privileged male was willing to approach her over the head of a cottage that his great-aunt had only used for summer picnics! His behaviour struck Tabby as being horribly cruel and unfeeling.

In any case, *she* might be an outsider but her son had rather more claim than she had to the property, Tabby reminded herself doggedly. Jake's illegitimate birth might have placed him outside their precious family circle but, regardless of that reality, her son had Laroche blood in his veins and he was entitled to a home on French soil. In addition, Solange Roussel had not left Tabby that cottage on the expectation that she would sell it straight back to Christien sight unseen. To Tabby, the very idea of immediately disposing of her inheritance seemed ungrateful and horribly disrespectful to Solange's memory.

'I'm not selling.' Forcing her head up, Tabby connected with his scorching tawny gaze. That fast, a sensation of heat sprang up low in her pelvis and lit every sensitive inch of her flesh with a burning physical awareness of his masculinity that was a pure torment to bear.

'Take a look at the cheque first,' Christien invited, the words thick with his accent, slightly slurred, faint colour accentuating the hard angle of his bold cheekbones.

Blinking in surprise, mouth running dry, Tabby only then noted the cheque he had tossed down onto the dining table in front of the window. Her mind was a complete blank.

'Take the cheque and I'll take you out to lunch.' Christien was aching for her and wondering if he would even make it out of the house without giving way to the megawatt sexual vibes filling the atmosphere.

Where had she heard that before? In her time with him, how many lunches and dinners had she never received? They had not been able to resist each other long enough to reach the restaurant. Once they had ended up in a lay-by. Another time he had done a U-turn in the middle of the road, cursing and laughing at the strength of his desire for her. During their affair, she had lost a stone in weight and had felt lucky to get the chance to rifle the villa's fridge while he'd been asleep.

'I'll *try* to take you out to lunch...' Christien rephrased, golden eyes a smouldering gleam below sensually lowered lashes, his vibrant smile suddenly flashing out to chase the gravity from his sculpted mouth, for he was recalling that U-turn as well.

When he smiled that stunning smile, it brought back so much remembered pain for Tabby that it hurt her to look at him. Having won her release from his spellbinding gaze, she shivered, folded her arms tight in front of herself, suddenly cold and scared inside.

'No, thanks…please take your cheque and leave,' she told him unevenly.

'You don't mean that…you don't *want* that,' Christien purred with immense confidence, all caution thrown to the winds in the face of his own hunger.

No, but she knew that she would never forgive herself if she did not resist him. He had taught her that a level of wanting that went beyond the bounds of common sense or pride was destructive. That he was being his typical arrogant self also helped. He sauntered back into her life after years away and just assumed that she would be as eager for him as she had been at seventeen. But she *was*, wasn't she? And he could feel that in her too, she conceded with a sinking heart, for when had he not been able to read her like a book?

Filled with fear of her own weakness, Tabby said abruptly, 'Is Solange's cottage close to your home at Duvernay?'

Christien frowned. '*Non*…miles by road.'

'Do you go there often?'

In answer, Christien growled with impatience. 'No. I want you to sell. If it is your wish to own property in France, I will instruct an agent to find somewhere more suitable for you.'

'You have no right to demand that I sell!' Tabby snapped in sudden furious denial of all the frightening raw feelings that his very presence was making her relive. 'And who are you to decide what's suitable for me?'

'I can't imagine what you could want with a dwelling in the remoter depths of the Breton countryside. I doubt if it is even habitable. It *has* been almost half a century since the property was used as anything other than a glorified summer house!' In a raw gesture of impatience, Christien raked long, lean brown fingers through his luxuriant black hair. 'Why won't you see sense? Only a Laroche belongs on the Duvernay estate!'

Paling, Tabby turned her head away, wondering why she was letting him make her feel as if she were something less than he was.

'In any case,' Christien murmured in scornful addition, having read a message of poverty in her faded T-shirt and worn jeans, 'You look like the money would be a lot more use to you.'

'How do you know that? You know nothing about me now!' Tabby flung back fiercely, furious that he was putting her down like that. 'What I want...what I need, *anything*!'

Christien dealt her a brooding appraisal, anger at her unexpected stubbornness driving him, for once she had done exactly as he wished without hesitation. '*Au contraire*, I know many things about you that I would rather not know,' he contradicted with a harsh edge to his rich drawl. 'That you're a compulsive liar—'

'No, I'm not. I just told a few fibs. You never *asked* me what age I was!' Tabby argued, feverish colour mantling her cheeks as she surged to her own defence.

Christien aimed a look of raw contempt at her. 'That you can't even take responsibility for your own actions—'

'Shut up!' Tabby suddenly hurled at him, half an octave higher.

'And you still lose your head when you are confronted with your flaws—'

'And you think *you're* so perfect?' Tabby hissed at him, rage jumping up and down inside her.

'No, I wasn't perfect, *ma belle*,' Christien conceded in a black velvety purr, scorching golden eyes locked to her outraged face. 'But even when I was at my most rampant I never ran two lovers at one and the same time. Sleeping with the lout on the Harley-Davidson while I was in Paris was sordid and sluttish...and not a trifling offence I felt I could overlook!'

The silence was charged with hard, hostile vibrations.

Tabby was staring at his lean, strong face with wide eyes of appalled disbelief. 'Say that again... I mean, I *didn't*... I didn't do what you just said I did with *any* lout on a Harley!'

'*En voilà une bonne*...that's a good one! The compulsive liar bites again,' Christien derided with a curled lip.

Grim at that degrading recollection, he strode past her back into the hall.

In a daze at what he had just let drop, Tabby halted in the sitting-room doorway. 'Did you really think I'd been unfaithful? How *could* you think that?'

'If you were easy with me, why shouldn't you be equally easy with someone else?' Christien lifted and dropped a shoulder, smouldering animosity laced with contemptuous dismissal in his insolent appraisal. 'And let us be honest...five days was a long time for you to go without sex, *chérie*.'

'I won't forgive you for talking to me like this—'

'I don't want forgiveness.' In fact, Christien felt forgiveness of even the most minor variety might be very, very dangerous to his own interests.

Tabby Burnside was nothing but trouble. She had no morals. That that should appeal to him was not a trait within himself that he ought to encourage. She would accept the cheque. Of course she would accept the cheque. However, if there were any further negotiations required, he would leave the matter in the hands of his English solicitor. After all, he was to marry to Veronique, who was a fine woman. Beautiful, honest, trustworthy. She would make an excellent wife. Eventually he would become a father and a grandchild might well lift his mother's spirits a little. Was that not what had prompted him to become engaged in the first place? Wild, hot sex, fights and seething attacks of emotion would never feature in his alliance with Veronique. That was *good*, Christien told himself.

For a long time after Christien had departed, Tabby stared into space. The lout on the Harley-Davidson? Could he have been referring to the English student, Pete? Pete and two of his mates had been staying nearby. Pippa and Hilary had become friendly with them and Tabby *had* gone out with Pete on his bike one evening when Christien had been in Paris. But that had been all. Why had Christien accused her of sleeping with Pete? How could he have believed that she would have behaved like that? Why would he have believed that when she had been so patently crazy about him?

Once more time was sliding back for Tabby and she was reliving that summer. After that first ennervating sighting of Christien in the village, Tabby had lived in a daydream inhabited only by her fantasy of Christien and herself. Her stepmother had become noticeably less unpleasant when Tabby had opted to stay behind at the farmhouse most evenings while everybody else had gone out. Tabby had gloried in the quiet and the privacy and the daring freedom of bathing naked in the big blue-tiled pool. She still remembered the wonderful cool of the water on her overheated bare skin. At the outset of the second week while she'd still been in the water swimming, the electricity had cut out.

Wrapped in a towel, she had been attempting to find her way through the rambling farmhouse back to her bedroom when she had heard a car pulling up outside. Assuming everyone had come back early, she had gone to the door, but it had been Christien out on the front veranda with a torch.

'I saw the lights go out and I guessed you'd be here alone. Join me for dinner, *chèrie*,' he murmured.

'But there's a blackout—'

'We have a generator.'

She stood there, teeth chattering with nerves, hair dripping round her. 'I'm all wet—'

'You would like me to dry you?'

'I'll need to get dressed.'

'Don't bother on my account.' In the light of the torch, mocking tawny eyes set below the lush black fringe of his lashes rested on her hot face. 'Are you sure you're not too warm in that towel?'

'You don't even know my name. It's—'

'Not important right now.'

'Tabby,' she completed shakily, taken aback by the intensity of his appraisal.

'You don't look at all like a little brown cat. You're smaller than I thought you would be, too,' Christien confided, inspecting her with the torch beam. 'But you have fabulous skin. Don't bother with make-up. I hate it.'

For Tabby, his appearance was her every dream come true and she was terrified that he would disappear while she was getting dressed. Giving her the torch, he told her he would wait in the car.

'I don't know your name,' she said when she climbed into his car.

'*Naturellement*...of course you do,' he contradicted with disturbing confidence.

'All right... I asked one of the locals who you were,' Tabby mumbled.

'Don't waste your best lines on me. I've heard them all before and honesty is fresher.'

'I don't know you... I shouldn't have got into a car with you,' Tabby exclaimed, because she was suddenly feeling very much out of her depth in his company.

'But I feel I know you so well already, *ma belle*. Every night of the past four I have watched you strip off and cavort naked in the pool down here.'

At the news that her swimming sessions had not been as private as she had believed them to be, Tabby gasped in shock. 'I beg your pardon—?'

'Don't be coy. I respect nerve and enterprise in a woman. I also admire a woman who knows what she wants and goes after it,' Christien breathed with a husky intimacy. 'And the simple ploy was remarkably effective...here I am.'

Her aghast embarrassment fought with her recognition of his apparent respect for what he had interpreted as an adventurous campaign to attract his attention. The temptation to pose as an enterprising go-getting woman triumphed over all common sense. She did not angrily demand to know how he could possibly have seen her bathing in a pool surrounded by a wall or ask him how on earth he could have sunk low enough to spy on her. She did not contradict his outrageously self-satisfied assumption that she had been breaking her neck to get off with him and, as mistakes went, hiding behind that fake image was her first mistake with Christien.

There was no great mystery about why she ended up in Christien's bed on their very first date either. She was so excited at dining alone with him in the incredibly opulent villa that she barely ate a mouthful but she *did* drink three glasses of wine. Nor did she have a prayer of resisting a guy with his seductive expertise. In fact she was a lost cause from the first kiss for nobody could kiss like Christien could.

'*Zut alors...* I am crazy for you,' Christien intoned with ragged emphasis, sweeping her off her feet in high romantic style as if she were not a healthy lump frequently scorned by her stepmother as being on the larger side of overweight. For that alone, for his simple ability to lift her without grunting with effort, she would have loved him.

'You enchant me,' Christien swore, so that she felt generous enough to try and hide the fact that the first time he made love to her and she lost her virginity without him noticing, it hurt. And when he seemed to suspect that things hadn't gone quite as well for her as he seemed to have expected, she pretended to go to sleep because she was so embarrassed.

So for her, it was not sex, it was *never* just sex, because the first night she went to sleep in his arms, she very much hoped that he would not want to do what they had just done very often. In the middle of the night, she crept out of the bed and he sat up and switched on the light. 'Where are you going?' he demanded.

'Er...back down the hill,' Tabby muttered, worried sick that Pippa would have reported her absence from the bedroom they shared.

'I don't want to let you go but... *Ciel!*' Christien groaned.

'What was I thinking of? To keep you this late was madness. How liberal are your family?'

Her father would have taken a shotgun to him without hesitation, but it would have been the opposite of cool to admit that. He was very disconcerted when she refused even to let him take her back in the car. She was even more dismayed when he insisted on walking her down the road to the very entrance of the farmhouse. 'Can I see you tomorrow morning for breakfast?' he asked.

'I'll try to make lunch—'

'You'll *try*? Was I that bad?' In the moonlight, Christien gave her a rueful grin that had so much charismatic appeal, it physically hurt her to leave him.

When she climbed in the window of the bedroom she was sharing with Pippa, Pippa was wide awake. 'Have you gone crazy?' the other girl hissed furiously. 'Did you think I wouldn't realise that you've been out all night with that guy in the flash sports car?'

'How did you find out?'

'I just watched you snogging him from an upstairs window! I'm been going out of my head worrying about you and wondering whether I ought to tell our parents you were missing,' Pippa censured angrily. 'What's got into you? Don't ever put me in a position like that again!'

What *had* got into her that summer? Tabby wondered with shamefaced regret. Mercifully, it had been a recklessness that had never touched her again. Disturbed by Tabby's unfamiliar behaviour with Christien, Pippa had moved into Jen's room instead. Tabby had been upset by her friend's defection, but not upset enough to turn her back on Christien. Her need for him had been all-consuming, her love total, and nothing and nobody else had mattered to her. Only living and breathing for him, she had slept through the daylight hours she'd often been away from him like a vampire in a coffin who only came into real being and secret life after nightfall.

Angry tears stung Tabby's eyes as she stared down at the cheque that Christien had left behind him. With hands that were all fingers and thumbs she tore it up into lots of little pieces. She had not even looked at it to see how much he had been prepared to pay for the cottage. He did not want her in France, but she had already made all her arrangements. How dared Christien assume that he could buy her off and make her do things she didn't want to do? How dared he call her easy to her face? *He* had betrayed *her*, but then he had never given her any promises of fidelity, had he? Nor, she noted, had he mentioned his staggeringly beautiful blonde Parisienne girlfriend.

She would go to Solange's cottage and she would use it for as long as she wished. It would be a mark of her respect for a sweet woman, whom sadly she had never got to know well. Perhaps at the end of the summer she would take stock on whether or not anywhere in the vicinity of Duvernay was the best place for her to embark on a new life with her son. But as for Christien Laroche, who had already caused her so much grief, he had better steer clear of her from now on!

CHAPTER THREE

A SLIM BLOND male of around thirty with steady blue eyes and an attractive grin, Sean Wendell walked Tabby back to the town car park. He groaned out loud when he realised what time it was. 'I'm going to have to rush off and leave you here... I have an appointment with a client.'

'No problem. You've been a terrific help and thanks for the coffee,' Tabby told him warmly, for her aunt's former work colleague had proved to be a positive goldmine of local knowledge.

Regardless of the fact that he was already running late, Sean followed her across to the ancient van packed high with possessions. He continued to hover while she climbed back into the driver's seat. 'Look, don't try to unload the van on your own,' he urged. 'I'll come over this evening and give you a hand.'

'Honestly, that's very kind of you but I loaded it up, so I should be able to unpack it again.' Colouring at the continued heat of Sean's admiring appraisal, Tabby closed the van door and drove off with a wave. She liked him but wished that he had taken the hint that, while she was always happy to have another friend, nothing more intimate was on offer.

It was four o'clock on a warm June afternoon. She had made

good time from the ferry port and Sean's linguistic prowess had speeded up her dealings with the *notaire*. Now, she was barely twenty kilometres from her final destination. However, as Tabby drove out of Quimper again a glimpse of a shop window full of colourful faience pottery sent her thoughts winging back to her childhood. Her late mother had collected the elegant hand-painted pottery for which the cathedral city was famed and every year a fresh piece had joined the display on the kitchen dresser. Shortly before their move to a new and much bigger house, Tabby's stepmother, Lisa, had disposed of the whole collection, along with everything else in the household that had reminded her of her husband's first wife. After her father's death, it had hurt Tabby to have no keepsakes with which to highlight her memories of her parents.

But on the day that she travelled through Brittany to claim her inheritance, it would have been impossible for her to forget that her mother's biggest dream had always been to own a house in France. Indeed, by the time that Tabby finally identified the half-timbered one-and-a-half-storey cottage that was screened from the quiet country road by a handsome grove of oak trees, she was very much in the mood to be excited and to be pleased with all that she saw.

The front door of her new home opened straight into a big room with a picturesque granite fireplace and exposed ceiling beams. It was full of character and Tabby smiled. Her smile dimmed only a little when she glanced through a doorway at a kitchen that consisted of a stone sink and an ancient range that did not look as though it had been lit in living memory. The washing facilities were equally basic. However, the final room on the ground floor came as a delightful surprise for it was an old-fashioned sun room with good light, which would make a wonderful studio for her to work in. Up the narrow twisting oak staircase two rooms lay under the eaves. She unlatched stiff windows to let in the fresh air before strolling back downstairs and out of doors.

The garden rejoiced in splendid countryside views, an orchard and a pretty little stream. It would make a wonderful adventure playground for Jake, Tabby reflected cheerfully. Having seen all that there was to see, she endeavoured to take sensible stock of her inheritance. Christien's description of the property as a 'glorified summer house' had been infuriatingly accurate for there was no central heating, no proper kitchen or bath. She had also rather hoped that there would be some furniture to supplement what little she had of her own, but apart from a couple of wicker chairs in the sun room the cottage was bare to the boards. On the other hand, the roof and walls seemed sound, her utility bills would be tiny and, once she was bringing in a decent income, she would be able to add a few frills.

Her good mood very much in the ascendant, Tabby sat down under a tree and took advantage of the provisions she had bought on the outskirts of Quimper. Her hunger satisfied by half a baguette spread with tomatoes and ham and washed down with water, she changed into shorts and a T-shirt in preparation for cleaning the room where she planned to stay the night. An hour later, every surface scrubbed, she unloaded her bed from the van. As the head and footboards were made of wood, getting them up to the bedroom was no mean task, but she persevered and indeed was finally struggling with what was left of her energy to drag up the mattress as well when a knock sounded on the ajar front door.

Having got the unwieldy double mattress squashed round the bend in the staircase, Tabby was lying across it to keep it there while she tried to catch her breath again. Determined not to let go of the mattress, she attempted to twist her head round and peer down to see who was on the doorstep, but it was an impossible feat. 'Yes?' she called, praying that it would be Sean Wendell arriving as promised to offer his male muscle.

'It is I...' A dark-timbred masculine drawl imparted with accented clarity and awesome cool. 'Christien...'

She was unable to see him and taken badly by surprise; dismay provoked Tabby into loosing a rather rude word. It was ironic that it was a word that she had never said out loud in her life before and she cringed at her own lack of control over her wretched tongue. In fact she just wanted the ground to open up and swallow her and a fiery blush enveloped her complexion. Had he tried, Christien could not have chosen a worse moment to spring a visit on her.

Entering the cottage, Christien angled his proud dark head back and wondered if she had a man upstairs with her. 'Are you planning to come down and speak to me any time soon?'

Feeling trapped and foolish, Tabby flipped over and struggled to wedge the mattress in place while she stretched forward as far as she dared in an effort to see Christien. But that movement was all that it took for the bulky item to spring free of her hold. The weight of the mattress against her back dislodged her feet from the step and as the mattress forced its passage back down the stairs at shocking speed it carried her with it. In dismay, she cried out but it was too late: the edge of the heavy mattress hit Christien hard on the knees, destroyed his balance and toppled him before he could move from its path.

Christien fell and he only managed to partially break that fall by bracing strong hands on either side of her startled face. Tabby was winded by the sheer impact of a well-built six-foot-three-inch male hitting the mattress and momentarily crushing the life out of her lower body.

'Zut alors!' Christien raked down at her with furious force.

For an instant as she careened down the stairs like a cartoon character on board a novel flying carpet the world had swum scarily out of focus, but now it had righted itself again and Tabby found herself gazing up into dark golden eyes as bright as gemstones in a masculine face handsome enough to take any woman's breath away. Her slight body stilled taut as a bow string beneath the heavy imprint of his. Something as power-ful as it was emotionally painful swelled inside her chest and her throat tightened, her mouth running dry. Physical memories were engulfing her to a level beyond bearing for her senses had gone off on a roller-coaster ride of rediscovery.

The clean, evocative aroma that was unique to Christien flared her nostrils: hard male heat braced with a faint exotic hint of citrus. The very scent of his skin was so immediately familiar to her that she was shaken by the leap of her own recognition even at that most primitive level. She searched his lean dark features, her attention lingering on his level ebony brows, straight nose, blunt cheekbones and stubborn jawline, and then she connected with his amazing eyes again and felt a deep, slow pulse begin a slow, dangerous beat way down low in her pelvis. Below her T-shirt, her nipples swelled and tightened into sudden embarrassing prominence. She didn't want to feel like that, indeed she could barely credit that she could still react to the primal charge of his raw masculinity to such an extent, but it was as though a chain reaction of response had kicked off inside her and, once started, there was no stopping it.

Tabby trembled, her hips succumbing to a tiny, involuntary upward shift and her slender thighs sliding a little further apart to better bear his weight in a movement as old as history itself. That wicked throb at the heart of her could not be denied even while she struggled to recapture her ability to think.

'What the hell do you think you are playing at?' Christien demanded wrathfully as in fierce, fervent denial of the burning heat of his own arousal, he began to lever himself up and back from her.

It was those words of his that were Tabby's ultimate undoing. The mere suggestion that she might somehow have choreographed a mattress to surf down the stairs and knock him off his feet was sufficient to send Tabby into a sudden helpless fit of giggles. Recalling how chillingly impressive Christien's air of grave authority had been before the mattress intervened, she was in stitches.

'You think this is funny...huh?' Christien growled with savage incredulity.

'I-Isn't it?' she prompted chokily.

A split second later, his hot, hungry mouth swooped down to possess hers and killed her near-hysterical amusement at source. He was pure erotic temptation. For the first time in almost four years, electrifying excitement seized Tabby. Her head spun and air rasped in her tortured throat. The explicit intrusion of his tongue in the moist interior of her mouth sent a wave of delirious hunger currenting through her slight body. Her last grip on reality snapped: suddenly she was reaching up to him and no longer a passive partner. Her arms locked round his lean, hard frame, her hands rising to shape his broad shoulders before her fingers snaked higher and delved deep into the black silk luxuriance of his hair to hold him to her.

'Christien?'

'Non...' In an abrupt movement, Christien wrenched himself back from her again. Breathing raggedly, he stared down at her, his smouldering gaze blazing gold, febrile colour accentuating the savage line of his hard cheekbones, ferocious tension written into every hard, angular line of his lean, strong face. In one powerful movement he vaulted upright, but it took every atom of will-power he possessed to step back from her. That acknowledgement both outraged and shocked him but, more than anything else, he was disconcerted by an awareness of exactly *what* had ripped his formidable self-discipline to shreds a moment earlier: that husky laugh of hers had snatched him back in time to that summer.

He had never forgotten that streak of bubbling, contagious joy that was so much a part of her nature, her childish habit of giggling at the most inopportune moments and in the worst of places, or her mysterious ability to lift him from his darkest moods. Loner and cynic though he was, he had basked in that warmth of hers, the extravagant, trusting ease with which she seemed to love. His hard, sensual mouth set into a tough line. Love as she had offered wasn't worth a damn but the sex had been out of this world, he reminded himself with bitter amusement.

'Why did you touch me?' Tabby condemned shakily.

'Why do you think, *chérie*?' The thickened note in his sexy drawl sent a responsive shiver travelling down her taut spinal cord.

'You shouldn't have. That's all in the past.' Shaking like a leaf in a cruel wind, Tabby scrambled off the mattress and turned away from him. Her knees were wobbling and her hands were trembling. Her reddened lips stung from the devouring heat of his and more than anything else in the world she just wanted to sink back into the lean, powerful strength of him and taste him over and over again until the terrifying ache of loss he had filled her with had finally evaporated and faded like a bad memory.

And that was *not* how she should be thinking about a male who had once used her and discarded her again with no more care or consideration than he might have utilised had she given him her body in a casual one-night stand. In fact it was frightening to recognise the longing still pent-up inside her and the extent of her own vulnerability. Where were her pride and her intelligence?

'How did you even know I was moving in today?' she demanded, desperate to keep herself busy and stooping down to snatch at the mattress and manhandle it up onto its side again.

Someone who knew that she had an appointment to collect the keys from the *notaire* had made the mistake of passing on that news to Matilde Laroche and Christien's working day had been interrupted by his distraught parent and her announcement. He had left his mother in the soothing hands of her doctor but his own patience had been sorely tested. Only once in his life had his late father attended one of Solange's rustic picnic parties, so his son could not see how the overgrown meadow outside could be regarded by the older woman as being in quite the same category as sacred ground.

'I can understand that you would want to take a look at your inheritance,' Christien remarked with studied calm. 'Naturally you're curious but I can't believe that you're planning to live here.'

'Why can't you believe it?'

*'Pas possible…*it's not habitable!' he retorted drily.

Out of the corner of her eye, Tabby studied him. His silk business suit was a trendy black pinstripe of exquisite cut that accentuated his wide shoulders, narrow hips and long powerful thighs. He looked absolutely gorgeous and, without her even realising it, her sneaky covert glance had become a full-on stare. Cheeks reddening as he elevated a questioning brow at the intensity of her appraisal, Tabby hefted one corner of the bulky mattress up onto the bottom step of the stairs again and slung him an expectant look. 'Are you going to give me a hand with this?'

Complete disconcertion pleated his level brows.

'Of course, it must be hard to stay fit when you're in an office all day.' Tabby sighed.

An utterly unexpected slashing grin banished the gravity from Christien's lean dark face. 'Do you really think I'm about to fall for a bait that basic?'

Riveted to the spot by the sheer charisma of that knowing smile, Tabby tried and failed to swallow. Closing his lean, shapely hands into the mattress, he hauled it up the stairs, negotiated with ease the bend that had caused her such grief and came to a halt in the room where the bed frame already stood assembled. As she reached the doorway he settled the mattress down onto the frame.

'Where did you find the bed? On a dump?' he enquired.

'It's old but it's solid.' However, her bed had come closer to the dump than she would ever have admitted. Virtually all of the elderly furniture and household effects in the van had come from her aunt's attic and garage, both of which Alison was clearing in preparation for letting her property.

'You still haven't told me what you're doing here,' Tabby reminded Christien as she bent to rifle the cardboard box of bedding in the corner and emerged with a folded sheet.

Christien studied the sheet she was unfurling and noted that it had been carefully mended with a slightly different colour of cloth. Did people still patch linen these days? He was more shocked than he would have liked to admit by the sight of that mended sheet. He had a vague Cinderella-like image of her sitting darning by candlelight and, in defiance of that unusually colourful flight of fancy on his own part, he spread his hands in a scornful gesture. 'Why are you wasting your energy with this? You *can't* live here—'

'*You* couldn't,' Tabby countered, tucking in the sheet at the corners with determined industry, because at least while she was attending to practicalities she was not gawping at him like a lovelorn schoolgirl. 'You'd be lost without your luxuries, but I'll be quite happy getting back to basics—'

'That's a double bed...who are you planning to share it with?' Christien demanded without warning.

An image of Jake's warm little body sneaking in below the covers first thing in the morning to cuddle up to her crossed Tabby's mind and her green eyes softened and her lush mouth took on a tender curve as she thought of her son.

Raw anger flaring and tensing his hard dark features, Christien strode forward to scrutinise her with brilliant dark golden eyes. 'If you choose to live on the Duvernay estate, there will only be one man in your bed, and that man will be me...*tu comprends*?'

In rampant disbelief, Tabby straightened to stare at him. 'Are you out of your mind?'

'Is that what you wanted...is that why you're here?' Christien purred low and soft, though the sting of that insolent enquiry cut like glass against her tender skin. 'You want to take up where we left off that summer?'

Without even thinking about what she was going to do, powered by hot, deep anger alone, Tabby slapped him. The crack of her fingers against his bronzed cheek sounded preternaturally loud in the hot, still room. 'Does that answer that question?'

Christien was so taken aback by that physical attack that he fell back a step.

The shock in his stunning golden eyes was patent and Tabby flushed. 'You *made* me do that—' .

Lean bronzed hands snapped over her wrists like handcuffs. 'Then I will have to make equally sure that you don't do it again.'

Tabby tried to pull free of his hold and failed. 'It *is* your fault that I hit you!' she condemned like a spitting wildcat in her frustration. 'You were very rude. I'm in my own house and I have every right to be here if I want to be. If you enter my home, I expect you to mind your manners—'

'Or you'll assault me?'

Still struggling without avail to slide her wrists free, she felt her face flame at that sardonic interruption. 'Can't I move to France without you getting the idea that I've only come here to chase you?'

Disturbingly, his wide, sensual mouth quirked. 'Perhaps I want to be caught, *chérie.*'

'But I don't want to get involved with you again—'

'Non?' Christien prompted in a husky undertone, employing his hands to draw her closer.

'Non...' Tabby told him insistently, but her heart was starting to beat very, very fast behind her ribcage.

'I can be very well mannered,' Christien murmured silkily.

'Not around me, you're not—'

'You burn me up, *mon ange...*' His arrogant dark head bent as he released one of her hands and raised the other to press his mouth to the centre of her small pink palm.

The heat of that teasing caress made her shiver. Time was running backwards for her. She pressed her thighs together on the hot, liquid sensation of melting at the very heart of her. Already she felt tender and swollen and shame pierced her as sharp as an arrow. She was passionate and so was he and once that had been a source of joy and discovery to her. She had believed that they were a perfect match, but now when she felt the blood run hot in her veins it scared her and she judged it a weakness in herself. As that almost unbearable longing for him held her there, her troubled gaze lingered on his downbent dark head. 'Don't do this...'

'Don't do what?' Christien husked. 'Don't do...*this*?'

He sank his other hand into her hair and tipped her head back to skim the very tip of his tongue over the full curve of her lower lip. His breath warmed her skin and she trembled.

'Or...*this*?'

He delved between her readily parted lips and she jerked and moaned, only to be racked by a shudder of frustrated longing as he lifted his head again.

'Tell me what you want, *chérie*.'

Her hand reached up of its own seeming volition and sank into his black hair. Stretching up on tiptoe, she drew him down to her, for she wanted his mouth on hers so badly that it hurt to be denied it. With an earthy groan, he lifted her up to him and crushed her mouth under his before he strode forward and lowered her down onto the bed. The moment he pressed her down on the mattress, the frame gave and collapsed with the most enormous crash down onto the floor.

Christien swore and snatched her back up again from the tumbled mattress. Still holding her slight body taut to his broad chest in a protective stance, he stepped back to the doorway and surveyed the disassembled bed with incredulous force.

'I forgot... I still had to tighten up the screws holding the frame together,' Tabby mumbled unevenly.

'You could've been hurt.' Christien set her down on her own feet again.

'I'm glad it happened...it stopped us doing something stupid,' Tabby asserted tightly.

Firm male footsteps sounded on the staircase. 'Tabby?' a familiar voice called. 'Are you OK? I saw the door open and just came on in when I heard the noise.'

A relieved smile driving the taut tension from her generous mouth, Tabby flipped round Christien's stilled figure and went to the head of the stairs. 'Sean...you're very welcome and I'm about to take shameless advantage of you. Are you any good with a screwdriver?'

Dark eyes veiled, Christien surveyed the young blond male with his self-satisfied smile and designer stubble and experienced a powerfully disturbing desire to kick him back down the stairs again.

'I brought my tool-kit with me...' Sean confided as he passed by Christien.

Christien was so pained that he almost winced. Who was this jerk?

'Sean...er, this is Christien.'

Neither man extended a hand. Each awarded the other a stiff but studiously casual nod.

Tabby tried not to notice that Christien made Sean look small, skinny and in need of a good shave.

'I'll sort the bed out...no problem,' the Englishman asserted, and started to whistle quietly.

'May I talk to you downstairs?' Christien murmured to Tabby.

Worrying at her lower lip, Tabby led the way, her slim back rigid.

'Is the whistling handyman going to be living here too?' Christien enquired flatly.

Tabby tensed. 'I don't think that's any of your business—'

'So I can just take care of him by going back up there and breaking his neck now, can I?' Christien incised.

Tabby paled in disbelief.

'I'm being straight. I don't want any other guy anywhere near you. Who is he?'

Tabby focused on scorching dark golden eyes and her mouth ran dry. 'You don't have the right—'

Christien swung back to the stairs. 'I'll go ask him—'

'No!' Tabby snapped in horror. 'He's a friend of my aunt's and lives locally… For goodness' sake, I only met him today!'

As far as Christien was concerned at that moment, nothing that he himself had done or said since he entered the cottage seemed to have had the smallest intellectual input from his brain. But her admission that her visitor was only an acquaintance cooled the white-hot, irrational anger that he was fighting to restrain.

Tabby walked right out to the silver Ferrari parked at the side of the cottage. 'I want you to leave…and I don't want you to come back—'

'Don't lie to me—'

Her small hands closed into tight, hurting fists of self-control as she fought her own weak inclinations with all her might. 'I won't sell this place, I'm staying…that's *all* you need to know—'

'So that we can both lie awake on the hot nights?' By the simple dint of moving forward, Christien cornered her against the wing of the car and backed her into contact with the sun-warmed metal. 'Tell me now,' he instructed in a raw-edged undertone.

'No…' Almost mesmerised by the smouldering heat of his golden eyes, Tabby stared back at him, pupils dilated, body humming with wild, hot, wicked awareness.

'Say it like you mean it,' Christien urged in a ragged undertone, leaning forward even as she leant back.

The front door slammed with a loud thud that made both of them leap back from each other in sudden mutual discomfiture.

Sean Wendell angled an apologetic grimace at Tabby. 'Sorry…the wind caught it!'

'He's a smart ass,' Christien growled with barely restrained menace.

Her colour high, Tabby walked away without another word.

She didn't dare look back at him, not when just turning her back on him had demanded almost superhuman will-power.

As the Ferrari drove off Sean rolled his eyes. 'Watching you two together is certainly an education—'

'Watching me with... Christien?' Tabby frowned. 'What are you talking about?'

'I don't think I've ever seen an attraction that powerful.' Sean remarked in wry fascination. 'I've just come out of a long-term relationship and now I know what was missing...the bonfire factor...stand back, feel the heat!'

Taken aback by the fact that her response to Christien was so painfully obvious that even a virtual stranger had recognised it, Tabby turned a fierce guilty pink. 'You misunderstood—'

'No, I don't think so, but I do know how to mind my own business.' With an easy grin, Sean asked her what she wanted to unload next from the van and she indicated the smart new furniture that she had bought specially for Jake's room in the hope of giving it greater appeal.

A couple of hours later, the van emptied, and alone again, Tabby stripped off and learned how best to wash her hair and all the rest of herself with only a sink and a saucepan to help with the task. As she climbed into her old-fashioned bed her thoughts were still full of Christien. The lure of the past always hit her hardest in weak moments: she was forever looking back to try and pinpoint the exact moment when her fairytale fantasy of everlasting happiness had begun to crack...

At the end of her third week of holiday, and a week of being with Christien, his friend Veronique had called in for a visit. Christien had been talking on the phone and Tabby had been lying half asleep with her head on his lap. She still recalled glancing up to see the lovely brunette in her trendy beige linen dress standing in the doorway with her bright smile and her even friendlier wave. Veronique had seemed so very *nice*, Tabby recalled with a rueful grimace. And of course, being just seventeen, Tabby had taken Veronique at face value and the other woman had found it easy to win her trust.

'I thought I'd find Eloise in residence... I shouldn't be saying it,' Veronique whispered like Tabby's new best friend the minute Christien went out of hearing, 'but I've been dying for Christien to meet someone new and you look so *happy* together! Oh, please don't get me into trouble by saying I mentioned her!'

It had taken Christien's childhood playmate only half an hour to plant the first seeds of distrust and insecurity. In no time at all, Tabby was hearing about the gorgeous Parisienne model whom Veronique had assumed Christien was still seeing, and the clever brunette was offering useful little nuggets of supposed girlie wisdom concerning Tabby's relationship with him...

'I don't want to butt in *but* I think I ought to warn you that Christien really hates being pawed all the time.'

'Mention other boyfriends...he loves competition.'

'He has a very short attention span where women are concerned...'

Of course, with a few well-placed questions it was not difficult for Veronique to penetrate Tabby's masquerade of being a twenty-one-year-old student at art college. Christien had never asked for any details. Why, oh, why had she ever pretended to be something she wasn't? Tabby asked herself unhappily. Why had she not sat down and thought before she'd parted her silly lips and lied about who and what she was to Christien the very first time that they'd spoken? She had believed that no guy in possession of a Ferrari and a fantastic villa would be interested in dating a seventeen year old fresh out of school. In her lively imagination, she had fast-forwarded her real life into the life she expected to be living four years in the future. After that initial bout of creative fiction, little more pretence had been required from her for they enjoyed a relationship rooted very much in the here and the now.

Until the final week when Christien went off to Paris on business, they had not spent a single day apart. There had been nobody to question where she was or what she was doing, for her father had been challenged enough to cope with his youthful bride's temper. In fact the older man had always seemed to be either hung-over or on the way to getting hung-over again, Tabby recalled with painful regret. Thanks to Lisa's tantrums their family friends had engaged in a frantic round of activity in an effort to gloss over the reality that they were on the holiday from hell. Only the other teenagers in the party had understood that something more than a shrewish stepmother and a desire for her own space had been powering Tabby's preference for remaining at the farmhouse alone every day and every evening.

'What do you like most about me?' Tabby asked Christien dreamily one evening.

'How do you know I like anything?' Christien laughed out loud when she mock punched his ribs before saying with striking seriousness, 'You never try to be something you're not. What you see is what you get with you and I really appreciate that...'

She was all smiles until it finally dawned on her that what he had just admitted ought to strike cold fear into her veins, because a male who prized honesty and sincerity was unlikely to be impressed by a teenager who had told him a pack of lies in an effort to seem more mature and sophisticated than she was. During those final days she was feeling very insecure because Christien *had* become quieter and more distant with her, making her suspect that he was getting bored with their relationship.

'I think he's going off me,' she confided brittily to Solange on that second visit to the older woman's villa further up the valley.

'Christien has a very deep and serious nature,' his great-aunt soothed. 'Complex men are not easy to understand, especially when they're young and hotheaded.'

When just a few days later the embarrassing truth of Tabby's true age was 'accidentally' exposed by Veronique, Christien hit the roof and unleashed a temper that Tabby had never realised he had. Perhaps, however, her worst moment of humiliation occurred when, without any forewarning whatsoever, Christien came down to the farmhouse determined to finally meet her relatives. Lisa wandered in topless from the pool to flirt with him and a drunken argument then broke out between her father and her stepmother. Christien was excessively polite and reserved. Agonisingly aware of the distaste he was concealing, Tabby shrank with shame on her family's behalf.

'Do I still consider myself dumped?' she asked in desperation as Christien climbed back into his elegant car.

'I went into this too fast. I need to think,' he ground out, capturing her willing mouth for a breathless instant that blew her away and then peeling her off him again with a grim look of restraint etched on his lean, strong face. '*Without* you around.'

'Don't expect me to sit around waiting for you!' she warned him shakily, suddenly very, very scared at the new distance she sensed in him and the tough self-discipline he was now exerting in her vicinity.

Christien sent her a truly pained appraisal that made her squirm. 'You sound so juvenile. I can't believe it took someone else to point out what I should have seen for myself.'

He went to Paris and he neither phoned nor texted her. Veronique implied that he was heading for a reunion with Eloise, who had spent most of the summer working in London. Tortured by his silence, Tabby was thrown back into the company of her friends for the first time that holiday. She did her utmost not to parade the reality that her heart was breaking. She never dreamt that the next time that she would see Christien, it would be in a hospital waiting room in the immediate aftermath of an unthinkable tragedy that left no space whatsoever for personal feelings or dialogue…

A towel knotted round his lean hips and still damp from the shower, Christien gazed unseeingly out the tall bedroom windows that gave the vast frontage of the Château Duvernay such classical elegance.

The mere awareness that Tabby was only a few fields away

on the edge of the rolling parkland that surrounded his ancestral home was making him restless. Thinking about her unshaven caller, Sean, it was finally dawning on Christien that he had just walked out and left Tabby alone with a strange man. A strange man with the hots for her as well. Wasn't there something weird about a guy who went visiting with a tool-kit clutched in one hand? And might not some men misinterpret Tabby's naturally playful friendliness as a come-on? *Mon Dieu*, why hadn't it immediately occurred to him that Tabby might be at risk? He had left her at the mercy of a smirking handyman who might be a real sicko! Discarding the towel, Christien began pulling on clothes.

Dim light could be seen burning both upstairs and downstairs in the cottage. Swinging out of his car, Christien walked up the path and then paused beside a gnarled tree to check out the hole in the trunk. He drew out a dusty key and then with a frown returned it to its hiding place again. Strong jawline at a determined angle, he made loud and clear use of the door knocker...

CHAPTER FOUR

WHEN THE KNOCKER SOUNDED, Tabby was curled up dozing on the wicker chair that she had brought through from the sun room.

Startled into wakefulness, she almost leapt out of her skin. Who the heck would come calling after midnight? Ought she to answer the door so late? Snatching up the bright patchwork crochet blanket she had draped over the chair, she wrapped it round herself, for she was only wearing a camisole nightdress.

It was Christien, black hair tousled by the faint breeze, brilliant golden eyes locking to her. Thud, bang, *crash* went her heartbeat, while her tummy see-sawed as though the floor had dropped away below her. Eyes glinting a glorious green from below a feathery fringe of tumbling hair the colour of honey, she stared out at him, soft, full mouth damp and pink.

'Why have you come back?' Tabby whispered unevenly.

Christien did not even need to think about that. He had come back because he could not stay away. He closed the door behind him. He reached out and detached her fingers from the colourful blanket. Thick black lashes cloaking his gaze, he slid the blanket slowly down from her narrow shoulders.

'Christien…?' she queried unsteadily.

His breath rasped in his throat as he scrutinised her lush, inviting curves. Unquenchable lust gripped him in a hold tougher than any vice. White cotton moulded her high, full breasts and the fabric was too thin to hide the rosy prominence of her nipples. He wanted to touch her, taste her, drive her insane with the same desire that burned in him. 'If Sean had still been here with you… I think I'd have ripped the bastard limb from limb,' he confided not quite levelly.

Tabby whipped the blanket back up round her again but her hands were shaking. 'I don't sleep around… I never have and I never will. You had no reason to think he'd still be here, but even if he had been it would be none of your business—'

'But I'd have made it my business, *ma belle*.'

Although she knew she should not, she looked up at him. The smouldering intensity of his dark golden gaze set off every sensual alarm bell she possessed but she moved not an inch. Indeed, she felt incapable of moving. For almost four years she had concentrated all her energies on being a loving mother to Jake and studying for her degree at art college. She had had to push herself very, very hard to cope as a single parent and a student, who also needed to work a part-time job. There had been little space for dating in her gruelling schedule, but then that had not really been a sacrifice when no ordinary male could dislodge Christien from her mind. Christien with his black hair falling over his bronzed brow, danger flashing gold in his stunning eyes, not a single note jarring the sheer, riveting perfection of his hard, all-male beauty. Christien, the ultimate of impossible acts to follow.

Dry-mouthed, she settled her focus back on the real live male in front of her. 'Why do you want to make me your business again?'

'I don't know.' A rough, humourless laugh was dredged from Christien. 'It's madness…but I'm still here.'

It shook her that Christien should say it was madness to be

with her again and yet stay. He was mere inches from her, drop-dead gorgeous and virile and, that close to him, she felt boneless.

'You should leave—'

'Should but *won't*.'

'Is that a threat or a promise?' she whispered.

'What do you want it to be, *mon ange*?'

His presence was both threat and promise and she knew it. She had never stopped wanting him, had never learned to hate him. How could she when she understood the very forces that had ensured they stayed apart? The enormity of the tragedy that had engulfed their families that summer had shattered the tenuous remains of their relationship.

'What do I want?' She wanted him, only him. It was a truth that was rooted so deep in her that even pride could not make her deny it. 'Take a guess...'

Eyes shimmering hard and bright, Christien snatched in a ragged breath. He reached out and lifted her right off her feet and up into his arms in a demonstration of confidence and unapologetic masculine strength that made her feel weak and wanton and dizzy.

He took her mouth with stormy hunger and pried her lips apart to ravish the tender interior. A violent shiver of response racked her. Her heart hammering, she stretched up to him to deepen that connection. It felt so good she was instantly, help-lessly addicted to her own craving for more. He pinned her up against the wall and his tongue plunged and withdrew between her readily parted lips with fierce, driving hunger.

Wrenching her stinging lips from his with a mighty effort, she shut her eyes, fighting to maintain even a shred of restraint. 'The whole world's spinning,' she mumbled.

In an almost clumsy movement that bore little resemblance to his usual sure, fluid grace, he peeled her back off the wall and clamped her to his big, powerful length. He held her tight, so tight she could barely squeeze air into her constricted lungs.

'I'm sorry... I feel out of control,' he grated.

Her arms linked round him then and a smile like the sunrise started inside her where he couldn't see it. This was the guy who rarely took more than one glass of alcohol because feeling anything other than in total command of himself was anathema to him. To make him feel out of control even momentarily was an achievement of no mean order and to hear him confess it was a joy.

'I'm never in control with you,' she whispered back with neither resentment nor pleasure, just acceptance that that should be the case.

Christien felt light-headed with a triumph as old as time itself. She was his, she was still *his*. He was not a guy who reasoned in what he believed were primitive sexist terms and he had never felt possessive around any other woman. But she was different and, with her, he was different too and that was a conundrum he had never wasted any time agonising over. He set her down in the bedroom where an old Anglepoise lamp burned on an upturned box next to the bed. He did not think of himself as imaginative but he was already picturing the bare room furnished with the kind of pretty feminine clutter she adored.

Eyelids sensually lowered over his dark golden gaze, Christien treated her to a fierce, intent appraisal that fired her very skincells with awareness of her womanhood. 'I take one look at you and I'm so hungry for you I'm in agony,' he confessed huskily, sinking down on the edge of the bed and drawing her forward to stand between his spread thighs.

Was that why he was still so very special to her? Tabby asked herself. His ability to look at her with a wondering appreciation that suggested that she was an incredibly gorgeous woman when she herself knew that she was just an ordinary one? A marvel made all the more striking by the simple fact that Christien himself was very much in a class of his own? Even in well-worn jeans and a beige cotton sweater, he exuded exclusive cool and bred-in-the-bone sophistication. He possessed that degree of pure masculine good looks more often seen on a movie screen. Men of his ilk usually gravitated towards classically beautiful women, but she was wildly, humbly grateful that something she couldn't see and couldn't begin to understand had brought him to her instead.

Vulnerable and almost dazed by the intensity of her own emotions at that instant, Tabby looked back at him. 'Christien...?'

'You're very lovely, *ma belle*,' he said thickly, reaching up to tug the band out of her naturally curly caramel-coloured hair.

'I'm not—'

'Shush...' He finger-combed her hair down onto her taut shoulders, leant forward to let his tongue penetrate between lips as sweet and inviting as juicy strawberries.

She shivered and leant into that kiss, knees wobbling under her, hands suddenly coming down to steady herself on his long, powerful thighs. The swollen tightness of her nipples hurt. The very thought of his expert hands on her made her tremble with eagerness and already she was way beyond rational thought or restraint.

'Please...' she heard herself say.

'I want to take my time... I've pictured this too often,' he murmured roughly.

Mesmerised, she stood there, gazing into gorgeous golden eyes shaded by luxuriant black lashes longer and more luxuriant than her own. Just like Jake's, she conceded, and her throat tightened and she knew that she would have no choice but to tell him about his son now. Intimidated by the thought, she blanked out her mind.

Reaching up, Christien brushed the camisole straps down over her slim forearms, baring the proud, creamy swell of her breasts. The fabric caught on the taut rosy peaks. On fire with wanting, she felt her nightdress fall to her hips and he vented an earthy groan of bold appreciation.

'Stop looking at me like that...' she gasped, racked by shamed embarrassment for the terrible hunger that kept her standing there, exposed and desperate for his touch.

'I can't...you *are* exquisite,' Christien ground out, hauling her to him and closing his mouth to a pouting pink nipple.

All the breath pent-up inside her escaped in a startled gush, her soft lips parting, her head falling back, sweet, intense sensation thrumming through her in a heady tide while the moist heat at the heart of her quickened. His hands on her rounded hips, he roved from one stiff, sensitive bud to the other and she whimpered in response to urge him on. There was only him and what he could make her feel, and what he could make her feel drove out all else.

Long fingers shaping and moulding her tender breasts, he took her lush mouth again and again and the hard, male urgency of his plundering kiss wiped her out. She clung, gasped, felt the nightdress fall away and cried out low in her throat as he let sure fingers explore the slick, wet flesh between her thighs. She was trembling, utterly seduced by the screaming demands of her own body. He brought her down on the bed and stood over her while he hauled off his sweater with something less than cool.

'*Ciel*... I forgot how it feels with you, *ma belle*.' Dark colour accentuating his proud cheekbones, he studied her with raw intensity.

'I've never forgotten.' Tabby was deliciously, wickedly aware of the size and the strength of his big, powerful body and the hard ridge of male arousal jutting below the tight jeans he wore left her weak with wanting. Belatedly conscious of her own nudity and the golden eyes flaming hungrily over her, she curled her legs up and he gave her a slashing smile of wicked amusement.

She could not take her eyes off him. His lean bronzed torso bore a triangular pelt of black curls across his pectorals. He was powerfully muscled but as sleek in movement as an athlete. His stomach was washboard-flat and dissected by a silky furrow of dark hair. She watched him unsnap his jeans, skim them down to reveal boxers and long, hair-roughened thighs and the shame of her own excitement almost overwhelmed her.

'You make me crazy for you...' Christien groaned, his rasping, sexy accent sending an evocative quiver down her spine.

He pulled her back to him. He made a praiseworthy effort to be cool, seductive and slow the pace with some seductive kissing, but her tongue twinned with his and he shuddered against her and ground his aching shaft into her pelvis with a raw growl low in his throat. Suddenly she was flat on the bed and he was devouring her with a wild, ravaging kiss. Her hunger went rocketing up the temperature scale and she rose up under him and sobbed his name below his marauding mouth, back arching in an agony of longing as he worshipped her breasts with his lips and his teeth.

'Please—'

'If I don't wait, I'll blow it,' Christien grated in raw warning.

'No...you won't.' She would have told him anything.

'*Oui*...just like the first time, like a stupid, over-eager kid, I'll *hurt* you!' Fabulous bone structure rigid, Christien glowered down at her as he struggled to maintain a grip on his fast-shredding control.

'That wasn't your fault.' Tabby pressed her lips to his strong jawline in a soothing gesture as natural to her with Christien as living. 'It was my first time and I should've told you but I was too embarrassed.'

Christien blinked. Her *first* time? When they met she had been a...virgin? One hundred per cent innocent, pure and untouched? And he hadn't noticed? He was stunned by the belated awareness that somewhere deep down where he had had no desire to probe he had always had that suspicion, but had never taken it out and faced it before. Why not? Was it possible that he had been reluctant to accept that amount of responsibility?

'Christien...?'

Golden eyes haunted by rare guilt, he steeled himself to back off, but her small hands were sliding into his hair, shaping his skull, and he looked down into luminous green eyes and fell victim to their enchantment instead. The drugging collision of their mouths ignited the hunger to a frantic fever again and her desperation only increased when he probed the hot, satin sensitivity between her thighs. She was in sensual torment, arching up to him, begging for more with every fibre of her being.

'I need to be inside you...' Dark blood delineating his hard cheekbones, Christien dragged her under him.

He plunged his swollen member into her damp, heated core and thrust deep. Sensual shock momentarily held her still. She could feel him stretching her and it had been so long that her own excitement was almost unbearable. His pagan possession thrilled her to the depths of her wanton soul. Her blood roared through her veins and her heart thundered as he drove her into his stormy rhythm. She was flying higher than she had ever flown and then she was crying out his name and her body was jerking, convulsing, breaking apart in a sweet, sweet rush of ecstasy. It felt so good, so wonderful it almost hurt and a surge of tears stung her eyes. His magnificent body shuddered over hers and she clutched him tight in the aftermath. It was as if she had been in suspended animation for almost four years and had suffered a sudden revival. She was in shock.

Christien emerged from the wildest, hottest orgasm of his life and struggled just to breathe again. He rolled over, carrying her with him, and stared down at her in a daze, pushing her tumbled honey-coloured hair back off her flushed, oval face with a lean brown hand that he noticed was trembling. That shook him even more.

Tabby drank in the musky, sexy scent of his damp skin and revelled in the familiarity even as a little voice shrieked inside her that she had just committed an act of insanity.

Christien pressed his lips to her smooth brow and rearranged her slight body over him. 'Once is never enough with you—'

'Don't be greedy,' she teased, snuggling into him like a homing pigeon, determined not to think about what she was doing.

'I should have guessed that you were a virgin when we met,' Christien breathed, for he was only just beginning to disentangle that startling reality from the miasma of misinformation with which he had deliberately fenced his memories of her in the intervening years.

'You didn't want to know...you thought it might commit you in some way,' Tabby whispered abstractedly. 'I told myself you hadn't noticed but I was really just trying to explain what I wasn't old enough to understand.'

It had been almost four years since Christien had been treated to that amount of blunt honesty and his even white teeth momentarily gritted together. As a rule women wrapped up the unpalatable truth around him and never ever voiced it. 'It wasn't like that...'

Of course, it had been, Tabby reflected painfully. She had been besotted, out of her depth and trying to be something she was not and he had taken what all young, virile males were programmed to take: sexual conquest of a willing woman. Everything that had happened between them had been inevitable according to their sex, right down to her having fallen head over heels in love and him having got bored with her.

'It was...and you got bored—'

His long, lean length had turned very tense. 'I didn't get bored...you went off with the lout on the Harley.'

'I *didn't*—'

Christien lifted her off him and dumped her down onto the mattress by his side. 'For once in your life, tell the truth—'

Infuriated, Tabby sat up. 'I *am* telling the truth!'

'Where is the bathroom?' Christien demanded.

'Downstairs.' Tabby compressed her lips, green eyes fiery. 'I went out for a ride with Pete, and Pippa and Hilary were with his friends on their bikes. It was just a night out and nothing happened—'

'*Ciel!* Don't give me that! I saw you snogging him in the village...little slut!' Christien suddenly shot at her with a passionate fury that took even him aback and was a far cry from the cool he preferred to show the world.

Tabby froze while Christien sprang out of bed and hauled on his jeans. She remembered that as she'd clambered off the motorbike that evening Pete had leant forward and kissed her before they'd parted. It had lasted only a second and she had not wanted to shoot him down in flames in front of his mates and hers by making a three-act tragedy out of something so small.

'You saw that...' she gasped in genuine horror. 'Oh, *no*!'

Unimpressed, Christien sent her a sizzling look of derision. 'Did you do it on the bike with him the same way you laid yourself across the bonnet of my car for me?'

'Don't be disgusting!' Tabby launched at him in a rage of quivering mortification and then she fell still again, agile brain working fast. It was like a missing piece of jigsaw puzzle suddenly slotting into place for her. But unlike with the average jigsaw that missing piece had changed the whole picture. Taken in isolation, what Christien had seen must have looked damning. During that week, he had been away in Paris and he hadn't been in touch and then he had seen her kissing someone else.

'Why on earth didn't you confront me?' Tabby slung at the lean bronzed back heading down the stairs.

'You think I would lower myself to that level?' Christien shot back at her in disbelief.

Tabby almost screeched her frustration out loud and raced in his wake.

Christien emerged in shock from his brush with the primitive plumbing facilities. 'There is no place to wash!' he condemned with incredulity.

'There's a sink and a geyser that gives hot water... I want to talk about Pete—'

'So that was his name...' Christien snarled. 'You tart!'

'Stop it!' Tabby launched at him. 'My friends were there and so were his and it was broad daylight. I went for a spin on his bike...that's all. That stupid little kiss you saw was all that *ever* happened between us!'

'You think I am about to believe *that*?'

'Why not? I didn't kiss him back but it didn't even last long enough for me to push him away...it was innocent. I was nuts about you—'

'And the biggest liar in Europe!' Christien countered with crushing effect.

She paled and then flushed beet-red with guilt for it was unanswerable. 'But not about that,' she persisted tautly. 'I wouldn't have gone with any other bloke and you should have known that. But then maybe you did and you just needed another excuse to put me out of your life.'

Christien swore in French but he had stilled too and doubt was touching him for the first time. Back then he too had believed she was too keen on him to stray. However, at the time newly aware of just how young she actually was, he had also known just how short-lived a teenage infatuation could be.

'Then you got the ultimate excuse to stay away, didn't you?' In Tabby's anguished gaze was the terrible memory of their meeting like strangers in the hospital waiting room thronged with those whose lives had been damaged by Gerry Burnside's drunk driving and for ever shadowed by the lost lives of those who had not survived that night.

Gerry Burnside had driven round a corner on the wrong side of the road and he had crashed the four-wheel drive head-on into Henri Laroche's Porsche. Tabby's stepmother, Lisa, had been the only adult who had not been in her husband's car and she had been having hysterics in the waiting room. Pippa had been shattered by the death of her mother and waiting to hear how the emergency surgery on her father had gone. Hilary and her little sister, Emma, had been huddled together, bereft of both their parents. Jen's mother had been badly injured as well and Jen had been praying for her survival.

Christien had appeared with Veronique Giraud, his beautiful

dark eyes bleak with shock and grief, and Tabby had wanted to go to him to hold him, but she had not had the nerve to reach out in that moment to the man she loved, who had lost his father through her father's drunken, inexcusable recklessness at the wheel.

'My father's death...the crash...it would never have kept me from you.' Lean strong face taut, Christien hauled her into the sheltering circle of his strong arms.

'I wasn't involved with Pete,' Tabby told him again, determined to make him listen to her.

Christien knotted one hungry hand into her hair and kissed her breathless, shutting out the uneasy feelings she had stirred up. He had no desire to rehash the past. All he could think about was the next time he would be with her and the time after that and how often he would be able to fly up from Paris to be with her. Here in his great-aunt's summer house on the Duvernay estate? Impossible! He would find her a much more suitable and far superior property elsewhere...

Somewhere in the early hours, Tabby opened her eyes and moaned with helpless pleasure beneath Christien's expert ministrations. 'Again...?' she mumbled, marvelling at his stamina and luxuriating in him being so demanding too.

'Are you too tired?' His gorgeous accent was as effective on her as the effortless way he had managed to turn her liquid with longing even while she was still half asleep.

'Don't you dare stop,' she muttered and he laughed huskily and pushed her to fever pitch before he finally, mercifully answered the great shameless tide of hunger he had roused and left her limp and dazed with an overload of satisfaction.

When Tabby wakened again, dawn had been and gone and when she stretched she discovered a dozen aches in secret places. She flipped over to survey Christien while he slept. Black lashes curled against a bronzed cheekbone, blue black stubble roughened his handsome jawline. The sheet was twisted round his hip, a muscular, long brown arm and a slice of hair-roughened chest exposed. Her chin resting on her folded arms, she suppressed a dreamy sigh. It was as if time had gone into reverse and she didn't really want to wake up and acknowledge the older, wiser individual she was supposed to be four years on.

He was the father of her son, so it wasn't surprising that she had never been able to forget him. In any case, it now seemed clear that only a stupid misunderstanding had separated them that summer. Such a little thing too that she could almost have screamed her frustration to the heavens: he had seen Pete kiss her and had assumed she'd been cheating on him. Of course that was Christien: the supreme pessimist and cynic always expecting the worst. Her lush mouth quirked. Oh, yes, she now understood why he would not even spare her five minutes on the day of the accident enquiry. His fierce pride would never allow him to overlook or forgive betrayal. For the first time, she also saw that the very ferocity of his rejection then had been revealing.

Last night, she had slept with him again. Over and over and over again. She was shameless, but she knew that if he woke up she still wouldn't say no to him. He was the only guy she had ever slept with but she was literally his for the asking every time and if she still loved him—and she suspected she did—was that so bad? Especially when fate seemed to be giving them a second chance? Or was it Solange who had given them a second chance? Had the older woman guessed that when she left the cottage to Tabby it would bring Christien into contact with her again?

Tabby smiled because a crazy happy feeling was bubbling up inside her. But then she tensed again for there was no denying that Christien was in for a major shock when she told him about Jake. She decided that she would prefer to spend some time with Christien *before* she made her big, stressful announcement. Just for one day, she bargained with her conscience, so that they could rediscover their relationship and sort out any other misunderstandings before she delivered the news that he was also the father of her three-year-old son. How was he likely to feel about that? Appalled? Pleased? But wasn't she rather putting the cart before the horse as well as being very presumptuous? What if... Christien had made love to her again out of simple lust? What if he just wanted to walk away from her again when he woke up? What if what they had just shared meant nothing at all to him?

Pale as parchment and feeling sick at that potential scenario, Tabby averted her gaze from him and crept out of bed. When she checked her watch, she grimaced for it was already almost nine. She had loads and loads of things to get done and very little time in which to accomplish them. Tomorrow she had to leave early to catch the ferry back to England again, she reminded herself doggedly. Lifting her overnight bag, she headed downstairs to freshen up and get dressed. She would call Alison from the public phone box she had noticed in the village and speak to Jake. She had to buy in wood and get the range going as well as stock up on basic groceries. In little more than a week's time she would be bringing Jake back over to France with her and she needed to make the cottage as welcoming as possible for his benefit.

Ought she to leave a note for Christien explaining where she had gone and when she hoped to be back from her errands? Wouldn't that make her seem a little clingy and desperate? She winced, feeling too vulnerable to lay herself open to the risk of rejection. It was better to do nothing at all. He knew where she was and he would have to go home for breakfast anyway as there was no food whatsoever in the kitchen. In any case, when she had made love with him the night before, she conceded painfully, she had demonstrated a remarkable ability to overlook the biggest stumbling block between them: the horrid accident in which his father had died. No matter how Christien felt, she was certain that his family would react to the news of his renewed involvement with her, not to mention the reality of her son's parentage, with horrified disgust. Fifteen minutes later, Tabby drove off.

She was recalling how, at the accident enquiry, Solange had made an embarrassed attempt to excuse her relatives' palpable hostility towards Tabby. 'My niece, Christien's mother, is under sedation today. Her suffering is terrible,' the old lady had confided. 'We all grieve for Henri, but in time the family will appreciate that many other people have also lost loved ones.'

When Christien wakened, he was surprised to find himself still at the cottage and even more surprised to find himself alone. He never, ever stayed the night with a woman. He could not initially credit that Tabby could have gone out and left him and he entered the sun lounge from which he had a clear view of the garden before he accepted that she was nowhere to be found.

The bright room was cluttered with all the paraphernalia of an artist and when he saw the miniature painting on display he stopped to study it in some amazement. He had never seen anything so tiny, perfect and detailed as that landscape. At least, not outside the giant elaborate doll's house that his mother had made her lifetime hobby. If the miniature canvas was of Tabby's creation, she was very talented, but he was convinced that she had to be wrecking her eyesight painting in such a minute scale and he knew he would waste no time in suggesting that she concentrate her skills on larger creations.

She must have gone out to buy something for his breakfast, Christien decided. He wandered back up to the bedroom and strode to the window when he heard a car. A silver Mercedes coupé had drawn up on the other side of the road. A slight frownline divided his level dark brows for Matilde Laroche owned a car very similar, although she had not driven herself anywhere since his father's death. At the same time, he could not help but uneasily recall her hysterical overreaction the day before to the revelation that Tabby was taking possession of Solange's property. His Ferrari was sitting parked out front. Really, really discreet, Christien, he mocked himself. *Bon Dieu*, it was madness to even let it cross his mind that his ladylike parent might be so off the wall that she would lurk outside the cottage like some weird kind of stalker! Even so, suddenly he was very keen to see the car registration, but by the time he reached the front door the Mercedes had driven off again.

Initially, Christien made the most of his time alone to make several calls on his mobile phone and arrange a trip to a property in the Loire Valley. It was picturesque and secluded and enjoyed spectacular views. Tabby was sure to leap at his offer because it would be certifiable insanity to do anything else. When another thirty minutes passed without her reappearance, he started to worry that something might have happened to her. Suppose she had climbed into that clapped-out old van and forgotten that his countrymen drove on a different side of the road from the British? He paled. Jumping into his car, he headed for the village a couple of kilometres away. Tabby would have passed through it the day before and if she had gone out to buy food, it was the most obvious destination.

There on the steep and narrow single street he had the edifying sight of seeing Tabby, looking very appealing in a short, frilled denim skirt and a white T-shirt, standing chattering and laughing while a grinning tradesman loaded up her van with firewood and admired her lithe, shapely legs. Nowhere could Christien see any evidence that she might have gone shopping to provide him with a breakfast or even that she was anxious to hurry back to the cottage!

Tabby saw the Ferrari and froze in dismay. Christien was watching her from the lowered window, designer sunglasses obscuring his expression, handsome jawline at a determined angle. He swung out of the car, six feet three inches of lean, lithe, gorgeous masculinity. A surge of colour warming her complexion, her mouth running dry as she remembered the passion of the night hours, she watched him approach. 'How did you know where I was?' she asked breathlessly.

'I didn't. I'm on my way home to Duvernay,' Christien murmured smooth as glass.

Tabby looked snubbed.

Against his own volition, Christien found himself smiling. 'I'll pick you up at twelve... OK?'

Warmth and animation leapt back into her expressive face. 'Where are we going?'

'I'd like that to be a surprise, *chérie*.'

When Tabby ought to have been cleaning the ancient kitchen range and scrubbing the terracotta floor tiles, she was washing her hair, daydreaming like a schoolgirl and dampening the single dress she had brought with her in the hope of getting the creases out of it.

Startlingly handsome in tailored cream chinos and a black shirt, Christien collected her and took her to an airfield where they boarded a small private plane.

'*You're* planning to fly us?' Tabby exclaimed in dismay.

'I've had my licence since I was a teenager... I do own an airline,' Christien reminded her gently.

'I don't like flying and, if I have to fly, I'm probably happiest in a jumbo jet,' Tabby confided with a grimace.

'It's a short flight, *ma belle*.' Christien dealt her a wide, appreciative grin that made her heart skip a beat. 'You have to be the only woman I've ever met who would dream of telling me that she hated flying.'

Undaunted by her nervous tension, he kept up a calm running commentary on the sights that she was too ennervated to take in during the flight. He flew with the same confidence with which he drove very fast cars. They landed at an airfield outside Blois where a chauffeur-driven limousine awaited them.

'Curiosity is killing me,' Tabby admitted. 'Where are you taking me?'

'Be patient,' he urged, linking long, lean fingers lazily with hers.

Some ten minutes later, the limo turned up a steep lane bounded on either side by vineyards and finally came to a halt outside an elegant house built of mellow golden stone and ringed by shaded terraces ornamented with urns of beautiful flowers.

'At least tell me who we're visiting...' Tabby hissed.

As Christien mounted the steps a charismatic smile slashed his lean, strong face. 'We're the only visitors.'

Recalling the astonishing pleasure of that beautiful mouth on hers, Tabby felt dizzy and it was an effort to think again. 'Then...what are we doing here?'

Christien pushed the door wide on a spacious tiled hall. 'I'd appreciate a feminine critique of this place.'

Assuming that the house was for sale, Tabby relaxed, flattered that he should want her opinion, but secretly amused that he should have chosen the inappropriate word, 'critique' for a property that even at first glance seemed to possess every possible advantage. It enjoyed immense privacy, a swimming pool and a hillside setting blessed with panoramic views of the wonderful wooded countryside. The interior was even more impressive. Fascinated, she strolled from room to room. It was an old house that had been renovated with superb style. Rich, warm colour, antique and contemporary furniture melded in a timeless joining. French windows led out to cool stone terraces and finally to one where she was surprised to find a uniformed waiter stationed in apparent readiness to serve them beside a table already set with exquisite china and gleaming crystal glasses.

'Lunch,' Christien explained with the utmost casualness as he pulled out a seat for her occupation. 'I don't know about you but I am very hungry. I usually eat at one.'

Tabby sank down and watched the waiter pour the wine. 'I thought this house belonged to someone else and you were thinking of buying it.'

A broad shoulder lifted in a fluid shrug. 'No, it's already mine but I've never been here before,' he admitted. 'Property is an excellent investment and I buy most of it through advisors sight unseen.'

'I can't imagine owning a house and not being curious enough to come and see it,' she admitted, reminded more than she liked of the vast material differences between them, something she had airily ignored and refused to consider important when she had first known him.

Over a sublime meal of endive salad followed by delicate lamb cutlets that melted in her mouth and a blackberry tart, Christien entertained her with stories of the rich history of the locality before moving on to describe the beautiful, tranquil water meadows of the Sologne as a nature lover's paradise. It was a hot, sultry afternoon and the sky was a deep, intense blue. Far across the lush valley she could see the fanciful turrets of one of the many châteaux in the area. Only birdsong challenged the silence and it was idyllic.

'You haven't offered a single opinion on this place yet,' Christien commented.

'It's fantastic…you've got to know that.' Tabby nibbled at her lower lip, colour lighting her cheeks as she squirmed on the acknowledgement that her standards might well lie far below his. 'But then, of course… I don't know what you're looking for.'

'What pleases you, *ma belle*.' Christien captured and held her startled upward glance. 'That's all I seek.'

Meeting those rich dark eyes framed by black spiky lashes, she could hardly breathe for the pure bolt of longing that shot through her and tightened her skin over her bones. Almost giddy with the force of her response to him, she took a second or two to register what he had just said.

'What pleases…*me*?' Tabby echoed, uncertain of his meaning.

In a graceful movement, Christien rose upright and stretched out a lean brown hand in invitation. 'Let's take another tour…'

He walked her slowly through the house again, but only on a superficial level was she appreciating the beautiful rooms and the stupendous outlook from every window. Her thoughts were in turmoil. Was he asking her to live with him here in this fabulous house? Why else would he care what pleased her in the property stakes? She sucked in a quivering breath in an effort to steady herself, but a wild burst of joy was thrilling through her.

'You like it here...don't you?' he prompted.

'Who wouldn't?' Tabby was so scared that she had picked him up wrong that she vented a discomfited laugh

'It might be too quiet for some, but it strikes me as the perfect environment for an artist. Peaceful and inspiring,' Christien murmured huskily.

It was little more than twenty-four hours since she had arrived in France. Could her eminently sensible and practical Christien be so impulsive? Could he have decided so quickly that he wanted to recapture what they had shared almost four years earlier? Did he, like her, feel bitter at the events that had driven them apart? Was he as greedy as she was to make up for lost time?

Tabby focused on the bottle of champagne in the ice bucket sitting on an occasional table and belatedly took note of the reality that he had chosen to stage the dialogue in the main bedroom. Coincidence? She didn't think so. She tried not to smile at how he planned even romantic gestures for she did not want to offend his pride. At seventeen she had once told him angrily that he had no romance in his soul at all and he had made extraordinary efforts to prove her wrong with surprise gifts and flowers and holding hands without anything more physical in mind. But she had always recognised the cold-blooded, purposeful planning it took for him to make an effort to do anything he saw as an essential waste of time.

'This property is also very convenient to Paris where I spend most of my working week.' As if to stress that leading declaration, Christien drew her back against his lean, muscular length.

The heat and proximity of his lithe, masculine frame tightened her nipples into stiff little points and stirred a dulled ache between her thighs. Trembling, she leant back into him for support. It seemed that he had spoken the truth when he'd told her that the manner of his father's death would never have kept him from her. Tears burned behind her eyes, tears of happiness, and her throat constricted. He was being crazily impractical and that was so out of character for him that it could only mean that he still had strong feelings for her.

Tabby stared hard into the mirror across the room that reflected them both: Christien, so straight and tall and serious and beautiful, her own reflection that of a woman so much smaller, decidedly rounder in shape and a great deal more given to smiles. 'This is so romantic…it must have taken loads of planning—'

'You used to say that the essence of real romance was not being able to see the strings that were being pulled to impress you,' Christien interposed.

'So I was too demanding at seventeen, now I give more points for effort and imagination like that lovely meal—'

When he spun her round and looked down at her, a tremor of almost painful awareness ran through her slight figure for she was weak with wanting. 'Do you, *chérie*?' he asked in a roughened undertone. 'Or when you hear what I have to say, will you accuse me of trying to manipulate you?'

'Perhaps I had better hear what you have to say first,' Tabby said breathlessly.

'I brought you here to suggest a very simple arrangement which would answer both our needs. I offer you this house in place of Solange's property…'

Her lips parted company. 'You've got to be kidding me.'

'No, you would be doing me a favour. A straight swop. Nothing as tasteless as money need change hands. I would prefer not to cut a business deal with you.' His brilliant dark golden eyes urged her to smile at that teasing assurance.

But Tabby had never felt less like smiling. She was also far too busy schooling her features not to betray how much he had wounded her and how bitter was the sting as her own foolish, extravagant hopes crashed and burned. His great-aunt's cottage in exchange for a luxury home five times its size and possessed of every opulent expensive extra? He wanted her off the Duvernay estate very, very badly. After the night she had spent in his arms, that continuing determination felt like a hard, humiliating slap in the face.

'I'd like to leave now.' Her green eyes shiny as polished glass in her determination to show no weakness or emotion, Tabby walked out of the bedroom into the hall. 'I still have so much to do back at the cottage. I have to return to England for a week tomorrow.'

Christien frowned, for she could not hide her sudden pallor. 'Tabby—'

'No, don't say any more or I'll lose my temper,' she warned not quite steadily. 'After all, you brought me here on false pretences and I'm not under any obligation to discuss ridiculous swops or business deals if I don't want to.'

'I did not say you were, but a fair and generous proposition rarely causes offence and usually deserves consideration. I hoped you'd be sensible.'

'And if I'm not, what then? Threats?'

'I don't threaten women,' Christien contradicted with icy disdain. 'You're being irrational. I want to keep the family estate intact and there is no shame in that objective. Nothing that happens between us will change that reality and I won't pretend otherwise.'

Rigid-backed, Tabby stepped out into the hot, still air and headed for the limousine, for she was desperate to be gone. Irrational? Was it irrational to feel unbearably hurt? Was her very presence within miles of the fancy château where he had been born such an offence? She felt sick at her own stupidity. Like a moth to a candle flame she had been drawn to him again. He had burned her before and after that warning it had been very naive of her to invite such pain a second time. But she was angry with him, so angry that she could barely bring herself to look at him and certainly not to speak.

Two hours later, he brought the Ferrari to a halt beside the cottage. As Tabby leapt out he followed suit at a slower pace. 'We have to talk this out,' he drawled with cool determination.

Two high spots of colour burning over her cheekbones, Tabby shot him a splintering glance. 'No, I don't want to talk to a guy who thinks of me as being something less than he is!'

'You have no grounds to accuse me of that.'

'Oh, haven't I?' A rather shrill laugh fell from her lips. 'You just tried to bribe me...you just tried to *buy* me!'

'It wasn't a bribe. In no way is that house I showed you intended as a bribe. But if I'm asking you to rethink your plans and relocate purely for my benefit, I must offer some form of compensation to make the inconvenience seem worth your while,' Christien proclaimed without hesitation.

'You are *so* smooth! How is it that you manage to make even the unacceptable sound acceptable?' Tabby demanded with furious resentment.

'I doubt that you would be reacting like this if I had not shared your bed last night. That has clouded the real issue at stake here.' Wide, sensual mouth compressing, Christien dealt her a brooding masculine scrutiny.

'You're right...*that* was a very big mistake.' Tabby slammed the front door loudly shut in his startled face and leant back against it in a tempest of angry, hurting tears.

'Tabby!'

As he rapped on the door she sucked in a steadying breath, but silent, stinging tears trekked down her quivering cheeks. In letting him stay the night she had regressed to the impulsive, reckless teenage years. She had forgotten all caution and common sense and flung her heart back at his feet. Did she never learn? Why was she so downright stupid around him?

Sean called her on her mobile phone at seven. The day before he had mentioned knowing the Englishwoman who owned the local art gallery and her daughter, who was a potter.

'Alice has asked us over for drinks. There'll be a crowd, there always is. You're sure to meet a few other creative types,' Sean told her cheerfully.

Tabby felt that company would distract her troubled thoughts from Christien and, although she went out with no expectation of enjoyment, she had an interesting evening. She met several artists living in the area, exchanged phone numbers and garnered useful information about where to buy art supplies. It was two in the morning when Sean brought her home. Only when she saw the lights flick on did she realise that Christien's Ferrari was parked at the side of the cottage. He climbed out, his long, powerful stride carrying him towards her at speed.

Tabby was very tense but determined to save what face she could and she moved forward with as easy and meaningless a smile as she could contrive. 'Christien...sorry I'm so late back—'

'*Zut alors...* I'm not!' he bit out, lean, dark handsome features taut with a scorching fury that took her aback. 'You almost had me convinced that I had misjudged you, but I've caught you in the act again. Where have you been all evening? In his bed? First one man, then another. You sleep with me and—'

'*Regret it,*' Tabby slotted in between angrily clenched teeth. 'Oh, boy, do I regret sleeping with you!'

Appreciating that he had been totally overlooked in the excitement, Sean peered out of his car, which was still parked by the roadside. 'Do you want me to stay, Tabby?' he called anxiously.

'See how you embarrass me!' Tabby snapped at Christien before she stalked back down the path to urge Sean to go on home and not worry about her.

Christien spread lean hands and swore in fast, furious French, demonstrating all the lack of tolerance typical of a male who had never in his whole charmed life been accused of causing anyone embarrassment.

Tabby unlocked the front door with a trembling hand. 'I don't ever want to see you again—'

'Why did you refuse to let me in when I brought you back from viewing the house earlier? You must have known that I would return here.' Christien stepped past her and then swung round to treat her to a fierce look of condemnation. 'Were you scared you might want to spend two nights with the same guy?'

In the moonlight, Tabby shivered with outrage. 'How can you talk to me as if I'm some slapper who goes with a load of different men?'

'When I'm around there's always another guy panting at your heels!'

'Just to think that your friend, Veronique, once told me that *you* liked competition!' Tabby recalled with bitter amusement. 'I guess that piece of misinformation was advanced with the same self-serving venom as all the other helpful advice she offered me.'

Christien had fallen very still. '*ça alors!* Veronique would never have said such a nonsensical thing—'

'Oh, wouldn't she? Your childhood playmate probably dug out her calculator in that cradle beside yours, worked out what a catch you were and decided right there and then that only she was going to profit. Who knows...who cares?' Tabby was mortified that she had let that petty bitterness out and paraded it for him to see. 'Obviously she knew you had a jealous streak a mile wide and guessed that nothing would kill our relationship faster—'

Febrile colour lying along his superb cheekbones, Christien threw back his broad shoulders and studied her with grim disfavour. 'It shames me to lose my temper as I just have and throw allegations that I cannot substantiate *but* I don't trust you—'

Tabby tilted her chin. 'And I won't stand for you accusing me of carrying on with other blokes.'

Eyes glittering gold with anger, Christien vented a harsh laugh. 'What do you expect me to think when you stay out this late and show up with another man in tow?'

'It amazes me that you can even ask me that when I'm the one who has never, ever had the luxury of knowing where I stand with you...yet you are *so* good at criticising my behaviour,' Tabby condemned with a slow, wondering shake of her head. 'Four years ago, you had another woman in your life called Eloise and you never once mentioned her existence to me. You got away with it too, because I was too scared to ask awkward questions—'

His lean, strong face was rigid. 'The minute I saw you it was over with Eloise and it was only a casual thing with her. I ended it soon after I met you. I don't know how you found out about her, but you only had to ask me. Unlike you, I would have been *honest*—'

Savaged by that reminder of her past dishonesty, Tabby twisted away from him and switched on the light. 'So I lied about my age and you know why, but that doesn't mean I can't be trusted—'

'No?'

'No...any more than it excuses you for implying that I'm a tart,' Tabby told him with spirit.

'Where were you until this hour?'

'I'm not telling you, I'm not answering your questions—'

'*Zut alors...*' Christien growled, raking long, lean, impatient fingers through the black silk luxuriance of his hair. 'What do you expect from me?'

Tabby was amazed that in spite of all she had already said he still had no idea whatsoever. 'Respect.'

Christien threw up his expressive hands, studied her with fulminating dark golden eyes, but, while he looked as though he could hardly wait to exercise his sardonic tongue on that ambitious request of hers, he stayed silent.

'Respect,' Tabby repeated doggedly. 'You made a mistake when you decided that I was cheating on you with that boy, Pete, that summer and you owe me an apology.'

'I...*do*?' Burnished dark eyes flared down into hers and she could literally feel the hum of his fierce pride threatening to blow the lid back off his temper again.

'Particularly for the way you treated me at the accident enquiry... I deserved better. You think about that—'

'*Tu parles*…the hell I will!' Christien raked at her and then, as though as disconcerted by that raw outburst as she was, he swung away.

'So that's respect and an apology,' Tabby listed in reminder, deciding to go for gold in the demand stakes. 'But if you want houseroom in my life, I want other stuff too…and I'm not sure if you could make the grade.'

Involuntarily, Christien almost grinned, wondering if she thought she could train him with her version of 'the carrot and the stick' routine. 'I score very high between the sheets, *ma belle*,' he breathed with husky insolence.

'But unfortunately an awful lot of life takes place outside the bedroom door and offering me a millionaire's residence in place of a tiny cottage was the last straw. Even though I've told you how I feel, you can't respect your great-aunt's wishes or my right to live where I choose,' Tabby spelt out, a great weariness enfolding her, for the stress of the past forty-eight hours and the lack of rest had drained her of her usual highwire energy.

'But—'

'All I want to do right now is jump off my soapbox, fall into bed and sleep like a log,' Tabby cut in heavily.

Christien bent down and swept her up into his arms to carry her upstairs. 'As I wouldn't like you to risk jumping, your wish is my command.'

'Put me down…' Tabby protested in weary frustration, so tired that she was very close to tears.

Christien settled her down on the bed and switched on the lamp. 'Possibly *I* was more at home in the millionaire's residence,' he remarked in a thoughtful concession. 'But you liked it too…don't lie.'

Tabby groaned and let her shoes slide off and drop to the floor. She could not be bothered arguing with him and she let her heavy eyes drift shut. Just to refresh herself for a moment, she promised herself.

Christien gazed down at Tabby while she slept, and sighed.

He unbuttoned her shirt and eased it off and removed her skirt. He studied the creamy swell of her breasts above her bra and the incredible peach bloom of her skin and suppressed a groan at his own lack of self-discipline. He wanted to get into bed with her. In fact the intensity of his own desire to be with her even when sex was out of the question unnerved him. He tugged the sheet up over her, put out the light and frowned at the un-curtained window and the front door that lacked any form of proper security. A grim look of disapproval crossed his lean, strong face. He knew that he had decisions to make.

CHAPTER FIVE

'LET ME UNDERSTAND THIS…' Nine hours later, Veronique Giraud studied Christien across the depth of her opulent riverside apartment in Paris. 'You want to break off our engagement for unspecified reasons?'

'Not unspecified. I've come to recognise that I'm not yet ready to commit to a marriage.' Christien's level dark gaze was filled with sincere regret as he surveyed his fiancée in her tailored business suit. 'I only wish that for your sake I had seen that reality sooner.'

'We haven't set a wedding date and I wasn't expecting to set one in the near future,' Veronique pointed out with admirable calm. 'You can take all the time you require to think this decision over.'

Relieved by her unemotional response, Christien expelled his breath. 'I appreciate that but I've had all the time I need to consider this and I must still ask you to release me from our engagement. I'm sorry that it has to be like this.'

After a moment of thought, Veronique gave a gracious nod of acceptance. 'There's no need for you to apologise. I wouldn't want to hold you to our agreement against your will.'

A warm smile of appreciation lightened Christien's grave aspect. 'I know you would never do that. We might have become engaged on a business and social basis but we have a strong friendship as well. I would hate to lose a friendship which I have always valued. But I will understand if you prefer to let that connection wane now.'

'I wouldn't dream of behaving that way. I won't pretend that I agree with the decision that you've reached, but neither will I make a fuss about it,' the self-contained brunette said briskly. 'However, I hope you won't be annoyed by my frank speech when I say that you will soon discover once again that that little madam is much more trouble than she is worth!'

Almost imperceptibly, Christien tensed. 'You can always be frank with me.'

'Even though I am saying things you cannot possibly want to hear?' Veronique's pale blue eyes had a hard sparkle new to his experience and his keen gaze narrowed.

'Even then.'

'Of course, I know it's the English girl again and I don't want to be crude, but why can't you just scratch the sexual itch and leave it at that level?' Veronique demanded in cold exasperation. 'I assure you that I require no confessions.'

Christien had to make an effort to conceal his distaste. 'Nothing is that simple.'

'But it *is*. It is you who are making it complex by being too conventional and expecting too much of yourself. What has come over you?' the brunette prompted with an air of concerned incomprehension. 'You yourself believe that your parents' relationship was unhealthily obsessive and your mother is *still* unable to function without your father. I understood that you wanted to guard against the risk of making such a destructive marriage—'

'I am not thinking of marriage,' Christien interposed in flat denial.

Veronique looked mollified by that assurance. 'Then why end

our engagement over something as trivial as an affair? Fidelity means nothing to me. I don't mind if you keep the Burnside woman as a mistress, for there are far more important matters in life!' she proclaimed with unhidden impatience. 'This situation is exactly why I offered to deal with that calculating little creature on your behalf.'

'Forgive me, but I will not discuss Tabby with you, nor listen to abuse of her.' His brooding dark eyes were veiled, his well-modulated speaking tone discouraging.

Veronique removed the huge solitaire on her engagement finger and set it down on the table with just the suspicion of a snap.

'It is yours…it was a gift,' Christien asserted. 'If you no longer want it, give it to charity.'

Veronique's thin lips stretched into an unexpectedly warm and reassuring smile. Rising, she tucked a slender hand into his elbow. 'At least I can now talk to you as a friend and perhaps you will listen with more patience. I *do* hope that we're still going out to meet our friends for lunch…'

'*So*,' Pippa Stevenson recapped, rolling her very blue eyes, 'although we've moved on nearly four years in our lives you're still happily falling for the Christien Laroche solid gold seduction routine.'

Tabby winced. 'It wasn't like that, Pip—'

'Lean, mean and magnificent, the guy most likely to succeed in business, in bed and every other place because conscience will never keep him awake,' her friend quipped with a cynically curled lip. 'You moving into Christien's neighbourhood is like a goldfish opting to go swimming with sharks!'

Tabby stiffened for, having let herself down very badly, as she felt, with Christien, she was less laid-back about the prospect of taking up permanent residence in the same locality. It was ironic that their renewed intimacy was likely to bring about the sale that he had wanted from the outset, she reflected unhappily. 'I may have to reconsider where Jake and I should live—'

'Considering your non-existent ability to resist Christien, I think that has to be the best news I've heard in a long time!' As Tabby flinched the redhead groaned in guilty embarrassment. 'I'm sorry... I am *truly* sorry. Believe it or not, I didn't invite you and Jake to stay here on your last night in England just so that I could make snide comments.'

'For goodness' sake, I know you didn't...' But as usual, Tabby recognised, her closest friend, who was burdened by a demanding job and the care of a disabled parent, was stressed out and exhausted.

'Whatever happens, I still feel that you ought to tell Christien that he has a son,' Pippa admitted in some discomfiture.

'I agree.' Tabby no longer required prompting on that score. Having reached that same conclusion, she almost smiled at her companion's surprise over her change of heart. 'When I decided to move to Brittany, I honestly did believe that I wouldn't see Christien again. I didn't think things through, which was foolish and short-sighted—'

'Easy enough to do in the circumstances.' Pippa gave her a look of understanding.

'But I *do* think it would be unfair to put Christien in an awkward position with his family...or perhaps a girlfriend over Jake while we're living so close,' Tabby revealed uneasily. 'I still have to work out how best to handle that.'

'It's Christien's own fault that he's likely to be the last to know about Jake. Naturally you were intimidated by the animosity that you met with when you attended the inquest into the crash.' Pippa frowned. 'That was so cruel—'

'But the way some people couldn't help feeling and probably will *still* feel about me,' Tabby emphasised with a grimace. Pippa dropped her gaze and neither woman chose to mention the reality that, since that accident, Tabby had also lost touch with their other friends, Hilary and Jen.

'They needed a focus for their bitterness and grief and Dad was dead, so I made the next best target,' Tabby continued.

'It's just I couldn't bear Christien or anybody else in his family to look at Jake in that same tainted light...as though he was something to be ashamed of, apologised for and concealed—'

'Why should he be? Your son is the mirror image of his very handsome papa. And Christien Laroche is not the male I took him for if he does not relish the sight of himself reprised in miniature,' Pippa opined drily. 'Furthermore, when Jake reveals his meteoric IQ and his deeply boring current obsession with fast cars Christien will experience such a shocking sense of soul-deep recognition that he will be flattered to death.'

Tabby cherished much less ambitious notions. She only hoped that once Christien got over the shock, he would be interested in getting to know his son. An hour later, sighing at the sound of her much-put-upon friend trekking downstairs again to fulfil yet another late-night demand from her domineering parent, Tabby climbed into the spare-room bed where Jake already lay fast asleep.

Eight days had passed since she had left France. Christien had tucked her into bed that last night and left her alone. Although that was what she had wanted, she had felt ridiculously abandoned the next morning and very sad driving away in the van. Indeed it had been a week during which Tabby had become increasingly angry with herself for her repeated failure to push Christien out of her mind, not to mention her reluctance to tell Christien that he was the father of her child. That smacked of a cowardice that Tabby was determined to confront within herself.

As Tabby drove off the ferry into France the following day she was keen to draw Jake's attention to the more unusual cars on the road to keep him occupied during the lengthy drive ahead. 'There's a Rolls Royce...' she told her son helpfully.

The little boy shifted excitedly in his seat.

'Are you excited about the new house?' Tabby asked.

'Can I jump on my new bed?'

'Forget it!' Tabby said with a grin.

The minute Tabby parked in the driveway at the cottage, Jake headed straight for the back garden with his football, eager to stretch his legs after being cooped up for so long. Tabby decided to let him burn off some energy before she took him indoors. In truth, she was afraid of seeing disappointment on his earnest little face. He was only three years old and it took adult imagination to see that the drab cottage had promise.

'Stay in the garden and don't go near the road!' she called in his wake, knowing her first priority would have to be the installation of a gate across the driveway.

Jake stopped and uttered a world-weary sigh that would have done justice to a little old man. 'I *know*... I'm not a baby now,' he muttered in reproach.

Entering the cottage while she thought about how shockingly fast Jake seemed to be growing up, Tabby came to an abrupt halt and stared with bewildered eyes at her unfamiliar surroundings. In panic she started backing outside again, believing that she had somehow contrived to gain entry to someone else's home. Only when she saw the gorgeous artistic arrangement of flowers beside the fireplace and the large envelope that bore her name in Christien's writing did she halt her retreat. In a daze, Tabby crept back inside again and snatched up the envelope to extract the card within.

'I respect your right to live where you choose...call me, Christien.'

A phone sat beside the floral offering. He had even had a phone line connected. The windows had been replaced and the walls had been painted in fresh colours. In a daze she looked around the room, which now was furnished with twin sofas and a handsome *armoire*. Dumbstruck, she peered into the kitchen and saw superb new freestanding units complete with discreet appliances and a beautiful dining set. A clock ticked on the mantel. The wine rack was packed with bottles. She looked into a fridge bursting with fresh produce and let the door fall shut again. Her son waved at her from the garden and she lifted a nerveless hand in response.

All of a tremble, she snatched up the phone and stabbed out the number that Christien had put on the card. As she waited for the call to connect she glanced into the little washroom and stopped dead. Because the 'little' washroom now appeared to encompass the enclosed porch beyond it as well and had a shower, marble tiles and a Jacuzzi that was state-of-the-art. A walk-in airing cupboard was packed with an array of fleecy towels and what looked very much like entire rows of crisp bed linen.

'Tabby…what do you think?' Christien purred as she hurried up the stairs with the receiver of the cordless phone clutched in her perspiring hand.

'I think… I think I'm hallucinating,' she mumbled, gaping at the rich wool carpet on the stairs.

'*Bien*… I thought I was having a nightmare when I first saw inside the cottage as it was,' Christien confided teasingly. 'A home fit only for a cave dweller—'

'Christien…there is just no way that I can accept any of this,' Tabby asserted in a wobbly voice. 'Have you gone out of your mind? This whole place has been torn apart and remodelled into far more than it was ever meant to be. It's so seriously trendy it must have cost a fortune!'

'It's my way of saying sorry for being pushy and welcoming you back to your new home, *ma belle*,' Christien murmured smoothly.

'How on earth did you even get into this place?' Tabby queried. 'Did you break in?'

Her bedroom had been embellished with a bed in which a princess would have felt at home and dressed with snazzy silk curtains and an over abundance of crisp white lace-edged pillows and sheets. The colour scheme was in her favourite shades of pale turquoise and lemon and she wondered dizzily if he had remembered that.

'Solange kept a spare key hidden in the trunk of the old tree in the front garden. I've removed it,' he confessed.

'Thanks for warning me!' Tabby sniped, but the reproof lacked bite because her voice was weak. 'I just can't believe you've done all this…and in such an incredibly short space of time.' She glanced into Jake's room, which, having already been furnished, had benefited a little less noticeably from fresh paint and polished floorboards. 'What are you expecting in return? Me in a gift box?'

His husky, sexy laugh vibrated down her spinal cord like a caress.

'How am I supposed to hand back new windows when you haven't left me the old ones?' Tabby demanded, looking out the bedroom window to note that a big glossy car had stopped out on the quiet road.

'When I want you to climb into a gift box for me, you can be sure I'll cut off all avenues of retreat—'

'But I can't accept a generosity that I can't match—'

'Are you discriminating against me because I'm rich?' Christien countered with mockery.

Tabby walked downstairs again. 'If I accepted all this stuff… well, it would make me feel like I'm in your power—'

'That works fine for me,' Christien slotted in without shame.

'Or like I owed you big time—'

'I can't say that that idea turns me off either. I know it's not politically correct but, if your conscience is heavy, I could give you a suggestion or two on how best to lighten—'

'Shut up!' But Tabby was laughing until she went over to the kitchen window to check on Jake, only to discover he was nowhere within view. 'Hold on a minute,' she urged Christien then. 'Look, I'll call you back!'

After distractedly pressing the 'hold' button, then discarding the phone, Tabby headed into the front garden. Relieved that Jake had not strayed round there as she had feared, she took the time to study the car still sitting parked because she couldn't help wondering what it was doing there. It was a Mercedes and a very expensive-looking model. She was heading for the side of the cottage where she assumed her son was playing when she saw Jake running out from behind the van. He was chasing his ball, which was bouncing down the sloping driveway towards the road.

'No, Jake...*stop!*' Tabby screamed at the top of her voice.

But her shout was drowned out as the engine of the Mercedes suddenly ignited and the vehicle moved off. Even knowing that she was too far away, Tabby made a frantic attempt to reach her son and prevent him from running out into the road in front of the car. But she was too late. With a protesting screech of tyres, the driver braked hard and swerved to avoid Jake and the Mercedes mounted the verge with a crashing jolt before coming to a juddering halt.

For a split second deafening silence held and then Jake broke it with a frightened howl. Tabby grabbed him up, sat him down on the driveway and told him firmly to stay there while she raced across the road to check on the driver. The car door fell open and a slender, middle-aged blonde lurched out, her white face a mask of shock.

'Are you hurt?' Tabby gasped and then, fumbling for the French words, used them as well.

The woman hovered at the side of the road and stared fixedly at Jake. Then she began to sob noisily. Curving a supportive arm round her and feeling quite sick herself at what had so nearly transpired, Tabby urged the woman indoors. She offered to call a doctor and when that suggestion was met with a dismayed frown asked if the lady would like to call anyone. That too was met with a silent negative and she was careful to apologise for having left Jake alone in the garden.

'It was not your fault. Children will be children,' the woman finally responded in English while she continued to study Jake as if not yet fully convinced that he was wholly unharmed. 'We must thank *le bon Dieu* that he is safe. He is...your son? May I ask what he is called?'

'I'm Jake. Jake... Christien... Burnside,' Jake recited with care.

The lady was trembling. She twisted her head away and fumbled for another tissue from the box that Tabby had set beside her, her thin hands shredding at it as she choked back another sob.

'You're in shock and I'm not surprised after the fright my son must have given you,' Tabby said worriedly. 'Are you sure I can't phone the doctor for you, *madame*?'

'Perhaps...if I could have a glass of water?' The woman snatched in a deep breath in a clear effort to calm herself.

'Of course.' Tabby returned with the glass and found Jake chattering about cars and holding the woman's beringed hand. Tabby introduced herself.

A strange little silence fell

'Ma-Manette,' the older woman finally stammered, suddenly awkward again, her reddened eyes lowering. 'Manette...eh, Bonnard. Your son is so sweet. He kissed me because he saw that I was sad.'

Tabby took the opportunity to explain to Jake why Madame Bonnard had been sad and why he must never, ever again run out into a road.

'Please don't scold Jake... I am sure he will be more careful in the future.' Although Manette Bonnard was smiling and it seemed a very genuine smile, her eyes still glistened with unshed tears.

'Do you have a little boy like me?' Jake asked.

'A big boy,' their visitor answered.

'Does he like cars?'

'Very much.'

'Is he taller than me?' Perceptibly, Jake was stretching himself up, his innate competitive streak in the ascendant, dark brown eyes sparkling.

'Yes. He is all grown up,' Manette Bonnard said apologetically.

'Is he a good boy?'

'Not all the time.'

'I'll be very tall and very good when I get grown up,' Jake informed her confidently.

Keen to see the older woman fully recovered before she got back into her car, Tabby offered her coffee. A rather dazed look etched in her fine dark eyes, their visitor nodded polite acceptance while trying to answer Jake's questions. Jake had no inhibitions about being nosy and, by dint of simply listening to the older woman's initially hesitant replies, Tabby learned that their guest lived in Paris in an apartment that had *twelve* bedrooms and also had a summer home in the area.

'Mummy...can I show Madam Bonnard one of your pictures?' Jake pleaded.

'If it would not be too much of an intrusion, *mademoiselle*,' Manette Bonnard interposed. 'I collect miniatures.'

Tabby got her first glimpse of the sun lounge since her return and discovered that in Christien's makeover even her studio had gained sleek storage units and a wonderful mosaic tiled floor. The older woman enthused at length over the two tiny canvases she was shown and was disappointed to learn that both were earmarked for a client.

'I must not take up any more of your time, *mademoiselle*,' their visitor finally sighed with regret.

'I like you,' Jake told Madame Bonnard.

Tabby was unsurprised that Jake was so taken with the older woman for Manette Bonnard had demonstrated flattering enthusiasm for her son's company and had made no attempt to hide her appreciation from him. But she was dismayed when their very emotional visitor looked as though she was about to go off into floods of tears again.

'Are you sure that you feel well enough to drive?' Tabby prompted with concern.

The older woman kept her head down and patted Tabby's hand in an uncertain but apologetic gesture. 'Please don't worry...you don't understand... I am sorry,' she muttered in confusion before she broke away to hurry across the road and take refuge in her car.

Tabby was relieved to see that the Mercedes drove off at a slow speed.

She darted back indoors intending to ring Christien back and then she fell still, the excitement in her discomfited eyes dwindling. Why did Christien always do what she least expected? She had been angry and hurt when she'd last seen him and she had believed that she could forget their night of passion and write it off as the result of her own foolishness. His arrogant assumption that he could make her do what she did not want to do had offended and mortified her and persuaded her that it was not possible for her to try to rewrite the past with Christien. But in the space of a week, Christien had turned all her expectations upside down.

He had gone to extraordinary lengths to demonstrate that he had accepted her right to live in Solange Laroche's cottage. He had transformed the humble little dwelling into a sophisticated and trendy property bristling with luxury extras. Of course, he had had no right to do that, but it scarcely mattered now, did it? After all, if she was planning to seek a permanent home elsewhere, she would be selling the cottage back to Christien and it would have to be at a price that did not take account of the improvements that he had made at his own expense.

In retrospect her own weakness with Christien seemed unforgivable and inexcusable. She had not told him about Jake. She had let her heart and her hormones carry her away and she had slept with him again. The Jacuzzi big enough for two suggested that Christien was very keen to repeat that experience. Only Christien had no idea at all that she was the mother of a three-year-old, who had already contrived to leave a muddy footprint on one of the slinky cream sofas. And she was not just any single parent either, she was the mother of *his* child. How was she to break that news to him? Especially with Jake under the same roof? She gathered Jake into a hug and rested her chin down into his dark silky curls. Her eyes were stinging.

'Our clothes are in the van,' her son reminded her. 'We'll go out and get our cases.'

Having fetched their luggage in, Tabby called Christien back.

'Why did you leave me on hold?' he demanded.

'I didn't... I must have pushed the button wrong,' she answered, her voice a little thick.

'I was worried that some disaster had occurred... What are we doing tonight?'

He was the only guy she had ever met whose voice could make her melt like ice on a griddle. 'Would you come here? About eight?'

'Do I have to wait three hours?' he groaned.

'Yeah...sorry.' She wanted Jake in bed and safely asleep before Christien arrived.

'We'll dine out—'

'Eat before you get here,' Tabby advised tensely.

'*Eat*? Before eight in the evening?' Christien demanded in disbelief.

'Stop being so French. I... I've got something serious I need to discuss with you.'

There was a short, intense silence.

'So have I...the outrageous concept of dining before eight and being told to feed myself when I've offered to feed you,' Christien quipped.

'I'll see you then...' Tabby drew in a slow, deep, steady breath and finished the call.

She unpacked one suitcase, two boxes of Jake's toys, bathed her son in the Jacuzzi and watched him fall asleep over the simple supper that she made. She carried him up to bed and tucked him in before taking a quick shower. Then she trawled through two more suitcases before she found the casual khaki skirt and white camisole top she wanted to wear. She put on make-up, which she usually didn't bother with. She wondered why she *was* bothering when the very last thing Christien was likely to be doing after she broke the news about Jake was notice her appearance.

A bag of nerves at the prospect of the confrontation that lay ahead, Tabby paced the floor. She froze when she heard his powerful sports car pulling up outside. Way beyond any concept of playing it cool, she opened the door and watched him stride towards her: a breathtakingly good-looking guy in a lightweight pearl-grey designer suit.

Christien sent her a slashing smile that had a devastating effect on her defences. 'I'm not stupid, *ma belle*. I've worked it out. You think you're pregnant!'

CHAPTER SIX

Transfixed by that charge, Tabby stared at him with wide startled green eyes, her dismay unconcealed. 'Er...you think there's a chance of that?'

'I didn't take any risks but I do know that accidents happen and you sounded as though you were crying on the phone.' Dark colour now delineating the hard angles of his superb cheekbones, Christien shrugged back his broad shoulders in a dismissive gesture as he read her expressive face. '*Mais non...* I can see that that isn't the "something serious" you referred to.'

'No...er, it wasn't.'

Black brows drew together over his clear dark golden eyes. 'You're ill?' he breathed in a roughened undertone.

'Healthy as a horse.'

'Then we've got nothing at all to worry about, *mon ange*.' Thrusting the door shut in his wake and without skipping a beat, Christien curved his hands round her slight, taut shoulders and pulled her to him.

Tabby snatched in a short, sharp gasp of air. *'Christien—'*

'Don't cry wolf with me. I was really concerned.' But there was no true anger in his accented drawl for when she was that close he believed that he could have forgiven her anything short of cold-blooded murder.

'I know, but—'

Moulding her slight body to him, he vented a husky groan of very male satisfaction as the surging peaks of her full breasts met the hard, muscular wall of his chest. His hands curved round her bottom to bring her into closer contact with the rigid thrust of his erection.

'*Zut alors*...being with you is *all* I've thought about since you phoned!' Christien dragged in a deep shuddering breath because all he wanted to do at that instant was sate the savage ache of his desire: push her back against the wall, lift her, sink into her over and over again. No more finesse than an animal, he acknowledged in shock at himself.

Weak with the same overwhelming hunger, Tabby trembled, awash with wild, mindless response to him on a half-dozen different levels. Fighting for the self-control to pull back from his lean, powerful body, she pushed her face into his neck, but the unique scent of his bronzed skin, of *him* was the headiest of aphrodisiacs. Her heart thumping like crazy, she rubbed against him, instinctively seeking relief from the throbbing sensitivity of her nipples.

Swearing barely audibly, Christien knotted long fingers into her hair to tip her head back. Smouldering dark golden eyes blazed down into hers and she stretched up to him as though he had thrown a switch somewhere inside her. He crushed her mouth under his, delved deep with his tongue in an explicit rhythm that made her knees buckle and damp heat pool between her thighs.

'I need to be inside you...' Christien growled and, backing to the sofa, he brought her down on top of him.

When she tensed and made a whimper of sound that just might have been the beginning of an objection, he was too clever to employ reason. Instead he pushed the camisole up out of his path and negotiated the hazard of the stretchy inner lining supporting her breasts. When the plump rosy-tipped mounds tumbled free, he groaned in raw male approbation of their bounty. Cupping the creamy swells, he used his tongue on her stiff, sensitised nipples and she gasped in tormented delight beneath his skilful ministrations.

'We *can't*...' Tabby mumbled in despair, fighting her own unbearable craving with all her might.

Christien hushed her and a sob caught in her throat as he stroked a tantalising finger across the taut wet triangle of fabric stretched between her thighs. 'I *love* your body, I *love* the way you respond to me—'

'I...*have* to talk to you—'

'I'll be much more receptive in an hour's time when I've recovered from nine days of deprivation,' Christien promised huskily.

Already he had her so excited she couldn't get oxygen into her lungs. He was touching her and she was lost in the ever-building flow of sweet, seductive sensation. Clutching his shoulders for support, she let her head fall back, helpless while he toyed with her.

'Tell me how much you missed me, *ma belle*,' he urged against her lush, reddened mouth, but she was way beyond speech. Her whole being was concentrated on the wicked joy of what he was doing to her.

At a fever pitch of desire, she was quivering all over. Heart racing, she gyrated against his expert hand, crazy with hunger as the throbbing ache at the heart of her drove her on with shameless eagerness. Knotting one hand into her tumbling hair, he plunged his tongue into her readily opened mouth, once, twice with explicit, erotic force...and it was enough to push her over the edge into a shattering release that wrenched a cry of ecstasy from her.

Only as the wild tremors of her climax and the mist of mindless pleasure receded did Tabby become aware of her mortal body again. He held her close, murmuring soothing, incomprehensible things in French as if he knew that, both emotion-ally and physically, he had turned her inside out. He tipped her back from him, smoothing her tangled hair back from her brow.

He sent her a slashing smile that made her heart lurch. 'Al-though you couldn't tell me that I was missed, you can certainly *show* me,' he murmured with wicked appreciation.

Tabby reddened to the roots of her hair. He was still fully clothed. She had been so out of it that the pleasure had been hers alone. In a clumsy movement, her face burning with shame and embarrassment at how out of control she had been, she scram-bled off his lap and pulled her camisole down from her bare breasts. While she stood there trembling from shock at what had happened to her in his arms, lean bronzed hands smoothed down her rucked skirt and then enclosed her clenched fingers.

Slowly, Christien turned her back round to face him. 'Your passion gives me a hell of a kick. Don't you know how rare it is? I don't want a woman who worries about creasing her clothes or wrecking her hair—'

'Basically, you're happiest with a trollop!' Tabby framed in a wobbly voice, and then she literally fled to the bathroom before she let herself down even more and burst into tears.

Even there she got no privacy. Christien opened the door a crack. 'We'll go out to dinner and lust over each other through-out at least five courses...will that make you feel better?'

A hairbrush gripped between her fingers, Tabby looked at her shameful reflection in the mirror and knew that nothing was likely to make her feel better. 'We can't go out... I have to tell you something...and you're going to hate me.'

Silence fell and grew thick and heavy outside the bathroom door.

'Is there another guy involved?' Christien enquired roughly.
'No.'

'No problem...there's nothing else I can't handle. I'm very shock-proof,' Christien asserted with complete confidence. 'Do we *have* to sit through a five-course dinner? I'm hungry but I'm infinitely hungrier...and needier for you.'

Her throat thickened. 'I'll be out in a minute. Open one of those bottles of wine.'

'You want me to wait upstairs?' A ragged laugh sounded from Christien. 'If I sound desperate, it's because I am. I'm in agony!'

'Just stay downstairs,' Tabby instructed unsteadily.

She shut her eyes tight, forcing back the tears that would have released her tension. She was convinced that no woman had ever made a bigger mess of a relationship. She loved him. She had never stopped loving him. She loved just about everything about him: his sense of humour, his forceful personality, the passion and energy that he brought into every aspect of his life, even that volatile streak of possessiveness that was so contrary to his cool façade. But he didn't love her. He lusted after her like mad and that was the height of her power over him.

When he'd arrived, she should have kept him at arm's length, maintained a formal distance that would have been more conducive to the confession that she had to make. What she had just done, what she had just allowed him to do to her, had been very unwise and wrong. But then in her own defence she still had no very clear idea of how she had ended up on that sofa with Christien. Any more than there was anything new in her shell-shocked reaction to her own behaviour with him. When Christien touched her, everything but him blurred out of focus and importance. However, this one time, Tabby thought painfully, just this *one* time she should have had enough gumption to stay in control for her son's sake.

'What's worrying you?' Emanating megawatt self-assurance and calm, Christien passed her a glass of wine when she came out of the bathroom, narrowed dark golden eyes intent on her troubled face.

'What's worrying me goes back nearly four years,' Tabby informed him tightly, tipping the wine to her dry lips but barely able to bring herself to swallow.

'You've just come back into my life. It would seem more sensible to leave the past where it belongs for now,' Christien drawled.

'I'm afraid that this is a piece of the past that's not going to go away and roll back up at a more convenient time,' Tabby mumbled and, feeling her knees going weak under her, she sank down on a sofa and stared into her wineglass. 'That summer, do you remember me telling you that I was taking the contraceptive pill?'

Disconcerted by that question, Christien frowned. *'Oui...'*

Tabby was embarrassed and she refused to look at him. 'It was the doctor's idea that I start taking it because I was having problems with my skin...acne. Well, I was given a three-month supply but I lost a packet somewhere, which meant that I ran out of them while I was still in France.'

'Ran out of them...?' Christien queried in bewilderment.

Tabby cringed, for it was hard to admit just how naive she had been in those days. 'I didn't think it mattered too much if I had to miss a couple of weeks. Unfortunately, I had this really stupid idea that the pills had a sort of cumulative effect after they'd been taken for a while.'

'Are you saying...?' Christien breathed in a seriously strained undertone. 'Are you saying that even though you were no longer taking the pills you believed that you would *still* be protected from pregnancy?'

As Christien's tone rose in volume, Tabby flinched. 'Don't shout at me... I know it was stupid, but back then I didn't know anything about stuff like that. When I was put on that course of pills, I didn't need to be interested in the small print because it never occurred to me that I would be relying on them as birth control... I didn't know you were about to come into my life!'

'I don't believe this. Why the hell didn't you ask *me* to take precautions?' Christien raked at her with incredulous bite.

'Well…'

His stubborn jawline clenched. 'I thought you'd be challenged to answer that—'

'No, just embarrassed. You'd told me that you disliked condoms—'

'*Zut alors!*' Christien exclaimed.

'And I didn't want to annoy you and I persuaded myself that there was no real risk.' Tabby loosed a sad, shamefaced sigh. 'I was seventeen and I couldn't imagine falling pregnant. I thought it couldn't happen to me and, of course, it *did.*'

That simple admission lay there like a stone thrown into a deceptively tranquil pond. A pond that was about to start churning up beneath the surface. Pale below his olive skin, Christien stared at her from the other side of the room, magnificent golden eyes shimmering with the ferocity of his tension.

Tabby fixed her discomfited gaze back on her wineglass and then she set it down in an abrupt movement.

'I found out that I was going to have a baby soon after I went back to England… I had morning sickness like…morning, afternoon and evening too,' she recalled in a small, flat voice. 'To cut the wretched long story short, he—'

'*He?*'

'Our son was born three weeks before the inquest into the car crash was held.' Tabby pleated her trembling hands together to keep them steady. 'I intended to tell you then—'

'*Bon Dieu*…why that late in the day? Why didn't I hear that I was to be a father months before that?' Christien shot at her rawly.

'You changed your mobile phone number. I tried to call the villa in the Dordogne but, by that stage, you had sold it and I had no other address or means of contacting you—'

'That's not much of an excuse. You could have made more effort.'

'I didn't have your resources to conduct an all-out search *and* I had other problems!' Tabby's temper was sparking in her own defence. 'In his will, my father left everything he possessed to my stepmother and when she realised I was pregnant she threw me out of the house in literally what I stood up in. I had just started art college and I had to sleep on a friend's floor until my mother's sister, Alison, took me in.'

'I am certain that she could have advised you on the best way to locate me…such as through the name of my airline.' Majoring in heavy sarcasm as he pointed that out, Christien was not yielding an inch.

'I think you're overlooking the fact that you dumped me like a hot potato after that car accident and never spoke to me again—'

'The crash had nothing to do with it. I saw you with that idiot on the Harley—'

'But I didn't know *how* it was with you, did I? I wasn't inside your secretive head with you!' Tabby scanned him with strained eyes that demanded his understanding. 'I wasn't aware that you believed I was seeing someone else. All I knew was that you wanted nothing more to do with me after the death of your father and mine. So you had better believe that I wasn't in any great hurry just then to track you down with the news that I was pregnant…because, believe it or not, I have my pride too!'

Christien was very pale. He raked a not quite steady hand through his luxuriant black hair, his dark eyes brooding and bitter. 'Why don't you just get to the point? So, you gave my son up for adoption!'

Tabby registered that she should have guessed that he would assume that she had put their baby up for adoption. After all, he had seen no sign of a child in her life when he'd visited her in London the previous month or when she'd stayed in the cottage over that first weekend. 'No, I *didn't* do that. I couldn't give him up. He's upstairs fast asleep…'

Black brows pleating, Christien gazed back at her, what she had just revealed too shattering for him to accept. *'Comment?'*

'I called him Jake Christien and your name is on his birth certificate. I planned to tell you about him when I attended the accident enquiry.' Tabby couldn't keep the bitter hurt out of her voice. 'But you wouldn't have anything to do with me—'

'What are you trying to say?' Christien was not focusing on what to him was an irrelevance. 'You are saying that you have our son...that there is a little boy *here* in this house? I don't believe you—'

'The day you visited me in London, he was at nursery school, and I left him in England with Alison when I made my first trip here.' Tabby rose to her feet as she appreciated that she might as well have been talking to a brick wall for all the listening that Christien seemed able to do.

'Right *now*, he is upstairs?' Christien questioned fiercely.

Tabby halted at the foot of the staircase and whispered, 'How...how do you feel about that?'

'That I can't believe that this is real because, if I start believing it, I might get so angry I lose my head with you.' Dark golden eyes glittering, Christien stared at her with deadly seriousness. 'I can't believe it's real because you slept with me last week without saying a word—'

A deep dark blush flamed over her face. 'I didn't mean to—'

He dealt her a derisive glance. 'I want to *see* him—'

'He's asleep... OK.' Intimidated by the anger flaring in his expectant gaze, she went upstairs and crossed the landing to push the door of Jake's room wider open.

Behind her, Christien stilled like a guy turned to stone. A night-light illuminated the bed. Jake seemed to be having a restive night for his little face was flushed, his black curls tousled, the sheet in a tangle round his waist. With strong, determined hands, Christien set Tabby out of his path and entered the room. Her heart leapt into her mouth as she wondered what he planned to do. For long, endless moments, he stared down at Jake and then at the long row of toy cars parked with military exactitude along the skirting board. He released a long, low, shuddering breath and then very slowly began to back out again.

The silence on the landing was so intense that it screamed.

Tabby hurried back downstairs.

Christien drew level with her again and looked at her, searing dark eyes hard with condemnation. 'You're the equivalent of a kidnapper who never asked for a ransom.'

Tabby blanched.

'Once again you lied to me, but this time the consequences were much worse,' he continued with harsh clarity. 'This time, an innocent child has suffered—'

'Jake has not suffered—'

'Of course, he has! He has had no father!' Christien slung back without hesitation. 'Don't try to tell me that that hasn't made a difference to my child's life. Don't try to make some sexist point arguing that a mother figure is more important—'

Caught unprepared by the cutting force of his attack, Tabby was pale as milk. 'I wasn't going to—'

'*Zut alors*…just as well!' Christien snarled. 'Not unless you want to hear how outraged I am at the knowledge that a stupid schoolgirl has been attempting to raise my son!'

'Don't you call me stupid.' Tabby's temper flared. 'I might not be a real brainbox like you, but there's nothing wrong with my brain—'

'*Isn't* there?' Christien incised at the speed of a rapier. 'You've already told me that, until your aunt offered you a bed, you were sleeping on a floor while you were pregnant. Had you contacted me, you would have been living in luxury. So *not* contacting me was an act of inexcusable stupidity!'

'Listening to you right now, not contacting you strikes me as having been a very clever decision. Being a filthy rich, smug four-letter-word doesn't make you any more acceptable!' Tabby shot back at him.

'Except in the parent stakes. Strive to focus on the main issue, *chérie*. Four years ago, it was your responsibility to protect our unborn child by taking no risks with your own health. Since when was sleeping on floors recommended for pregnant women?'

Compressing her lips, Tabby turned her head away.

'But in the present, our primary concern must simply be Jake...*not* how I feel about your lies or how you feel about me. This is about Jake and *his* rights.' Christien lifted a forceful brown hand to stress his point. 'And his most basic right was his father's care, which you chose to deny him.'

Tabby knotted her trembling hands tightly together. Her palms were damp, her eyes felt scratchy and her throat was so tight it was hurting. No matter how hard she attempted to make herself she could not hold Christien's outraged dark golden gaze. It was as if he had got her by the throat and stolen every excuse she might have employed before she even got the chance to think any up. Jake and *his* rights. No, she had to admit that her son's right to know his father had only occurred to her in more recent times when she had had to face the fact that Jake would soon be reaching an age when he would be asking awkward questions.

'The way you felt about me, I didn't think you'd want to know about him.' Tabby knew she sounded accusing, but she could not help it for she did not think it was fair for him to refuse to acknowledge that his treatment of her had naturally influenced her expectations and her opinion of him.

'That decision was not yours to make—'

'OK... I went to the accident enquiry determined to tell you that you were the father of my son but you couldn't even give me five minutes of your time—'

As Tabby made that reminder the angular lines of Christien's fabulous bone structure hardened into prominence below his olive skin, but he stood his ground. 'That is not the point—'

'Excuse me, that is *exactly* the point!' Tabby argued fiercely, recalling the terrible feeling of humiliation she had experienced that day and stiffening in sick remembrance. 'I was ready, willing and eager to tell you about Jake. I think you need to remember what a louse you were to me that day—'

'I did and I said nothing—'

'And nothing was precisely what you deserved and got for treating me like the dirt beneath your feet!' Tabby hurled furiously. 'I practically begged you to speak to me in private in spite of the fact that your awful snobby relatives and friends were all lined up with you and shooting me looks of loathing as if *I*, rather than my father, had been the cause of that ghastly accident!'

Christien was rigid and pale with rage. '*Ciel!* That day I was too busy grieving for my father to concern myself with the behaviour of other people—'

'You didn't give a damn! I was eighteen and I was alone in a foreign country and I was grieving too.' Tabby was shaking, raw with pain and the need to justify her own actions and defend herself. 'But you talk now and you behaved then as if you had cornered the grief market. You lost a father. Well, at least you were able to look back on your memories of him with respect and affection. I was denied even that because my dad got drunk and destroyed a lot of other lives as well as his own!'

Christien spread two lean hands in a movement of angry rebuttal. 'I did not even notice how others were behaving. If you think that grief was all that lay behind my distance with you that day—'

'Don't you shout at me!' Tabby interrupted wrathfully.

Hauling in a furious breath, Christien then froze in bewilderment at the strange noise he could hear emanating down from the floor above. Tabby was quicker to recognise and react to her son's frightened howl and she raced for the stairs in automatic maternal pilot. She found Jake sitting bolt upright in bed, tears running down his pale, scared face.

'The car...the car ran me over!' her son sobbed, letting her work out for herself what had caused the nightmare that had wakened him from his sleep.

Tabby tugged his small, trembling body into her arms. 'It was just a dream, Jake...just a dream. The car didn't run you over. You're safe. You're all right. You got a fright but you weren't hurt,' she told him with a note of soothing and determined cheer in her quiet intonation.

But the consequence that she had feared from the minute she ran to her son's bedside was already happening. Although Jake had stopped crying as soon as she'd put her arms round him, he was now struggling for breath and wheezing. Worse, because he was not yet fully awake and still recovering from the effects of his nightmare, he was all the more distressed by his physical difficulties.

CHAPTER SEVEN

CHRISTIEN WAS PARALYSED to the spot by shock as he watched Jake fight to get air into his skinny little chest. As Christien had not even a nodding acquaintance with what fear felt like, his fear on his son's behalf hit him as hard as a bullet from a gun. He watched Tabby grab up what looked like an inhaler and tend to the little boy. *His* little boy.

'What's the matter with him...what can I do?' Christien demanded, sick to the stomach with the force of his concern.

'You don't need to do anything. Jake's fine.' Tabby's squeaky tone was a leaden but obvious attempt to conceal her anxiety sooner than increase the risk of Jake getting more upset. 'It's just a little asthma attack and the medication in the bronchodilator will help put it under control.'

Unimpressed and constitutionally incapable of standing around doing nothing and feeling helpless, Christien stepped out onto the landing, dug out his mobile phone and hastily called a doctor.

Even as his son's breathing difficulties subsided Christien discovered that he could not take his attention from Jake. In appearance the little boy was unmistakably a Laroche. His black curls ran down into a peak at the hairline just as Christien's did. His eyes were just like his paternal grandmother's—dark, liquid and very expressive. His olive skin was in direct contrast to Tabby's fair colouring and the pure lines of his bone structure were already hinting at the strong features that could be seen in the family paintings. However, in apparent defiance of those genes from a tall, well-built family, Jake looked shockingly small and slight to Christien, who had had very little to do with young children. But then illness had probably stunted his son's growth, Christien reflected sadly.

Tabby's tension was beginning to drain away when Christien sat down on the other side of Jake's bed as though it was the most natural thing in the world. Jake stared at the tall, dark male in his city suit with huge surprised eyes.

Tabby was annoyed that Christien was pushing in just when she had got her son calmed down. 'Jake...this is—'

Christien closed a hand over Jake's tiny one and breathed shakily, 'I am your papa...your father, Christien Laroche—'

'Christien!' Tabby hissed in a piercing whisper, shaken by the ill-considered immediacy of that startling announcement. 'If you upset him, it could cause another—'

'Daddy...?'

Jake was studying Christien with big, wondering eyes.

'Daddy... Papa. You can call me whatever you like.' Satisfied to have introduced himself and claimed his rightful place in his son's life, Christien smoothed a thumb over the little fingers curling within his. He smiled. Jake began to smile too.

'Do you like football?' Jake piped up hopefully.

'Never miss a match,' Christien lied without hesitation.

Feeling excluded for the first time since her son had been born, Tabby watched in a daze as Jake and Christien proceeded to demonstrate that the gap between three years and twenty-nine years was not so great as any mere female disinterested in sport might have supposed. But then Christien was bright enough and smooth enough to sell sand in a desert. A bell sounded and she jerked in surprise, only then appreciating that the cottage now possessed a doorbell.

'That will probably be the doctor.' Christien vaulted upright.

'You called out a doctor?' Tabby questioned in some annoyance.

'Don't go, Daddy,' Jake protested worriedly.

Tabby hurried downstairs and opened the door to a suave medic in a suit. Jake clasped in one strong arm, Christien hailed the older man from the top of the stairs, and from that point on, as the French dialogue whizzed back and forth too fast for Tabby to follow and Jake was examined, Christien was in charge. Apart from the occasional question relating to the treatment Jake had received in London for his asthma, Tabby was required to play little part in the discussion that took place.

Finally, having shown the doctor out again, Tabby returned to Jake's bedroom. Christien held a silencing finger to his lips. Her son had fallen asleep in his father's arms. That Christien had won Jake's trust so easily shook Tabby. 'Let me tuck him in.'

'I don't think it would be a good idea to risk waking him up again,' Christien asserted.

Tabby was tempted to snatch Jake from Christien's arms and she was ashamed of her own streak of childish possessiveness. 'You can't be comfortable lying there like that.'

'Why not? Are you the only one of us allowed to show parental affection?' Christien queried, smooth as silk, dark golden eyes flaming satiric gold over his son's downbent head. 'I have a lot of time to make up with Jake. I won't miss out on a single opportunity that comes my way. If *he* is comfortable, I will lie here all night and I really don't care how uncomfortable I get or how you feel about that.'

Hot colour flooded her cheeks. He had thrown down a gauntlet but it was not one she was willing to pick up as yet. She was moving in uncharted territory. Christien had accepted that Jake was his without a single word of the protest she had expected or even a demand for further proof. That was good, she told herself. That he should be angry was natural, she told herself in addition. On the surface, Christien might seem to be handling her bombshell very well but, in reality, he had to be in shock too and he needed time to adjust. It would be foolish of her to argue with him before he had even had the chance to think through what being Jake's father would demand from him.

Tabby sat down on the chair by the wall. She wanted to cuddle Jake, reassure herself that he was fine again, but instead Christien had him and she felt constrained. 'There was really no need for you to contact a doctor,' she remarked. 'It was a very mild attack—'

Christien gave her a hard look of challenge, his strong jawline set firm. 'I can afford the very best medical attention and I intend to avail myself of it for my son's benefit. I would like him to see a couple of consultants. I want to be sure that he receives the best possible treatment.'

'Don't you think that you should discuss that first with me?' Tabby was fighting her own resentment over his high-handed attitude with all her might, for she did not want to be unreasonable.

'For three and a half years you have made all the decisions on our son's behalf and I am not impressed by the value of your judgement.'

Tabby set her teeth together. 'You're not being fair.'

'You kept Jake and I apart by denying me all knowledge of his existence. As a result, my son was forced to go without many advantages that I believe he should have enjoyed from birth,' Christien enumerated coldly. 'How can you expect me to think in terms of being fair to you? Were you fair to him?'

'There is more to life than money. Our son has always had love.'

'A very selfish love,' Christien pronounced with lethal derision. 'Both I and my family would have loved him. You have also deprived him of his cultural heritage—'

'What on earth are you talking about?' Tabby was staring

fixedly at him but her throat was convulsing with tears held at
bay only by will-power.

Christien dealt her a grim appraisal. 'He speaks neither the
Breton language nor French. He is the only child born to a proud
and ancient line in this generation. He will mean a great deal
to my family—'

'Are you so sure of that? Are you sure they'll be pleased to
hear that you have an illegitimate son and that his mother is
Gerry Burnside's daughter?' Tabby cut in painfully.

'In France, children born outside marriage have the same
rights of inheritance as those born within it. My family are
more likely to be shocked that I should have a son who only
met me today, a son who speaks not one word of our language
and who does not know what it is to be a Laroche,' Christien
completed with icy conviction.

A chill ran down Tabby's spine and then spread into her
tummy to leave her feeling both cold and hollow. Lashes screening her pained and confused gaze from his, she surveyed them
both: the man and the little boy with the same distinctive
colouring. She watched Christien smooth back Jake's mop of
curls and, noticing that his hand was not quite steady, appreciated that he was not as in control as he would have liked her
to believe.

'He looks so like you,' she could not help muttering.

'I know.' Christien sent her a blistering look of condemnation. 'How could you do this to us?'

'Christien—'

'No, you listen to me,' he broke in, low and deadly in tone,
for he did not need to raise his voice to make her shiver. 'From
the hour he was conceived, he deserved the best we both had
to give. His needs transcend your wishes and mine. You should
have recognised that before he was even born. But now that I
am part of his life, you will not be in a position to forget who
and what comes first again.'

That sounded threatening. Tabby wanted to argue with him

and demand to know exactly what he meant. However, she did recognise that he had voiced sufficient grains of hard truth to give her pause for thought. But, regardless, he was a man and she reckoned that there was no way he could really understand how fearfully hurt and humiliated she had been on the day of that accident enquiry when he had acted as though she had never meant anything to him. He had made her feel about an inch high and fiercely protective of Jake. She had assumed that Christien would have been even more scornful had she announced that she had given birth to their child. After all, he had demonstrated a complete lack of respect or caring towards her, so why would she have credited that he would react with any greater generosity to his young son? But then he had believed she had started seeing another guy and she had to make allowances for that.

When Tabby woke up, she was lying fully dressed on top of her bed with a bedspread pulled over her. After she'd fallen into a doze, Christien must have carried her through to her own room. It was already after nine in the morning and she scrambled out of bed. Jake's tumbled bed was empty, his pyjamas lying on the floor. Frowning, she sped down the stairs and discovered that she was alone in the cottage. Panic tugging at her as she recalled how Christien had accused *her* of being no better than a kidnapper in keeping him and his son apart, she was almost afraid to read the note that she saw lying on the hearth. Christien's abominable scrawl informed her that he had taken Jake out for a drive in the Ferrari. Slowly, she breathed again. What could be more natural than Jake getting a run in his father's boy-toy car? Christien doing something so predictable and male made her feel a little more secure.

It was a beautiful hot sunny day and she took a green sundress from the wardrobe and went for a shower. Christien was so angry with her, so bitter. Would he ever get over that? Would he ever look at events from her point of view and appreciate that she had done what she believed was best? Was Jake to be their only link now? Well, at least Christien seemed keen to form a relationship with Jake, she told herself bracingly. Really that was what was most important. But her eyes ached and burned with unshed tears.

When she heard a car outside, she hurried straight to the door and was surprised to see Manette Bonnard walking up her path with a gaily wrapped parcel clasped in one hand. 'I wanted to thank you for your kindness and understanding yesterday. I hope you have no objection but I have brought a small gift for your son,' the older woman said tautly. 'May I talk to you, *mademoiselle*?'

In bewilderment, Tabby tensed and then, with a rather uneasy smile of acquiescence, she invited her visitor in.

'I'm afraid that I concealed my true identity from you yesterday. I was too embarrassed to admit who I was,' the blonde woman confessed in a troubled rush. 'My name is not Manette Bonnard. I lied about that. I am Christien's mother, Matilde Laroche.'

Tabby was betrayed into a startled exclamation.

'I drove over here to spy on you,' Matilde admitted tightly, discomfited colour mantling her cheeks. 'I thought you had no right to be in this house. I thought you had no right to be with my son.'

As Tabby wondered if the older woman was aware that Christien had spent the night with her that weekend that she had first visited her inheritance, never mind passed the night before under the same roof as well, she could no longer look her visitor in the eye. Worst of all, she could not think of a single thing to say to her either.

'Although I knew nothing about you and had never met you, I told myself four years ago that I hated you because…well, because of who you are—'

As Matilde's eyes filled with tears Tabby took her trembling hand into a sympathetic hold. 'I understand… I really *do* understand—'

'I was mad with grief and it twisted me. But perhaps I was also afraid that I was on the brink of losing my son to a young woman when I was least willing to part with him,' Matilde breathed shakily. 'But that is not an excuse. When I saw how very young you were yesterday, I was surprised, but I was shocked when I met your little boy.'

Christien's mother removed a photograph from her bag and extended it. Tabby studied the snap of Christien as a child of about five or six with a fascination she could not hide.

'Jake is the living image of his father,' Matilde commented.

Thinking of the gift that Matilde Laroche had brought and the acceptance of Jake that that telling gesture conveyed, Tabby just smiled. 'Yes, he is.'

'I am so ashamed of the way I have behaved. I felt my punishment when I recognised my grandson, who is a stranger to me,' Matilde admitted with deep regret. 'For how long has Christien known about Jake?'

Tabby winced. 'I'm afraid that I only told him last night.'

'A long time ago, my aunt, Solange, tried to talk to me about you and Christien and how accidents happen and how we must forgive and go on with our lives, but I was too stubborn and full of self-pity to listen.' Matilde Laroche's guilt was etched in her troubled face.

Tabby urged the older woman to sit down.

'Henri always drove very fast,' she confided. 'Far too fast to stop in the event of an accident.'

As the silence stretched Tabby gathered her courage and began talking too. 'That night my father had a dreadful argument with my stepmother over dinner. She stormed out of the restaurant and caught a taxi back to the farmhouse.'

'So that was why your father's wife wasn't in his car when it crashed.' Slowly, Matilde shook her head. 'I always wondered about that.'

'I'm not making any excuses for Dad but I would like you to know that, until that holiday, I had never seen him drinking to excess,' Tabby said in a quiet voice. 'Dad had remarried very soon after my own mother's death. That summer he was very unhappy. He and my stepmother weren't getting on and I think he turned to alcohol because he realised that his second marriage had been a terrible mistake.'

'Was he happy with your mother?'

'Very...' Tabby's eyes watered. 'They were always talking and teasing each other. He went to pieces when she died. I think he rushed into marriage with Lisa because he was lonely and he couldn't cope—'

'I was like that after Henri went,' Matilde muttered unsteadily and she patted Tabby's hand as if in gratitude for her honesty. 'I couldn't cope either, and since then my grief has been my life. When I saw Jake, I understood that life had gone on without me and that I had caused those closest to me a lot of unhappiness that they did not deserve.'

'You really don't mind about Jake, do you?'

Matilde Laroche studied her in amazement. 'Why would I mind? He is a wonderful child and I am overjoyed that he has been born.'

'Christien has taken Jake out this morning,' Tabby revealed.

The older woman stood up. 'I would not like to intrude by being here when they return. But I am sure you have already guessed that, if you are generous enough to allow it, I would be very happy to have the opportunity to become better acquainted with you and my grandson.'

Tabby grinned. 'We'd be happy too.'

'Will you tell my son about what happened yesterday?'

'No. I think it's bad for Christien to know absolutely everything,' Tabby heard herself admitting, before it occurred to her that such facetiousness might not go down well with his parent.

But Matilde's gaze had taken on a surprised but appreciative gleam of answering amusement and she chuckled as she took her leave of Tabby.

As the morning wore on, and there was still no sign of Christien and Jake reappearing, Tabby became more and more jumpy. She told herself that it was a nonsense to imagine that Christien would have taken off with their son just to teach her a hard lesson, but her imagination was lively and her conscience too uneasy to give her peace. It was noon before she heard a car pulling up and she rushed to the door.

Sheathed in black denim jeans that fitted him like a second skin and a trendy shirt, Christien swung out of a scarlet Aston Martin V8 and scooped Jake out of the car seat fixed in the rear. Tabby's jaw dropped. Last seen, her three-year-old son had been the possessor of a cute mop of black curls. Since then he had had a severe run-in with a barber and not a curl was to be seen.

'What have you done to him?' Tabby heard herself yelp accusingly.

Christien angled a look of pure challenge at her. 'I trashed the girlie hairstyle…you might not have noticed but boys aren't wearing pretty curls this season.'

'It looked girlie,' Jake told his mother slowly but carefully, and he even pronounced it just as his father must have done complete with French accent. Her little boy then carefully arranged himself in the exact same posture as his unrepentant father.

'Girlie is in the eye of the beholder,' Tabby remarked.

'Girlie is girlie,' Christien contradicted.

Christien, she understood, was staking possession on his son and ready, even eager, to fight any attempt to suggest that he might have overreached his new parental boundaries. But, grateful for their return and blessed with great tolerance, Tabby was willing to overlook Christien's current aggressive aura for the sake of peace. She surveyed the two males who owned her heart with helpless appreciation. She missed her son's curls but had to admit that the cropped style was much more boyish. Christien? Christien looked irresistibly sexy and fanciable. Her mouth ran dry. Her breathing quickened. Involuntarily she remembered how she had felt on that sofa and her knees quivered and her face burned with mortification over her own weakness.

'What time did you get up this morning?' Tabby enquired, dredging her attention from him.

'Jake woke up at seven and I took him out for breakfast. Lock up,' Christien urged. 'I want to take you for a drive.'

Tabby did as she was asked and climbed into the passenger seat of the powerful car. 'Where else did you go this morning?'

'Daddy showed me his cars. I got little cars and he's got big cars,' Jake volunteered chirpily.

Jake was already calling Christien Daddy and he said it with such pronounced pride. From the corner of her eye, Tabby watched Christien's handsome mouth curve with eloquent satisfaction. Evidently the morning had been spent in a male bonding session composed of laddish haircuts and car talk. Tabby did not begrudge them their mutual appreciation. She was delighted that they had got on so well.

When Christien drove through a colossal and imposing turreted entrance, Tabby tensed and dragged herself from her preoccupation. 'Where are we?' she questioned even though she already knew, for at the end of a very long, arrow-straight drive lined by trees sat a château.

'We're home!' Jake announced.

'Sorry?' Tabby gasped.

'Duvernay. I needed a change of clothes earlier and I brought Jake back here before we went out for breakfast,' Christien advanced with the utmost casualness.

She had a delightful image of Christien playing it cool over breakfast in some café while Jake attempted to mirror his every action and expression.

'It's very big...' Tabby went on to remark because, the closer the car got to the ancient building at the end of the drive, the more enormous the château seemed to get.

'Where will I sleep?' Jake asked.

'I'll show you later,' his father responded.

Tabby froze at that casual assurance. Christien brought the car to a halt and sprang out. He lifted out Jake. A rather rotund lady with a big, friendly smile was approaching them. Christien introduced Tabby to Fanchon, who had been his nurse when he was a boy. Jake planted a confident hand in the older woman's and, beneath Tabby's disconcerted gaze, woman and child headed off into the gardens.

'I wanted to speak to you without Jake present,' Christien explained.

Her oval face flushed and set, Tabby came to a halt in the vast marble entrance hall and fixed angry green eyes on Christien. 'Why is my son asking where he is going to sleep? And why did he refer to your home as *his* home?'

'It is a challenge to keep a secret with a chatty three-year-old around.' Christien pressed open a door and stepped back in invitation.

'Well, what I heard was more of a fantasy than a secret!' Tabby retorted sharply, entering a terrifyingly elegant reception room furnished with loads of antiques.

'Is it? Duvernay is where my son belongs.'

Tabby collided with the cold glitter of Christien's challenging appraisal and her tummy gave a frightened lurch. 'At present, our son belongs with me—'

'Long may that arrangement last,' Christien remarked softly, and there was something in his intonation that made goosebumps rise at the nape of her neck. 'Children need their mothers as much as they need their fathers.'

'Thank you for that vote of confidence.' Tabby tilted her chin but her heart was starting to thump very fast and her chest felt tight. 'Although I have to admit that I haven't a clue why you should take the trouble to tell me that.'

Christien was very still. 'I'm prepared to be generous and make you an offer—'

'I'm not very fussed about the kind of offers you make,' Tabby declared with complete truth.

'Either you hear me out or my lawyers deal with this situation. Your choice,' Christien traded, smooth as silk.

'We don't have a situation here.' Tabby's hands closed so tight in on themselves that her nails carved dents into her palms. 'I was the one who told you that Jake was your son and you can see him as often as you like. I'm pleased that you want to spend time with him and I can't see why you need to talk about bringing lawyers in.'

'Naturally not. However, I want Jake and you to live with me—'

A disconcerted laugh fell from her dry lips. 'You can't always have what you want—'

'You think not?' A winged ebony brow quirked in open defiance of that statement. Hard dark golden eyes surveyed her. 'If you can't even accept that I have the right to make terms that will enable me to see more of my son, you will leave me with no choice but to challenge you for legal custody.'

This time, Tabby could not have laughed had her life depended on it for she was shattered by that warning assurance.

CHAPTER EIGHT

TABBY IMAGINED TRYING to fight Christien for custody of Jake and almost winced for she only had love to offer. She struggled to stay calm and make allowances for Christien's anger with her while curiosity prompted her to say, 'What exactly are your terms?'

Christien sent her a slashing smile as if she had already lain down at his feet and awarded him victory. She wanted to slap him so badly that her palm tingled with longing.

'You and Jake move in with me—'

'*Move in?*' Tabby repeated. 'Quantify "moving in" from my point of view.'

'I get to buy you boxes of sexy lingerie and you get all the sex you can handle...as well as a lifestyle most women would envy.'

The tingle in Tabby's palm had become almost unbearable. 'What happens when you get bored?'

'We remain civilised.'

'I'm not civilised. Right now I just want to kill you for having the sheer nerve to suggest I would agree to a casual arrangement of that nature—'

'Even though it is what you want too?' Christien chided. 'Why else did you choose to come to Brittany?'

'I beg your pardon?'

'You could've sold the cottage and never set foot here with our son. Instead you brought him to a property within three kilometres of Duvernay. Your choice of location speaks for itself, *ma belle*.' Christien sent Tabby a knowing look that sent a tide of chagrined colour up into her cheeks at the same time as it made her want to scream at him in a very unladylike fashion. 'It's obvious that you were as eager to see me again as I was to see you—'

'That is untrue!' Tabby slung at him shrilly.

'The first chance you got, you went to bed with me again.'

'Drop dead, Christien.' Tabby stalked past him.

'*Zut alors*...the first chance I got, I went to bed with you too,' Christien drawled. 'Even being furious with you doesn't stop me lusting after you every hour of the day!'

'Every hour?' Tabby queried involuntarily.

'I even dream about you,' he growled.

Tabby concealed the grin that had come at her out of nowhere. If lust was all he could feel, she was happy that it should be a source of hourly torment for him. But on that same thought, the desire to grin ebbed fast. *Was* it possible that she had cherished a subconscious hope that she could be with Christien again in Brittany? Did he know her better than she knew herself?

Whatever, she was in no position to consider an uncommitted relationship with Christien. Everything she did affected Jake and her son was already coping with big changes. In bringing him to France, she had taken him away from all that was familiar. However, she had made the decision to do that with a clear head and the belief that a fresh start would benefit both of them. All right, getting involved with Christien again had been foolish, but at least she could own up to her mistake and guard against repeating it. Jake would be terribly hurt if he got used to his parents being together and they broke up again. He would be damaged by yet another change of home and lifestyle. Their son needed to feel secure.

'Us rushing into a relationship that might turn uncivilised within a few months would be very hard on Jake—'

'I'm sure you'll make a special effort to tell the truth at all times and avoid snogging guys on motorbikes,' Christien murmured with sardonic cool.

'I'd rather be with a bloke who didn't think that *he* was so perfect that it was my job to make all the effort to make things work!' Her green eyes were bright with defiance at his hurtful reminders of her own mistakes, for she was furious that he took no account of his own less than perfect record. 'There's nothing left to discuss, is there? Roll out your lawyers.'

Luxuriant black lashes semi-veiled the simmering golden eyes flaming over her feverishly flushed face. His lithe, well-built body rigid as he reacted to the rebellious challenge she provided, Christien snapped his hands over hers and pulled her close. Bemused by that sudden move in the midst of a serious discussion, Tabby looked up at him in disbelieving bewilderment. 'What do you think you're doing?'

'You need telling, *ma belle*?' Christien chided huskily.

Clamped to his powerful muscular frame, Tabby was insanely aware of the hard male heat of his erection. She knew she ought to push him away but she could not muster the willpower. Hot, melting longing was pooling at the very heart of her. He sank possessive fingers into her caramel-coloured hair and took her soft, ripe mouth by storm. He dragged her down so deep and fast into the passion that she moaned out loud in mingled hunger and fear. She wanted to shimmy down his lean, powerful physique, tantalise him to the edge of desperation and then arrange herself on the nearest horizontal surface like a wanton, willing reward. If anything, the very strength of her need for him scared her enough to make her yank herself back from him.

'*D'accord*... OK,' Christien grated as though the novelty of her new ability to resist him were the equivalent of having a loaded gun put to his head. 'Moving in includes a wedding ring.'

Shock made Tabby blink in slow motion and left her dizzy. 'I don't know much about proposals but I think you ought to have mentioned that about ten minutes sooner. It *was* a proposal of marriage...wasn't it?'

Christien raked brown fingers through his black hair, his molten gaze pinned to her with seething intensity. 'What else?'

Face burning, Tabby endeavoured to dredge her eyes from his riveting dark good looks. Well, at least he wasn't putting up any pretences. Evidently lust was well up to the challenge of getting him to the altar. 'Are you sure about this?'

'If we marry, we'll be providing a proper family environment for Jake...' Christien emerged from a deeply satisfying fantasy of having Tabby on call twenty-four hours a day. He saw her reclining across his gilded four-poster bed upstairs, rushing to Paris for sexy lunch break meetings at his apartment, accompanying him on long, boring business trips to enliven the hours he spent airborne and those spent between the sheets.

Tabby was still in a daze and afraid to believe that he meant what he was saying. 'Yes but—'

'Our son needs both of us.' He would also need a nanny, Christien conceded, permitting a small glimmer of reality to tinge what was fast becoming an erotic daydream.

A wedding ring *would* be a true commitment on his part, Tabby thought. A little glow of happiness started to expand inside her. Why had Christien not made it clear that he was talking about marriage from the outset? Her embryo glow dimmed a little. She had a shrinking suspicion that he might only have come up with the marriage idea as a last resort. A last resort to get her into bed and keep her there until familiarity bred contempt?

Paling, Tabby could not bring herself to meet Christien's eyes. He would be furious, and excusably so, if he knew what she was thinking. At the same time, she found it hard to credit that he was willing to give up his freedom solely for Jake's benefit. And even if he was, it would take more than sex and a praiseworthy wish to be a good parent to hold a marriage together. But then wasn't it also possible that she was misjudging Christien? He might not be in love with her, but that did not mean that he did not have warm feelings for her.

'What about us?' Tabby asked abruptly.

'Us?' Christien looked blank.

'You and me...how you feel about me,' Tabby muttered awkwardly.

Christien vented a husky laugh and treated her to a downright lascivious appraisal that radiated sexual heat. 'Hungry,' he growled without hesitation.

'That's not quite what I meant. When I mentioned how you feel about me...hmm...' Tabby steeled herself to forge ahead and rise above all mortification because it was very clear that he was not about to give her any help.

'What are you getting at?'

'Er...love.' Tabby finally got it out.

Instantly, Christien recoiled. 'What's love got to do with it?'

Tabby's heart sank. Rarely did anyone receive an answer that bristled with such clarity. Talk about slamming the door shut on her dreams! One reference to love and he backed off six feet and could not conceal his revulsion. Even so, he had proposed...after a fashion. Instincts she was ashamed of urged her to accept first, get smart with him about terms later. But he was being so shallow about something that she took very seriously. She wanted her marriage to have the best possible chance of lasting until she was old and grey.

'The civil ceremony will take ten days to organise,' Christien commented.

'I haven't said yes.'

Emanating confidence, Christien bent mocking dark golden eyes on her. 'I'll make the arrangements...now come here.'

Christien began to pull her inch by inch back to him, his hungry gaze devouring her. Tabby breathed in deep. She knew that she was facing a definitive moment in her relationship with Christien. She had never planned anything with him, had never demanded anything from him either. Loving him from the first, she had let her heart rule her head and had then suffered the consequences.

But now Jake had to be considered. Christien himself had stressed that their son's needs should be placed ahead of their own more selfish desires and doubtless that was why he had decided to propose. Unhappily, Tabby could not bring herself to believe that their marriage would last six months on so shallow a basis as sex. If Jake was not to be torn apart by a divorce, Christien would have to be prepared to make more effort.

'Right at this minute, I'm not actually saying yes to marrying you,' Tabby told Christien tautly.

Black brows pleating, Christien jerked back from her again. 'Then what *are* you saying?'

'I'd like to say yes but I just don't think I can. We don't have enough going for us—'

'We have a son and dynamite sexual attraction!'

'If it doesn't work out, it will hurt Jake most of all...a lot of husbands and wives end up hating each other when they split up—'

'Are you always this optimistic?' Christien asked very drily.

'I'm putting Jake first like you said we should.' Tabby thrust up her chin. 'If I did marry you, I know I'd try hard to make it work. But I'm not convinced you would do the same—'

Christien was getting riled. 'Why the hell not?'

'You're spoiled. Life's a breeze for you. You're good-looking, rich and successful and you're just not used to having to make an effort in relationships—'

Christien's stubborn jawline was at an aggressive angle. 'But naturally I *could* make that effort if I had to.'

'Dragging me into the nearest bed wouldn't count,' Tabby returned in some embarrassment, but she knew it needed to be said.

'Since when did I have to drag you?' Christien derided silkily. 'We're talking in circles here, *ma belle*.'

'No, we're not, you're not listening to what I'm saying. I want to marry you, but not if it's likely to end in tears so that Jake suffers for my having made the wrong choice—'

'I can't offer you some miracle guarantee—'

'If you'd loved me, I wouldn't have needed any more.'

'I can make you happy without love,' Christien murmured with immense assurance.

'How far would you be prepared to go to make me happy?' A germ of an idea had occurred to Tabby.

'I'm no quitter.'

At least, she consoled herself, in the radius of his father's unquestioning confidence Jake was highly unlikely to suffer from low self-esteem.

'You said it would be ten days before we can get married. So you've got that amount of time to persuade me that I should marry you—'

'Persuade?' Christien frowned. 'I don't follow.'

'You've got from now until the ceremony to convince me... while we occupy separate beds,' Tabby hastened to add.

The silence pulsed like a live thing.

Christien angled a sardonic scrutiny over her. 'This is a joke...right?'

Tabby stiffened. 'No, it's not a joke. You see, we've never had a normal relationship—'

'"Normal" is defined by separate beds?'

'The very fact that that is the first thing you home in on proves that—'

'I'm a guy and honest enough to admit that separate beds have zero appeal?' Christien slotted in darkly.

'I'd just like us to spend time together, go out to dinner and stuff... I've never had that.' Tabby compressed her lips on that grudging admission. 'Not with anyone. Before I met you, I went around with a crowd but it wasn't really dating and then I fell pregnant.'

Christien had gone very still. 'What about after Jake was born?'

Dully amused at how little he understood about how much parenthood had changed her life, Tabby released a rueful laugh. 'Single mothers aren't high on the hot list of babes in the eyes of male students. I didn't have time to date anyway. I was studying, looking after Jake and working several nights a week to bring in some cash.'

Without the smallest warning, Christien was feeling gutted by guilt and a reluctant awareness of the privileged existence that he took quite for granted. He could easily imagine how he would have felt being saddled with the care of a baby as a teenager and he almost shuddered. She had had to be responsible way beyond her years. Jake's conception had deprived her of all freedom and fun. That she had still got through college was a tribute to her.

'Don't think that I didn't get asked out, because I *was* asked!' Tabby wanted him to know that.

'So why didn't you go?'

Tabby grimaced. 'Blokes tend to assume you're a sure thing if you already have a baby. After I got that message, dating seemed more trouble than it was worth.'

His lean, strong face was taut. 'You don't have to answer this...but have you ever been with anyone but me?'

Glancing up in surprise, Tabby collided with his intent gaze and blushed to the roots of her hair before uttering a sheepish negative.

Something in his chest tightened and he dragged in a deep, ragged breath. He swung away. His son had been as good as a chastity belt. He was ashamed that he was pleased that she had never been to bed with any other guy. After all, self-evidently, he had wrecked her life at seventeen. Ironically that had been the one and only time that he had ever chosen to rely on a lover to take precautions. Why? In certain situations condoms were inconvenient and he had thought of his pleasure rather than her protection.

'D'accord...' Christien squared his wide shoulders like a male ready to assume an unpleasant duty. 'So I demonstrate that I can make you happy without sex... I hope you're not expecting me to be happy too.'

'You might be surprised.'

'Not that surprised,' Christien drawled.

They lunched with Jake at a polished table in a grand dining room lined by rather gloomy ancestral portraits. Even so, she did recognise that the men were a pretty fanciable bunch. After the meal, he informed her that they were flying to Paris.

'Don't be annoyed with me... Jake has an appointment with a specialist this afternoon,' Christien imparted.

'That was quick.' Tabby had no desire to question anything that might benefit her son's health. 'Money talks—'

'Not in this instance. The specialist concerned is a family friend.'

Her face flamed with embarrassment. They called in at the cottage so that she could pack, for he had suggested they stay the night in the city. Zipping shut the bag, suppressing a groan at the noisy sound of Jake spilling his Lego bricks over the tiled floor, she turned round to see Christien watching her from the bedroom doorway. He looked incredibly tall and dark and lethally attractive. Her mouth ran dry, tummy muscles tightening.

'You're never going to live here,' he commented.

Tabby tried to shrug as though she didn't care either way.

'I always play to win...' he murmured silkily.

Her lashes lowered over her eyes as she evaded the stunning directness of his gaze. A ripple of awareness ran down her spine in the heavy silence. The sexual buzz in the atmosphere was intense and her heart was thumping like mad. She drew in a quivering breath. Her nipples were pushing in stiff little points against the lace of her bra cup and a wave of hot pink washed her face.

She watched his brilliant eyes darken and shimmer. He extended a lean brown hand and she grasped it, let him tug her forward.

'We shouldn't,' she said shakily.

'What's a kiss, *ma belle*?'

Downstairs she could hear Jake making 'vroom-vroom' sounds while he played with his cars. Christien leant down. His breath warmed her cheek. She was so excited she stopped breathing. Without laying a hand on her, he tasted her lips, suckled them, savoured the eagerness with which she opened the moist interior to him. She strained up to him, electrified by the penetrating sweep of his tongue, the greedy ache stirring between her thighs in response.

'Christien...' she whimpered shakily.

'Stop acting like a hussy...this is our first date—'

'A first date?' Tabby parroted.

Crhistien frowned. 'You asked me for what you called a normal relationship—'

Tabby was nonplussed. 'I *did*?'

'A request which was in effect a direct challenge for me to redo what I seem to have got very wrong the first time around four years back—'

'It...it *was*?'

Christien laughed. 'So you had better learn how to say no... loud and clear. It takes two to play this game and I need all the help I can get.'

Bemused chagrin warming her face, she dropped the heavy bag at his feet and preceded him downstairs. Her body felt heavy on the outside and tight and achy on the inside. In her mind separate beds had already fallen in stature from being a common-sense precaution to being a rather naive and narrow-minded embargo. It was slowly dawning on her that on that score she had no right to feel superior to him: she might love him but, when it came to the lust factor, she was as guilty as he was.

CHAPTER NINE

TABBY AND CHRISTIEN went to Paris with the nursemaid, Fanchon, in tow. The specialist, an expert in the field of childhood asthma, gave Jake a brief examination and booked him in for tests the following day.

Christien owned a seventeenth century town house on Ile St-Louis. It had an incredible location on a picturesque tree-lined quay overlooking the Seine. Admitting that he had several calls to return, he left her to dress for dinner in a guest room. She put on a slender white dress with a plaited brown leather belt that hung low on her hips, and when she tucked their son into bed he wished her goodnight in careful French.

Sleek and handsome in a designer suit, Christien came forward to greet her when she walked into the imposing drawing room. A portly older man stood smiling beside the trays of glorious rings spread out in front of the windows to catch the best light.

Christien curved a light arm to her spine. 'I want you to choose your engagement ring.'

'Wow...you're being so conventional,' she mumbled to cover her delight and surprise with a little cool.

'Maybe it's *too* conventional... If you prefer we can scrap the ring idea,' Christien countered very seriously.

'Don't be daft... I was only teasing.' Having registered that facetious comments could get her into trouble, she hastened over to the rings and fell madly in love with a diamond in a wonderful art deco setting.

'Take your time,' Christien censured, distrusting impulses.

'No, this is it...this is the one,' she insisted. 'It's my favourite era.'

He took her to an exclusive restaurant for dinner.

'This is how it should have been the first night... I should have waited,' Christien conceded. 'But I couldn't keep my hands off you—'

'Let's not talk about stuff like that.' Tabby was getting short of breath just looking across the table at his lean dark features and the aura of sexy confidence he exuded.

'I want to marry you,' Christien said harshly. 'I really *do* want to marry you.'

'But I don't want it to be just because of Jake or...' But she bit back the word 'sex' for suddenly she could see how unfair she was being. He didn't love her, but she was pushing as if she thought pressure might somehow change that and, of course, it wouldn't. If lust and his son were all she had to hold him, maybe she was just going to have to come down to earth and get used to that reality.

She scarcely knew what she ate at that meal. She saw other women glancing at him, admiring that hard bronzed profile, the grace of the lean hands he used to express himself while he talked. An intensity of love that was almost terrifying filled her.

'Shall we go to a club?' he asked over coffee.

'Not in the mood.' She didn't trust herself to look at him in the cab. She wanted him. She wanted him so badly it hurt to say no to herself. He followed her into Jake's room. From the floor he retrieved the worn white stuffed lamb that Jake had slept with since he was a baby. He slotted it in beside their son and straightened his bedding.

'*Bon Dieu*... I can't believe he's ours,' Christien confided huskily. 'When I think about him or look at him I have that same sense of wonder I used to have as a child at *Noël*...at Christmas.'

Her eyes prickled. 'Thank goodness... I thought it was only me who could get soppy about him.'

In the corridor, Christien paused, lean, powerful face taut. 'If I had known you were carrying my baby, I would have been there for you,' he asserted in a driven undertone. 'But that day at the accident enquiry, I didn't trust myself to be alone with you—'

'But why?' she whispered, breaking into that emotive flood.

'I was angry as hell. I believed that you'd two-timed me with the biker. I'd let that conviction destroy even the good memories I had of you,' he admitted grimly. 'I was still very bitter. I didn't want you to know what I was feeling.'

He had freed her from the fear that he had rejected her that day because she was Gerry Burnside's daughter. She knew how strong his pride was, but he had told her more than he probably realised. All those months later, he had still been furious and bitter over her supposed betrayal. The longevity of those emotions suggested to her that she had meant something rather more to Christien Laroche than a casual summer lover.

'But I can see that you thought I was cruel. That was never my intention. I didn't appreciate that I had the power to hurt you that day,' Christien completed.

She stretched up on tiptoes, linked her arms round his neck and raised shining eyes to his. 'I know. Thank you for my gorgeous ring.'

With infuriating control, Christien set her back from him again. 'We have an early start tomorrow.'

It was a warm night and she wasn't in the mood to go to bed. Earlier in the evening, Christien had given her a tour of the apartment and there was a pool in the basement. She descended the stairs and used the atmospheric lighting to illuminate the glorious pool shaped like a lake. Never had she seen a stretch of water look quite so enticing.

Stripping where she stood, she padded down the Roman steps and sighed with appreciation as the cool, silky water washed her overheated skin. She swam a length and then let her eyes drift shut while she floated.

'You'd better vacate the water if you don't want to be ravished,' Christien's husky drawl warned.

Her eyes flew wide and she flipped over with an ungainly splash. He was hunkered down by the side of the pool, bronzed hair-roughened chest bare. He vaulted upright again.

'This is my equivalent of a cold shower,' he told her bluntly. 'You're looking at a guy on the edge, *mon ange.*'

Her face suffused with colour as she noticed the bulge of male arousal delineated by the tight black denim. He unsnapped the waistband, undid the zip with obvious difficulty. Again she noticed the silky furrow of black hair that ran down over his flat, taut stomach. Dragging her half-embarrassed, half-appreciative attention from him, she swam for the steps. Only as she emerged from the water did she appreciate her own nudity and how provocative it must seem to Christien that she had not even set out a towel with which to cover herself.

Christien was stopped in his tracks by the sight of her. Her hair was a thick, damp tangle round her animated face and her skin had the luscious glow of a sun-ripened peach.

'I swear I didn't know you were coming down here,' Tabby muttered feverishly. 'I swear it.'

'Stand up...drop your hands...show me what I want to see.' Christien's rich dark accented drawl was bold and rough-edged.

She met burning golden eyes and her heartbeat quickened and her head swam. She arched her spine, let her hands fall to her side, listened to the indrawn hiss of his breath with an inner stab of feminine satisfaction. 'It's our first date,' she reminded him.

'So I'm a sure thing, *ma belle.*' His gaze clung to the creamy swell of her voluptuous breasts and lingered on distended pink nipples still beaded with water. A groan broke low in his throat. 'In fact, I'm a pushover... I'm the sort of guy who gives his all on a first date.'

'Are you?' Tabby shivered although she was not cold. She was, however, very wound up. She knew she ought to run like hell. He was putting out vibes like placards: go...or else. She had to be a wanton hussy because just the thought of his knowing hands on her left her giddy and weak. Standing there naked in front of him while he looked her over, she felt shameless, but it was very exciting too.

He reached for her in one sudden movement. He took her mouth with sexual savagery, penetrating fast and deep between her lips with an urgency that sent the blood drumming in a crazy beat through her veins. Trembling with desire, she let herself be carried over to the padded bench by the wall. He spread her there and knelt to lick the crystalline water droplets from her breasts and toy with her pointed pink nipples. He tipped her back and spread her thighs to trace the lush, swollen flesh below the soft curls that crowned her womanhood.

As she lay there open to him, her face burned. *'Christien—'*

'You've got shy,' Christien teased with hungry appreciation and he located the tiny bud that was unbearably sensitive and wrenched a startled gasp from her.

Hot, almost painful sensation was tugging at her every sense, making it more and more impossible for her to concentrate on anything but her own pleasure.

'This is one more reason why you have to marry me,' Christien growled with raw satisfaction. 'You're down here at two in the morning because you can't sleep for wanting me and I'm the same. We belong together.'

'But—'

'Don't you dare say "but" to me,' Christien told her bossily. 'You can stuff the separate beds too.'

He slid a finger into the slick heat of her and she was lost.

He employed his mouth and the tip of his tongue on her most tender place. Writhing in abandonment, she moaned like a soul in torment and clutched at his hair. Pleasure as she had never known had her in its grip and she couldn't speak, couldn't think, couldn't handle anything but the incredible impact of what he was doing to her. Then, when she was way beyond any form of control, he lifted her up as though she were a doll, turned her over to arrange her exactly to his liking and drove his hard shaft into her tight, wet sheath from behind.

'Oh...*oh*!' Tabby cried out in sensual shock as he held her fast and delved deeper with every sure stroke.

His ruthless domination was indescribably exciting. Setting up a pagan rhythm, he proceeded to drive her out of her mind with excitement. She hit a high in a blinding instant of shattering release and her entire body convulsed in an explosive orgasm. Her legs just collapsed under her at that point. With an understanding laugh, Christien pulled out of her, threw himself down on the bench and lifted her up to bring her back down on top of him.

'I'm so hot for you, I feel like an animal,' he confessed raggedly.

She whimpered as he eased back into her passion-moistened depths.

'Am I being too rough?' he groaned.

'No... I'm passing out with pleasure,' she managed to mumble.

Reassured, he pushed her hair off her damp brow, kissed her and spread her thighs a little more to deepen his penetration with an earthy groan of appreciation. *'Moi aussi, ma belle.'*

The wild pleasure began to build afresh for her. When his magnificent body shuddered with the raw excitement of his own release, he sent her flying to the same uncontrollable heights of fulfilment a second time. It was a burst of ecstasy so intense that her eyes were awash with tears in the aftermath. Clasping him close and glorying in the wondrously familiar scent of his hot, damp masculinity, she knew that she never wanted to let him go.

'We're sleeping together tonight too,' Christien delivered, pressing a kiss to her temples, lacing his fingers into her tumbled hair and then smoothing the tangled tresses again. '*Ciel!* Suppose one of us was to die tomorrow…imagine how we would feel if we had slept apart.'

That very suggestion was too much for Tabby in the emotional mood she was in and she sobbed, 'Don't ever say anything like that!'

'I was only kidding.' Christien hugged her so tight that breathing was an impossibility. For a sickening second he had been jarred by the thought of how he would have felt had she been in that car with her father and his friends that night almost four years earlier, and it was as if he had been punched in the gut by a iron fist.

'But stuff like that happens—'

'We've already come through a lifetime of bad luck and we're together again,' Christien drawled forcefully, but he was wondering uneasily what was the matter with him.

Why was he talking and thinking the way he was? It was weird. He felt decidedly queasy about the amount of unfamiliar emotion assailing him, never mind his own imaginative flight of folly that had caused her to burst into tears in the first instance. Of course, he was fond of her. Naturally. There was nothing wrong with affection, was there? She lapped up stuff like that too, he reminded himself, relaxing again. The hugs, the hand holding, the cards, the flowers, all the stupid, meaningless mush. He hugged her, held her hand and resolved to have flowers sent to her in the morning. He was really only catering to *her* needs and only a miserable, selfish bastard would withhold the little touches that made her content.

He carried Tabby into a big walk-in shower. 'By day you can be as proper as a Victorian virgin but at night, you're mine,' he told her.

Her body had a sweet, lingering ache of satisfaction that filled her with languor. A towel wrapped round her in a sarong, he took her back up to his room. There he unwrapped her again with the care of a male performing a symbolic act and slid her beneath the sheet. Shedding his jeans, he climbed in beside her and hauled her close. Love spread through Tabby in a warm wave of security. Nestling into him, charmed by the fact that he was holding her hand even though it was not really comfortable, she went straight to sleep.

Christien woke to find his three-year-old son staring at him from the foot of the bed.

'What are you doing in Mummy's bed?' Jake asked, wide-eyed.

'She had a nightmare,' Christien responded glibly.

'What happened to her nightie?' Jake demanded.

'It fell off...when she was having the nightmare,' Christien told him boldly, but a faint flush of colour underscored his superb cheekbones.

Tabby, who had woken up too, started to laugh.

'You're supposed to be supporting me here,' Christien breathed in a meaningful undertone out of the corner of his handsome mouth.

'You'll have to do better than that to get support!' Tabby spluttered, for she was in the grip of helpless giggles.

Christien held her until she subsided: Tabby under one arm, their son, who seemed to find giggles highly contagious, beneath the other. Should he call his own mother to tell her that he was marrying Gerry Burnside's daughter? He was no coward, but he felt more like sending a note and keeping his distance until the hysterics were over and the tears had dried. Phoning, he decided, would be the safest and kindest first line of approach. Did he then risk taking Tabby for a brief visit? For perhaps ten minutes? He refused to contemplate the possibility of Tabby being slighted or hurt. Ought he to say something to that effect to his mother beforehand? Above Tabby's vulnerable head, he grimaced and his possessive embrace became even more pronounced.

That afternoon, Christien shepherded Tabby and Jake into his mother's apartment. It seemed less gloomy than it had been on his last visit. The curtains were no longer half shut and some of the blinds that blocked the sunlight had been raised. He could only stare when his parent walked to greet them, looking quite unrecognisable, not only because she had a tentative smile on her face, but also because she was wearing something other than black for the first time in almost four years: a dark blue dress.

'*Madame...*' Tabby murmured cheerfully, offering her cheek French-fashion for his elegant mother's salutation.

'Tabby...' Christien's parent murmured in warm welcome, kissing her on both cheeks. 'Please call me Matilde.'

Jake opened his arms for a hug. Matilde knelt down to oblige and informed the little boy that the French word for grand-mother was *mamie*.

Christien could not credit what he was seeing. It was picture perfect. It seemed too good to be true that the very first time his parent laid eyes on Tabby, she should greet the younger woman like a cherished family member. But there it was: his mother was enthusing over Tabby's engagement ring and listening to Jake's chatter while their son hung onto the older woman's hand.

Christien cleared his throat. Both women gave him an innocent look of enquiry.

'*Non*...the show is over,' Christien pronounced drily. 'I'm not fooled. I'm not that stupid. The two of you have met before!'

'How did you know?' Tabby demanded in exasperation.

A rerun of Veronique's first meeting with his parent after their engagement had replayed in Christien's memory. Although she'd known the brunette since childhood, his mother's polite reception of her future daughter-in-law had had little warmth. A belated deduction that came as a sincere shock to Christien led him into a rare indiscretion.

Christien studied Matilde in surprise. 'You didn't like Veronique...'

The older woman was taken aback by his lack of tact in referring to his former fiancée on such an occasion and then she sighed in answer. 'Even when that young woman was a little girl, I thought she was sly.'

'So how did you meet Tabby?' Christien asked, only casually wondering why Veronique had such a very bad track record when it came to befriending her own sex. Sly?

'Ask us no questions and we will tell you no lies,' Tabby interposed at an instant when, ironically, she was gasping to ask a curious question on her own account. Veronique? Had Christien and his parent been referring to the same woman whom she had met in the Dordogne?

Matilde announced that she wanted to throw a party to celebrate their engagement. As a distraction it was very successful, particularly as Christien was also caught up in silencing his son's innocent attempt to tell Matilde that Tabby had had such a bad nightmare that her nightie had fallen off.

Having left Matilde's apartment, Tabby and Christien were in the lift before Tabby had the opportunity to say, 'Veronique... was that the same Veronique I met years back?'

Christien gave her an uncommunicative nod of confirmation.

So he *had* been seeing the other woman. Tabby almost winced. She was disappointed in him. All right, Veronique had been beautiful and stylish and clever, but she had also been a cold, nasty piece of work as Tabby had found out to her cost after that car crash when she had gone up to the villa in the hope of seeing Christien again. But there it was, deserved or otherwise, evidently Veronique had finally got what she had wanted all along: her chance to shine with Christien as something other than a good mate. For once, however, life appeared to have handed out its just deserts for Christien had obviously been less than impressed, Tabby reflected with a satisfaction that was only human.

But that satisfaction was just as swiftly replaced by a disconcerting stab of unease that prompted her to say, 'I gather that
you and Veronique were together a while back…so I don't have
anything to do with you breaking up with her, do I?'

'*Ne fais pas l'idiote*…don't be silly!' Telling all, Christien
had decided, would only cause distress. In fact it was a kindness to keep quiet for Tabby was happy and an awareness of
how recently he had been engaged to Veronique would only
make her very *un*happy…

On the night of their engagement party, Tabby twirled in front
of a giant gilt-edged mirror in the grand salon at Duvernay and
then twirled again for good measure.

Courtesy of Christien's generosity, an antique Cartier diamond necklace of deco vintage encircled her throat. It looked
fabulous and her dress had a to-die-for glamour that thrilled her.
Ruby-red in colour, it bared her shoulders, hugged her shapely
figure to perfection and fell into a flirty hem round her ankles,
scoring on all three counts of being feminine and sexy and chic
into the bargain. But without Matilde, she would never have
had the nerve to enter the high fashion emporium on the Rue
St-Honore where she had found the gown.

The past eight days had been hugely enjoyable for Tabby and
jam-packed with activity and entertainment. With Christien she
had picnicked below the chestnut trees in the Jardin des Tuile-
ries, visited Disneyland Paris with Jake, toured fabulous art col-
lections and on one memorable occasion had gone out clubbing
until dawn. They had talked about her career as an artist and
stolen hungry kisses behind doors like guilty teenagers. They
had spent virtually every daylight hour together with Christien
making up business hours most evenings and Tabby was now
fully convinced that she had had very good taste when she'd
fallen in love with him almost four years earlier.

He had become so romantic since then too, she thought blissfully. He kept on sending her flowers and buying her little gifts,

like the teddy bear with the silly smile that he had said reminded him of her…and big gifts like the diamond necklace and a gorgeous deco bronze of a dancing woman. With Matilde Laroche being so welcoming, Tabby truly felt as though she was becoming part of a family again and that it should be Christien's family was a source of real joy to her for it healed the wounds of the past.

In between times, and regardless of the reality that she had yet to officially give her agreement to marrying Christien, their wedding plans had marched on with Matilde in enthusiastic charge. Tabby's actual spoken agreement had come to seem quite unnecessary. In just thirty-six hours, they would undergo a civil ceremony in the *mairie* or town hall, and that would be followed by a church blessing.

Tabby could hardly wait for the wedding, not least because she and Christien would finally be able to make love again. They had both learned an embarrassing lesson by letting Jake catch them in the same bed before she had a wedding ring on her finger. Not the least of their punishments had been Jake's earnest suggestion that he keep his mother company at night in case she had another nightmare. Indeed Tabby and Christien had reached the conclusion that it was their duty to set their son an example until that magical moment when they could freely point out that married people slept in the same bed.

Christien appeared in the doorway, a sleek and spectacular masculine vision in an Armani evening suit.

'Show-stopping,' he pronounced with intense appreciation when he saw her in the ruby-red dress. 'You look hot and you're mine, *ma belle.*'

The party took off like an express train and the best champagne flowed like a river in flood. Jake got a little over-excited at all the attention he was receiving and had to be reprimanded once or twice. Christien's relatives were generally very much in the older age group and Tabby found them old-fashioned and formal but kindly and inclined to treat her son like a little prince in waiting. Christien had invited only a handful of close friends to the engagement celebration because it was being staged so close to the wedding. Tabby had only contrived to invite one guest of her own: Sean Wendell. Her aunt and her boyfriend were flying in just for the wedding before they travelled on to Australia but unfortunately Tabby's friend, Pippa, was unable to leave her father to manage on his own.

Veronique Giraud staged her entrance when the party was in full swing. Tabby noticed the sudden silence that fell and she glanced up. She was dismayed by the other woman's arrival for she had had no idea that the brunette had been invited. Sporting a stunning black and white evening gown, Veronique headed direct for Christien. As she crossed the floor she performed a couple of fluid teasing steps to the music and extended her hand to Christien. Striding to meet her, he accepted her invitation.

Tabby knew how to jive but had never learned how to do anything else. She had ignored Christien's effort to persuade her that she could easily learn the steps because she had not wanted to risk making a fool of herself at their engagement party. The sight of Veronique smiling while she gracefully circled the floor in Christien's arms sent a shard of angry envy and hurt darting through Tabby.

Indeed, just watching Veronique Tabby could feel herself regressing to the intimidated teenager she had been almost four years earlier. On the day that she was to fly back home with her widowed stepmother, she had hurried up to the Laroche villa to make a desperate last ditch attempt to see Christien before she had to leave France. After all, he had not called her, nor had he been answering his phone.

Veronique had come to the door in the wake of the manservant. 'What do you want?' she demanded rudely.

Tabby was shocked for, up until that point, the brunette had always been pleasant. She found herself asking if she could see Christien as if she was asking for Veronique's permission to do so.

'It's over. Isn't it time you accepted that you've been dumped? He doesn't want to see you.' Veronique dealt Tabby's white drawn face and shadowed eyes a scornful scrutiny and her lip curled. 'He thinks he may have to change his mobile number to shake you off!'

At that confirmation that her calls had been received and that the other woman was as aware of that fact as she was of Christien's evident determination to ignore those same calls, Tabby died a thousand deaths inside herself. Already sick with grief over her father's demise and the appalling suffering of her bereaved friends, she was torn apart by the pain of Christien's rejection for she had never needed him more than she needed him then. She turned to leave at that point but Veronique was the kind of female who specialised in kicking her victims even harder when they were already down.

'Surely you didn't believe that Christien Laroche would get serious with a cheap little scrubber like you? Do you believe in Santa Claus as well?' Veronique sneered.

Tabby dragged herself out of the past and back into the present and threw back her slim shoulders. She was not a teenager any longer and in a day and a half she would be Christien's wife. In those circumstances she could afford to overlook the brunette's spiteful nature and be gracious. After all, whether she liked it or not, it looked as though Veronique was still firmly entrenched in the ranks of Christien's friends and would have to be tolerated.

Some of the older guests were leaving and, having bid them goodnight, Christien was hailed by a friend. Tabby left him to it and returned to the ballroom alone. Veronique was coming towards her and Tabby felt pride demanded that she stay still long enough to acknowledge the other woman with a polite smile.

'Oh, *do* let me see the ring Christien gave you!' Veronique exclaimed with mocking insincerity.

'I'm sure you're not really interested,' Tabby said uncomfortably, feeling horribly small and squat when she had to tip her head back to look up at the tall brunette.

'But naturally I'm dying to make a comparison.' The brunette extended a hand on which a large solitaire diamond glittered on her middle finger.

'Sorry...a comparison?' Tabby stared at her in confusion.

'This is the ring I wore when *I* was engaged to Christien. Look closely at it, expect to see it back on my engagement finger again, because when you screw up as a wife he'll divorce you and I'll comfort him,' Veronique forecast.

Tabby was paralysed to the spot. 'When were you engaged to Christien?'

'Right up until a little scrubber came out of nowhere clutching her bastard brat!' the brunette advanced nastily. 'It pays well to be fertile, doesn't it?'

CHAPTER TEN

ALL THE COLOUR in Tabby's face had faded away. Giddy with the force of her disturbed emotions, she turned on her heel and walked away from Veronique.

Veronique was lying. Of course, Christien couldn't have been engaged when Tabby had come back into his life. Christien would have said so. Christien was always such a stickler for honesty. There was no way he could have been Veronique's fiancé, no way on earth! Dry-mouthed and trembling, Tabby lifted a glass of champagne off a waiter's tray and downed it in one.

She espied Christien out in the entrance hall and sped out there at the speed of light to catch him on his own before anyone else could intercept him. 'Veronique just showed me her engagement ring—'

Christien vented what sounded like a French swear word. 'I was planning to tell you after the wedding, *ma belle.*'

Tabby studied him in sick disbelief and took a step back from him. 'You mean…it's *true*? You were engaged to her? When did you and her split up?'

'We'll discuss this later in private,' Christien decreed, distrusting the overwrought wobble in Tabby's voice and the furious look of hurt and condemnation in her green eyes.

'When did you break it off with her?' Tabby snapped.

His lean, strong face clenched. 'What I had with Veronique is not relevant to what I have with you.'

'She just called me a scrubber for the second time in my life...and this time, thanks to you, I *deserve* it!' Tabby accused, but her voice was shaking because her heart felt as if it were breaking up inside her.

'Veronique called you a...*what*?' Christien growled in raging disbelief. 'You must have misheard her—'

'Like heck I did. She called me one four years ago as well. Imagine you being so dumb you didn't even realise she was determined to hook you that far back. But as far as I'm concerned now she can have you back...*and* she's welcome to you!' Tabby slung in fierce conclusion before she stalked back into the ballroom.

Dark anger flaring, Christien went to find Veronique.

'I'm sorry, but Tabby is lying to you.' Veronique sighed in sympathy. 'I think she must be feeling jealous and she's made up this nonsense in a silly attempt to destroy our friendship. Don't be too hard on her. Quite naturally, she's feeling insecure.'

His narrowed gaze probed the gleam in her pale blue eyes. *Sly?* His lean, strong face was grim. 'I am satisfied that Tabby is telling me the truth. If you abuse her again or spread gossip about her or our child, I'll sue you through every court in France until you're ruined.'

Veronique had gone white with shock.

'I make a bitter enemy and I will protect her with the last breath in my body.' Christien's intonation was cold as ice. 'Leave my home. You're not welcome here.'

Having submerged herself in the crush of dancers to evade the risk of Christien's pursuit, Tabby emerged at the far side of the floor. She helped herself to another glass of champagne and drank it down in the hope that the alcohol would help her stay smiling until the last guests had departed. At the far end of the room Matilde Laroche was chatting with relatives. The older woman did not deserve the embarrassment of the newly engaged couple having an open fight at the party she had arranged.

Unfortunately, however, reflections that caused Tabby a great deal of pain and humiliation were already bombarding her from all directions. Christien could only have decided to marry her because of Jake. No wonder Veronique hated her guts! Doubtless Matilde had kept quiet about his having been engaged to Veronique because she also believed that Christien should marry her grandson's mother.

Christien found Tabby taking refuge out on the balcony beyond the ballroom and he breathed in deep when she spun away refusing to look at him. 'Veronique wasn't invited this evening and I made the initial mistake of crediting that she had gate-crashed in a spirit of goodwill. But I told her to leave and she's gone and I assure you that she will not trouble you again—'

'Go away... I hate you!' Tabby gulped back the sob threatening her voice.

'Tabby—'

'Did you or did you not sleep with me when you were engaged to another woman?' Tabby demanded shakily.

In the moonlight, Christien almost groaned out loud.

'You lying, cheating...when I think of the grief you gave me when I lied about my age four years ago and here *you* are...' Words failed Tabby in her angry distress and she stalked past him.

A lean hand snapped round her elbow. 'Don't do this to us. Just let it go. I remained silent about Veronique because I didn't want to wreck things—'

Tabby tried to pull free. 'Let go of me!'

'I can't let you walk away in this mood—'

'I'll scream if you don't!'

Christien removed his hand with a flourish. 'This is insane. You know how it has been between us from the minute we met again.'

'Lust!' Tabby fired at him in disgust.

Tears were threatening to flood her eyes when she returned to the ballroom. Sean stopped in front of her. 'What's up? Are you all right?'

'Dance with me,' she begged.

The music was slow and Sean groaned. 'I'm no good at these ones.'

Tabby wrapped her arms round his neck and mumbled, 'Just shuffle.'

'Have you had a row with Christien?'

'Why would you think that?'

'Oh, no good reason…just he's standing at the edge of the floor looking furious with both hands clenched into fists as if I'm making a pass at you,' Sean said.

'Ignore him.'

'He's a big guy and hard to ignore. He is also *very* jealous. I noticed that the first time I met him. If I let a single finger stray, he'll haul me off the floor and kill me, so try not to stumble or do anything that he might misinterpret.' Sean sighed.

'He's not jealous…why would he be jealous of me?'

'Possibly because he's one of those intense types who goes overboard when he falls in love—'

'In love?' A sour little laugh fell from Tabby's lips.

'He's been bitten deep by it too. Doesn't like to see you laughing with another bloke either,' Sean remarked even more uneasily, holding her back from him at a careful and circumspect distance.

The minute the music paused, Christien strode up and Sean released her with patent relief. Tabby collided with scorching golden eyes and twisted her head away, but Christien was too fast for her and he drew her close.

'I know you're angry with me...but don't start flirting with other guys—'

The champagne was bubbling through her like petrol hitting a bonfire. 'I'll do as I like!'

Christien closed his arms round her. *'Fais ce que je dis...*do as I say. Stay calm—'

'I want to scream at you,' she gasped chokily.

'Scream all you like...just don't flirt. It drives me crazy—'

'How can you act jealous of me after the way you've behaved? When did you get engaged to *her*?' Tabby snapped at him like a bristling cat ready to pounce on prey.

'We should talk about this when you've sober—'

'Are you suggesting I'm drunk?'

'No, I'm doing you the justice of assuming that you only screech when you've had too much champagne,' Christien murmured tautly.

'Answer my question—'

'We got engaged six months ago. It was—'

Tabby lifted her arms and brought them down to break his hold. Frozen-faced and rigid-backed, she walked away. The last hour of the party seemed to fly. Later she could not have said whom she spoke to or what she said, but her cheekbones ached with the smile she kept glued in place. Six months, was all she could think in an agony of jealous hurt. *Six months!*

When the final merrymaker departed, Christien closed a hand over hers and urged her into the library. She snatched her fingers free of his, folded her arms and finally threw her head high to stare back at him. 'I can't marry you now...'

He lost colour, lean, darkly handsome features setting hard. 'I would have told you about the engagement after the wedding. It wasn't important but I knew that you would regard it in a different light—'

'Your engagement to another woman wasn't important?

Wasn't the least you owed her fidelity? And didn't I deserve honesty? Do you think I'd have had anything to do with you if I'd known you belonged to someone else—?'

'*Belong?* What am I? A trophy?' Christien made a sudden angry slashing movement with one brown hand, his frustration unconcealed. 'Last year, Veronique and I talked about how we had got into the habit of using each other as partners on certain social occasions. We were friends and it worked well. We discussed marriage from a practical point of view. I needed a hostess and she valued high social status and a husband who would not interfere in her career, for she is ambitious. We decided that we could have a successful marriage without the emotional entanglements that so often lead to disillusionment—'

'It sounds like one very creepy arrangement to me,' Tabby sniped.

'Fidelity was not required from me. It was not part of our agreement.' Glittering golden eyes sought and held hers, willing her to listen and understand. 'I tell you that only because I don't want you feeling guilty about what happened between us—'

'Veronique told you that you could sleep around?' Tabby gave him an aghast appraisal. 'And you accepted that? That's disgraceful!'

'Not in her opinion. Veronique does not attach importance to such matters.'

'Well, it's just as well that I'm not marrying you, because if you played away on *me*, I'd make your life hell!' Tabby launched fiercely. 'In fact hell would feel like a four-star paradise by the time I'd finished with you!'

It threw her off balance when Christien seemed to almost smile at that threatening declaration. 'I know,' he acknowledged. 'But tell the average single male that he can have a beautiful, accomplished wife and do as he likes behind closed doors with other women and he'll go for it...until he finds that there's something better—'

'Well, I think it's disgusting!' Tabby spun away.

'But I'm with *you* now—'

Tabby vented a humourless laugh. He was only with her because all Veronique's beauty and accomplishments had proved to be worthless in the face of a three-year-old son in his own handsome image. If Jake had not existed and Tabby had been willing to settle for being a kept woman in that opulent house in the Loire valley, Christien would have stayed engaged to Veronique and he would eventually have married her. She could not forgive him for that. She just could not forgive him for choosing to marry her solely for the benefit of their son. After all, she was not his friend, who inspired his respect and admiration as the brunette did!

There was nothing Christien would not do for Jake. She had seen his relief when the consultant had told them that Jake's asthma was unlikely to get worse and that he looked set to outgrow it. Christien adored his son. He didn't say it, didn't need to say it, just lit up with tender pride and protectiveness around Jake and got down on his knees to play with toy cars as if it were the most fun he had ever had. Her wretched eyes misted over. No, she could not fault him for loving Jake. That would be unfair. But she had a right to her own self-esteem and it was being battered into the ground by the cruel confirmation that the only true interest the guy she loved had in her was her wanton talent for meeting his every passionate demand in bed.

'I'm really sorry that you've been upset by this,' Christien breathed grittily. 'But it doesn't touch us. Can't you see that? I wasn't in love with Veronique and she wasn't in love with me either. I offended her pride by rejecting her. But you and I...we have so much more—'

Her throat ached. 'Yeah...great sex.'

'*Zut alors*...don't talk like that, don't try to talk down what we have.'

'I've never forgotten the way you dumped me four years ago,' she confided tightly. 'You didn't even have the grace to tell me. You let me come up to your family's villa chasing after you—'

His black brows pleated. 'When...when was that?'

'The day I flew back home with my stepmother, Lisa. Veronique met me at the door. I had to face the humiliation of your very good friend telling me I'd been ditched and that you were going to have to change your mobile phone number to shake me off!'

Christien took a hasty step forward and reached for both her hands. 'Veronique had no right. She went behind my back. I never discussed you with her, nor would I have allowed her to speak to you in such a way. But at the time I did believe that you were seeing another guy,' he reminded her. 'I wasn't expecting you to come to the villa—'

'I don't care. You hurt me then...and tonight you hurt and humiliated me again and I can't forgive you...*won't* forgive you!' Tabby's aching eyes were wide to ensure the gathering tears stayed out of sight and she didn't trust herself to listen to his arguments in his own defence. He was downright gorgeous and she loved him, but just then she hated him too. Trailing her fingers free, she yanked the ring off her finger before she could lose her nerve and set it down on the console table beside her.

'No...' Christien grated.

Tabby fled upstairs. She wouldn't let herself cry. She took a nightdress from her bedroom and stole across the corridor to Jake's room where she knew she would not be disturbed. Distressed as she was, she was asleep within minutes of climbing into the twin bed next to her son's. Around dawn she wakened and went for a shower to freshen up. Her head was sore. Too much champagne, just as Christien had said. The night before, she had been all drama and brave defiance. Now in the cold light of day she was trying to imagine what it would do to Jake if the promised wedding failed to take place. He was so excited. And it was not as if Christien were in love with Veronique. But what would it do to her to love Christien without return for years on end? It would humble her, damage her confidence.

The second time she wakened, she was back in her own bed and she sat up in bewilderment. His back turned to her, Christien was lodged by the windows, the curtains partially opened to let the sunlight flood into the elegant room.

'I moved you in here because we have to talk,' he breathed harshly.

'No... I don't know what to say to you—'

Christien swung round. The lines of strain grooved between his nose and mouth were matched by the brooding darkness of his gaze. 'I should have asked you just to listen. I'll do the talking.'

Tabby looped a straying strand of hair off her brow in an effort to hide that she was still reeling from the way events had overtaken them the night before.

'That day four years back, when you tried to see me at the villa and Veronique spoke to you instead, I was probably drunk. After I'd dealt with the formalities of my father's death and my mother shut herself away here demanding to be left alone, I spent the rest of that hideous week drunk.'

Green eyes huge, Tabby gaped at him because he had told her something she would never have suspected for herself, for he always seemed so much in control. 'Perhaps I should've thought of that. Naturally you were having trouble coping—'

Christien dug lean hands into the pockets of his well-cut trousers. 'It was getting by without you I was struggling to handle,' he ground out in a driven undertone.

The silence stretched and stretched.

'*Zut alors*... I was planning to marry you and then I saw you with the biker and it all went pear-shaped on me. When our fathers died in that car accident, I wanted you,' he bit out. 'But pride wouldn't let me have you, so I drank myself into a stupor to ensure I didn't weaken.'

Tabby blinked. She was transfixed. He had been planning to marry her?

Christien shrugged a broad shoulder with something less than his usual grace. 'I didn't like feeling like that. I watched my mother sink into despair without my father. They had always been very close and for a while after his death she did not want to live without him. It was terrifying to watch. I decided I didn't want to feel like that about any woman *ever*.'

'I can understand that…' Tabby mumbled, and yet she could offer nothing to match his unhappy experience.

Her stepmother had had shallow affections. Aside of a few noisy crying jags, the discovery that she was not as prosperous a widow as she had hoped had infuriated Lisa and ensured that her grief had been even more short-lived.

'Were you serious when you said you were planning to marry me then?' Tabby prompted hesitantly. 'I mean, you were furious with me for lying about my age. How *could* you have been thinking about marrying me?'

'How not?' Clear dark golden eyes met hers in fearless acknowledgement. 'I still wanted you. In the end that's all it came down to.'

Still wanted her but much against his will, she translated. But she was still deep in shock. While being very moody and unsentimental about it, Christien was nonetheless giving her riveting information about what he had felt for her in the past. He was so tense, though, that she felt a sudden shout might shatter him to pieces and she was touched.

Christien expelled his breath in a slow, measured hiss. 'Once you lied to me about your age because you didn't want to lose me. In the same way I chose to hold fire on telling you that I was engaged to Veronique on terms that you would never understand. Why? *I* didn't want to lose *you*.'

'Didn't you?' Her voice felt all strangled inside her throat.

'That summer we were first together, I was in love with you.

What else could it have been? That kind of madness that means you can't bear to be apart for even a few hours?' Christien rested shimmering golden eyes on her. 'I wouldn't admit it to myself but I had never felt for anyone what I felt for you—'

Her nose wrinkled and she made a frantic attempt to fight the tears threatening. 'Oh Christien…' she said thickly.

'When Solange left you the cottage, I used it as an excuse to see you again in London. I had no need to make that a personal visit and I could have made more effort to discourage you from moving to Brittany—'

'But I was *so* determined to make a new life here… I think that you weren't the only one of us hiding from the truth—'

Christien spread graceful brown hands in an inconclusive motion. 'Nothing went to plan then…but then I had no true strategy. Around you, I don't think straight,' he confessed with fierce reluctance. 'I just needed to see you, be with you, make love to you, and that first time I did not even recall that Veronique was a part of my life!'

Tabby scrambled off the bed, crossed the carpet and closed her arms round him tight. She was satisfied for, to her way of thinking, he had not had a normal engagement with the other woman and she could not judge him for his lack of fidelity to a woman who had told him that he might do as he liked.

'But I ended my engagement to Veronique immediately afterwards. I felt guilty but I didn't hesitate,' Christien confirmed.

'*Immediately* afterwards?' It was though yet another weight fell from Tabby's troubled heart, for she needed to know that she could trust him.

'I saw her in Paris and came back to Brittany that evening but you had already left the cottage. Unfortunately something foolish I said out of guilt to Veronique—that I was not thinking of marriage with you—very probably made her even angrier when she learned that I had in fact decided to marry you just as fast as I could.' Christien volunteered with a grimace.

'That's right…at that point you were dreaming of refurbishing the cottage into a delightful residence for a convenient mistress…am I right?'

Beautiful dark golden eyes glinting with wariness, Christien finally nodded.

'You see, I know you… I *know* how your mind works,' Tabby warned him with newly learned assurance. 'The idea of marrying me only came after you found out about Jake and when you realised I wasn't up for the living-in arrangement—'

'Can't you tell when a guy's ready to do anything to get you?'

'Nope… I need it spelt out.' Tabby was hardly breathing as she said it, for she was beginning to believe her wildest dreams had come true without her even appreciating it. It was the way he was looking at her.

Christien scooped her up and sat down on the edge of the bed with her cradled in his arms. 'I love you, *ma belle*. I love you like crazy.'

Tabby heaved an ecstatic sigh. She had not even dared to hope and there he had been sneakily hiding his feelings from her. 'You should have told me that ages ago—'

'It took me a painfully long time to appreciate how I felt—'

Tabby gazed up at him with a dreamy smile. 'I thought it was Jake… I thought you were only marrying me for him—'

'No, he's fantastic, but you are in a class all your own,' Christien confided thickly. 'I want to marry you to make you mine—'

'What do you think I am…some trophy?' Tabby teased.

'My trophy.' Framing her face with not quite steady hands, he tasted her lush mouth with a hungry fervour that threatened to blow her away.

Tabby quivered. 'I love you so much,' she finally told him.

'You *do*?' His charismatic smile flashed out and his beautiful eyes were tender on hers. 'Even though I've screwed up on innumerable occasions?'

'I like it when you screw up—'

'You were supposed to tell me I *don't*...feed my ego,' Christien lamented.

'Your ego is healthy enough—'

'I'm mad for you,' he breathed raggedly.

'We'll be married tomorrow—'

'Tomorrow might as well be a hundred years away. I ache with wanting you—'

'It'll be a very exciting honeymoon,' Tabby promised shamelessly, nestling close to provoke, really loving his desperation.

'We could go for a drive, *mon amour*,' Christien groaned. 'Book into a hotel—'

'No...your mother has me booked into a beauty salon for half of the day as it is—'

'That's stupid...you're gorgeous just the way you are. Don't let them cut your hair.'

Tabby glanced up to see Jake peering round the edge of the door at them.

'Kissy stuff.' Jake pulled a face. 'It's yucky!'

'I think we should start as we mean to go on. Lock the door on him and let your nightie fall off again,' Christien informed her huskily.

'I'm worth waiting for,' Tabby swore with a cheeky smile. She curved into the wonderful reassuring warmth and strength of his big, muscular body and, when Jake hurtled over to join them, gathered Jake in close as well. She was loved. She was loved by both of them, which just made her feel incredible.

Her wedding outfit was a two-piece composed of an embroidered and beaded fitted bodice the same rich green as her eyes and a flowing ivory skirt. An emerald and diamond tiara was anchored to her head, her diamond necklace was at her throat and her wedding present from her groom was the superb diamonds that hung from either ear.

Christien could not take his appreciative gaze from her. He led her up the steps and into the *mairie* for the civil ceremony

as though she were a queen. The church blessing followed in
the little chapel down the street. Holding hands, they posed for
photographs afterwards, her eyes shining, his eyes resting on
her with pride and a love he couldn't hide.

The reception was held in the Ritz Hotel in Paris. Alison Davies and her boyfriend looked on in surprise as Tabby took all
the luxury and the attention in her stride. Indeed, the bride's
bubbly personality and assurance were much admired and, in
her radius, the groom was less cool than his reputation suggested. His less discreet relatives hinted that parental opposition had kept the young couple apart. Their guests began talking
of the match as a '*grande passion*'. That Tabby was penniless
and neither stick-thin nor a classic beauty had been noted. That
Christien looked at his bride as though she were as irresistible
as Cleopatra was also noted. That Tabby had succeeded where
the much-disliked Veronique had failed was sufficient to ensure that she would become a great social success.

Before leaving the hotel, the bridal couple entrusted their
son, Jake, to the care of his grandmother, Matilde. A limo
whisked them to the airport where they boarded Christien's
private jet for their flight to a honeymoon hideaway in the
Tuscan hills.

Only when the jet was airborne did Christien remove a letter
from his inside pocket. 'This was delivered to me just before
the reception. It's from my great-aunt, Solange—'

'Solange?' Tabby echoed in disconcertion. 'How could it be?'

'Solange wrote it the same day that she changed her will so
that you could inherit the cottage. She instructed the *notaire*
that her letter was only to be given to me in the event of our
marriage.'

Tabby was challenged to translate the letter written in the
old lady's spidery handwriting.

Christien came to her rescue. 'In opening, Solange apolo-
gises to me for leaving a part of the Duvernay estate outside
the family—'

'She *does*?' Tabby exclaimed.

'And goes on to congratulate me for marrying you, thereby reuniting the cottage with the estate again—'

'Oh, that's *magic*!' Tabby was tickled pink. 'Obviously you only married me to get the cottage back.'

'Solange concludes by advancing the hope that we enjoy a long and happy life together and states that she always knew we were made for each other.' A rueful charismatic smile curved Christien's handsome mouth. 'She must have guessed even then that I loved you.'

Tabby's eyes stung. 'I wish I had,' she muttered. 'I'd have stormed past Veronique and confronted you that day. You'd have been too drunk to play it cool and you'd have admitted that you had seen Pete kissing me…and we'd have got it all sorted out there and then.'

With a sigh, Christien pulled her into his arms and held her close. 'I was a real smart ass in those days and I was fighting loving you. I'm more mature now—'

'I suppose I was too young to get married then.'

With incredible tenderness, he kissed the sprinkling of tears off her cheeks. 'I adore you. I appreciate you so much more now. Think of all the time we have ahead of us, *ma belle*.'

Her sunny smile began to blossom again and his own slow-burning smile broke out, stunning golden eyes lingering on her with intense appreciation. She found his mouth, dallied there with deliberate provocation, listened to his breathing fracture.

'Make mad, passionate love to me,' she whispered.

'Hussy…' Christien growled adoringly, and he carried her into the sleeping compartment because she was laughing so hard that she could hardly walk.

* * * * *

The Italian Boss's Mistress

CHAPTER ONE

A TEAM HAD flown over to Naples to bring Andreo up to speed on his latest acquisition, Venstar.

Tensions were running high for there was not a single Venstar executive present who did not feel that his job might be on the line. The ruthlessness that distinguished Andreo D'Alessio's brilliance in the business world was a living legend.

'This should help you to fit faces to the senior staff when you come over to visit us,' one of the directors said with a rather nervous laugh as he passed over a company newsletter adorned with a photograph of key personnel.

Andreo D'Alessio studied the front page with keen dark eyes. Only one woman featured in the line-up and he only noticed her in the first instance because she messed up the picture. She was very tall and her stooped and self-effacing stance shrieked all the awkwardness of a very skinny baby giraffe striving in vain to hide its overly long limbs. Heavy framed spectacles dwarfed her thin, earnest face. But what had caught Andreo's attention was her pronounced untidiness. Stray riotous curls stuck out from her head hinting that her hair was in dire need of a good brushing. His frown deepening, he went on to note that her ill-fitting suit jacket was missing a button and the hem on one leg of her shapeless trousers was sagging. He almost shuddered. The epitome of cool elegance himself, he was less than tolerant of those who offended his high standards.

'Who is the woman?' he enquired.

'*Woman?*' Andreo was asked blankly and he had to point her out in the photograph before his companions made the necessary leap in understanding.

'Oh, you mean... *Pippa!*' a Venstar executive finally exclaimed as though challenged to recognise the reality that the senior staff actually harboured a female in their ranks. 'Pippa's our assistant finance manager—'

'You don't tend to think of her as being a woman...has a brain like a calculator. An academic high-flyer who thinks of nothing but work,' a director proclaimed with appreciation. 'She's absolutely dedicated. She hasn't taken a single holiday in three years—'

'That's unhealthy,' Andreo cut in with disapproval. 'Stressed and exhausted employees operate below par and make mistakes. The lady needs a vacation and HR should have a word with her about smartening up her slovenly appearance.'

Jaws dropped. Paunches were sucked in and jackets smoothed down for none of the men was quite sure which imperfections might put one at risk of attracting the clearly very dangerous label of being 'slovenly'. An uncomfortable silence fell. Slovenly? *Was* Pippa slovenly? Nobody had ever really looked at Pippa long enough to have noticed one way or the other. That she was an economics prodigy and very efficient was all anybody had ever cared about.

Still scanning the picture to note the level of personal care as displayed by the male contingent of the line-up, Andreo found yet more scope for censure. 'I don't believe in the concept of dressing down because it doesn't impress clients. I don't want to see jeans in the office. A smart appearance implies discipline and it *does* impress. This man here could do with a haircut and a new shirt.' He pointed out the offender in an impatient tone. 'Attention to self-presentation is never wasted.'

Almost every man in the room decided to go on a diet, get a haircut and buy a new suit. Andreo, all six feet five inches of him, after all, could be seen to practise what he preached. Lean, mean and undeniably magnificent in a to-die-for Armani designer suit, Andreo was an impressive enough sight to inspire the younger men with an eager desire to emulate him. Ricky Brownlow, however, who was far too vain of his blond good looks to believe himself in need of either a diet or a haircut, concealed a self-satisfied smile. He had just worked out how he could promote his current lover over Pippa's head without attracting undue criticism.

'The HR department also needs to set new targets. I want to see a *very* rapid improvement in Venstar's abysmal record of promoting women to executive level,' Andreo concluded.

When her immediate superior, Ricky Brownlow, invited her into his office and broke the bad news, Pippa was betrayed into a startled exclamation. 'Cheryl...is going to be the new finance manager?'

Ricky nodded in casual confirmation as if there were nothing strange about that development.

Cheryl Long? The giggly brunette who currently acted as her junior was now to become her *boss?* That bombshell sent Pippa into severe shock. After all, she herself had been Acting Finance Manager for almost three months and she had had high hopes of the position being made permanent. Until that moment she had had no idea that Cheryl had even applied for the job.

'I thought that I should let you know before HR informed you through official channels,' Ricky added in the tone of a man who had gone out of his way to do her a favour.

'But Cheryl has hardly any qualifications and only a couple of months of experience in the section...' Pippa was quite unable to conceal her astonishment.

'New blood keeps the company fresh and sharp.' Ricky Brownlow frowned at her in reproof and a painful flush lit her fair skin.

A slender young woman with shaken blue eyes and vibrant auburn curls scraped back from her brow and held tight by a clip, Pippa walked back to her desk. She *could* have taken losing out to a superior candidate, she told herself urgently. But was she just being a bad loser? Shame at the fear that she might be that petty consumed Pippa, who suffered from a conscience more over-developed than most. Self-evidently, she decided, Cheryl Long had talents that she herself had failed to recognise.

The animated buzz of dialogue around Pippa reminded her of the party being held that evening to welcome Andreo D'Alessio and she suppressed an exasperated sigh. She had never liked parties and she liked work social occasions even less. However, now that she had been turned down for the job that she had naively assumed was in the bag, she had better make an appearance at the celebrations lest other people start thinking that she begrudged Cheryl her good fortune.

Cheryl was about to become her boss. Pippa swallowed the thickness building in her tight throat. For goodness' sake, had she screwed up somewhere so badly that she had blown her own promotion prospects right out of the water? If that was the case, why hadn't she been told and at least warned of her mistake? Cheryl was going to be her boss. Cheryl, whom Pippa had had to be rather stiff with on several recent occasions for her incredibly long lunch breaks and shoddy work? Cheryl, who seemed to spend half the day chatting and the rest of it flirting with the nearest available male? Cheryl, who was mercifully on leave that day...

Pippa sank deeper and deeper into shock. Hothoused as she had been from preschool level right through to university, and always expected to deliver exceptional results, failure of any kind threw her into an agony of self-blame and self-examination. Somehow, somewhere, she was convinced, she had fallen seriously short of what was expected of her...

'I wish he was more into publicity and we had a better photograph of him,' one of the project assistants, Jonelle, sighed in a die away voice that set Pippa's teeth on edge. 'But we'll see if he lives up to his extraordinary reputation when we see him in the flesh tonight—'

Her companion giggled. 'He's supposed to have bought his last girlfriend a set of diamond-studded handcuffs...'

Pippa had no need to ask who was under discussion for Andreo D'Alessio's exploits as an international playboy, business whizkid and womaniser were very well documented for a male who went to great lengths not to be photographed. Her soft full mouth curled in helpless disgust. The man that offered *her* diamond-studded handcuffs as a gift would find himself skydiving without a parachute. But then no man was ever likely to offer her diamond-studded sex toys of any description, and very grateful she was too not to be the type to attract that kind of perverted treatment! Just listening to another female agonise in fascination over a male set on reducing her sex to the level of toys for fun moments made her feel ill.

'I bet he's an absolute babe.' Jonelle had a dreamy look on her pretty face. 'Hot stuff—'

'I bet he's small and rather round in profile just like his late father,' Pippa inserted with deliberate irony. 'And the reason that Andreo D'Alessio doesn't like publicity is that he loves the rumour that he's much bigger and better looking than he really is.'

'Maybe the poor guy is just sick of being chased for his megamillions,' Jonelle opined in reproach.

'And maybe he wouldn't be chased at all if he didn't have them,' Pippa mocked.

Mid-morning she was called to an HR interview. Informed for the second time that her application to become Finance Manager had been unsuccessful, she felt grateful but still a little surprised that Ricky Brownlow had been kind enough to forewarn her of the disappointment coming her way. When she asked if there had been any complaints about her work performance, the older man was quick to reassure her.

'And that's very much to your credit when one considers events in recent months,' the HR director continued in a sympathetic tone.

Picking up on that oblique reference to her father's death in the spring, Pippa paled. 'I've been lucky to have my work to keep me busy.'

'Are you aware that you haven't utilised your holiday entitlement in several years?'

Her fine brows pleated and she shrugged. 'Yes...'

'I've been asked to ensure that you take at least three weeks off effective from the end of this month—'

'Three weeks...*off?*' Pippa gasped in dismay.

'I've also been authorised to offer you the opportunity of a sabbatical for six or twelve months.'

'A...a sabbatical...are you serious?' Pippa exclaimed in an even greater state of disconcertion.

Impervious to Pippa's discouraging response, the older man went on to wax lyrical about the benefits of taking a work break. He pointed out that Pippa had not taken a gap year between school and university and had in fact commenced employment at Venstar within days of her graduation.

'You spend very long hours in the office.'

'But I *like* working long hours—'

'Nevertheless I'm sure that you will enjoy de-stressing during your holiday in two weeks' time and that you'll consider the opportunity of extending your break with a sabbatical. Think of how refreshed you would be on your return to work.'

De-stressing? Ultra sensitive, Pippa picked up on that word and wondered if that was why she had been passed over in the promotion stakes. Did she come across as stressed to her colleagues? Irritable? Or was it that she seemed lacking in management skills? There had to be a reason why she had been unsuccessful—there *had* to be! Whatever, she was not being given a choice about whether or not she took a holiday and that bothered her. Why now and not before? Was there concern that she might not adapt well to the new command structure in the finance section?

Deeply troubled by her complete loss of faith in her own abilities, Pippa worked through her lunch hour and when, around three that afternoon, she glanced up and saw the empty desks around her, she frowned in surprise.

'Where is everybody?' she asked Ricky Brownlow when she saw him in his office doorway.

'Left early to get ready for the party. You should be heading home too.'

Pippa hated to leave a task unfinished but then she recalled the events of the day and the holiday that had been pressed on her. That had been a hurtful lesson in the reality that she was not indispensable. Rising from her desk, she lifted her bag. She had reached the ground floor before she appreciated that the rain was bouncing off the pavements outside and, in her haste to depart, she had left her coat behind.

Too impatient to wait on the lift again, she took the stairs. The finance floor was silent and she was walking towards the closet where her coat hung when she heard Ricky Brownlow's voice carrying out from his office.

'When I was in Naples, Andreo D'Alessio made it very clear that he likes sexy, fanciable women around him,' Ricky was saying in a pained, defensive tone. 'He took one horrified look at the piccy of our Pippa Plain in the company newsletter and it was clear that she would never fit the executive bill in his eyes, so I backed Cheryl's application instead. Cheryl's less qualified, I grant you, but she's also considerably more presentable—'

Pippa had frozen in her tracks. Pippa... *Pippa Plain*?

'Pippa Stevenson is an excellent employee,' a voice that she recognised as belonging to one of the older directors countered coldly.

'She's an asset as a backroom girl but her best friend couldn't call her a looker *or* a mover or shaker. She has all the personality of a wet blanket,' Ricky Brownlow pronounced with a viciousness that flayed Pippa to the bone. 'To be frank, I didn't think we'd be doing ourselves any favours if we ignored D'Alessio's sexist preferences and served up Pippa Plain to him on his first day here!'

Shattered by what she had overheard but even more terrified of being found eavesdropping, Pippa crept back out to the corridor and fled without her coat. In that one devastating dialogue, she had learned why Cheryl instead of herself was to be Venstar's next finance manager. *Pippa Plain?* Her tummy rolled with nausea but she refused to let herself cringe. Ricky Brownlow had laid it on the line: unlike Pippa, Cheryl was extremely attractive and popular with men. The curvaceous brunette's looks rather than her ability had influenced her selection.

A cold, sick knot of humiliation in her stomach, Pippa swallowed hard and blinked back stinging tears. It was so unfair. That job had had her name on it and she had worked darned hard for promotion. Nobody had the right to judge another person on their appearance. It was utterly wrong and against all employment legislation and Venstar deserved to be sued for treating her so shabbily. She imagined standing up at a tribunal and being forced to relate Ricky's demeaning comments and compressed her lips with a shudder of recoil. No, there was no way that she would take the company to a tribunal and make herself an object of sniggering pity.

Her best friend couldn't call her a looker... Pippa Plain? Was that a fact? Doubtless Ricky would never credit that when she was fifteen years old a modelling agency had offered her a lucrative contract. Of course, her father had been outraged by the mere suggestion that his daughter would engage in what he deemed to be a lowbrow career. But for the eight years that had followed Pippa had secretly cherished the memory of her one stolen day of rebellion against Martin Stevenson's strict dictates. She had gone to the agency in secret and let them make her up and do her hair. She had watched in fascination as cosmetic magic and clever clothing had transformed her from a pale, skinny beanpole into a glowing, leggy beauty. Then the old lech of a photographer had made a pass at her and sent her fleeing for home again, convinced that everything her father had said about the dangerous corruption of the modelling industry was true.

Why shouldn't she try to effect even some small part of that transformation on her own behalf? She could attend the party looking her best just to confound Ricky Brownlow and that sexist louse, Andreo D'Alessio. How could a man be so stupid that he put beauty ahead of brains even in a business capacity?

Standing in the rain getting absolutely soaked through, Pippa dug out her mobile phone and rang her friend Hilary. Hilary Ross was a hairdresser and when asked if she could squeeze Pippa in for a last-minute hair-rescue mission, she was so taken aback by the request that she gasped, 'Are you being frivolous at last? Is it Christmas or something?'

'Or something,' Pippa confirmed a little unevenly. 'I'm going out tonight and it's really important.'

Hilary had a heart the size of a world globe and told her to come straight over, while adding that Pippa should have known better than to think that she had to phone and ask one of her oldest friends for an appointment. 'Especially when you only make the effort to get your hair done about once a year!' she teased in conclusion.

Pippa caught an underground train that would take her to Hilary's salon in the west London suburb of Hounslow. As she was jostled by other passengers while she stood in the aisle because there were no seats available Pippa's teeming thoughts were troubled. Sad though it was to acknowledge, she was relieved that her father was not alive to be shamed and disappointed by her failure to win promotion. But then when had she ever managed to meet her parent's expectations and make him proud of her? she asked herself with pained and guilty regret.

Her mind travelled back almost six years to the summer that her family life had been destroyed. She had been just seventeen when her parents and three other families had gone on their final holiday together to the Dordogne region of France. Her friendship with Hilary Ross stretched back as far as their childhoods. The Ross family had been part of the group that had gone to France and as the holiday had been an annual event there had been no reason to suspect that that year would be any different from any previous year. But that particular summer everything that could have gone wrong *had* gone wrong. In fact it had been a disastrous vacation for all concerned but nobody had had the nerve to admit that and it had still lasted almost the full six weeks.

No sooner had they arrived in France than her then best friend, Tabby, had got involved in a passionate secret fling with a French guy staying nearby and had become so besotted that she had scarcely noticed that Pippa had been alive for the remainder of their stay. During that same period, however, Pippa had had her heart broken and her self-esteem smashed without anybody even noticing.

But the conclusive life-altering event of that fatal holiday had been the dreadful car accident that had left Pippa's mother dead and put her father into a wheelchair. Tabby's father, Gerry Burnside, had got drunk and crashed a car full of passengers, shattering the lives of all his friends. Pippa had been much closer to her mother than she had ever been to her harsh and demanding father and she had been devastated by her mother's sudden death. Before the crash her father had been a science teacher and an active sportsman and he had never managed to come to terms with his disability.

Furthermore, as a young man Martin Stevenson had wanted to be a doctor but had narrowly missed out on the exam grades required. From the hour of Pippa's birth, her father had been determined that his daughter should live out his dream of be-coming a doctor for him and she had been pressed into doing her academic best from a very early age. But the consequences of that appalling car accident, which had also claimed the lives of Tabby's father, Hilary's parents and both Jen's and Pippa's mothers had traumatised Pippa and she had had to tell her father that she could not face a career in medicine.

The cruel intensity of her father's disappointment had been almost more than Pippa's conscience could bear and his bitter-ness had been terrible to live with. For nearly six years after-wards, Pippa had nonetheless been her parent's main carer. But, no matter how hard she had worked to please him with high grades in the economics degree she'd pursued and with tender care of his needs at home, he had never forgiven her for turn-ing her back on the chance to become a doctor. Pippa remained wretchedly aware of what she saw as her own shortcomings. She was totally convinced that the really gutsy woman whom she wanted to be would have been fired by an unquenchable de-sire to study medicine after that car accident rather than put off for life and convinced that she was too soft to last the course.

When she made herself remember just how much she had once adored France, she could hardly credit that she had not visited the country of her own mother's birth since that tragic summer. She had even made excuses to avoid attending Tab-by's wedding. Thankfully, however, Tabby's husband, Chris-tien, brought his wife over to London on regular visits, so Pippa had been able to maintain contact with her friend. But wasn't it really past time that she came to terms with her mother's death and visited Tabby and Christien at Duvernay, the Laroche fam-ily's beautiful château in Brittany? How often had her friend invited her? Her conscience twanged. Shouldn't she spend at least part of the holiday she had to take with Tabby in France?

'Oh, no, this is the day you close at lunchtime and I com-pletely forgot!' Pippa groaned in dismay when Hilary, having met her at the door of her tiny apartment took her across the passage into the hairdressing salon, which was strikingly silent and empty. 'For goodness' sake, why didn't you remind me that it was your half-day?'

Hilary was small and slim with enormous grey eyes and spiky blonde hair that had the very slightest hint of blue to match her T-shirt. Only a year Pippa's junior, she actually looked barely eighteen and she grinned. 'Are you kidding? Do I look that patient? You're finally going out on a date and I can't wait to find out who the bloke is!'

Pippa stiffened. 'There's no bloke. It's the big party for the new MD tonight—'

'But you were all out of breath on the phone and I thought you were excited—'

'Not excited...upset,' Pippa conceded jerkily. 'I bombed out at work, I fell *flat* on my face—'

'What on earth—?'

'I didn't get the job,' Pippa muttered in a wobbly undertone and then the whole unhappy story came tumbling out.

Hilary listened and tried not to wince while she dug into a cupboard in the tiny staff room and poured Pippa a stiff drink from the brandy someone had given her at Christmas.

'I don't touch it, you know I don't...' Pippa attempted to push the glass away.

'You're as white as a sheet. You need a boost.' Hilary pressed her down into a seat by the washbasins and deemed a change of subject the best policy. 'So you want to knock 'em dead in the aisles at Venstar tonight—'

'Some chance!' Wrinkling her nose at the taste, Pippa drank deep and the unfamiliar alcohol ran like fire down into her cold, empty tummy. Like the warmth of her friend's sympathy, however, it was a soothing sensation and she was incredibly grateful that she had ignored her father's withering sarcasm and had attended her first school reunion just a few months earlier. After Tabby had made a permanent move to France, Pippa had been delighted to meet up with Hilary again at the reunion and learn

that the blonde also lived in London. After that tragic car accident, their paths had been forced apart and Tabby and Pippa
had lost touch with Hilary and with the fourth member of that
teenage friendship, Jen Tarbert.

'Even blindfolded, you could knock 'em dead,' Hilary repeated with determination, trying not to think unkind thoughts
about Pippa's deceased father. However, it was an unfortunate
truth that even when Pippa had been a child her parent had been
a domineering bully with a wounding tongue and he had done
a real hatchet job on his daughter's self-esteem.

While Hilary washed her hair, Pippa remembered to ask after
her friend's kid sister, Emma. 'How's she doing?'

Hilary chattered on happily about the teenage sister she
adored before saying, 'Will you let me do your make-up too?'

'If you don't mind...'

'Why would I mind? I *love* doing faces!'

'Well, you can only do your best—'

'With a bone structure as good as yours, I would hope so.'
Hilary watched Pippa stiffen and sighed before she pressed another brimming glass of brandy into the redhead's hand, told
her that she was far too tense and hustled her upstairs to her
cluttered apartment.

'I'll have to rush home to get changed,' Pippa remarked.

'You haven't got the time. You'll be late enough as it is.' Hilary hurried into her sister's bedroom and plundered the packed
wardrobe there to emerge with a strappy dress in a glorious
shade of turquoise.

'I can't borrow anything that belongs to your sister!' Pippa
protested.

'Emma decided that this made her look too old and you
know how picky teenagers are...there's no way she'll ever wear
it now.'

'I wouldn't feel comfortable in a style like that,' Pippa muttered.

'Lighten up, Pippa,' Hilary urged in a pained tone. 'You're

young and you can wear just about anything with your figure. It's not a revealing dress, so what are you worried about?'

In Pippa's opinion any garment that bared her shoulders, her thin arms and the sheer pitiful tininess of her breasts *was* much too revealing. Yet, her friend was being so kind and supportive that she was reluctant to reject her generosity. Both women wore the same size in shoes but, yet again, there was a great gap between their personal preferences. Hilary adored shoes with high heels whereas Pippa rarely wore heels because she already stood five feet eleven inches in her bare feet. A pair of three-inch high gold beaded sandals were set beside the dress and then Hilary showed her guest into the bathroom to enable her to take a shower before her transformation commenced.

Almost two hours later, and only after Pippa had donned the contact lenses she carried in her bag but rarely utilised, Hilary whisked the towel off the mirror and marched Pippa in front of it. 'You look totally, incredibly gorgeous and if you argue about that I swear I'm going to have a fight with you!'

In shocked silence, Pippa stared at her colourful reflection. 'I don't look like me—'

'No offence intended, but that's only because "me" neglects her hair, never wears make-up and can't be bothered dressing up!'

Pippa's eyes stung a little but she could hardly blink for the amount of mascara on her lashes. She swallowed hard and said gruffly, 'Thanks. I don't look like a loser and you wouldn't believe how much that means to me.'

Andreo D'Alessio was bored. He was also in a very bad mood.

He had not asked for a party. He had not wanted a party. He disliked surprises and he did not think that surprise parties had a role to play in the business world. He was not entertained by long speeches either. He had even less time for flattery and employees in a high state of excitement, particularly when it was obvious that a healthy proportion had overindulged in alcohol before attending the event. Having left the conference hall with the excuse of an important call, he was crossing the hotel foyer when he saw the ravishing redhead. Then he saw her, so stunning that she stopped him in his tracks.

Hair the rich colour of heavy cinnamon silk tumbled to her shoulders in a smooth, shining fall that reflected the light and framed an oval face of perfect symmetry. Her eyes were the clear, bright blue of the midsummer sky, her full mouth painted coral-pink to highlight the invitation of her soft lips. Her height alone would have attracted his attention for she was unusually tall for a woman. Nearly six feet in height, Andreo calculated with appreciation, and still confident enough to wear high heels. Of all things he abhorred the absurdity of trying to match his own very tall, well-built frame to that of some tiny, birdlike creature half his size. The redhead with her taut white shoulders, slender feminine curves and wondrously endless and shapely legs would *fit* him to perfection...

That fast, voracious male hormones kicking into lusty overdrive at the enervating prospect of the precise intimate fit of the gorgeous woman he was watching, Andreo decided that he was surveying his next lover.

Pippa gazed into the crowded conference hall, which was buzzing with Venstar employees, and wondered if anyone would even recognise her. With the curls she loathed straightened by Hilary's expertise with a blow-dryer, her spectacles discarded and in borrowed finery, she looked different. The amount of male attention she had attracted since her arrival at the vast hotel had made her very aware of that fact.

Unfortunately, the girlie dress made her feel horribly exposed and self-conscious. She wasn't used to men staring at her and all her life she had been shy. Got up in a no-nonsense trouser suit with work-related issues providing the framework for every dialogue with male colleagues, she had managed fine. But, shorn of that sensible façade, it was a challenge to appear impervious to the lustful appraisals she was receiving. Her chin tilting, she was on the brink of entering the hall when sudden silence fell within. Seeing the man moving towards the podium on the platform, she decided to stay where she was until he had finished making his speech.

As the speaker took up position Pippa stared and then laughed out loud. Oh, dear, Jonelle and every other woman fantasising about the physical attractions of the billionaire Andreo D'Alessio were suffering a very big let-down indeed to their wild fantasies.

'Care to share the joke?' a male voice urged lazily by her side.

Pippa stiffened in surprise for she had not noticed that there was a man standing that close and she felt far too awkward to turn her head to look at him direct. 'I was just thinking that a lot of people must have been very disappointed with Andreo D'Alessio,' she said a little breathlessly.

Disconcerted, Andreo frowned. 'And why would you think that?'

Something in that accented drawl sent a tiny little shiver of warning down her spine and might have silenced her had not Pippa been in the mood to be sharp, rather than soothing. 'I suppose that I should've said that the women will be disappointed. He's not even a little bit fanciable,' Pippa remarked with some satisfaction.

'No?' At that point, Andreo believed that she was only pretending not to know who he was. After all, the Venstar shindig had kicked off over an hour earlier and he had been the centre of attention from the outset. He assumed she was making a move on him and, having been subjected to some strange pick-up routines in his time, he was curious to see where she planned to travel after such an opening.

'No, he's downright short. In fact, he's so small, he would look more at home sitting under a mushroom dressed all in green like a leprechaun,' Pippa pronounced.

Belatedly, Andreo realised that she was studying Salvatore

Rissone, whom he planned to put in charge of Venstar after the business had been restructured. 'Height is not everything.'

'He looks like he's rather too fond of his food as well,' Pippa added with a cruelty that was quite unlike her. 'And he's definitely going bald. No wonder he doesn't like publicity photos. He's not exactly Mr Universe, is he?'

'Movie-star looks are not required in business.' Andreo was angered by her unkind comments about Sal's homely appearance. 'He is a fine man—'

'No, he's *not*,' Pippa cut in with growing heat. 'Andreo D'Alessio is a very rich man and the only reason people talk him up is because they're either hugely impressed by his money or...' As she spun round, giving way to her hurt resentment of Andreo D'Alessio to address her companion direct, she looked at him for the first time and what she was about to say went clean out of her mind again.

It was rare for Pippa to be forced to look up at a man. But what sent her brain into free fall was the sheer dazzling effect of this particular male animal up close. From the bronzed skin enhancing the lean, hard, elegant planes of his proud cheekbones to the stubborn masculine angularity of his jawbone, he was strikingly handsome. His mouth was wide and firm, his brows level and dark to match the gleaming luxuriance of his cropped black hair. But it was the piercing quality of eyes dark as ebony and accentuated by a frame of lush inky lashes that entrapped her.

'*Or...?*' Andreo collided with her turquoise gaze and found his annoyance mysteriously evaporating beneath the onslaught of those spectacular eyes. She was staring up at him in the most uncool way, her response to his sexual magnetism patent in her dilated pupils, and amused satisfaction gripped him.

She really *didn't* know who he was. She really had mistaken Sal Rissone for him. She was not teasing him or trying to capture his interest with a novel approach. Perhaps he was at risk of turning into one of those painful guys who took himself much too seriously, Andreo reflected abruptly. He decided that he ought to be challenged rather than antagonised by the unusual experience of hearing himself criticised. It certainly made a change from the fawning flattery that had been his lot throughout the evening.

'Or...?' Pippa was magnetised by his proximity and inexplicably feeling very short of breath.

'You were saying that people talk up Andreo D'Alessio because he is wealthy and *because*...?'

'His reputation scares them half to death,' Pippa filled in jerkily.

'What have you got against Andreo?'

'You're an Italian, aren't you?' Somewhat belatedly, Pippa connected his delicious growling accent to his likely nationality. Delicious? The dark timbre of his deep, low-pitched drawl was impossibly sexy. Thrown by the strange emergence of thoughts that seemed to have no direct input from her brain, she shifted off one foot onto the other. Without the smallest warning, she felt her nipples snap tight into stiff little buttons inside her bodice and her cheeks burned hot while she wondered what on earth was happening to her.

'I am.' Andreo continued to study her. No matter how hard or how long he studied her, her colouring was a source of continual fascination to him: that glowing cinnamon hair and those turquoise eyes enhanced by skin that had initially been pale as milk but that was now flaring a soft rose pink. It had been a long time since he had seen a woman blush and he was intrigued. 'You work for Venstar?'

Pippa nodded but she was extremely tense. 'You referred to Andreo D'Alessio as if you know him personally...'

He was Italian, Pippa was thinking in dismay. He had to work for D'Alessio and, if he was part of the initial wave of imported employees, he was unlikely to be a junior member of the team. Her tongue darted out in a nervous flicker over the soft underside of her lower lip.

Andreo found himself imagining that moist pink tip tracing an erotic path of exploration over his bared skin. The sudden throb of his aroused sex startled him for he was long past the teenage years when self-control in the radius of a beautiful woman had often been a challenge. 'Perhaps I'm just curious to know what you have against a man you've never met,' he breathed almost harshly.

Pippa tossed her head, cinnamon tresses spilling back against her slim white shoulders. Cautious as she was trying to be, it was already too late because the alcohol in her bloodstream was firing her every response with an unfamiliar aggression. 'How do you know I've never met him?'

Andreo elevated a fine black brow. 'You...h*ave*?'

'No, I haven't, but I don't need to meet him in the flesh to know that he's a sexist dinosaur, who discriminates against women to make himself feel more powerful!' Pippa slung bitterly.

CHAPTER TWO

DISCONCERTED, ANDREO FROWNED down at the woman maligning his reputation as a fair employer. His ebony eyes glinted with golden highlights. He stifled an instinctive urge to slap her down so hard verbally that she would never again dare to make such an unjust charge against him. '*Dio mio...* That's a loaded accusation to make against a man whom you can know virtually nothing about.'

Pale as death and almost as taken aback as she could see he was by her angry outburst, Pippa dropped her head and muttered, 'Excuse me...'

As she began to move away Andreo swung round to effectively bar her passage. 'Don't rush away,' he urged.

What the heck had come over her? Pippa was asking herself in consternation. Only a mad woman would hurl an accusation like that about the boss at a work function! That wretched brandy had gone to her foolish head and loosened her tongue. Naturally she was bitter about the reasons why she had been passed over for promotion but, if she had no intention of making a formal complaint, she needed to keep her lips sealed for her own protection. 'Look, I—'

'You haven't even told me your name,' Andreo incised, noting the slight tremor of the pale slender hand she had braced against the wall.

After that crazy bout of outspokenness, only a suicidal idiot would gave a truthful response to a name, rank and number request that would identify her, Pippa conceded in dismay. Her head was beginning to pound in response to the increasing level of her stress. What was she to tell him? Pippa Plain? Pride brought up her head again as she remembered what her late mother had often called her. 'It's Philly...'

'Philly,' Andreo sounded out, rolling the syllables huskily together. 'I like it. Let me buy you a drink and convince you that Venstar's new owner walks on water even in his spare time—'

'Is he really that full of himself?' Pippa interrupted with aghast turquoise eyes.

'You have a problem with confident men?' In the act of frowning, Andreo again found himself questioning his own self-image.

'If by confident you mean arrogant, yes, I have a problem—'

'Andreo isn't arrogant. He is secure in himself and assertive,' Andreo pronounced with approval, ushering her in the direction of the quiet bar by dint of a light hand that only momentarily brushed her spine. 'But you must tell me why you referred to Andreo D'Alessio as sexist—'

Eager to avoid that controversial subject, Pippa murmured hurriedly, 'You haven't even told me your name yet...'

As if he already knew how much he off-balanced her, Andreo sent her a slanting grin.

Her heart hammered so hard and fast that she felt momentarily faint.

'It's Andreo, I'm afraid,' he supplied.

'Is that like...a common name in Italy?'

'Very much...every other guy is called Andreo,' Andreo groaned with silken mockery, surveying her from below the deceptively sleepy fringe of his black lashes, dark golden eyes vibrant with concealed amusement.

Pippa was fascinated, exhilarated and scared all at one and the same time. She had not even noticed him ordering a drink for her and when a waiter offered her a cocktail in a tall, thin glass she accepted it without comment and let the sparkling liquid moisten her throat.

'Are you married?' Pippa heard herself ask Andreo with all the effortless cool of a giant weight dropping from the sky. Having heard other women talk, she knew it was the one question that a sensible woman should always ask when she met a man for the first time.

He laughed out loud. 'You're so subtle...of course I'm not married. Tell me why you think Andreo D'Alessio is a dinosaur—'

'I don't want to talk about that.'

'I do.' Andreo stared down at her with the daunting force of will that came as naturally to his domineering nature as the need to breathe.

'I don't...' The tingle in the atmosphere gave Pippa a wicked thrill. She couldn't take her eyes off him and she felt as if she were locked into a live electric current.

Shimmering dark golden eyes rested on her. 'I'll get it out of you,' Andreo intoned with innate conviction in his own powers of persuasion. 'Do you always take shameless advantage of the fact that you're beautiful?'

Pippa spluttered on her drink and glanced up at him, riveted to the spot, her lovely eyes unguarded. 'Sorry...?'

He was chatting her up. She could hardly believe it. A guy who was a dead ringer for her ultimate fantasy male was flirting with her. And she didn't know how to handle it, had not a clue how to respond, so she smiled up at him, smiled and smiled and smiled, suddenly terrified that he might lose interest and walk away again. Wasn't it time she enjoyed what other women took for granted? Wasn't it time she took account of the reality that she was young and single? The admiration in his appreciative gaze was like a shot of adrenalin in her veins and balm to her wounded ego. Pippa Plain? *Who?*

That knowing feminine smile that appeared to suggest that she was aware of exactly the effect she was having on his libido tensed every muscle in Andreo's lean, powerful body. It had been a long time since sexual hunger had hit Andreo with that intensity and it had a mixed effect on him. Rigid with throbbing arousal, he wanted to behave like a caveman and thrust her back against the wall and crush those ripe coral lips under his again and again and again before he dragged her off somewhere much more private. But while his hot-blooded nature revelled in the rare heat of his desire for her, his intellect was in direct opposition. He liked to be in control, he *always* liked to be one hundred per cent in control.

'Santo Cielo,' he murmured thickly.

The ragged edge to his deep voice sent yet another responsive shiver travelling through Pippa. She meshed with scorching dark golden eyes and her mouth ran dry and her knees turned weak as water under her. For the first time in twenty three years she understood what it was like to be really wanted by a guy. And she didn't know *how* she understood, how she could possibly recognise the rough edge of desire stamping his lean, hard features and the passionate intensity of his stunning eyes. But although she had only just met him, she was attuned to his hunger with every humming fibre of her physical being. What she was feeling terrified her and excited her in equal parts.

'Let's get out of here...' Andreo breathed, deciding in the space of a moment that he could plead a prior engagement to escape the party.

He extended a hand to her. She could not think straight but still she closed her fingers into his, unable to resist her own need to touch him. She quivered, tormented by the nagging ache she barely comprehended at the very heart of her body, and stared down at their linked hands while she strove to get a grip on herself again.

'This is crazy,' she mumbled shakily.

Andreo's mobile phone sounded up the tune his fourteen-year-old kid brother had fed into it to announce that he and *only* he was calling. Anybody else calling at that instant would have been ignored but Andreo was always ruefully aware that in the eyes of Marco, who was less than half his own age, he had more the standing of a father than a brother.

Even white teeth gritting, Andreo released Pippa's hand with an apology for the interruption and dug out his phone to answer it. His sibling plunged straight into outlining the mathematics question he was struggling to answer. Suppressing a groan of disbelief, Andreo flipped over a flyer lying on the bar counter and jotted down the problem on the blank side of the sheet.

'My little brother...he's in boarding school and sometimes he needs a hand with his work,' he explained taut-mouthed to Pippa.

Blinking, only slowly emerging from the daze induced by her own screaming hormones and her wild response to Andreo, Pippa hovered by his side. She was shattered by the acknowledgement that she had been on the very brink of going off with Andreo. A guy she had only just met, a guy she knew nothing about! She was incredulous at her own reckless behaviour and appalled. Anyone might have been forgiven for thinking that she had lost her wits the same moment she'd first laid eyes on Andreo!

'Marco...' Andreo could feel Pippa's sudden withdrawal as much as if she had slammed a door shut in his face. He had to fight to keep the exasperated edge from his intonation as his impatient little brother asked him how long it would take for him to solve the problem for him.

In the act of emerging from shock to plunge into embarrassment instead as she wondered how the heck she was to retain Andreo's interest while also telling him that she had changed her mind about going any place with him, Pippa noticed that Andreo was in the act of striving to differentiate trigonometric functions on the flyer.

'That line's in error,' she muttered with a slight frown as she drew closer to him.

Andreo froze in astonishment. 'Is that a fact?' he challenged.

Pippa filched the pen from between his fingers and at lightning speed ran through the question to emerge with the answer while at the same time succinctly explaining where he had gone wrong in his calculations.

Andreo breathed in very deep and slow. He was better than ninety-nine out of a hundred people at maths and he had just met the hundredth in the unexpected guise of a very lovely and tactless redhead. Was he a chauvinist bastard?

'Andreo...' Marco breathed in wonderment, having overheard the entire dialogue and haltered by no such reservations. 'Whoever she is she's a real whiz at this stuff. Not one of your usual airheads, is she? Make sure you get her phone number for me!'

As Andreo finished the call it occurred to Pippa that she had not been very diplomatic. Tabby, who seemed to have been born knowing how the male mind worked, had once told her that men had very tender egos and that, if you really, really liked a guy, you should always leave him space to save face. Aware that she had steamrollered over him, she almost winced.

Over the top of her head, Andreo saw two members of his personal staff lurking by the door of the conference hall, visibly anxious to rope him back into the festivities but understandably reluctant to interrupt him and his companion. He pressed her round the corner of the bar where they were no longer within view.

'We should separate and return to the hall for ten or fifteen minutes...practise discretion,' Andreo ground out half under his breath, while gazing stormily down into her beautiful face, his reluctance to part from her palpable, 'but I don't want to let you out of my sight for a second in case I lose you, *cara*.'

Unaccustomed to being treated like a *femme fatale* whom no mere male could resist, Pippa just giggled, convinced that he was teasing her. Hands snapping to her elbows, Andreo backed her into the phone cubicle behind her and hauled her close.

'What are you doing?' she gasped in stark disconcertion.

'What do you want me to do?' Andreo enquired in a husky, ragged undertone, languorous golden eyes hot with invitation on hers.

Held in intimate contact with every lean, hard angle of his big, powerful frame, Pippa discovered in shock that she just wanted to be even closer to him, indeed so close that she might qualify as an extra layer of his skin. This time around she understood why her breasts felt heavy and almost swollen. She recognised her own desire for him and her face burned with mortification but nothing could kill the raw, wicked longing quivering through her in a thousand tiny stinging needles as her body came alive in ways entirely new to her.

'Philly...?'

Tempted beyond all bearing by promptings that she had never been forced to deal with before, Pippa let her arms slide up to link round his strong brown neck and eased closer into the hard, unyielding strength of him. With a stifled Italian curse, Andreo succumbed to that frank invitation with all the volatile passion that lay at the heart of his nature.

Pippa might have been new to passion but no victim could have been more eager to seek her fate. He took her softly parted lips under his and thrust them apart with the forceful onslaught of his. The sweet, unbearably rousing invasion of his tongue into the moist interior of her mouth made her heart give a heavy thud and tightened her every muscle. All of a sudden her entire body was alive and throbbing with near-painful excitement and greedy for more of what she had never had.

With a reflexive shudder at the amount of strength it demanded from him and rigid with fierce desire, Andreo yanked himself back from her. Heavily lidded golden eyes swept her bemused face and lingered on the soft, swollen red of her ripe mouth. 'Ten minutes...and you stay within view the whole time,' he warned thickly. 'Then we leave together.'

Blinking like a woman emerging from a dark spell of enchantment, Pippa let herself be walked back across the foyer and finally into the busy hall. The clumps of chattering people seemed to evaporate from their path at magical speed and Andreo only came to a halt when they reached a vacant corner table. There he snapped his fingers to hail a passing waiter and order her a drink. Momentarily, his imperious show of command took her aback.

'Now don't move from here until I come back, *cara mia,*' Andreo instructed in a low-pitched drawl. 'It would be so easy for us to lose each other in this crush.'

'Are you worth waiting for?' Pippa heard herself enquire in a teasing undertone for she could only be amused at being spoken to as though she were a feckless child likely to wander off and get lost without his guidance.

'Don't laugh. This is not funny.' Andreo was angry that she could seem unconcerned at the same risk and equally infuriated by his own lack of cool. He wanted her. But the level of that wanting was already more than he felt comfortable with. As his mobile phone broke into Marco's colourful signature tune again, he worked out how best to pin her down in the short term.

'Do you think you could help my little brother with his homework again?' he asked. 'He speaks excellent English.'

Touched by that request, Pippa grinned and extended her hand for his phone. Sipping at her drink, she talked Marco through what remained of his assignment while she watched Andreo on the other side of the room watch her in turn. Every time she saw that proud dark head angle in her direction, scorching dark golden eyes burning up the distance between them, her mouth ran dry and her heart raced. Venstar bigwigs surrounded him and the portly little man she had earlier identified as D'Alessio, but in that almost anonymous sea of people she was conscious of only one very individual male: Andreo.

Everything she was feeling was so outrageously new to her. Nothing had ever seemed so wonderful and miraculous as the simple fact that Andreo appeared to be as impressed by her as she was by him. No matter how hard she tried to reclaim her usual sterling common sense, it was overwhelmed by the outrageously girlish giddy excitement leaping and dancing through her bloodstream.

She had not known a guy *could* kiss like that. She had not known that a guy could actually make her feel like that. Oh, yes, she had heard women describe certain men as irresistible, but she had scorned the belief that any male could have such an extreme effect on her. But even while she had disbelieved those claims, she had always secretly longed to be proven wrong, she acknowledged dizzily. And when Andreo had kissed her every skin cell in her body had responded with breathtaking enthusiasm. All that had kept her upright was the reality that she had had her arms wrapped round him and he was strong enough to bear her weight.

While she studied Andreo from afar her blue eyes sparkled with wondering satisfaction when he immediately directed his gaze to her as though some sixth sense had warned him of her appraisal. His charismatic smile set fireworks off inside her tummy and made her heart thump as frantically fast as though she had run a marathon.

'Will you give me your phone number?' Marco prompted in a wheedling tone. 'You're much better at explaining this stuff than Andreo is.'

Lounging back against the edge of the table, her burnished fall of hair fiery as flames against her fair, delicate skin, the vibrant blue dress a simple understated frame for her superb long-legged figure, Pippa was attracting a great deal of both male and female attention. But not one of the star-struck men admiring her would have dared to approach her while Andreo D'Alessio watched her with such blatant possessiveness in his arrogant gaze and a flashing intimate smile on his firm, hard mouth.

Pippa had just finished talking to Marco when Andreo rejoined her. Drawing level with her, he barely broke his stride as he closed a lean brown hand over hers to urge her towards the exit. She heard the buzz of speculative voices break out as they passed by together. But then he was incredibly handsome and, as nobody had approached her while she'd been alone at the table, it seemed fair to assume that none of her colleagues had recognised her without her curls, her spectacles and her serviceable suits.

When the lift doors closed on them, she leant back against the cool metal wall because the fresh air-conditioned atmosphere was making her head swim to a dismaying degree.

'You still haven't told me why you suspect Andreo D'Alessio of being prejudiced against women in the workplace...'

In disconcertion, Pippa blinked. 'I thought you'd have forgotten about that by now—'

'I never forget anything,' Andreo confided.

'Well, do your best to forget that,' Pippa mumbled ruefully. 'I was indiscreet—'

'You can trust me,' Andreo purred.

'A little bird told me your namesake—'

'My namesake? The little guy who reminded you of a leprechaun?'

Reassured by that light-hearted sally, Pippa nodded and tried with some difficulty to concentrate. 'The word is that the big boss only likes pretty women to make it up the promotion ladder—'

'That's a four-letter word, *cara*!' Andreo incised in bold disagreement.

When it came to their mutual employer, he was evidently very strong on the loyalty front. As that was an old-fashioned quality that she admired, she could not think less of him for it. Lashes carefully lowered, for she wanted the topic closed, she murmured soothingly, 'I'm sure you're right.'

'I know I'm right.' Andreo continued with conviction.

Pippa almost smiled at his absolute certainty.

Andreo reached out and used her own hands to draw her close to him again. 'I like the way you feel against me, *carissima...*'

Powerfully aware of his abrasive masculinity and the hard muscular strength of him, she rested against him, suddenly weak with wanting. 'Me too... I mean, I like being close to you too.'

He laughed with husky appreciation, slid long fingers into the thick fall of her hair to tug her head back and look at her again. Beneath the harsh lights in the lift, the clarity of her blue eyes mesmerised him for he could read every passing thought: the shy uncertainty laced with the stubborn bravado of her pride and deeper still...the feverish hunger for him that she could not hide.

He devoured her mouth with an urgency that left her reeling. She could not spare the time or the energy to breathe and she lost herself in the earthy taste of him, revelling in the eagerness of her own desire. When he straightened to walk her out of the lift again, she let her head rest against his broad shoulder while she drank in air to aid her starved lungs.

Her mind was in turmoil. She could barely believe that what she was feeling was real but was at the same time impossibly greedy for that no-longer-connected-to-planet-earth sensation to continue. He employed a card to open a door that led into a very luxurious suite.

Not having until that moment taken the time to consider *where* he was taking her, Pippa was aghast to appreciate that he had accommodation in the hotel itself and that she had unthinkingly allowed him to bring her back up there with him.

'Are you expecting me to stay the night with you?' Pippa demanded in dismay.

CHAPTER THREE

ANDREO DEALT PIPPA a level challenging appraisal. 'That's entirely your decision.'

Colour swept Pippa's face and she could have bitten her tongue out in embarrassment. Of course that was *her* decision! It was a good half-century since women had been raised to think that what a man expected a woman should invariably try to deliver. She walked over to the tall windows that overlooked the spectacular city skyline but she could only think of how foolish she must have sounded to him. Like a nervous virgin who had never been alone with a man in a hotel suite before? All the heat drained from below her fair skin to leave her pale.

Unfortunately, Hilary had only managed to make her over on the outside with a smooth sophisticated façade and inside she was still the same old Pippa Stevenson, she acknowledged. Pippa, who had attended an all girls' school and whose evenings and weekends had been filled with extra classes and academic study, rather than social events and flirting. Boys had always seemed as remote and strange to her as alien entities and she had never learned what to say or how to behave around them. At the age of seventeen she had been humiliated by the young man she'd been infatuated with and, from that day on, hurt pride had become her strongest source of protection.

Time might have moved on but once bitten twice shy had proved to be her motto. Since then she might as well have been living on a single sex planet, she conceded ruefully, for she had never again risked pain or rejection. For almost six years she had been her father's carer and while it was true that the older man had demanded that she devote all her free time to his needs and his interests, it was equally true that she had not offered much of a protest. It had been easier to be a dutiful daughter and accept without question that she was the 'big strapping lass' her parent had often called her and highly unlikely to appeal to any man. From the age of twelve, when she had first shot up in height to tower over all her classmates like a lanky beanpole, Pippa had loathed her extra inches and had pointlessly longed to be small and dainty like her pretty mother.

But now, for the first time, she shook free of that memory without regret and reminded herself that Andreo appeared to admire her just as she was. She stole a covert glance at him and collided with smouldering dark golden eyes and her mouth ran dry. He was breathtakingly handsome.

Andreo watched her, for she was so still that she might have been a living breathing statue. Her feathery lashes lowered above the pale perfect line of her cheekbones and she looked incredibly vulnerable. It was obvious that she was having second thoughts. Was there another guy in her life? Someone to whom she felt she owed loyalty? Whatever, he chose patience over the risk of losing her altogether. 'Perhaps I should just take you home,' he murmured evenly.

Pippa went rigid, for that unexpected offer only heightened her tension. Go home? It would be the sensible thing to do. Yet her whole being rebelled against the concept. *Sensible* Pippa. When had she ever been anything else? And where had it got her? She had become a workaholic with no social life and no man had looked twice at her either. When had she ever felt for any male what she was feeling now?

'Is there anyone else?' Andreo breathed, his tension palpable.

'No...' She drew in a slow steadying breath. 'You?'

'No.' The blonde who had last shared Andreo's bed was modelling in Mexico and he saw no reason to confess that the lady had become yesterday's news at the exact same instant that he'd seen her successor before him.

The atmosphere buzzed.

'I don't believe that I've ever wanted any woman as much as I want you, *bella mia*,' Andreo confided with raw honesty.

'I want to stay...' Pippa whispered in a rush and, shaken though she was by the force of her own craving for him, she was equally entrapped by the simple acknowledgement that she still had a whole new dimension of life to explore. Her body seemed to be developing responses all of its own. The fabric of her dress felt abrasive against the taut peaks of her breasts and there was a swollen heaviness low in her pelvis that made it a challenge for her to remain still.

'You won't regret it.' His slashing smile of satisfaction was sufficient reward for her agreement. Her heart hammered so hard inside her ribcage that she felt dizzy. He was so beautiful and when he looked at her she felt beautiful too. She crossed the room on lower limbs that felt as unreliable in the support stakes as bendy twigs. She was trembling but she reached for his silk tie like a woman who meant business, a woman who knew exactly what she was doing.

Averse to her clumsy approach, his wretched tie refused to cooperate and went into a tight, immoveable knot. Just when she was on the brink of screaming for a pair of scissors, lean brown fingers intervened and jerked loose the knot with apparent ease. He cast the tie aside and drew her raised hands into his own to fold her back into his arms. She was as boneless as a rag doll until he crushed her into the hard, muscular wall of his chest, one masculine hand knotting into her bright hair to angle her head back. Then she shivered, stretched up to him, helpless in the thrall of her own wild anticipation.

His expert mouth swooped down to taste hers again and a soft moan of encouragement broke low in her throat. He traced her lips, penetrated them and a series of little gasps were torn from her as she clung to him to stay upright. He bent down and swept her up into his arms.

'Aren't I too heavy?' she mumbled through swollen, stinging lips and a sense of wonderment as dangerous as a hypnotic spell. He was, she was convinced, 'the one', the one special guy who she had always hoped and prayed might be waiting out there for her. The guy she was going to fall madly in love with. The guy who was hopefully going to fall madly in love with her. Well, maybe not madly, she adjusted hurriedly, fearful of hoping for too much and ending up with precisely nothing as a punishment for daring to be so ambitious. Even if he fell just a little bit in love with her, she would be content, she swore to herself.

'Light as a doll, *cara mia*... I'm just an unrepentant show-off,' Andreo teased as he strode into the elegant contemporary bedroom next door and set her down again onto her own feet.

One of her shoes had fallen off and she kicked off the other, but he had already stepped back from her to unbutton his shirt. Eyes wide, she became his audience. Her toes curled in the luxury carpet while she watched as the shirt fell open to display a sleek bronze wedge of masculine torso, his powerful pectoral muscles delineated by a triangle of rough dark curls. Her tummy flipped and she felt alarmingly short of breath and very hot. Knees wobbling, she backed up until her legs hit the edge of the bed and she sank down on the luxurious mattress.

'What...?' A wicked smile slanted over his wide, sensual mouth and golden eyes gleamed from below dense black lashes. 'Did you want to take off the shirt for me?'

'No...er... I'm not into shirts,' Pippa framed, dry-mouthed

and serious, for she had decided there was nothing less cool than struggling with male apparel.

'You can always practise on my tie, *cara*,' Andreo teased with intense amusement for he had found her lack of dexterity and the inexperience implied by that trait endearing.

'Is that a fact?' Pippa strove to match his mood with a quip while acknowledging that his sheer masculine presence both thrilled and intimidated her.

'Any time...' Andreo husked, strolling forward with all the formidable and yet daunting grace of a prowling tiger to lean down and close his large hands over her smaller ones and raise her upright.

That close to him her nostrils flared on the clean, husky male scent of his lithe, lean physique. She quivered, a curl of heat igniting low in her stomach. Shorn of her shoes as she now was, he struck her as awesomely tall and broad.

'*Santo Cielo*...you've shrunk a little,' Andreo mocked. 'But promise me that you will always wear those heels around me. Seeing you top all the guys around me gives me a high—'

'It...*does?*'

'*Sì.* You looked as disdainful as a queen too.' He shed his shirt and reached behind her with complete calm to unzip her dress for her.

'Couldn't we put the lights out?' Pippa mumbled in as humorous a tone as she could manage, the cooler air brushing her spine merely reminding her that when the dress went she had only one more layer left to hide behind.

Andreo actually laughed out loud. 'You've got to be kidding, *bella mia*!'

Perspiration beaded her short upper lip. 'I guess I was...'

He skimmed the straps down from her taut shoulders and let her slinky little blue dress fall to the carpet. He spread long fingers to frame her cheekbones. 'You are stunning...'

But Pippa had already closed her eyes sooner than risk seeing his disappointment when he saw how thin and flat-chested she was when stripped back to her bra and briefs. Nerves strung high, she shivered and he gathered her up into his arms and came down onto the bed with her cradled across his hard thighs. He tasted her mouth long and slow and the forbidden heat in her tummy flickered up again in spite of her tension.

'Sexy...' Andreo growled, appreciating the satin-smooth softness of her delicate white skin.

Nobody had ever called her that before and the temptation was too great: her lashes lifted on bemused eyes as blue as sapphires. 'Sexy?'

'Very...' He found everything about her sexy: her hair, her eyes, her height, her incandescent smile, the air of fragility that she exuded that gave him a curious urge to open doors for her, the sort of courteous but unfashionable stuff he normally only did in the radius of his female relatives.

Mesmerised by the intensity of his dark golden appraisal, she missed out on the deft movement with which he unclipped her bra. 'Honestly...?'

As her firm little breasts were bared his breathing fractured. Air chilled the tightly beaded tips and she looked down at her own bare flesh in dismay before bringing her hands up to cover herself from his intent appraisal. 'Lights...' she said in a wobbly voice.

'I love your body...' Andreo told her.

Feverish colour flooded her cheeks as she scrambled off him and dived with more haste than elegance below the fancy quilted spread and tugged it back up to her chin.

Andreo elevated a level dark brow and surveyed her with a frown. Her cinnamon hair was fanned out like polished silk round her face, which was hot pink to her hairline. Her eyes were evasive.

'I think I need a drink,' she gasped, amazed that after all the alcohol she had imbibed she still felt almost as sober as the proverbial judge.

Andreo sprang upright and strolled over to the mini bar to

withdraw a chilled mineral water. Opening it, he emptied it into a crystal tumbler and wandered back to extend it to her.

Clutching the spread to her, Pippa accepted the glass. She did not have the nerve to tell him that she had expected to receive an alcoholic beverage. 'You must be thinking I'm a little strange,' she muttered in a rush.

'Why would I think that?' Drinking water from the bottle he had helped himself to, Andreo rested his lean hips on the edge of the cabinet opposite while he contemplated her tense and embarrassed face.

No way was she having another intoxicating drink. He liked his partners to know what day it was. But there was another guy in her life, he was sure of it. That was why she was so jumpy. His competitive spirit soared into the ascendant. He would talk his way into that bed with her tonight. He might only get this one chance to pull her and once the deed was done, it would squash the competition. And if she didn't squash the competition after the event, he most assuredly would take care of that necessity for her. He didn't share and she was his. *Dio mio*, never before had he kissed a woman in a public bar or been so challenged to restrain his overwhelming hunger to possess her. Together they were hotter than a volcano and if she didn't yet appreciate that fact, he would soon teach her to do so.

The silence stretched and with the galling cool of an expert interrogator he made no attempt to break it.

Pippa sat up in a driven motion and hugged the spread beneath her arms. 'There's something I ought to mention...'

Andreo tensed. He really did not want to hear about the other man. Everything she told him would linger in his memory and annoy him. He didn't know how he knew that. He didn't even know why he was thinking that, for he had never been one of those weird possessive types. But he did know that he did not want to hear the low-down on her soon-to-be-ex-boyfriend. 'I don't believe in exchanging stories about other lovers.'

'Neither do I...and I'm not even sure I should make such an

issue of this…but—' Pippa sucked in a jerky breath and shot
him an anxious glance '—it seems only fair to warn you that I
haven't done this much.'

Andreo was touched. He didn't want to hurt her pride so there
was no easy way of telling her that she had made her relative
lack of experience pretty obvious. He was fine with that. But
then he was a very open-minded guy, he reflected.

'In fact…' Pippa hesitated, worrying at her full lower lip
with her teeth, her quiet voice dropping lower and lower in level
until he was leaning forward without realising it to catch her
words. '…to be really, *really* frank, I haven't done this at all…'

His winged black brows pleated. 'Say that again…'

'Ever,' Pippa concluded.

'You're telling me that you've never spent the night with a
guy you've just met before?'

'Yes, but not just that,' Pippa interposed a shade irritably for
he was being exceedingly slow on the uptake when she wanted
him to get the message faster than the speed of light. 'Apart
from the fact that I'm not promiscuous—'

'Hey…hold it there, I was not making a judgement,' Andreo
slotted in, lying in his teeth for he never, ever got involved with
women who slept around.

'But that…well, that I've never slept with a guy before…
I'm, er, you know…' Pippa shot an almost pleading glance at
Andreo but, while showing every sign of granting her one hundred per cent of his attention, he did not seem about to help her
out '…a virgin…'

'A…a what?' Andreo frowned in evident bewilderment. 'Did
you just say what I thought you said?'

Bearing a close resemblance to a stone image at that point,
Pippa nodded, twin high spots of self-conscious colour bloom-
ing over her cheekbones. He looked really shocked and she had
not been prepared for that reaction.

'But you're not a teenager.' Andreo seemed to be sinking
into deeper shock with every second that passed.

'*So?*'

A virgin. She was a virgin. He was blowing it. He ought to be taking this confession in his stride, not staring at her as if she had just leapt fully formed out of a medieval painting. She looked so anxious and she was blushing like mad and something inside him just twisted. In one bold movement, he rose upright and moved forward to come down on the bed beside her.

'It's not a problem,' Andreo asserted, fishing below the spread to gather her back into his arms but with rather more circumspection that he had utilised moments earlier.

It was not a problem, he told himself. Why should it be a problem?

'Honestly?' she pressed unevenly.

Lust fought with innate decency inside Andreo and the guy he liked to think he was surfaced for the first time in longer than he cared to recall. 'You need to think about this—'

'No, I don't.' Pippa closed her arms tightly round him and resisted the urge to scream that she had spent all her adult years thinking and thinking and thinking and hardly ever just *doing.* The very feel of his long, lean body next to hers made her heart speed up. She gazed into dark golden eyes enhanced by spiky black lashes and breathing normally became a distinct challenge. In fact just looking at him unleashed a flock of butterflies in her tummy and that was followed up by a wanton, warm, melting sensation that pierced deep enough to make her blush and squirm.

'Why me?' Andreo framed, inching down the spread while he kept her preoccupied and burying his hungry mouth against the delicate ridge of her collar-bone where a tiny pulse was flickering like crazy. The very scent of her soft skin enthralled him.

Jerking, she gasped in oxygen like a drowning swimmer and then buried her face in the cropped luxuriance of his black hair. Her entire body was humming like a race car engine revving up and she couldn't concentrate. 'I don't know...'

'Yes, you do...' Andreo countered.

And he was right, she registered in dim surprise. She wanted him more than she had ever wanted anything or anybody: it *was* that basic.

Andreo thrust the spread from his path and paused to admire the succulent pink nipples he had uncovered. 'You're exquisite...' And he rubbed those stiff, swollen buds with knowing fingers before lowering his dark head to lave them with his tongue.

Her spine arched up to him and she cried out in sensual shock at the sheer intensity of sensation. Her fingers dug into his hair and she flung her head back. He toyed with the tender tips while he kissed her again with erotic thoroughness, very much a male staking a claim and taking his time. She wrapped her arms tight round him, crushing her sensitised, tingling breasts into the hard, abrasive wall of his chest and letting her hands trace the breadth of his muscular shoulders and the long, silky smooth line of his strong back.

'I promise I'll make it good, *cara*,' Andreo swore, pulling back from her and springing upright to shed his well cut trousers.

Soft mouth voluptuous and red from the hungry urgency of his, she stared at him. From his superb torso to his taut, flat stomach, lean hips and powerful thighs, he was all hard muscle and sleek bronzed skin: magnificently male. His boxer shorts could not conceal the virile evidence of his male arousal. Untouched by an atom of her self-conscious shyness, he skimmed off that final garment and all the curiosity she had never owned up to possessing was fully met. Eyes wide, face burning, she dropped her head again. For goodness' sake, how on earth...?

He tossed back the spread beneath which she had again taken refuge. She connected with smouldering dark golden eyes and suddenly she was stretching up to welcome him back to her, her body tight and hot and restive in ways she did not even understand.

'How virginal is virginal?' Andreo husked.

'On a scale of one to ten…ten being the ultimate…probably almost ten,' she said breathlessly.

'Your skin is as translucent as porcelain.' Andreo explored the pert mounds of her small breasts, lingered to tease her distended pink nipples with his expert mouth. 'You're so delicate, so sensitive there. I love that.'

She couldn't lie still beneath his ministrations. Heart thundering, she arched into his caresses, eager for more, shameless in pursuit of that ever more seductive pleasure that built and built to a level that was almost a torment. 'Kiss me…'

He savoured her lips, let his tongue tangle with hers, laughed with earthy appreciation as she dragged him down to her with impatient hands, hungry for the weight of him over her, the firm, hard pressure of his mouth, and denied it.

'You said you'd never wanted anyone as much as me…' she reminded him shakily. 'Was that a lie?'

'I want you to feel the same passion but you're too impatient,' Andreo growled, sliding a hand beneath her restive legs to tug up her knees and remove her briefs. 'We have all night, *bella mia.*'

Her hips shifted against the sheet as she sought helplessly to quell the ache at the very centre of her. She was insanely aware of every sensitised inch of her throbbing body: the straining buds of her breasts still wet from his attentions, the swollen dampness between her thighs. She pushed up against his big, powerful frame, adoring the unyielding contours of bone and rippling muscle below his bronzed skin, wildly conscious of the rock-hard rigidity of his bold erection.

Golden eyes glittering, Andreo lifted away from her as though she had burned him, aggressive jaw-line set at an angle. 'I intend this to be special.'

It was as if a fever had hold of her and her temperature were out of control. She wanted so desperately to touch him and all that had been holding her back was fear of doing something wrong. She headed back into the heat and strength of him and let her mouth trail from a muscular shoulder down over his hair-roughened chest. There she paused to snatch in an erratic breath and lick and kiss her path across his taut ribcage where…he closed his hand into her hair and dragged her back up to him before she could really start experimenting.

'Independent woman,' he whispered in a tone of raw discovery.

He was a control freak but he was gorgeous, she thought dizzily. She studied the black hair she had disarranged, the riveting eyes, high, proud cheekbones, arrogant nose and classic and willful masculine mouth and inside she turned boneless. 'So I'll lie back and think of…?'

'Me…you think about *me*,' Andreo instructed with complete seriousness and he kissed her and refused to consider why he had said something so naff.

He reacquainted himself with her slender, seductive curves. In the process, she gasped air in shallow bursts and he forced her to stop thinking and just feel and what she felt was extraordinary in its very intensity. His fingers flirted with the damp curls at the junction of her slim, restive thighs and she moaned out loud, her hips rising off the mattress in a yearning movement as old as time.

'Oh, please…!' she gasped.

At last, he touched her where she most needed to be touched, exploring the moist, silken heat at the heart of her where the ache was a torment. Heat and wanton pleasure engulfed her as he utilised a lean finger to probe her tight depths, opening her for his skilled caresses until she felt like honey heated to boiling point and on the brink of spontaneous combustion. It was the sweetest torture she had ever withstood because just when she believed the heights of pleasure could not climb any higher, he would prove her wrong.

'I'm mad for you,' Andreo groaned, rising over her and tipping her back from him in one smooth motion.

She felt him, hard and smooth and demanding, enter her.

The sharp, rending pain took her aback and her blue eyes flew wide in dismay.

Andreo stilled as a whimper of protest was dredged from her. 'Shall I stop?'

'No...' There was too much of him and she had known that and she shut her eyes tight, waiting until the pain of his intrusion had lessened yet savouring the wonderfully erotic feel of him inside her.

'I don't think I'm supposed to be enjoying myself this much when you're not,' he muttered in ragged masculine apology.

And she almost laughed and knew beyond a shadow of a doubt that she was going to fall in love with him if she hadn't already. 'It's OK...' she whispered shakily.

'Amore...' Andreo pressed his lips to her damp brow. 'You're very brave—'

'Greedy for you,' she confided guiltily, rising up to him to invite a deeper invasion, controlled by her own desperate need for fulfillment.

He surged into her again and she arched and gasped in shock at the rich, sensual tide of sensation. He prolonged her pleasure with every art he had ever learned. Hot and hungry for him, she succumbed to his pagan rhythm with helpless abandon. The burn low in her pelvis had become a tight knot of delirious excitement, dragging her higher and higher until her heart was thundering in her ears. She hit a pinnacle and drowning pleasure rocked her with wave after wave of ecstasy. As he drove himself into a shuddering release, she held him tight, dazed and oddly proud and incredibly happy. She had had a wonderful time trashing her sensible former self and she had not a single regret.

She dozed off to sleep without realising it. Sliding back into bed, Andreo shook her awake again. 'It's only midnight,' he told her in teasing reproof. 'How can you be so tired this early?'

Snuggling back into him, Pippa went pink and avoided his too-shrewd gaze. She knew that it had to be the amount of alcohol she had consumed that was making her brain feel as if it were filled with cotton wool and her eyelids behave as though they had lead weights attached to them. 'Sorry...'

Andreo arranged her back against the pillow and smoothed her tumbled hair back from her brows. 'What we just shared was fantastic for me but I have a confession to make...'

Her lashes swept up on his serious expression and her heart sank. 'You're married?'

'Dio mio...'

His angry look of reproof soothed her fears so she moved to what was the next-worst scenario in her mind. 'Cheating on your girlfriend?'

'I don't cheat,' Andreo declared loftily, choosing to overlook the reality that a purist might deem him still, in the strictest sense, involved with Lili because he flatly refused to dump anyone by phone.

'Then what...?'

He grimaced. 'The condom broke. Too much enthusiasm on my part... I very much doubt that there will be any repercussions but I thought I ought to warn you.'

Pippa lay very still. 'The...er...*broke*?'

Andreo employed several rather more apt and descriptive expressions that made her face heat with embarrassment.

'I have a clean bill of health. No need to worry about that angle. I've always taken precautions,' he continued levelly. 'But obviously there is a risk that I could have made you pregnant.'

The very sound of that unexpected word, 'pregnant', shook Pippa rigid. An embarrassed little laugh escaped her because she could not begin to imagine so far-reaching a consequence as a little baby resulting from a defective condom. 'I'm sure I'll be fine...it's not that easy to get pregnant. There's two women in my section attending an infertility clinic,' she extended in a rush of abstracted confidence. 'It seems that these days quite a few women have problems conceiving.'

When Pippa had laughed, Andreo's blue-shadowed aggressive jaw-line had clenched. 'The women who marry into my family don't have problems of that nature.'

Pippa pushed her face into a bare brown muscular shoulder to hide her helpless grin. So, he was the contemporary equivalent of a caveman, who confused fertility with virility, was he? That was so sweet. She had to resist an inexplicable urge to hug him tight. 'Are you fond of children?' she asked, her amusement suffering a sudden check.

'I'm one of five...what do you think?'

He was ducking the issue but, just as her amusement had vanished, she had no desire to probe more deeply. She had only been ten years old when she had decided that she wouldn't ever want to have children. In her teen years, she had been quite open about the fact but had too often found herself under attack and forced to defend what were essentially private views on the subject. He might well feel as she did, mightn't he? Perhaps he had had a miserable childhood as well and, like her, shrank from the risk of inflicting similar suffering on a child of his own...

Andreo attempted to read her tranquil expression for he had discovered that for the first time in his life he was extraordinarily impatient to hear a woman's opinion on a topic he usually avoided like the plague. He almost groaned out loud when he registered that it was the tranquillity of sleep that had reclaimed her. He recalled her patience with his decidedly irritating little brother and he found himself smiling. He was willing to bet that she was crazy about kids.

Furthermore, why had he been worrying when she was patently unconcerned by that unfortunate glitch with the condom? What did she know that he didn't? Most probably, he decided, she was too shy to tell him that at the current stage of her cycle there was precious little chance of conception having taken place.

* * *

Pippa wakened to the sound of her mobile buzzing only inches away from her head.

While acknowledging that she had a headache and felt as though she had engaged in some very over-active sport, she fumbled for the phone and half sat up to answer it. 'Hmm?'

'Did you sleep well, *bella mia*?' an awesomely familiar masculine drawl enquired in a tone as smooth as black velvet.

At the same time, Pippa struggled to adjust to the additional revelation that she was stark naked and lying in a bed in an only vaguely familiar hotel room. 'S-sorry?' she stammered.

'I ordered breakfast for you,' Andreo continued with quiet assurance. 'It should be waiting for you next door about now.'

Dazed blue eyes now huge and appalled, Pippa stared down at the phone in her hand and blinked rapidly. 'I thought maybe... er...maybe I dreamt you up,' she confided unsteadily.

'Your dreams are that exciting?' Andreo teased in an intimate undertone, flagrantly ignoring signals from his personal staff that his presence was awaited in the boardroom.

'For goodness' sake...what time is it?' Pippa exclaimed.

'Half-past nine, sleepyhead...but don't worry, I'm happy to give you the day off.' A reflective smile on his wide, sensual mouth, Andreo was picturing her as he had seen her before he'd left his suite. All tousled and flushed and beautiful even while still asleep. She had been exhausted, he recalled. She should spend the day in bed recouping her energies.

'Half-past *nine*? A day off...are you kidding?' Pippa framed in a rather high-pitched response.

'We're dining out tonight and I want you to be rested,' Andreo countered with all the masterful cool of a male who felt it was his business to ensure her well-being.

Had she signed over her soul to him as well as her body the night before? She flinched in shame and growing shock. 'Andreo... I appreciate that you have to be senior to me at Venstar but I don't take days off just because I'm tired—'

'But you will today, *cara*,' Andreo intoned, waving away the executives hovering in the doorway with a censorious frown as he concentrated on his call.

'Why?' she whispered shakily.

'Why?' Andreo queried in frank astonishment for, in his own opinion, he had only made a tiny request. 'If for no other reason then to please me, of course!'

Since when had pleasing a guy been one of her priorities? Since you fell for tall, dark and domineering, who wasn't a dream last night!

'Look, it's not convenient for me to chat right now. But I have a surprise to share with you tonight over dinner. I think it'll make you smile. Leave me your address so that I know where to pick you up,' he instructed before he concluded the call.

Oh, boy, was he in for a surprise! No way was she taking a day off the same day that Cheryl assumed management of the finance section. Shaking her buzzing head, Pippa set her phone down and then as swiftly snatched it up again. As it was already after nine, she needed to call work and make her excuses before saying when she *would* be in. Calculating how long it was likely to take her to travel home and get changed before trailing all the way back across the city to begin work at around lunchtime if she was lucky, Pippa winced and abandoned that idea. Almost throwing herself out of bed, she raced about picking up her clothing and hurtled into the bathroom. It would be faster and simpler if she simply *bought* a new outfit to wear!

Into the shower she went, determined to think of nothing but her goal of getting into work as fast as possible, but her self-discipline crumpled while she washed. Every movement reminded her of the intimate ache at the heart of her body from Andreo's passionate possession. She was torn between mortification and a guilty sensation of happiness that seemed wholly inappropriate in the circumstances. Alcohol had banished her caution and her inhibitions and she had gone to bed with a male she had only just met. His interest had turned her head and she was shocked at the speed and ease with which her pride and moral principles had fallen in the face of temptation. Hadn't she behaved like a tramp?

But she discovered that she could not be that hard on herself. Not every romance was strictly conventional, she told herself urgently. Andreo seemed as wildly attracted to her as she was to him and he had called her first thing and he wanted to take her out to dinner that very evening. Reaching for the towel as she left the shower, she saw her reflection in the mirror and wrinkled her nose at the dizzy grin on her own face. All right, so he was gorgeous, she bargained with herself, but wasn't that all the more reason to make an effort to keep her foolish feet on the ground?

Fully dressed and having paused only to print her address on the writing pad by the bed, she entered the elegant reception room next door and came to a startled halt. An exquisite arrangement of roses adorned with an envelope carrying the name 'Philly' met her attention first. Even as she breathed in the glorious scent of the wonderful old-fashioned blooms, she was taking note of the incredible number of breakfast choices on the table. Having no idea what she would like, Andreo, it seemed, had just ordered up everything for her.

Without warning, her eyes stung with tears and, with a choky little laugh of embarrassment over her own teeming emotions, she dashed away that betraying moisture. Her hand not quite steady, she reached for a fresh roll and buttered it and drank down one of the fruit juices. But it was just no use trying to block out the thoughts pressing in on her: Andreo was, indeed, pretty special. She could not remember when, if ever, any man had made such an effort on her behalf. Her own father had not given two hoots when his own last-minute demands first thing in the morning had ensured that she'd rarely had time to eat before she'd rushed out to work.

'You might as well learn it now,' Martin Stevenson had told

her with excruciating bitterness more than once over the years. 'Life's *tough*.'

Cocooned in her warm, happy feelings about Andreo, Pippa went shopping. In fast succession she bought a black trouser suit, comfortable loafers and fresh underwear in the same store that had supplied her entire wardrobe. She really hoped that it wasn't her dress sense that had drawn him because she had never had a flair for choosing clothes or doing her hair or make-up, she conceded ruefully. How superficial in his judgements was a guy who looked as though he had sprung live from a glossy magazine of sophisticated, classy, handsome men? Possibly dating Andreo was likely to demand a lot from her...but since when had she not been up to a challenge?

Chin at an upbeat angle, Pippa entered the Venstar building with a decided smile lurking in her clear blue eyes. In the lift she stood beside two women talking about the employee meeting that was being held on the third floor. The events room that was always used for large staff gatherings was packed. Pippa slipped in at the back just as a middle-aged director lifted a welcoming hand to announce, 'Andreo D'Alessio, Venstar's new president!'

Pippa saw Andreo, *her* Andreo, rise from his seat at the top table. Magnificent in a pale grey business suit worn with a dark blue shirt and toning silk tie, lean, sardonic face grave, he made her heart leap and her tummy fill with butterflies. Trying to keep a silly smile from forming on her lips, she felt quite ridiculously proud and possessive of him. Only when she was about to look away rather than risk other people noticing who she was staring at did it finally dawn on her that *her* Andreo was striding forward to raise a silencing hand in response to the thunderous tide of applause.

For a long, timeless moment, she assumed that he was acting as spokesman for his employer and then the director addressed him as, 'Mr D'Alessio' and all such hope died. Disbelief made her eyes huge and her mouth fall open and, inside her suit jacket, her heart seemed to be running a one-minute mile so noisily that it was interfering with her hearing.

The finance project assistant, Jonelle, shifted closer to speak to her. 'Go on, admit it. For a bloke as hot as Andreo D'Alessio, just about any woman would stretch a point and consider donning diamond-studded handcuffs! I mean, you wouldn't throw him out of bed, would you?'

Pippa tried to laugh off the comment but her voice had vanished and her lips were too slow and clumsy to shape words for her. But then, had she been able to rescue her vocal cords and make sound, she would have sobbed with raging unbelief and pain.

CHAPTER FOUR

SHOCK WAS ROLLING over Pippa in a suffocating, chilling tidal wave: *her* Andreo was Venstar's president, the fabulously wealthy Italian entrepreneur and womaniser, Andreo D'Alessio!

Gutted by that revelation and much too devastated to immediately react, Pippa listened dully to Andreo giving a short, witty speech about his plans for Venstar. *Her* Andreo? Since when? Sick with shame and the most terrible sense of hurt and betrayal, she shivered, cold to the very centre of her bones, even her skin clammy. Why had he lied to her? Why had he let her think that he was just another employee? How could he have done that to her? What sort of sick, perverted sense of humour did the guy have?

Only then did she remember that she had made the first error in mistaking the small, portly man at the podium for Venstar's new owner. She had then made critical remarks about Andreo D'Alessio. Was that why he had slept with her? The ultimate put-down? Her tummy gave a nauseous roll. How very funny he must have thought he was being when he'd assured her that Andreo was a very common name in Italy and she'd swallowed his stupid lie whole!

Across the room, Andreo's attention was caught by the apricot glint of her bright head. His recognition of her was instantaneous even though her hair was caught up in a rather juvenile pony-tail and her face was bare of make-up. Having assumed that she would do exactly as he had asked, he was disconcerted. In fact, he frowned. Why the hell hadn't she remained at the hotel? Even as he looked he saw her spin away and almost cannon into a group of people in her haste to leave the room. Of course, he conceded grimly, she would immediately have learned who he was.

Instinct urged Andreo to follow her, but he was determined not to make a parade of their relationship during office hours. He was aware that his blatant pursuit of her the night before had been far from discreet. Annoyance flared in him at that grudging acknowledgement. Philly *should* have listened to him and taken the day off. Why was she so stubborn? Now instead of discovering his identity over a relaxing meal, she was finding it out in rather more challenging circumstances.

'I find it hard to believe that your being late today was accidental,' Cheryl Long was informing Pippa in a sharp tone at that exact same moment. 'I wasn't able to show the Kelvedon project figures to senior management because I had no idea that you had sent the file back to Acquisitions. That caused me a *lot* of embarrassment!'

Staff nearby stiffened at that unjust attack but Pippa was much too devastated over what she had just discovered about Andreo to feel the full bite of Cheryl's outrageous accusation. She said nothing because she would have felt foolish defending herself against such a ridiculous charge.

'I'd like you to use my old desk from now on,' Cheryl added, determined, it seemed, to get a reaction out of her subordinate.

'Fine.' Pippa began to clear out her desk drawers.

Cheryl allowed a small smile to play over her burgundy lips and murmured with studied casualness and in an almost friendly tone, 'Oh, I'll need a copy of the presentation you planned to give at this afternoon's meeting for Mr D'Alessio's benefit.'

'I'm afraid I haven't prepared one,' Pippa replied.

'But you *must* have done...' the brunette asserted, her smile falling away at ludicrous speed.

'No, I hadn't got around to it.' Pippa saw no reason to point out that had she been given the job of manager, she would have devoted all of the previous day to that most important task.

Cheryl gave her a furious look of disbelief and, turning on her heel, she stalked across the room and entered Ricky Brownlow's office with only the smallest warning knock.

'Life around here is going to be hell,' Jonelle forecast gloomily to nobody in particular.

'I never thought she'd be such an unbelievable cow,' someone else whispered aghast. 'I mean, she's always been good for a laugh.'

'I can't understand how on earth she....' Jonelle fell silent, possibly appreciating that such remarks were tactless within Pippa's hearing.

In the uneasy silence, Pippa relocated her possessions to her new desk.

'What did you think of Andreo D'Alessio's girlfriend last night?' one of the other women asked Jonelle with determined cheer.

'The redhead? She was sex on legs. Every bloke in the place was drooling over her to the most disgusting extent,' Jonelle lamented. 'If that's the standard of the competition, what hope have us more ordinary types got with him?'

'None at all, I should think.' The older woman chuckled. 'I got the impression that as couples go those two were rather well matched.'

'Matched? In height, I suppose you mean.' Jonelle pulled an unimpressed face.

'Come on...he could hardly bear to take his eyes off her for longer than twenty seconds. She's got him tagged and good luck to her. Didn't she remind you of anyone?'

'Like who?'

'There was just something very familiar about her. I don't know what it was but I thought that maybe she was a model and I'd seen pictures of her somewhere.'

'She didn't remind me of anyone,' Jonelle retorted.

Pippa had grown tense, but her tension ebbed as the subject was dropped. Of course, nobody was going to recognise her, she told herself bracingly. She busied herself with work that she herself had given Cheryl the previous week. The task was well beneath her ability and, in failing to engage her brain, ensured that as she emerged from the shock of having discovered Andreo's true identity her angry pain only became more raw at the edges.

Never in her life had she felt more humiliated. Andreo had deceived her with a cruel and heartless masquerade. He had lied to her and betrayed her trust. But what kind of an idiot had she been to trust a guy she had only just met? What she had believed to be a wonderfully special and romantic encounter now seemed much more like a sleazy one-night stand. Hurt distaste filled her. He was a notorious womaniser. How come she hadn't at least recognised that reality?

After all, he had been as sleek and sophisticated as the legendary Casanova. Her soft, full mouth compressed. She had been too naive to recognise Andreo D'Alessio for what he was. But where had her intelligence been? He had handed out orders with the cool authority of a male used to people jumping to do his bidding. Arrogant, confident, forceful in personality. His hotel suite had been very large and opulent. The roses and the expensive array of breakfast choices had been the lavish gestures of a rich man, accustomed to using his wealth to impress a woman. And she *had* been impressed, hadn't she? Without warning, a hot tide of moisture hit the back of Pippa's eyes in a stinging flood.

Getting up from her desk, she headed straight for the cloak-room. There she stared at herself with loathing in the mirror until those weak tears had receded of their own volition. How could she be hurting so much? So the fairy tale had been an illusion. And she was *surprised*? As her late father had often reminded her, life was tough. What she had to do was move herself on and focus on something else. But what? Her lacklus-tre future with a company that had refused her promotion and moreover suggested she take a lengthy career break? That was when Pippa decided that at the end of her three weeks of leave she would not be returning to work at Venstar.

Instead, she would hand in her notice and make a fresh start elsewhere. Some place where looks did not count more than ability and where hard work and results were rewarded. Some place where she had *not* slept with her boss. Settling her trem-ulous lips into a firmer line, Pippa steadied herself. That was *his* fault too…that she had betrayed her principles and ended up sleeping with her employer. An amount of anger that left her downright giddy shot through her in a re-energising surge. In retrospect she could not credit Andreo's reckless behaviour and she knew then that she would know no peace until she con-fronted him.

She took the lift up to the executive floor. It was almost lunch time and the corridors were busy with people hurrying back and forth. She headed straight for the managing director's of-fice, knocked once on the door and entered before anyone could try to prevent her.

Taken aback by that sudden interruption, Andreo swung round from the computer screen and focused on Pippa instead. On a slender woman dressed all in black with eyes as bright and blue as sapphires and a mouth that even unadorned was as inviting as a ripe cherry.

He smiled because he was pleased that she had come to him and then wondered why she was wearing a suit at least a size too large for her.

It was his smile that first threatened Pippa's tenuous self-control. That he could still smile when she felt lacerated was almost more than she could bear. But that smile was also a trip wire for it had megawatt charm and she found herself staring at him, drinking in his lean bronzed features and the stunning impact of the dark golden eyes welded to her. A host of intimate recollections drowned out her anger. Suddenly she was back where she had been the night before, blushing like mad and as overwhelmed by the power of her own frantic response as an adolescent in the presence of her idol.

'Philly...' In one strikingly graceful movement, Andreo rose to his full height and extended his hand.

The name he employed broke her spell. 'It's Pippa, actually, Pippa Stevenson,' she told him in a high, unnatural voice. 'Andreo...how could you have lied to me the way you did?'

Andreo let his hand fall back to his side, keen eyes narrowing, for he did not like her tone. 'I didn't tell you a single lie,' he countered.

'But you knew that I hadn't the smallest suspicion that you were Andreo D'Alessio. If you weren't prepared to tell me the truth, you should've left me alone.'

'But you didn't *want* to be left alone, *cara mia*,' Andreo traded smooth as polished jet, wondering why she was making such a fuss over news that would delight any normal woman. So, instead of being a nine-to-five worker, he owned the business. So, instead of being reasonably successful, he was a mega achiever. So, instead of earning a good salary, he was filthy rich and in possession of a private jet and an array of luxury homes. What was there to complain about? And where the hell did she think she was coming from when she accused him of lying? He had been careful not to tell her a single untruth.

Tension was pounding out an enervated beat at Pippa's temples but she lifted her head high and she breathed in deep. 'You are my employer and I had a right to know that.'

'*Dio mio*...what a fuss you are making about nothing!' Andreo censured, a satiric dark brow elevated in a manner that would have warned the wary that his patience was running out.

'Nothing?' Pippa gasped, jolted into agonised reaction by his bold refusal to acknowledge the damage he had done.

'Between us and after last night, it *should* mean nothing, *carissima*.' Andreo rephrased as he strode forward to reach for her clenched hands.

Pippa sidestepped him and spread her arms wide in angry condemnation. 'You're even worse than I thought you would be—'

'And what's that supposed to mean?' Andreo demanded.

Pippa kept her eyes wide and fixed in focus because tears were damming up again behind them. Tears of rage and disappointment. He was not the guy she had thought he was. 'I would never have spent the night with you if I had known I worked for you. Do you make a habit of sleeping with your employees?'

'Per meraviglia...' A faint but perceptible rise of blood illuminated his high cheekbones and his tall, powerful length went rigid. Blazing golden eyes seared her in punishment for her daring to ask such a question. 'Never before have I become intimate with a member of my staff!'

'I wish I could say I believed you but it's difficult,' Pippa admitted curtly. 'Particularly when it's obvious to me that you haven't the faintest idea of the boundaries that a decent employer should respect!'

'Your anger I will take, but your insolence I *refuse* to accept,' Andreo murmured in icy warning.

Pippa trembled and her hands knotted into tighter fists. 'You're not even ashamed of yourself, are you?'

Andreo surveyed her steadily. 'Do I have regrets about spending the night with you? No. I had too good a time. I don't consider our relationship a mistake. As far as I'm concerned the fact that I employ you is virtually irrelevant as an issue. I own many different businesses and employ many thousands of workers and my time here at Venstar will be brief. You will neither gain nor lose by my interest.'

'Oh? And how do you make that out?' Distress made Pippa's voice rise half an octave. 'If a colleague was to recognise me as the redhead with you at last night's party, I could never hold my head up again! My only consolation is that I wasn't recognised and that nobody knows what a fool I made of myself!'

Andreo closed lean brown hands over hers in a deliberate move that prevented her from walking away again. He could not imagine how her co-workers could possibly have failed to identify her and he could only believe that she was kidding herself on that score. Enough was enough, he decided in growing frustration. It was time she calmed down and stopped attacking him. 'You didn't make a fool of yourself. That isn't how it was between us. Why are you talking like this? Two people met and succumbed to the same potent attraction—'

'It's not that simple—'

Andreo stared at her with level intensity. 'It *is* if you want it to be, *cara*.'

Painfully aware of the rich, dark pull of his sensual attraction, which was all the more devastating when backed by his powerful personality, Pippa wrenched her hands free of his with positive violence. 'I don't want it to be. You pretended to be someone you weren't. The guy I *thought* you were doesn't exist. I wouldn't have been attracted to a sexist playboy like you in a million years!'

As she attempted to move away Andreo blocked her path and scorching golden eyes assailed hers in a look as aggressive as an assault. 'I think you had better explain that condemnation in language I can be sure I understand.'

Her throat convulsed but she stared back at him in agonised defiance, the sense of loss tearing at her only increasing her bitterness and armouring her with more obstinate determination. 'You cost me my promotion even before you arrived in this building. I heard one of the men who met you in Naples telling a director how unimpressed you were by my picture in the company newsletter and how you preferred sexy, fanciable women in executive posts...'

'That is a complete fallacy.' Pippa Stevenson? Her name had set off a faint familiar bell in Andreo's memory. The company newsletter. He remembered that publication and leafed through the documents on his desk in search of the copy that he had retained.

'I applied for the management position in my section,' Pippa continued unsteadily. 'A job which I had already been doing for some months and which I had every reason to hope would become mine on a permanent basis. Instead the promotion went to another woman, who is not only junior to me in status and unqualified but, also, very much prettier—'

'*Dio mio*...this photo does nothing for you! In this guise even I would be challenged to recognise you,' Andreo confessed with a frown of exasperation. 'But I made only one reference to your appearance that day in Naples. I did not make a single politically incorrect or provocative comment about pretty or sexy women in management, I assure you. I only said that you looked slovenly—'

'I beg your pardon?' Pippa exclaimed in a stricken tone of wonderment.

'And, unfortunately, you *do* look rather untidy in this picture,' Andreo breathed, standing his ground, shooting from the hip in self-defence.

Slovenly? She could not believe he had employed that word as a description of her appearance. Moving forward to snatch the newsletter from him, she gasped, 'What's wrong with me?'

'I shouldn't need to tell you. Look at your hair...it's all over the place.' Andreo found himself studying her while she pored over the newsletter picture and noticed that once again her hair presented, at first glance at least, a rather mussed appearance. Tiny cinnamon curls clustered at her hairline and a rebellious wave was threatening to ruin the once-smooth fall of the silky strands on top of her head. Far from being straight, he registered, her hair seemed to be exuberantly curly.

'Slovenly...' Pippa repeated sickly.

Andreo found that that hurt intonation hit him like a four-car pile-up but he was bone-deep stubborn and as angry with her as any male wholly unaccustomed to female censure could be. 'There's a button missing from your jacket and the trousers look like you slept in them. You don't look very smart. That's *all* I said.'

Painful colour had drenched her cheeks. She bit down hard on the soft underside of her lower lip and tasted blood. That photo had been taken barely a week after her father's death and she had rushed into the room, all breathless and apologetic and the last to join the line-up. It was an old trouser suit and she could see that it was not flattering. But that word, 'slovenly', mortified her and she was appalled that he could be so cruelly inconsiderate of her feelings.

'That is the sole remark that I made,' Andreo asserted, deciding just then that he would never, ever again comment on an employee's personal appearance without very serious forethought.

Whatever, he had cost her the job of Finance Manager even though he was refusing to acknowledge it, Pippa reflected unhappily. He had to know just how eager the Venstar executives were to please him. His criticism would have been sufficient to put a large question mark over the advisability of raising her to managerial status.

'I want to repeat that I passed no inappropriate comments relating to my supposed physical preferences in female employees,' Andreo completed with sardonic clarity.

Pippa remained mutinously silent. He might have what it took to pull women in a very big way, but he was also very much one of the guys: earthly male, athletic, dazzlingly confident, popular with his own sex. A male-dominated culture operated at executive level within Venstar. If Andreo *had* chosen to make Jack-the-lad jokes about women at that session in

Naples, she was well aware that he could not have chosen a more receptive audience.

'I *assume* that you accept that,' Andreo prompted with speaking emphasis.

A laugh that was no laugh at all fell from her lips. 'I don't know if I do. Your behaviour last night made it clear that you don't consider yourself bound by the standards that the average employer would automatically respect.'

Andreo threw up his arrogant dark head. 'I don't accept that contention.'

'Why should you when you're so convinced that no rules whatsoever should apply to you?' Pippa shot at him with a fierce, tremulous edge of accusation to her voice. 'You seem to believe that you have a God-given right to do exactly as you please regardless of how it might affect others. What about my rights? You're my boss and, had I known that, what happened between us would never have happened. I wouldn't have dreamt of making an exhibition of myself with you in front of the people I have to work with either!'

'*Dio mio*, what is done is done...' Andreo entrapped and held the distressed blue of her gaze with smouldering golden eyes.

'It should never have happened,' Pippa mumbled chokily, striving with all her might to disconnect from the heated charge of his magnetic appraisal. 'And slovenly means grubby...and I have never been less than clean in my whole life—'

'I never said that you were...just a little untidy. I was not aware that the word had any other connotation.' Andreo could not credit the effort he was making to placate her. He was annoyed with her. He had every reason to be annoyed with her but he still found himself closing his arms round the general space she occupied as slowly and sneakily as if he were about to try and hug dynamite.

'I am *not* untidy...what are you doing?' It shook Pippa that even in the wake of all her proud words of rejection little miniature fireworks of wild anticipation started fizzing low in her tummy the minute he put his arms round her.

'Tell me you don't want this,' Andreo growled sexily.

Her body was all hot and quivery and eager and shamed colour warmed her cheeks at that awareness. Her breasts felt heavy and tender, the straining peaks tautening into hard little points of betrayal below her jacket. 'Stop looking at me like that,' she pleaded.

With a husky laugh, Andreo bent his handsome dark head and teased her soft lips open with shattering carnal expertise. 'We need to talk. We could have lunch instead of dinner, *cara*—'

'No...'

'Dinner is such a long way away...why should we be that patient?' Andreo's breath fanned her cheek as he came back for a more intimate sortie, letting his tongue delve an erotic path between her lips and making her vent an involuntary moan.

'Back off...my career and my reputation are important to me and this is a mug's game,' Pippa muttered shakily, desperate for another kiss but fighting the lure of him with all her might, knowing all too well just how much she was likely to hate herself if she let him come between her and her wits a second time.

She could smell the evocative male scent of his skin, awesomely familiar to her, shockingly exciting. She felt dizzy and emotional and she wanted to throw herself the last six inches that separated them. She could feel him willing her to do it too. He had an attitude problem. She knew that now. A big backlog of her misguided predecessors had flattered his ego and taught him that he could talk and laugh and seduce his way out of awkward moments. He was manipulative, utterly without conscience, ruthless enough to go to any length to win. He was *not* Mr Wonderful, Mr Perfect, that one very special guy she had believed he was.

But even though she knew all that, resisting Andreo was tearing her apart at the seams. He had taught her to want him and she had been bitten deep by her own yearning. She felt achingly vulnerable and furious with herself for not having sufficient will-power to put him in his place.

'*Amore*...let's not make heavy weather of this,' Andreo drawled, his glorious Italian accent skimming down her sensitive backbone and just tying her up in pathetic shivering knots of responsiveness. 'In your heart, you know very well that you're going to forgive me for all my supposed sins.'

Fury with him and her own weakness made the tears she had held back for well over an hour surge free in a dismaying flood. Without thinking, she wiped her eyes with the back of her hand and dislodged one of her contact lenses. 'Oh, no!' she groaned and dropped down onto her knees. 'Don't move... I've lost a lens!'

Andreo dropped down into an athletic crouch and picked up the tiny lens from the polished wood floor. 'I have it,' he murmured, removing a sheet of paper from the desk and folding the lens into the pocket he had fashioned for it. 'So you wear contacts...'

Pippa wondered if he had ever made a pass at a woman who wore spectacles before and then sucked in a stark breath of despair, wishing that she had the power to regain control of her own brain. 'I'm not about to forgive you,' she stated between gritted teeth. 'I don't want to see you again. I just want to forget that last night happened—'

'Go ahead...we can have a hell of a time rediscovering the joys and reliving the highlights tonight, *bella mia*.'

'Why won't you listen to what I'm saying?' Pippa demanded in fierce frustration, still down on her knees as she tucked the folded paper into her jacket.

'Whether you knew it or not, you signed up for more than one night when you shared my bed.' Andreo rested brilliant dark golden eyes on her in challenge. 'I still want you. You still want me. While I can't understand how your colleagues could have failed to recognise you at the hotel last night, I'm willing to be discreet if that's what you prefer—'

'Stop trying to tempt me,' Pippa cut in a fierce accusing tone even while she leant almost imperceptibly closer to him. 'I wouldn't waste ten minutes of my time on a guy who gives women sex toys for his amusement!'

His black brows drew together, lashes dropping low over his amazing eyes. He gave her a slashing grin that made her want to hit him and pin him horizontal to the floor at one and the same time. '*Sex…toys?*'

'The diamond-studded handcuffs… I read about them in a newspaper,' she informed him thinly.

'Shame on you, *cara mia*. You've been reading real trash,' Andreo murmured in unembarrassed silken reproof. 'And I hate to be the one to disappoint you but you're about as ready for sex toys as I am for celibacy!'

Vaulting upright, he stretched down a hand to help her up too. But in almost the same moment Pippa heard the door open and a male voice address Andreo in his own language. She almost died on the spot and shot right under his desk to curl up into a remarkably small ball.

Sal Rissone made a praiseworthy effort not to let his attention touch on the woman hiding under Andreo's trendy glass desk.

'Just pretend that she's as invisible as she thinks she is,' Andreo told him in Italian.

'Am I allowed to ask what she's doing there?' his childhood friend enquired, deadpan.

'Protecting herself from the embarrassment of being seen in my office. She…she gets hyper about crazy things,' Andreo murmured almost defensively, shrugging a broad shoulder. 'She's a sensitive woman.'

Sixth sense warned Sal not to crack the rather coarse joke brimming on his lips. Self-evidently, Andreo had decided that hyper was cute and sensitive and worthy of respect. Andreo, who thought women were interchangeable commodities pretty much put on earth for his sole enjoyment, was making excuses for one so off-the-wall she was hiding under his desk. Andreo, who had such very pronounced ideas of what he liked and what he disliked. Sal could not wait to call his wife and share the news that Andreo was acting as strangely today as he had the night before.

Seconds after the door closed on Sal's departure, Pippa shot out from her hiding place. Standing up, she smoothed herself down with shaking hands while refusing to award Andreo a single glance and walked straight back out of his office again. After all, what more was there to say? She had made her feelings clear. Furthermore, she was all too painfully conscious that she had a very low resistance threshold to those sleek, dark, gorgeous good looks of his.

Mid-afternoon, instead of working, she found herself staring into space, utterly, frighteningly shorn of her usual great concentration. She tried to boot Andreo back out of her thoughts but he hung in there as if he were tattooed on her brain cells. She was furious with herself. He had no shame. He would not agree that he had been an irresponsible, selfish toad in refusing to admit that he was her boss. So now she knew what the surprise he had been planning to break to her over dinner would have been...

Yes, now she knew and she also had the unarguable proof of how basically unimportant he had deemed the whole issue to be. Brow furrowing, she reconsidered that angle as she recalled his insistence that the attraction between them should take priority over all else. Hadn't he also sworn that she was the only employee he had ever been involved with? Taken together with his behaviour, didn't those facts suggest that Andreo might be genuinely interested in her? For goodness' sake, was she already falling back into that demeaning trap of dreaming that her wildest fantasies could come true?

How naive could a woman be? Andreo D'Alessio was a rat! A sleek smooth rat. He was also very, very rich and he had a very bad reputation with women. How likely was it that such a male had even vaguely decent intentions towards the stupid, trusting virgin who had flung herself into his bed the very first time they'd met? Pippa paled. She was ashamed of her own desperate desire to believe that she could trust him. Hadn't she learned anything at all since she was seventeen?

That last summer in France she had fallen in love for the first time. A student staying in the neighbouring village, Pete, had been four years older, blond, good-looking, a motorbike fanatic. For a whole month, she and Hilary and occasionally even Jen had hung out with Pete and his mates. Tabby had met the boys too, but once her friend had met Christien, who was now her husband, Tabby had spent all her time with him.

Pippa had fallen like a ton of bricks for Pete. He had held hands with her, kissed her, acted as though he was interested in her and her life. Perhaps she ought to have questioned why he'd been so keen to encourage her to talk about how worried she'd been about Tabby, who had embarked on a wild affair with Christien. Tabby with her caramel-blonde hair and voluptuous figure had always attracted the guys and she had come out with them all again only because Christien had been away on business.

That day, Pete had taken Tabby on the back of his bike instead of Pippa. Although he had pretty much ignored Pippa, she had honestly thought he was just being friendly. So when he had kissed Tabby right in front of her, she had been shattered, but pride had made her hide her pain. Tabby had had no idea that Pippa had regarded Pete as her boyfriend and she had said afterwards, 'I was annoyed when Pete came on to me but he told me he'd been waiting his chance with me all summer and I felt really sorry for the poor bloke…because, let's face it, the only bloke in the world for me is Christien.'

The hardest thing that Pippa had ever done was pretend indifference to the humiliation that Pete had inflicted on her. Pete had just used her to pump her for information about Tabby and as an excuse to call at the farmhouse where they'd all been staying in the undoubted hope of running into her friend again. What little faith Pippa had had in her own judgement of the opposite sex had taken a hammering, for Pete had made it painfully obvious that he'd felt absolutely nothing for her.

Surfacing from those wounding recollections, Pippa looked up with a dazed aspect to her bespectacled blue eyes when she saw the post boy poised in front of her desk holding a gigantic basket of flowers.

'Wow...' Jonelle gushed with inquisitive eyes. 'Is it your birthday or something?'

Gulping, Pippa scrambled upright. She detached the envelope from the basket handle and tore into it with hands that she could not keep steady.

'Text me your address...finish early?'

There was no signature and it was not his handwriting but she knew the glorious arrangement was from him because she did not know another living soul in the country who could have afforded to spend that much on flowers. Her knees felt wobbly and she dropped back into her seat. She decided that it would be more dignified to ignore both the gesture and the message, but she was horribly conscious of just how badly she wanted to dig out her mobile phone and text him. She had never had a guy to do that with.

'Call for you, Pippa...' Jonelle announced, having answered the extension on what was now Cheryl's desk.

Pippa took the call.

'Do we have to sneak around?' Andreo complained huskily. 'My English grandmother used to say, "Tell the truth and shame the devil".'

'It's a pity her outlook didn't rub off on you!' Pippa whispered in a controlled hiss while she slid her forefinger into the long ringlet that had broken loose from her pony-tail and wound bright strands of hair round and round in a frantic, enervated spiral.

'I had to throw all my staff out of the boardroom to call you—'

'Did I ask you to?' But an appreciative grin tugged at Pippa's mouth.

'I need to use *my* phone!' Without any further warning, Cheryl simply snatched the receiver from Pippa's hold and stabbed a punitive finger down on the cut-off button.

In astonishment, Pippa wheeled round. 'There was no reason to do that—'

'Wasn't there?' Cheryl gave her an enraged scrutiny. 'Thanks to you I've just gone through the worst ordeal of my life!'

'Sorry?' Pippa was now noticing how hot, bothered and tearful the pretty brunette looked.

'I gave my presentation and that sarcastic bastard, D'Alessio, blew me away with the most awful questions. I couldn't answer them and he treated me like I was stupid…it's your fault that I wasn't well enough prepared!' Cheryl was sobbing in noisy earnest long before she reached the end of that impassioned outburst.

In the ghastly silence that stretched through the section, Ricky Brownlow hastened up, his discomfiture in the radius of Cheryl's distress palpable. 'Miss Long's upset and she doesn't know what she's saying. Pippa…er… I'm sorry about this. I'm sure Cheryl will want to apologise to you later when she's feeling more herself.'

As the blond man urged the crying brunette into his office, Cheryl was heard to loudly deny any desire to apologise to Pippa for *anything.*

'Since when did Ricky get so chummy with Cheryl?' someone asked.

'Seems she found out the hard way that she couldn't do Pippa's job. Serves her right too.' Jonelle sniffed. 'I'm more amazed she had the nerve to even apply for it!'

Pippa's mobile phone buzzed. Instead of answering it, she switched it off. It would be Andreo and she did not trust herself to check that it was and still ignore his call. Stuffing her phone back into her bag, she went back to work. As she was leaving an hour later Cheryl sidled up to her, her eyes and her nose still pink, her resentment barely concealed as she forced out grudging words of apology for her verbal attack.

Pippa was as gracious as she felt she could be but the brunette's behaviour had merely underlined her own conviction that her own days of working at Venstar were strictly numbered. When she got home to the terraced house that she had once shared with her late father, she phoned out for a pizza. She loosed her wayward hair, finger-combed her curls and shed her suit in favour of a T-shirt and shorts. Making herself comfortable, she rang Tabby at her Breton home and asked if she could come and stay with her friend and her husband for a while.

'I can't believe you're finally taking a holiday and coming over to see us!' After the ghastly day at work that Pippa had endured, Tabby's bubbling delight warmed her.

Following that call, Pippa studied her familiar surroundings and finally conceded that she was bored and dissatisfied with her dull existence. She decided that that was most probably why she had gone off the rails with Andreo D'Alessio and ditched her principles. Alcohol had played its unfortunate part too, she told herself grimly. It was not that *he* was so impossibly attractive, but more that he had caught her in a weak moment.

Just for once she had longed to do something different, something adventurous, something that wasn't sensible. Everything else in her life was certainly sensible. Right down to her very wardrobe and rarely varied routine. Her grandparents and her parents had been comfortably off and, thanks to their canny financial planning, she owned her home outright, enjoyed a healthy savings account and could afford to take her time about job hunting. In twelve days' time, she would be in Brittany. While she was over there, shouldn't she explore the possibility of living and working in France for a while?

No sooner had that idea occurred to Pippa than her thoughts

leapt ahead of her. She was free to do as she liked and rather than burn all her boats at once and risk selling her terraced home, she could let it out to tenants instead. Her late mother had been French and Pippa had grown up bilingual. All things considered, launching a fresh phase of her life across the English Channel would not be quite as risky for her as it would be for others, she decided.

Her front doorbell buzzed. Her mouth watering at the prospect of a slice of pizza, she answered it and then fell back a step in surprise and confusion.

Andreo took advantage of her disarray to push the door back and stride into the hall. Tall, broad-shouldered and lean-hipped, his proud dark head at an angle, he rested brilliant golden eyes with speaking satisfaction on the basket of flowers that she had carted back from the office and then he switched his bright gaze to her.

'You aren't dressed yet, *cara*,' he commented in his lazy drawl.

'I'm not d-dressed because I'm not going anywhere.' At the nervous stammer of her own voice, flames of pink burnished Pippa's delicate cheekbones. 'And I've already told you that... why are you so persistent?'

CHAPTER FIVE

ANDREO ALMOST LAUGHED out loud. In asking him that question, could Pippa be serious?

Sexual desire was like a juggernaut inside him, driving him back to her with relentless force and determination. Lean dark face taut, he raked his incisive gaze slowly and carefully over her. He had to admit that she was a far cry from the sultry beauties he usually took to his bed, women who devoted much of their day to the maintenance of a groomed and flawless appearance. Her cinnamon mop of explosive curls was tousled and curiously appealing to him. She wore not a scrap of make-up and she was barefoot. Not even her nails were painted. Her T-shirt and shorts were not of the designer variety either.

But her candid eyes were bright as sapphires against her flushed skin and her soft pink mouth was vulnerable and full. Well washed and faded, the T-shirt moulded her supple curves and delineated pouting breasts rounded as apples and crowned with stiff little nipples.

His all-male body responding with fierce enthusiasm to that provocative evidence that his preoccupation in her was wonderfully matched by hers in him, Andreo murmured thickly, 'I want you too, *bella mia.*'

The whole time that Andreo had been engaged in looking her over with the arrogant assurance of a male well aware of his own breathtaking magnetic attraction, Pippa had found herself welded to the spot with her heartbeat accelerating, her mouth bone-dry and her breath coming in jagged little bursts.

Clad in designer casuals of faultless sophistication, he looked incredibly handsome: cropped black hair glinting below the downlighters, level brows accentuating the masculine perfection of his hard cheekbones and the blue-black shading of his bronzed skin where it roughened in true masculine style round his aggressive jaw-line. She could literally *feel* his stunning eyes on her and the intensity of his appraisal fired a charge of helpless quivering excitement inside her. Her spine was in a rigid curve, slim shoulders thrown back, an attitude she only then appreciated pushed her braless breasts into prominence. The tingling of her sensitive flesh made her gaze lower and a hot wave of scarlet washed her cheeks when she realised why he was staring at her: the shameless distension of her nipples was obvious even through the cotton of her top.

'I don't want you...' she gasped in belated denial, lifting one hand in a blind betraying gesture to steady herself against the wall behind her.

Andreo was incensed with her. 'All I want right now is food—'

'Liar!' Pippa proclaimed.

Andreo sent her a smouldering appraisal, dense black lashes low over burning gold. 'It is polite to make a civilised pretence of patience, *cara mia.*'

Civilised? Since when had he been civilised? Even the alcohol in her bloodstream the night before had not dimmed her awareness of his powerful personality and emphatic individuality. Staring back at him, for all her spoken defiance entrapped by the sheer impact of his exotic dark good looks and sexual vibrancy that close, Pippa shivered. 'Don't pretend with me.'

He quirked a sardonic brow. 'You need me to tell you that, since early this morning, I've been on fire with a very powerful urge to carry you back to bed and sate my every fantasy?'

'I'm not the kind of woman whom men have fantasies about,' Pippa told him with a stony disdain edged with a raw, angry regret that she fought to keep to herself. For at that very moment she longed to be the sort of female who *did* inspire men with such fervour and admiration.

'I only know what you do for me and what we found last night *was*—'

'Just sex.' Pippa thrust up her chin as she forced herself to make that blunt interruption, determined as she was to ensure that he received no opportunity to turn her foolish head again with false flattery. 'That's all it was.'

Andreo was outraged. Times without number he had slept with women and thought in exactly those terms, but no woman had ever treated him to a similar description. He felt insulted beyond relief and furious with her. '*Dio mio*. Why so coarse?' he demanded with seething bite. 'Together we discovered something exceptional. You were a virgin—'

Pippa paled with anger at that embarrassing reminder of the lack of experience that had evidently encouraged his reluctance to accept that she could know what she was talking about when she rejected him. 'Do you have to drag that up?'

'It is relevant. You *chose* me as your first lover,' Andreo reminded her, infuriated by her efforts to brush him off as though he had been some tasteless and misjudged one-night stand.

Her oval face flushed a hot and mortified pink.

Andreo was quick to press his advantage. 'I was concerned then that you would have regrets but don't let that come between us now, *amore*.'

'My choosing you as my first lover meant nothing...nothing at all,' Pippa disclaimed with lacerated pride.

Andreo learned that he could travel from rage to a torn sense of tenderness that threatened to gut him and he loathed the revelation. He knew by her unhappy eyes that she was lying to him but he could not work out why. 'Then why look at me the way you do?'

Pippa went rigid. 'What way?'

A very male smile slashed his lean, strong face. 'I need to draw pictures?'

Temper leapt through her in an energising roar. 'Perhaps you do.'

His molten golden gaze snared hers and her heart crashed against her breastbone as though someone had thrown a panic switch deep down inside her. 'Even the way you look at me speaks to me of your hunger for me...'

'It's only sexual attraction, nothing I can't bury again any time I want to!' Pippa stabbed back in fearful retaliation.

'So...bury me,' Andreo invited in husky challenge, angling down his proud dark head and claiming her full parted lips, prying straight between them with the erotic immediacy of an expert.

For a split second she remained stiff as a coat-hanger and then she trembled violently, shifted forward in a clumsy movement and let her hands close in a feverish embrace over his wide shoulders to steady legs that she could no longer depend on. She moaned as he used his tongue to probe the sensitive reaches of her mouth. The ticklish throb of her tender breasts made her instinctively press into the tough, muscular wall of his hard, masculine body. Fierce sensual excitement currented through her slim body and the intimate ache between her thighs intensified.

Andreo snatched his head up and drew in a stark lungful of air, a suppressed shudder racking his lean, powerful length, a raw Italian curse almost impelled from him by the disciplinary demands of restraining the force of his hunger for her. Shimmering golden eyes locked to her hectically flushed face and swollen mouth. 'You were saying...?' he prompted lethally, hoping like hell that she was a good loser so that he could triumph twice over and just haul her off to the nearest bed.

'Saying?' The word meant nothing to her for Pippa was not thinking just then. Her pale slender fingers stretched up and speared into his luxuriant black hair to yank him back down to her again. 'Kiss,' she told him, all of a quiver against him, hot and restive and in need, all her powers of concentration bent on the single-minded, necessary goal of dragging him back into her arms.

Andreo murmured something husky in Italian and gazed down at her with sizzling satisfaction, glorying in his sensual power over her, neatly choosing to overlook that he had been cursing hers over him just seconds earlier.

'Please...' she framed in uneasy bewilderment, brow indenting, for she had been unlocked from the erotic lure of him long enough by that stage for rational thought to be threatening a return. As the phone began ringing she winced, for she felt as if the slightest external annoyance might tip her over the edge and make her scream or break down.

'You're on a sensual high...coming down hurts, *amore*,' Andreo breathed as he recognised the source of the bemused tears in her eyes.

Shock shrilled through her. It had not occurred to her that the fever pitch of desire that he could rouse her to so easily had another side to the coin: the torment of unsated hunger. Suddenly limp, she rested against him, devastated by her own capacity for passion. He had been in her life barely twenty-four hours and already he had turned it and her upside down with feelings and sensations that she had never dreamt she might fall victim to. It was truly terrifying.

Andreo smoothed a hand over her down-bent head in a soothing gesture. An answering machine clicked on and a man's deep pitched voice broke the humming silence in French.

'Pippa? It's Christien. I need a private word with you...'

Her head came up in surprise and she pulled back from Andreo. The speaker was Tabby's husband. As he was not in the habit of making personal calls to her, Pippa was afraid that something had happened to Tabby and concern sent her flying to the phone. 'Christien?'

But, cool and calm as was his wont, Christien informed her that he was willing to come over to London on the day she wanted to travel and bring her back to France with him that same evening if she would accompany him on a maternity shopping trip on Tabby's behalf. Her lively friend had her own quirky dress sense and Christien might be the living image of the Parisian's legendary sophistication, but he had never yet managed to buy his adoring wife anything to wear that she actually liked.

'Tabby's pregnant again? My goodness...' Pippa had to struggle to keep the dismayed disapproval out of her voice. After all, if her friend was soon to give birth to a *third* child at the tender age of twenty-three years, it was hardly Pippa's place to comment. However, she was seriously tempted to ask Christien if an annual baby was a perquisite of Tabby having married into the top drawer of French society to which he belonged. Surely her poor besotted friend could only be expecting yet again because a mini football team of kids was what Christien's unquenchable masculine ego demanded? Tabby might be blissfully happy with Christien but Pippa put that down to Tabby's loving nature.

'I'll let her tell you all about it herself,' Christien countered finally to bridge the awkward silence that had fallen. 'You're very quiet. Does a shopping trip in my sole company promise to be more than you can stand?'

Beneath Andreo's steady appraisal, Pippa turned a guilty brick-red. Christien had seduced Tabby as a teenager and broken her heart. Their past misunderstandings had been resolved before their marriage a couple of years back but Pippa had never really warmed to her friend's husband. That Christien himself should have guessed that fact, however, mortified her. 'Don't be silly. Your wife's my friend, for goodness' sake—'

'Just tell yourself that you're doing it for Tabby's benefit.'

Christien's cool, condescending amusement rarely failed to set Pippa's teeth on edge. 'Don't worry. I've never considered your hostility as an issue personal to me... I know you dislike men.'

At that declaration, Pippa's eyes almost shot out on stalks and she sped into the kitchen to gain the privacy to hiss, 'Is that what you think? Well, let me disabuse you of the suspicion that I'm either gay or a man hater—'

'I wasn't aware—' Christien sounded startled and well he might have done, for when he had brought his wife over to London in recent years Pippa had always been very quiet in his presence.

'In fact right now I'm involved in a passionate affair with an Italian guy!' Pippa asserted in defiant retaliation, hurt and offended by what he had said and desperate to disprove it.

At that rather shattering announcement, Christien just laughed out loud, smoothly assured her that she had misunderstood his meaning but that he was delighted to hear that her private life was flourishing. As she walked back into the hall, mentally kicking herself for rising to Christien's provocative bait, Tabby's husband arranged to pick her up on the relevant date. Wondering if her embarrassment over her wild outburst would have subsided even partially by then, she cast aside the cordless phone.

Out in the hall, Andreo had heard most of that exchange. Initially he had only been surprised that Pippa could speak French with the speed and verbal virtuosity of a native but his mood had soon turned dark and stormy. Who the hell was the French guy she was chattering to? Why on earth had she looked *so* guilty? Evidently this Christien character was married to her friend yet she had seemed most unhappy to learn that her friend was pregnant again. Weren't women usually overjoyed by that sort of news? Why had she gone into the kitchen to continue the dialogue in urgent secretive whispers? Her discomfiture at the risk of being overheard had been pronounced.

Was she in love with her friend's husband? It struck Andreo

as a quite likely scenario. In love with a married man and fighting it or in love and flirting like mad with the misbehaving bastard but idealistically resisting temptation and refusing to let the relationship become sexual? Was that why she had thrown her virginity away on a total stranger? In a bout of rebellious frustration over the male she could *not* have? *Dio mio*, even worse, Andreo reflected with bitter anger flaming through him like a burning arrow of provocation, had he, Andreo D'Alessio, been only a sexual substitute for some other man? Might that not explain why in the aftermath Pippa should be so very determined to try to deny and indeed forget their intimacy?

Her heart rate picking up speed, her throat dry, Pippa focused on Andreo's lean, dark, devastating profile. She remembered begging for that beautiful, tormenting mouth of his. It had taken him only moments to reduce her to the level of a wanton again. She made herself recall how she had clung and sobbed in the frantic clutches of the sweet agony of ecstasy he had given her the night before and her palms grew damp and her face burned hot as the heart of a fire. All of a sudden she knew why she had hurled that crazy lie at Tabby's husband. Why had she said she was having a passionate affair with an Italian? Her subconscious mind had spoken out loud what she did not have the courage to admit even to herself: she *wanted* to have that affair with Andreo!

'Is there someone else in your life?' Andreo demanded with shocking abruptness.

Taken aback, Pippa breathed, 'Why are you asking me that?'

Andreo settled veiled dark eyes on hers and the strangest little frisson of incipient threat feathered down her taut spinal cord. 'Is there someone?'

'No...of course there isn't... I don't even know why you would ask me again,' she muttered, almost smiling at the realisation that he saw her as rather more irresistible than she saw herself.

Andreo's lean brown fingers clenched into a fist and thrust

into the pocket of his well-cut chinos. After what he had over-heard, she had to be lying to him. Yet she looked so innocent! He gazed steadily back at her until she had the grace to blush and drop her head. It infuriated him that he should still be as hungry as hell to feel her slim white body under his again.

Pippa tried to be really brave. 'I'm... I'm very drawn to you...'

Andreo shrugged a powerful shoulder, stubborn jaw-line at a punitive angle, eyes bright with hard gold challenge. 'You said it was just sex, *amore*. That's good enough for me.'

Pippa paled. It wasn't good enough for her. She wanted more. She wanted an open ticket, a proper relationship, the chance of a future with him? Maybe even wedding bells? Did dinosaurs still walk the earth? Or had he stolen her every brain cell? Fu-rious with him for forcing her to face how deep his hold on her already went, she pulled open her front door. 'You're my boss. Let's leave it at that,' she told him woodenly.

Dark fury claimed Andreo for a long, timeless moment. She blew hot, she blew cold. How dared she do that to him? How dared she try to play him at his own game? In that instant, in proud, angry denial of his own fierce, flaring reaction to yet another rejection from her, Andreo was tempted to snatch her up into his arms and carry her into the bedroom and put the 'you're my boss' embargo to the ultimate test. It was his belief that she would crumble. She was *his* woman. Didn't she know that? His every aggressive instinct assured him that he could prove that to her. As soon as he got the chance, however, he intended to check out the identity of the married French guy.

When Andreo had gone, Pippa slumped. She felt horribly let down. Somehow she had lost the plot, for the instant she'd advanced he had seemed to change tack and cool off instead of responding to her greater honesty. Now she could only feel embarrassed that she had harboured naive girlish dreams about a male whose interest in her was unashamedly sexual. She had heard some women say that it was perfectly possible to enjoy sleeping with a guy without emotion getting involved. But she had only shared a bed with Andreo once and already her emotions were in absolute turmoil and he seemed to be occupying her every waking thought. There was a lesson to be learned there, she reflected unhappily.

'I need time to bone up on the latest projects.' The following morning, Cheryl angled a bright, determined smile at Pippa. 'You'll have to stand in for me at today's meeting.'

Secure in the knowledge that she had no intention of remaining at Venstar, Pippa was able to tolerate Cheryl's barefaced cheek in demanding that she take her place in the hot seat.

Ricky Brownlow accompanied Pippa into the lift, clearing his throat to say, 'The directors asked for you specifically. Miss Long was nervous yesterday and Mr D'Alessio became quite impatient with her.'

In the act of wondering why Ricky now seemed to take it upon himself to make excuses for Cheryl, Pippa drew in a short sharp breath at the more challenging news that Andreo would be present at the meeting.

She saw him the minute she entered the room. He looked spectacular and she found it almost impossible to drag her eyes from his lean, powerful face. In a navy business suit, silver-grey shirt and silk tie, he stood more than half a head taller than the men around him. The high heels she had selected from the back of her wardrobe that morning clicked on the polished wood floor. He swung round and watched her progress towards the circular conference table: a tall, slender woman with a tumbling mane of cinnamon curls and blue eyes concealed behind large spectacles with dark frames that only accentuated the delicacy of her fine bone structure and the purity of her skin.

For a split second, when Andreo studied her without any hint of familiarity, Pippa believed she was about to succumb to an attack of stage fright, and then a director voiced an enquiry, helpfully prompting her into her usual working efficiency. She delivered a detailed breakdown of the figures that had caused Cheryl such grief a day earlier. Nobody was left in any doubt that she knew her field inside out and backwards.

On that same score, Andreo suffered a rare attack of conscience for he could not disprove Pippa's belief that his criticism of her appearance had led to the promotion of an unsuitable candidate over her head. Yet he could barely credit that a single censorious comment from him *could* be responsible for the downright stupid decision to appoint Cheryl Long to a position for which she was demonstrably unfit.

As silence fell in the wake of the question-and-answer session Pippa studied Andreo, wanting him to look at her, needing him to notice her, shaken by how fierce that craving was. His intent dark golden scrutiny rested on her for only the briefest moment. But for Pippa, while that moment lasted it was as though their companions just faded out from her awareness. Butterflies broke loose in her tummy and an irresistible urge to smile almost overcame her self-discipline.

'You have an exceptional grasp of financial planning,' Andreo acknowledged with approval.

An unearthly silence fell round the table.

At the compliment, Pippa turned pink with pleasure. Andreo sprang upright and shifted a lean staying hand in an indication that he would like her to remain behind. Almost unbearably conscious of the veiled curiosity of her companions, she hovered until he finally turned back to her. 'I'd like to discuss your future with Venstar over dinner this evening. We'll go straight from the office and eat early...if that suits you?'

'Er...yes, of course,' Pippa muttered hastily, wondering under what terms she was being invited. Strictly business as she herself had requested? She could not fault his present attitude to her. His attention had not lingered on her once and now, in receipt of her agreement, he swung away to deal with someone else. He was driving her out of her mind, she conceded wretchedly. He was behaving like her boss and she couldn't bear it! Yet wasn't that how she had asked him to behave? But she couldn't handle being treated as though she were merely another anonymous employee. She felt absolutely gutted when he no longer looked or smiled at her.

'You want me too...' Andreo had told her and he had been much more on target than she had been prepared to admit. Was she guilty of being a closet romantic who needed to dress up sex with more lasting feelings? For a deeper relationship was not on offer, was it? How could it be? Andreo had been upfront about the fact that his time at Venstar would be brief. He wanted to go to bed with her again. He had been outstandingly frank on that score and why should he not have been? He *was* a notorious womaniser and the last guy alive on whom a sane woman would focus romantic expectations. Why couldn't she meet him on the same ground and accept that all she would ever share with Andreo would be a physical relationship? In ten days she would be packing to leave London for France and embarking on a new phase of her life. Why didn't she just reach out and take what she wanted for the next week and a half?

An affair limited by time boundaries that would ensure that she did not get too involved and as a result...hurt. An affair on *her* terms. She would be in control. It wouldn't, it couldn't get messy within the space of a few days. In such a truncated time frame there was surely no room for complications or pain. Her chin came up, eyes alight with hope and pure bubbling happiness. She could have him for a little while, enjoy him the way one enjoyed luxurious chocolates and then go back on a normal healthy and sensible diet.

'U were right. I want u 2,' she texted Andreo before she could lose her nerve.

Travelling in his limo across the city Andreo read that message with pleated dark brows and wondered why she had changed her mind. Had his suspicion that she was hooked on her friend's husband been way off target? It seemed it might well have been and he winced, wondering why he had been so unusually fanciful. Undoubtedly there was a more reasonable explanation than that which had appealed to his more cynical streak. Was he becoming overly distrustful of women? Almost simultaneously, the grim mood that had settled over Andreo and that he had refused to acknowledge evaporated. He pictured Pippa as she had looked in the conference room that morning: sunshine firing her vibrant hair, eyes bright as gemstones against her fine porcelain skin. Even the most fleeting thought of her stirred a dulled ache of arousal in his groin.

'Wise woman. C u l8r,' he responded by text.

His PA called Pippa to tell her what time she would be picked up at the rear entrance. The afternoon drifted past Pippa while she lost herself in a daydream. By the time she emerged from the building, having spent an inordinate amount of time fussing with her hair, she was on a nervous high of anticipation. A chauffeur swung out of the long silver limousine waiting by the kerb and opened the passenger door for her. Endeavouring to act as though limos were two a penny in her world, she climbed in.

Andreo surveyed her with burnished golden eyes framed by black spiky lashes. He looked incredibly handsome and her heart raced so fast she felt giddy and breathless.

'So now you're mine on request, *bella mia…*' he breathed, savouring the syllables in the most impossibly sexy style.

As he urged her into connection with his big powerful frame, she blushed at the reality that she could barely wait for him to touch her. He meshed one long-fingered hand into her bright hair and claimed her lips with hungry, driven urgency. She shivered and pushed up against him, temporarily so bereft of anything but her own overwhelming need to connect with him again that the move was instinctive.

'We have business to discuss,' Andreo groaned, drawing back from her.

'What sort of business?'

But the limo had come to a halt and the dialogue was shelved until they were seated at a corner table in a fashionable restaurant.

'You've suffered an injustice at Venstar. If that was—indirectly—my fault, I can only apologise. Unfortunately, the company's choice of candidate, however inappropriate, cannot be deprived of the job without good reason and establishing grounds takes time,' Andreo murmured dryly. 'In the short term it makes more sense for me to find a better position for you in another company.'

Pippa had grown very tense. 'I don't need your help—'

Andreo expelled his breath on an impatient hiss. 'I'm not offering help. I'm trying to redress a wrong. There's a subtle distinction.'

An uneasy flush had lit her cheekbones. She was convinced that he only felt he ought to intervene on her behalf because she had slept with him and that belief mortified her. 'What's done is done... I can look after myself—'

'I'd also like to see you achieve a status commensurate with your abilities—'

'Don't you think that I can manage that on my own?' Pippa was angry at being patronised. 'You're not responsible for me—'

'Maybe I *feel* responsible.' Andreo surveyed her with brooding dark eyes. 'But naturally I'll respect your wishes.'

Unexpectedly, amusement afflicted Pippa and melted her annoyance. 'Will you really? Even though you think my wishes are rubbish and you really hate people disagreeing with you? Will I have to grovel to get back in with you again?'

Andreo's appreciative gaze narrowed to a blazing sliver of raw gold. 'Just share my bed, *amore*. I've thought about nothing but you for thirty-six hours.'

Her mouth ran dry, a wanton flame lighting low in her pelvis.

'Are you hungry?' Andreo asked thickly.

'Not really but...' Her voice faded for Andreo had already sprung upright.

Three minutes later, he had swept her back out of the restaurant and settled her back into the limo. Without hesitation he had shown her that he would not allow conventional expectations to come between him and what he wanted. The atmosphere between them sizzled. She felt dizzy with wicked anticipation.

CHAPTER SIX

ANDREO HAD TAKEN a penthouse apartment for the remainder of his stay in London.

He opened the door on the vast impressive hall, linked his lean fingers with Pippa's and walked her down to a bedroom as big as the entire ground floor of her home. She hovered in the centre of the carpet, suddenly desperately shy, realising that alcohol had blunted her inhibitions on the night of the party.

'Every time I look at you, I want to take your clothes off,' Andreo confided, shedding his tie and his jacket and tossing both aside with flattering enthusiasm.

She blushed to the roots of her hair. 'I'm glad I didn't know that at the meeting today. You seemed so distant.'

Andreo laughed huskily, strolling forward with easy assurance. 'Now you know why... I have a very active imagination. All guys are the same, *cara mia.*'

He untied her wrap top, took it off and tugged her closer. She kicked off her shoes, felt her skirt give at the waist as he unzipped it. When she stepped out of the skirt, he flipped her round, clamped her to his all-male muscular frame and crushed her mouth with passionate hunger below his.

That first sensual onslaught blew her away. His tongue delved between her lips in an elemental imitation of a much more sexual possession. Clinging to him, she shivered in the circle of his strong arms like a leaf in a high wind.

'I never knew I could feel like this...' Pippa whispered helplessly.

His lean, strong face was taut with intent. His shirt hung unbuttoned and loose to reveal a bronzed wedge of hair-roughened chest. He tasted her swollen mouth again while he reached behind her to undo her bra. When he lifted his proud dark head to look at her, her hands whipped up to cover herself but he caught them in his and drew them down again.

'I want to look at you,' he told her boldly.

Never had she been so conscious of being naked as she was standing there in front of Andreo, her bare breasts crested by shamelessly swollen pink nipples. 'Andreo...'

'*Dio mio*...you're even more exquisite than I remembered.' He sank down on the side of the bed and pulled her down onto his thighs.

At the first touch of his expert fingers on the tender crests straining for his attention, she gasped, weak and quivering with wanting. He closed a hand to the silken explosion of curls at the back of her head and tipped her over one arm. The heat of his mouth hungrily engulfed the throbbing pink buds to tug on the sensitive peaks. His hand cupped and shaped her pouting breasts, rubbing and teasing the stiff crests. The tormenting pleasure of his knowing exploration made her back arch. She moaned her response and speared shaking fingers into his cropped black hair.

He lifted her up and brought her down on the bed. Standing over her, he ran down the zip on his well-cut trousers. She lay there watching him, slim hips shifting in a restive motion against the spread below her. She was unbearably aware of the swollen moist heat at the heart of her. In one impatient movement, he dispensed with both trousers and boxers and the breath snarled up in her throat when she registered the extent of his fierce arousal.

'I want you *so* much, *cara*.' Like a lithe bronzed warrior ready for action, he came down on the bed beside her and skimmed a possessive hand over her tummy to trail along the edge of the modest white panties she wore. Leaning over her, he rearranged her so that he could remove that final garment. The hot gold of his eyes wandered at a leisurely pace over her rose-tipped breasts and the cluster of copper curls crowning her womanhood. There was a quiet sure confidence and sensual threat about his every move that made her burn and crave.

'You should wear jewel colours and silk. I shall buy you gorgeous lingerie, *amore*,' he murmured huskily.

'I wouldn't wear it...' she told him, shocked.

'You don't know all that I could make you do yet.' A slashing grin curved his beautiful mouth as he voiced that bold belief. 'Where did the wild adventuress at the party go?'

'Sorry?'

Golden eyes mocked her self-conscious colour. 'You stayed a good girl a long time...why me?'

The wicked amusement in his darkly attractive features was incredibly seductive. 'I like the way you kiss...'

Andreo drifted down closer, helplessly drawn by the warmth of her appreciation. 'Anything else, *amore*?'

A dreamy smile slid across her softened mouth. Just the whole incredible package, she thought helplessly and she wrapped her arms around him. 'I'm not telling...'

'Are you sure of that?' He shifted against her in a sinuous movement that sent her heart racing and her body quivering with wanton longing. She stretched up, the tender points of her breasts grazed by the rough black curls outlining his powerful pectoral muscles.

'You like *that*,' Andreo purred like a prowling, playful tiger, outlining her lower lip with the tip of his tongue and then penetrating between with a delicious force that stole everything she possessed.

'And that,' she confirmed shakily.

He ran his hand over her tummy to the nest of curls below and let his fingertips flirt there until she slid her thighs apart with a needy little moan. He stared down at her with smouldering sexy eyes of pure satisfaction. 'Do you know what I like best? That I'm the only guy you've ever had,' he confessed with primal force. 'You wouldn't believe how exciting I find that, *carissima.*'

'That's old-fashioned...' But even though she tried not to be, indeed reminded herself that theirs was only a casual affair, she was pleased by that confession. She was grateful that she hadn't ended up with a male who found her inexperience a bore.

'Maybe I'm an old-fashioned guy...deep down where it doesn't show,' Andreo affixed hastily, suddenly wondering where that strange thought had been born. Old-fashioned... him...since when? Since he had looked around his rarefied social circle and worked out that almost all the men had slept with the exact same women? Since he had decided that he did not want to marry a female who had trekked through all his friends' bedrooms as well?

'It doesn't show,' she whispered, shifting up to his caressing hand in helpless encouragement.

He skimmed the tiny sensitive spot below her feminine mound and dallied there with tormenting expertise. Suddenly she was no longer up to the challenge of speech. Breathing in irregular little fits and starts, her writhing body was on fire with a need that he alone controlled.

'Andreo...' she framed, awesomely aware of the rigid hardness of his straining sex against her thigh, shivering with desire as the sweet, agonising ache of her craving became more than she could withstand in silence.

'It's OK... I can't wait either,' he breathed raggedly.

Rising over her, he sank his bold shaft into the slick wet heat of her and released a wondering groan of satisfaction. *'Amore...'*

Madly excited by him, she arched up to meet his powerful thrust. She couldn't get enough of him. Nothing had ever felt so good to her or so right. She tried to hold back the animalistic little cries wrenched from her as he drove her to his stormy sexual rhythm, but she couldn't. He sent her spiralling into a convulsive climax. Ecstasy sent her hurtling into wave on wave of exquisite sensation. His magnificent body shuddered and he vented a harsh groan of masculine satisfaction at the height of his own climax.

'You make me feel incredible, *amore*,' Andreo purred, stretching over her and then freeing her from his weight, only to haul her back to him with one strong arm. 'I want to have you again and again and again... I feel so greedy.'

Giddy, she hugged him tight until the world settled round her again and then she lay there sleepily smiling while he smoothed her tousled hair, told her how amazingly sexy those curls were and dropped tender kisses on any part of her within reach. She looked up at him with dazed eyes and there was a kind of fear in her then that she had not felt in years and years. What she had just experienced with him had been earth shattering passion and glorious fulfillment but sixth sense told her that she ought to ration herself on him.

'You're a very restful woman,' he teased, lifting her off the bed to accompany him into the opulent bathroom. 'Very mysterious too. Where, for instance, did you learn to speak colloquial French?'

'From my mother...she was born and bred in Paris.'

'Was the Frenchman who phoned you a relative?'

Pippa frowned in surprise. 'No, he's married to a friend. I've never quite taken to him—'

'But didn't I hear you arranging to meet him next week?'

'He asked me to visit his wife's favourite maternity shop with him and help him choose some outfits as a surprise for her.' Pippa sighed. 'I just couldn't credit that she was expecting yet another kid. That'll be number three and she's only twenty-three...'

Andreo had relaxed but he was ashamed of his own suspicions about her relationship with her friend's husband. He decided that he had met far too many calculating women, who would go to any lengths to capture a rich man whether they wanted him or not.

Pippa watched him switch on the power shower in the big cubicle and simply reach for her again. He acted as if he owned her but what shook her most was that she liked him acting that way. He was protective and, when he wanted to be, gentle in a way she had never associated with his sex, especially with a guy who was so innately masculine and aggressive at other times. He made her feel like a cross between a spun glass ornament in need of constant care and a sexual enchantress because he couldn't even share the shower with her without getting aroused again.

He was her perfect dream guy. She had not been wrong about that. He was gorgeous, fantastic in bed and he treated her as though she was as irresistible as Cleopatra. It was no wonder she was already halfway to being infatuated. Given very little encouragement, she thought in shrinking dismay, she would fall head over heels in love with him and make a complete ass of herself!

'We'll order in some food... I don't think I could be trusted in a public place with you yet, *bella mia*.' Having enfolded her in a fleecy towel, he lifted her hands and pressed his lips to the centre of each palm, looking down at her from beneath dense black lashes longer than her own with a provocative gleam in his teasing gaze. 'But I've got you all evening and all night...'

Pippa tensed, imagining sleeping in his arms, waking up with him and deciding that she could not indulge herself in that amount of intimacy with him. 'I'm not staying the night,' she told him in a rush.

'Why not?' One arm carelessly curved round her, Andreo was already punching out a number on the phone by the bed.

'I don't stay the night... I mean, I...prefer to go home to my own bed,' she declared.

Andreo slung the phone back down. 'How would you know what you prefer? I've got to be the first guy you've stayed with—'

'I just prefer it... OK?' She worried at her lower lip anxiously.

His strong bone structure taut, Andreo veiled his fulminating gaze and wondered if his own sins were coming home to roost. As a rule, he never invited his lovers to stay the night. Staying over added a whole different dimension to a relationship and he liked to keep things casual. So why had he invited her?

'No problem.' Jaw-line at an aggressive angle, Andreo ordered in Thai food without asking her what she wanted.

Luckily, Pippa adored Thai food. Sitting cross-legged on a big swanky sofa, clad in a towelling robe, she ate with appetite and she asked Andreo how he had come to have a brother so much younger than he was.

'Marco was a surprise package when my mother was in her forties. My father died when he was five, so Marco turns to me a lot,' Andreo said. 'We have three older sisters, all married, all very given to spoiling little brothers and he was turning into a horrible precocious brat. So I persuaded Mama to send him away to school. He's much improved.'

'What was it like being one of five children?' she prompted curiously.

'Fun...it would've been more fun, though, if a couple of the bossy sisters had been boys,' he drawled with mockery. 'Some day I'd like a big family.'

Pippa gave him a startled look. 'I don't want kids at all,' she confided without thinking, reacting to her own surprise that a guy like Andreo D'Alessio could admit to such an unfashionable ambition.

Andreo was frowning. 'You don't want kids...*any*?'

Feeling awkward, she added with rather forced amusement, 'I'm more into my career.'

'So what are you planning to do if I have got you pregnant?' Andreo enquired with a derisive edge to his dark, deep drawl.

Pippa paled. 'That's not going to happen...why are you saying that?'

'Because after that mishap on the contraceptive front the night before last, it's a distinct possibility and I'd appreciate knowing right now up front,' Andreo incised with angry emphasis, 'what the score is likely to be if you *do* conceive!'

Pippa pushed away her plate and scrambled off the sofa. Her restive fingers worked feverishly at the robe's over-long sleeves, which were threatening to engulf her hands. 'I don't like this conversation.'

'*Per meraviglia!* You think I do? But I've asked a fair question,' Andreo bit out rawly.

Furious with him, mortified and feeling threatened by the subject under discussion, Pippa spun on her heel and headed back to the bedroom. Gathering up her clothes in haste, she hurried into the bathroom.

Before she could get the door shut, however, Andreo appeared, lean, powerful face set hard. 'I think that you could give me an answer...'

'How can I answer a crazy question like that?' Pippa almost sobbed at him in her discomfiture and distress. She had made what was for her a casual admission and had without the smallest warning found herself plunged deep into moral issues that she had never had to consider before. His contemptuous attitude both hurt and infuriated her.

Locking the door behind her, she pulled on her clothes, tears lashing her eyes.

When she emerged, Andreo had also got dressed. Drop dead gorgeous in a silver-grey shirt and black cargo trousers, he strode forward, a look of cool exasperation in his scrutiny. 'This is insane, *cara*—'

'Well, don't look at *me* when you say that! I want to go home... I've called a taxi.' Sidestepping him, Pippa fled out into the hall.

'I'm not letting you go like this. Perhaps I shouldn't have said anything...but how was I to know it was such a controversial subject?' Andreo threw up lean brown hands to accentuate his astonishment. 'Most women *like* babies!'

Pippa wanted to slap him. 'I like babies too... I just don't want one of my own!'

Andreo strode across the wide glossy hall floor and rested his hands on her rigid shoulders. She was trembling. 'You'll change your mind—'

'No, I won't!' she told him fiercely.

She pulled away from him. Her mind had already thrown her way back to memories she rarely visited and lodged on a painful image of her mother crying and calling herself a rotten mother because she had been unable to make theirs a happy home.

Andreo settled scorching golden eyes on Pippa's pale, frozen profile. The intercom by the front door buzzed.

'That'll be my taxi...'

'Walk out now and I won't phone you tomorrow,' Andreo threatened without hesitation. 'If you walk, we're finished.'

To her everlasting shame, Pippa stopped dead in her tracks.

Andreo spoke into the intercom and said that she would be down in a few minutes.

Coming to a halt behind her, he closed both arms round her. She went stiff, resisting him with every fibre of her will-power, but the weakening started like a melting sensation deep down inside her. She wanted this guy. She wanted to be with him and she wanted his good opinion too, which was why it hurt to lose it over an issue that struck her as being as crazily remote as the risk of pregnancy. 'I've already told you...it's not that easy to fall pregnant...are you listening to me?' she demanded sharply.

'*Sì*. I'm listening.'

'My mother was never able to conceive again after she had

me and my grandmother tried for ten years before she had my mother!' she protested feverishly.

'That doesn't mean that you're likely to have similar problems.'

As the fierce tension holding her rigid began to give she curved back into his lean, powerful frame. She was of too practical a nature to sustain an argument about a situation that she could not imagine developing. Andreo slowly turned her round to face him. He splayed long fingers to her taut cheekbones. 'You scare me...you scare yourself, *amore*—'

She didn't know why but the wretched tears just broke free then and cascaded down her cheeks. With a driven groan, he hauled her close and she choked back a sob, drinking in the gloriously familiar scent of him like an addict. 'You're too serious,' she told him chokily. 'Just looking for trouble is like asking for it.'

Molten gold eyes assailed hers. 'Come back to bed...'

'My taxi...'

He pressed her down on the fancy wrought-iron chaise longue ornamenting the hall and called the doorman in the foyer. She sat there shivering, shocked at the woman she was somehow changing into against her own volition. She had said she was going home. She should have carried through on what she had said she would do. Andreo swung back to her, all male, powered by resolute determination that mocked her own. While he'd been on the phone, he had unbuttoned his shirt again. He stood there in front of her and simply shed his clothes where he stood.

'I want to go home for the night,' she mumbled unsteadily, sounding like a little child trying to talk herself into running away.

Slowly he raised her to her feet. She hovered, letting him peel off her garments one by one.

'No, you don't...you want to be with me, *amore*. Walking away was tearing you up,' Andreo reminded her with lethal assurance, and then he bent and caught her up into his arms to power back towards the bedroom. 'Week nights, you can go home, but weekends you're mine from start to finish. Sorry, but that's how it is.'

'It's a Thursday,' she muttered weakly into the smooth brown shoulder she was already pressing her lips against.

'Sorry, I didn't hear that...'

'It's Thursday.'

In the act of arranging her on the bed with the care of a connoisseur, Andreo elevated an incredulous black brow at that announcement. 'You need to consult a calendar, *cara mia.*'

'It *feels* like a Friday night,' she whispered in sudden decision, surrendering to his sheer animal vibrancy and ferocious resolve and amply rewarded by his lazy smile of approbation.

Pippa plucked a coral-pink rose from Andreo's latest floral offering and wedged it into the buttonhole on her new blue jacket. Matched with a slim short skirt and fitted to her small waist, it gave her figure a flattering definition that she was unused to seeing.

Her terraced home was awash with flowers that perfumed every room. At least once every couple of nights she had made a supreme effort to tear herself from Andreo's side around dawn and visit home to obtain fresh clothes. She would always bring back all the flowers he gave her and arrange them into vases. In the hall mirror she studied her reflection, absorbing the happiness in her eyes and the silly smile that just the thought of Andreo summoned up. Tension compressed her lips then instead. Indeed she gave herself a stern look. In little more than thirty six hours she would be flying off to France, not only to enjoy her holiday with Tabby and Christien, but also to take her first step towards forging a fresh existence. But leaving Andreo promised to be the toughest thing she had ever had to do...

Yet wouldn't that only be because most ironically *she* would be the one to get in first and end their affair? Andreo had not yet betrayed any sign of boredom with her and why should he have? On her terms, the past nine days had been full of fun and passion and special moments. She was determined not to forget a single second that she had spent with him and had committed every single detail with religious care into her diary. However, nine days were also a very short period of time and she reckoned that Andreo had decided that it would be more convenient for him if he simply let their affair continue until the date of his own return to Italy arrived. Of course, as she had not even told him yet about her own plans, he still had no idea that she was on the very brink of leaving both Venstar and London herself.

Why hadn't she told him? Perhaps she had been afraid that if he knew he might seek to replace her with someone who would be available for a little longer. At least she wasn't fool enough to start imagining that someone as essentially ordinary as she was could possibly have any hope of a more lasting future with a male of Andreo's legendary reputation.

No, she had made the sensible decision that she would make the utmost of every precious minute of her time with him but neither look for nor indeed hope for anything more. In return for her common-sense outlook, her careful, honest acceptance of her own limitations, she had had nine incredibly wonderful days living a fantasy existence with a guy whom...a guy of whom she had become very, *very* fond. That was all. Only a very stupid woman would have let herself fall in love with Andreo D'Alessio. And she wasn't stupid, was she?

A limo was waiting at the kerb when she emerged from her home. Quite unconscious of the curtains twitching at the neighbours' houses, she scrambled in and called Andreo on the car phone.

'I told you I'd get the train,' she scolded softly.

'I want you to conserve your energy for me... I'll see you at one for lunch.'

Even his rich, dark, accented drawl sent a little responsive quiver down her spine. 'Hmm...' She smiled while she thought about how much she enjoyed eating out in the exotic restaurants at discreet locations that Andreo chose for their daily assignations. 'Can't wait.'

A sudden silence seemed to fall when she reached her desk at Venstar. But then of recent she had progressed from being the first to start work in the morning to being the last to arrive and the first to leave. Furthermore, since the simple work she was currently being allotted was way below her capabilities she was free to daydream as much as she liked.

'You know that's a really fantastic suit you're wearing...it's *so* funky!' Jonelle commented rather loudly.

Pippa gave the blonde a sunny smile of abstraction. 'I think so too.'

Her colleague cleared her throat. 'It looks very like a Versace outfit I saw in a shop window last week. Is it... I mean, Versace?'

Pippa shrugged without interest for she had never been into fashion. 'I don't know. I haven't looked at the label,' she said truthfully.

After all, Andreo had presented the outfit to her with the far more interesting news that he had *had* to buy it because it was the exact shade of her eyes. Apparently he had stopped the limo in traffic and got out the instant he'd seen it, so very probably the suit had featured in a window display. Whatever, Pippa kept on seeing a dazzling image of Andreo casting aside all cool sophistication and shouting at his chauffeur to stop and she thought such impetuous behaviour was incredibly romantic. It would have been true to say that had Andreo bought her a garment adorned with zebra stripes she would have been so affected by his going to so much trouble on her behalf that she would have worn it out of gratitude.

At that abstracted response, Jonelle and her equally inquisitive fellow listeners stared at Pippa in near disbelief.

'You're also wearing Jimmy Choo shoes,' Jonelle dared, gazing enviously at the strappy works of art adorning Pippa's slender feet.

'The heel snapped off my shoe when I was out for lunch yesterday,' Pippa confided.

'I wonder if my heel snapped off would a total miracle take place in the street for little old me!' With that acid comment, Cheryl shot Pippa a look of sullen resentment before she stalked out of the office.

Cheryl's spiteful attempts to upset and humiliate Pippa and provoke her into leaving Venstar had got her nowhere, for in the mood that Pippa had been in of late, she would not have noticed Cheryl had she stood on her head and screamed. In vain did Cheryl complain about the very long lunch hours that Pippa now took. Pippa would mutter something vague about having lost track of the time and drift off looking very much as though she was existing on another mental plane entirely.

Minutes later, Andreo's brother, Marco, phoned Pippa. It had to be about the sixth time he had called her. On the first few occasions he had asked for help with maths assignments, but since then their dealings had become more casually friendly and his latest request was for advice on what to buy for a six-year-old niece's birthday. Ten minutes later, Jonelle answered the phone ringing on Cheryl's desk and went off in search of the brunette. When neither Cheryl nor Ricky were to be found, Pippa received a call from a director asking her to go to the meeting room on the top floor to make herself available in Cheryl's place for the client due to arrive.

In the act of stepping into the lift she discovered that Andreo was stepping out. Although it was only a matter of hours since they had last seen each other, she still could not drag her attention from his hard, handsome bone structure and she was utterly ensnared when she met his riveting dark golden eyes.

'Is it long until lunch time?' Pippa muttered, having left her watch behind in his bedroom.

Andreo lifted a lean hand and brushed a stray curl back from her cheekbone with a slow, heart-stopping smile. 'Too long... where are you heading?'

'The meeting room. Lester Saunders is due to arrive and Miss Long can't be contacted.'

'That could be Venstar's biggest advantage over the competition,' Andreo drawled with cutting dark humour, following her back into the lift to accompany her.

Minutes later, Andreo pushed back the door to allow Pippa to precede him into the comfortable room set aside for important appointments.

Halfway into the room, she stopped dead to gape at the man and woman writhing in passion on the sofa. Ricky Brownlow pulled himself up in consternation when he saw Pippa but his partner, Cheryl, gave Pippa a defiant look. 'Don't you know when to make yourself scarce?'

'Don't you?' Andreo breathed smooth as silk when he strolled forward into view and proceeded to sack the guilty couple for gross misconduct.

Pippa had not even suspected that Ricky, who was a married man, and Cheryl might have been having an affair. While they slunk out, Pippa straightened the room for the client's imminent arrival.

'You were shocked. You really don't listen to the rumour mill, do you?' Andreo murmured. 'Even I had heard that Brownlow was believed to have pushed Cheryl for your job because it would make it easier for them to spend time together. It only remains for me to appoint you back to Acting Finance Manager—'

Pippa stiffened. 'No...no, I don't want it now. Not this way and not when you and I are...er...involved.'

Andreo quirked a questioning brow. 'That's not a sensible decision.'

'I think that's *my*—'

'No, you should start thinking like the career woman that you keep on telling me you are, *cara*,' Andreo countered with sardonic bite, and left her.

While Pippa dealt with Lester Saunders, however, she asked herself why it was that she had automatically rejected the job that she had longed to have just two short weeks earlier. Was she that committed to her plans to relocate in France? Or had Cheryl's appointment soured her on the idea of remaining at Venstar? Whatever, she could see that she did owe Andreo an explanation. After all, hadn't she told him that he was responsible for her loss of promotion? Naturally he wanted her to accept the position that he believed should have been hers in the first instance.

As soon as she was free, Pippa headed off to see Andreo, only to be told that he was busy and that she would have to wait. She took a seat and wished she had simply phoned Andreo direct instead of going through businesslike motions.

The receptionist leant across her desk to whisper confidentially, 'I shouldn't say but Mr D'Alessio is with his girlfriend. Apparently she's just back from working abroad.'

'Really?' Jolted and then realising that she could only be hearing office gossip, Pippa grinned. 'Tell me more.'

'She's Lili Richards...you know the famous model. You wouldn't *believe* how breathtaking she looks in the flesh!'

'Lili Richards...' Pippa had never heard of her.

'You could see how close she and Mr D'Alessio are.'

Pippa's interested smile had grown a little fixed round the edges. 'Could you?'

'Yes. The minute she saw him, she just dived on him. A reaction most of us could sympathise with. Let's face it, he's to die for,' the receptionist said dreamily. 'And with his wild reputation, I bet she's been worried sick that he would find someone else while she was away...'

Pippa's mobile pulsed in her pocket. She took it out. It was Andreo calling and her tension dissolved. Honestly, an attractive woman visited him and the office grapevine went mental on colourful rumours!

'I can't make lunch,' Andreo informed her without any preamble.

Pippa's brow indented. 'But I wanted to talk to you—'

'Unfortunately, some business has come up. I'll call you later... OK?'

Pippa opened her dry mouth but no sound emerged.

'OK?' Andreo prompted, sounding cool, distant and impatient.

'OK,' she almost croaked and he rang off.

Her hand trembling, Pippa put her mobile back in her pocket and slowly rose upright.

'The boss and Lili Richards are about to leave!' the receptionist was gasping into the phone for someone else's benefit.

No, she wasn't going to hang about behaving like a possessive girlfriend who didn't trust him. She began to move down the corridor. All along it heads were emerging from offices. Every employee on the floor seemed to be angling to get a first-hand look at Andreo and his visitor. Pippa backed into a clump of indoor plants and hovered. He had said he had business and if he said he had business, she believed him because she trusted him absolutely. She was only hanging around to celebrity-spot.

Andreo strode into view and hit the lift button. He was not alone. A woman who looked even to Pippa's unappreciative gaze like a fantasy pin-up was clinging to his arm. She had a mane of baby blonde hair and flawless features. She was just beautiful, just really, really, really beautiful, Pippa conceded in a daze. A famous model, yes, she looked as if she would be famous. There was something unearthly about someone that beautiful who did not even seem to be wearing make-up. Something rather sick-making too...

Maybe Lili Richards was really spoilt and had made it difficult for Andreo to avoid taking her out to lunch. Maybe she was a client, a family friend...a sister, cousin, childhood playmate? Maybe Andreo had been bullied into it. Maybe he was being kidnapped.

While Pippa watched, Lili slid caressing hands beneath Andreo's suit jacket with the familiarity of a lover confident of her welcome. Making it patently obvious that she couldn't keep her sex-starved hands off him, she stretched up to kiss him with similar enthusiasm...at which point Pippa could no longer stand to look.

'Looks like they're headed for the nearest bed!' she heard someone laugh.

Forty seconds later, Pippa was horribly sick in the cloakroom. She reeled dizzily back from the cubicle wall and struggled to get a grip on herself. But indelibly etched on her mind's eye was Andreo and his girlfriend. Two very beautiful human beings perfectly matched. Dear heaven, how could she have believed in him, trusted him? Pippa Plain...just when had she allowed herself to forget that that was her nickname?

Feeling like a robot, she freshened up as best she could and went off to clear her desk.

'Is it true that Ricky and Cheryl have been sacked?' Jonelle gushed.

'Yes.'

'So you'll be the new manager, then,' Jonelle assumed.

'I don't want the job any more.'

'Of course...you're seeing Mr D'Alessio,' the blonde murmured soft and low and admiring.

Pippa froze.

'We worked out it was you at the party by the second bunch of flowers,' Jonelle confided with an appreciative giggle. 'You really know how to surprise people, don't you?'

'Yeah... I just dumped him,' Pippa responded, wondering how long it would take for word of Lili's existence to work back to the finance section.

She went home and phoned HR to tell them that no, sorry, do what they will, she wasn't coming back *ever*. Then she undressed and put the designer suit, the shoes and all the dripping flowers and the cards she had saved into a bin bag. Pulling out a couple of suitcases, she began to pack. Unable to tolerate even the minor risk of Andreo trying to see her again, she decided to check into a hotel for the night. But before she left her home, she had the bin-bag collected for delivery to Andreo's apartment. Not that she imagined that either he or Lili would get out of bed to answer the doorbell.

CHAPTER SEVEN

PIPPA LEANT ON the ancient stone balustrade bounding the shaded terrace at Duvernay and tried to suppress all her unhappy and self-pitying thoughts in appreciation of the wonderful views stretching in every direction.

The château's glorious formal gardens were surrounded by rolling green fields that in turn gave way to apple orchards said to produce some of the best cider in the world. The remainder of the vast Duvernay estate, the ancestral home of Tabby's husband, Christien Laroche, was the equivalent of a densely wooded nature reserve. But only a few miles to the west lay the jagged Breton coastline of rocky cliffs, sandy coves and picturesque fishing ports.

Her fabulous bedroom suite was worthy of a five star hotel and she had been royally entertained. For two long weeks she had done her best to put on a cheerful front for her hosts' benefit, for who wanted to entertain a miserable, weepy guest? Unfortunately, being in the company of a very happy married couple had only made her feel more betrayed, more alone and more depressed.

Christien Laroche had been incredibly nice to her. In fact

Tabby's husband had been so much kinder than the rather arrogant character whom Pippa had recalled from the past that she had honestly wondered whether Christien had guessed that his wife's childhood friend was suffering from a broken heart.

Yes, Pippa was no longer kidding herself: she had fallen madly in love with Andreo. She had pretended she was in control when she was not. But common sense told her why she had never actually got around to making arrangements to let her London home and why she had been waiting to the last possible minute to hand in her notice at Venstar. It would only have taken one encouraging word from Andreo to persuade her to drop any idea of making a permanent move to France. Neither her pride nor her intelligence had got a look-in when it came to Andreo D'Alessio.

While his lovely girlfriend had been abroad and unavailable, Andreo had used Pippa to fill the vacancy in his bed and satisfy his sexual needs. She despised herself for having surrendered her body so easily. What had seemed so very special now seemed cheap and tawdry. Andreo had lied about being free of other entanglements but then as she was well aware many otherwise upright men thought nothing of the lies that went hand in hand with infidelity. And she could not accuse Andreo of having promised her love or any kind of a future.

So why on earth had Andreo repeatedly attempted to contact her since she had left London? Surely he had guessed that she had found out about Lili? Yet he had initially texted her innumerable times. When that had failed to draw a response he had left half a dozen messages on her mobile phone. Messages that had sounded genuinely anxious about her apparent vanishing act. What on earth had he been playing at? Had the dustbin bag she sent him not been explanation enough? She had changed her phone number but had reluctantly passed on her new one to Marco when he had begged as hard as a fourteen-year-old boy could beg not to be made to pay for his big brother's sins.

Tabby wandered out onto the terrace with a pretty toddler

maternally anchored to one hip. While her five-year-old son, Jake, bore a close resemblance to his darkly handsome father, Jolie, her one-year-old daughter, had her mother's toffee-coloured hair and lively green eyes.

'I *love* this dress.' Tabby smoothed an appreciative hand over the garment chosen by her friend from her favourite maternity shop, for it was styled to flatter the rounded shape of a woman more than four months pregnant. 'I'm so grateful you went shopping with Christien. Left to himself, he always goes for fancy formal stuff and in this climate I prefer casual and comfortable.'

'The summers here are warm.' Pippa tossed her damp hair with her hand to cool the nape of her neck. In the act of tilting her head back, she was assailed by a sudden giddiness that forced her to steady herself on the balustrade with both hands.

Oh, dear, she thought fearfully, lashes lowering to conceal the anxious look clouding her eyes. More than a week had already passed since she had first noted that her period was late in arriving, an event unusual enough to rouse her concern. In addition, she had felt rather queasy on several occasions. Now she had had a minor dizzy spell. She knew the most common signs of pregnancy as well as most young women. However, she also suspected that her emotional highs and lows and even worry might well be making her imagine symptoms and could also have interfered with her system.

'You like Christien better than you used to, don't you?' Tabby prompted with amused satisfaction.

Dredging herself from her uneasy thoughts, Pippa smiled. 'I've only really got the chance to get to know him properly since I came to stay.'

'He's so confident that he used to set your teeth on edge and I can understand that after the way your dad treated your mum and you.' Tabby sighed with sympathy. 'I don't blame you for distrusting men with strong characters.'

Pippa was disconcerted because Tabby seemed to be alluding to an issue that Pippa had believed was a Stevenson family secret.

Reading her friend's expression, Tabby winced. 'Oh, no, you didn't realise I knew about—'

'Dad and his other women?' Pippa strove to look unconcerned.

Tabby grimaced. 'My stepmother let the cat out of the bag during that awful final holiday. Her flirting with your father to annoy mine didn't exactly add to the friendly atmosphere. I felt so sorry for your mother.'

'She was a gentle soul and miserable with Dad.' Pippa discovered that she could feel almost grateful for the opportunity to finally express her pain on her late mother's behalf. She would never forget overhearing her father telling her mother that he was entitled to stray when he had such an unattractive wife. 'He could say very cruel things.'

'It was his way of controlling you and your mum,' Tabby opined. 'But a man can be strong without needing to hurt and humiliate women.'

'I know that.' But Pippa was only agreeing in the hope that that would conclude a subject that went too close to the bone for comfort. There had been nothing weak about Andreo, but that had not prevented him from hurting and humiliating her, she reflected painfully.

'Do you?' Tabby gave her a troubled look. 'Or has your dad's big, scary shadow fallen over your relationship with the Italian bloke you won't tell me about?'

'I just had a fight with… Andreo…no big deal,' Pippa quipped with forced lightness of tone, because her fierce pride would not allow her to confess the truth to Tabby, who was secure in her husband's obvious love for her and their children.

Starved of even such minor facts by her friend's reserved nature, Tabby could not hide the strength of her desire to know more. 'Did you even give Andreo the chance to say sorry?'

Pippa went pink with discomfiture and then decided to tell

a little white lie for the sake of peace. 'Actually...we're talking again. He phoned me last night—'

'Oh, that's marvellous!' Tabby gave her much taller friend a delighted hug of approbation. 'I wish Christien and I could get the chance to meet him...'

At that opportune moment, Jolie tugged at Pippa's cotton trousers and provided a welcome distraction by holding up her arms to be lifted. Pippa looked down into the little girl's trusting gaze and sunny smile and obliged. Jolie had all the confidence of a child who was growing up in an atmosphere of love and contentment. Pippa reckoned that granted the same background to her childhood she herself would have developed a healthier self-esteem.

'Come and play cars,' Jake urged in turn. 'Jolie can watch.'

Tabby rested most afternoons but it was her nanny's day off and she looked tired. Ignoring her half-hearted protests, Pippa took the children back indoors to give her friend a break.

After dinner that evening, Pippa thanked Christien and Tabby for their wonderful hospitality. In the morning she planned to board a train to the Dordogne to visit her mother's burial place for the first time. Following that she would head to Paris and seek accommodation and a new job. Christien had already offered her the use of his Paris apartment and lucrative employment, but Pippa preferred not to mix friendship with the acceptance of favours she could not return.

'Do you think I could persuade Hilary to come for a visit?' Tabby asked wistfully outside Pippa's bedroom door.

'She'd love to come, but between her little sister and the hair salon, she's very tied down,' Pippa explained ruefully. 'I wish one of us had heard from Jen but she seems to have disappeared off the face of the earth.'

'She was always very shy but I'm sure she'll get in touch eventually. In the meantime, you and me and Hilary should plan a proper get-together for the new year,' Tabby suggested before she said goodnight to Pippa.

Pippa was emerging from the shower when she heard a helicopter coming in to land. There was nothing unusual in that. The owner of an international airline, Christien flew himself most places and so did many of his social circle.

Clad in a cool white cotton nightdress, Pippa was setting out clothes for the morning when a hasty knock sounded on the door and Tabby appeared wreathed in a big grin. 'I've got a fantastic surprise for you!' her friend carolled like an excited schoolgirl. 'Close your eyes!'

Suppressing a sigh, Pippa did as she was asked. 'Can I open them yet?'

'Not until you hear the door close again...and don't feel you have to hurry down for breakfast in the morning!' Tabby giggled.

As the door snapped shut Pippa was picturing a beaker of hot chocolate topped with melted marshmallows or some such sentimental reminder of their childhood. But when her lashes swept up she got a severe shock. Instead of a soothing night drink, Tabby had delivered a six-foot-five-inch male to her guest's bedroom.

'Tabby's very sweet,' Andreo murmured smooth as black ice.

Just one look at him and Pippa felt as if she had been knifed. He was the male she had craved against her will for two endless weeks. The male she had simultaneously craved and hated, whom she had last seen being pawed by the beautiful Lili. Her tummy flipped in rejection of the cruel images flooding her memory. Angry pain was no true barrier against his hard male beauty and that raw physicality of his that made her senses sing. His charcoal grey business suit was tailored to a designer fit over his broad shoulders, lean hips and long, powerful thighs. He looked totally spectacular and her mouth ran dry.

'How the heck did you find out where I was?' she demanded fiercely. 'I didn't tell anyone!'

'When you were last on the phone to Marco, he heard someone address you in French—'

'I'll never forgive him for telling you—'

'Be fair, *bella mia*. You only asked him not to divulge your new phone number and he did respect that. I had to lean on him a little before he mentioned hearing French being spoken—'

Pippa dealt him an aghast look of reproach. 'You bully... he's only fourteen!'

'And even at that tender age, Marco has a healthy regard for family honour and loyalty,' Andreo delivered dryly.

'You still haven't explained how you discovered I was here—'

'I had your background investigated—'

Pippa stared back at him in disbelief. 'You did...*what?*'

'You have strong connections to France through your own family tree. Your friendship with Tabby and Christien Laroche made this an obvious port of call—'

'I can't believe that you dared to come here—'

'I dare...believe it, *amore*,' Andreo incised.

'Nor can I imagine what crazy stories you told to talk your way through the door—'

Andreo dealt her a look of hauteur. 'What need had I to tell stories? Your friend seemed unsurprised to see me,' he stated grimly. '*Santo Cielo*... I had only to say who I was and she offered to take me up to your room!'

Severe embarrassment claimed Pippa. Her own little white lie about Andreo having phoned the night before to heal their differences had come back to haunt her. Naturally Tabby had assumed that Andreo's arrival would be a wonderful surprise for Pippa and that she herself was helping along a lovers' reconciliation.

Brilliant golden eyes clung to her fast-reddening face. 'Care to explain that? Or am I supposed to assume that every guy who calls here asking for you is shown straight up to your bedroom, no questions asked?'

Infuriated by that dig, which pierced right to the heart of her belief that she had already made an enormous fool of herself over him, Pippa lost her temper and swung up her hand.

'*Don't...*' Closing lean fingers round her wrist before she could deliver that potential slap, Andreo sent her a hard look of censure and voiced that single word with icy restraint.

Pippa retrieved her arm from his hold, rage and mortification united inside her now. She was so mad with him that she could hardly catch her breath to speak. 'Get out of here, then!'

'No...' His refusal was cool and level.

'Then I'll move to another room...'

'If you like... I'll fish my bedtime reading out of my case and settle down for the night,' Andreo murmured soft and smooth.

Temper had taken Pippa to the door, but at those words that seemed to offer an unknown threat she stilled, her brow indenting. 'What are you talking about?'

Reaching past her, Andreo opened the door, swept up the leather case and garment bags draped over it and lifted them into the room.

'Andreo?' Pippa queried in bewilderment, unable to comprehend why he should suddenly remove the pressure on her and behave as if what she did was immaterial to him.

'You don't appear to grasp how angry I am with you,' he breathed in sudden warning. 'You owe me an explanation and a grovelling apology—'

Pippa folded her arms with a jerk. 'I don't think so.'

'And in the absence of said grovelling apology, I am likely to sink as low as a guy can sink—'

'Tell me something I don't know! I've already seen you swarming all over your blonde girlfriend!' Pippa suddenly slung at him with such feeling rage and pain that her voice had a crack in it.

Andreo studied her with fixed attention, eyes a shimmering gold below spiky black lashes. 'Correction. She was swarming over me. So you *did* see me with Lili. I wondered about that—'

'You said you couldn't go out for lunch with me because you had business to take care of...some business!' Pippa bawled at him full throttle.

'Lili was with me when I phoned you. Within her hearing I could hardly tell you that I was taking her out to lunch to dump her.'

To dump her? *To dump her?* Those magical words echoed in ringing decibels through Pippa's brain and made it quite impossible for her to think of anything else. He had been planning to *end* his relationship with Lili Richards?

Andreo sent her a grim glance. 'Of course, had you stayed in the same building, not to mention the same country you would have found that fact out for yourself because I would have brought you up to speed on events when I saw you that night.'

Momentarily, Pippa had been silenced. She had to angle back against the high bed for support because her legs felt shaky. Andreo had chosen her in preference to that gorgeous blonde fantasy woman? As a statement of intent, it was almost more than she could credit and then a little native wit crept back in to remind her that he had sworn that he was free of involvement with any other woman.

'You lied to me,' Pippa condemned. 'When we first met I asked if you were involved with anyone else and you said no.'

'As far as I was concerned it was true. Lili knew she would be travelling for a couple of months. Our relationship was casual. We agreed that if either of us met anyone else we would be free to follow it up. I met you. Lili said she met no one, but I suspect that what she really meant was that she met no one worth mentioning,' Andreo completed with rich cynicism.

So, according to his version of events, Lili had just existed in the background of his life, a casual bed partner when she'd been physically available. Surely that was all that she, Pippa, could have been to him as well? Had she not originally decided to allow their relationship to run only until she left for France? Hadn't that been the most sensible attitude? After all, Andreo was not looking for a long-term relationship with her either. It was better to be the one leaving than the one who was left.

In any case, how could she trust a word he said about Lili

Richards? Since when was it possible to believe anything a man said when it came to the *other* woman in his life? How many times had her late father lied to her trusting mother and persuaded her that an affair had been over when it had been in fact still continuing? Or even that his extra-marital activities had existed in her mother's imagination alone? How many times had he voiced arguments that had sounded credible but that had eventually turned out to be cruel, unfeeling lies?

'Any comment?' Andreo murmured flatly.

Pippa shot him a driven glance, imagining how she would feel watching him leave her again only to recoil from that prospect. No matter how bitter and suspicious she was, she still had to fight a demeaning desire to keep him with her. Ashamed of her weakness, she tilted her chin. 'Coming here was a waste of your time!'

Andreo frowned. 'I don't believe I've ever had a more one-sided dialogue with a woman. You don't even appreciate what you've done.'

'What *I've* done?' Pippa echoed with incredulity.

'*Sì*. Without a word of warning or explanation to anyone, you vanished into thin air—'

'I handed in my notice and I returned your gifts…didn't that all speak for itself?'

'That you were annoyed about something? Didn't it once cross your mind that when you disappeared I'd be worried sick about you?'

Pippa jerked up a rebellious shoulder. 'Why should it have done?'

Savage anger flared in Andreo's censorious gaze and he moved closer. 'We were in a relationship. I gave you no reason to believe that I would do anything to hurt or betray you. *Dio mio*…you trusted me enough to give me a key to your home!'

Her throat closing over on a flood of tears, Pippa focused on a point to one side of him for she did not want to be reminded of how easily she had initially given her trust.

'When you didn't answer my messages I went to your home to check that you weren't lying there ill. I could see that you had packed and left in a hurry and that remained a source of genuine anxiety to me.'

Involuntarily, Pippa glanced up and encountered scorching golden eyes of contempt that froze her to the spot.

'At that point I had no idea that you had already terminated your employment with Venstar. Concern prompted me to hire private investigators in an effort to trace your movements. Of course, a less honourable guy would just have sat down and opened your diary and read it from start to finish!'

Those final terrifying words hung there in the air while Pippa stared back at Andreo as if he had just developed horns and cloven feet. Every scrap of colour had ebbed from her face. 'My... my diary? You *know* I keep a diary?'

'It was hard to miss. There it was beside your bed—bright pink and furry and adorned with the words, "My diary" and a tiny girlie padlock which I could break with one finger.' Andreo seemed to positively savour that description and assurance.

'You saw my diary...' Pippa was sick with horror at him having got that close to her every written secret thought, especially when her every written secret thought had recently related to him. Why had she given him the key to her home? Why had she not had the wit to hide her diary away?

'Saw it and lifted it—'

'Lifted it?' Pippa gasped strickenly.

'It's just amazing the way you're finally giving me the attention I deserve, *cara mia*,' Andreo remarked silkily.

Pippa was paralysed to the spot. 'Did you break the padlock?'

'Not as yet but it strikes me as the most straightforward solution to your refusal to talk—'

'I'm not refusing to talk...where's my diary?' she steeled herself to demand.

'In my case—'

'You brought it with you?'

Andreo gave her a silent nod of confirmation.

Pippa breathed in very deep and thought fast but there was just no way out that she could see. 'I'll do just about anything to stop you reading my diary.'

'That's what I reckoned too,' Andreo confided, deadpan.

'Will you just give it back to me?' she prompted very softly and gently.

'No. Right now, it's a negotiating tool and a guarantee that you think and listen and eventually account for your behaviour,' Andreo delineated without hesitation.

Her teeth gritted and her fingernails flexed and bit into her palms.

'But in the short term, I'm willing to grant you a little breathing space. After all, it's late, we're in someone else's home and you're obviously ready for bed. We can talk tomorrow—'

'I'm leaving in the morning for the Dordogne—'

'I know. Tabby did mention how close I'd come to missing you,' Andreo interposed evenly. 'Isn't it fortunate that I have a home in the same region? You'll be able to travel down with me.'

At the mere idea that she might be willing to travel anywhere with him, Pippa breathed in so deep and long that she was almost convinced she would burst.

'Is it OK if I have a shower?' Andreo enquired, setting his case down on the luggage rack by the wall.

'You *can't* sleep here!' Pippa exclaimed, blue eyes huge.

'No problem. Perhaps you'd do the honours with our hostess and request a separate room for me.'

Pippa paled and tried to steel herself to the prospect of rising to that challenge. Tabby would be embarrassed by her assumption that her guests would happily share the same bedroom. Pippa would be embarrassed asking for an arrangement that was the equivalent of a public announcement about the hostile state of her current relationship with Andreo. Colour warming her cheeks, she dropped her head.

'You might as well sleep here tonight. It's a big bed and it's late and Tabby and Christien have probably already gone to bed,' she muttered grudgingly.

As he watched her visibly squirm at the idea of approaching her friend unholy amusement at her discomfiture made Andreo say with exaggerated courtesy, 'I wouldn't dream of it. It's obvious that you're uncomfortable with the idea.'

Pippa snatched in a steadying breath but she was relieved that he had sufficient sensitivity to appreciate how difficult she would find such a situation. 'It's all right. I'll be fine,' she said woodenly.

Andreo shed his jacket and tie, unbuttoned his shirt. He had been so angry when he'd arrived, and he still was, but all of a sudden he just wanted to laugh out loud. He very much doubted that their hosts had gone to bed at eleven at night. It was inconceivable to Andreo that he would allow other people's opinions to influence his behaviour, for he was fearless when it came to pursuing any course in which he knew himself to be in the right. It was evident that Pippa was much more vulnerable and he studied her with keen interest. Covered from head to toe in a shapeless garment that would have looked at home in a coffin, she was scrambling into the bed in extreme haste.

While he stripped with the most shocking lack of self-consciousness and not a decent ounce of the extreme awkwardness that Pippa felt he ought to have been suffering in her presence, she turned her back on him to glare at the wall. But the image of his lithe bronzed masculinity travelled with her as powerfully as if he still stood in front of her. She was furious with herself for being severely tempted to sneakily spy on him while he undressed. After all she had said and done, what sort of sense would that make?

But then was there any sense at all to what was happening between them now? Suppose he was telling her the truth about Lili Richards? Why, after all, would he follow her all the way to France if she had only been the two-week equivalent of a one-night stand? Maybe he had been planning to visit the country anyway: he did own a house in France, she reminded herself.

She lay in bed, tossing and turning, listening with one ear to the distant sound of the shower running in the connecting bathroom. It shook her that she couldn't get her thoughts into any kind of reasonable order. She was in total turmoil. In search of an explanation, she looked back to the outset of their affair...

She had spent ten consecutive days with Andreo D'Alessio. Only work hours had intervened and they had soon alleviated that problem by stealing at least two hours together around midday. In retrospect she was shocked at the feckless attitudes she had fallen into. Andreo had wanted her and that had been that: she couldn't have cared less about Venstar. For the entirety of those ten days she had lived entirely for Andreo. They had not spent a single night apart. The one evening on which she had suggested that she ought to go home, Andreo had wasted no time in dissuading her from the notion.

Never before had she been so indescribably happy. That reality spoke for itself, her more sober self interposed at that point. Happiness of that magnitude was not meant to last and once she had tasted the best she should have known that it could only get worse from there on in. How much worse? Andreo was an unrepentant womaniser...and there was a possibility that she might be expecting his baby!

No, no, *no*! Pippa shrieked inside her mind, fighting to throw that scary thought back out again. The chances of her being pregnant were very small, she told herself doggedly. If her cycle did not return to normal soon, she would consider approaching a doctor. A little voice she did not want to listen to reminded her that her own mother might only have conceived once but that conception had actually taken place when her parents had only been together for two short weeks!

Andreo sauntered out of the bathroom. All that stood between him and total nudity was a pair of seriously trendy Armani boxers. Pippa stared. She preferred distracting herself to suffering what she regarded as almost hysterical fears relating to pregnancy, or almost as bad, succumbing to a need to mentally dissect every blasted minute she had ever spent in his company. Her mesmerised attention roamed over the hard contours of his strong, muscular shoulders, broad, powerful chest, the flat slab of his stomach and long, strong thighs. Lean muscle rippled in the smooth bronze expanse of his back and narrow hips as he closed his case and straightened, a magnificent male animal in his athletic and sexual prime. The tip of her tongue slunk out to moisten her dry lower lip. She was conscious of the heated, heavy rise of excitement low in her pelvis, the aching pulse of moist responsive heat.

'No...' Andreo said softly.

Her reactions slowed by her distance from rational thought, Pippa blinked and focused on him. 'Sorry?'

'I'm off limits. You would have to get down on your knees and beg before I would forgive you for your behaviour—'

'Off limits?' Pippa was unable to credit her own hearing. 'Get down on my knees and beg? What for?'

'Sex...sex with me, *amore*.' Andreo tossed back the sheet and came down beside her, black hair tousled, stunning dark golden eyes burnished to sizzling gold. 'Don't think I don't know when you want me—'

Pippa turned the same colour as a ripe beetroot, yanked up a pillow and tried to thump him with it. 'That's utter nonsense!'

'And how violent you can be when you don't get it.' Removing the pillow from her fevered grasp, Andreo tossed it behind his head and stretched with the flexing, fluid grace of a prowling tiger. Angling a knowing appraisal at her, he smiled with unholy complacency.

In one furious jerk, Pippa sat up. 'You know nothing about me—'

'I know you kept *every* single flower and card I ever sent you, even the dying blooms,' Andreo commented smooth as silk.

'So what?' she raked at him. 'I hate waste!'

'Tabby said you had been inconsolable since your arrival but trying hard to cover it up,' Andreo added.

Ready to claw like a wildcat, Pippa launched herself at him and hissed scornfully, 'There's no way Tabby would say something like that to you…she's my friend!'

Andreo took advantage of her proximity to close strong hands round her forearms and tip her down on top of him.

Sudden silence fell. Her hands had come down on his chest to steady herself, slender fingers spreading on warm, hair-roughened muscles. Her breath caught in her throat. When her startled blue eyes collided with his burning gold scrutiny, the atmosphere was electric and the fight and the anger went out of her as surely as if he had pulled a switch.

Andreo meshed a lean-fingered hand in the tumble of her cinnamon-coloured curls and stole one devastating, passionate kiss. Breathing shallowly, he freed her reddened mouth again and lifted her back onto her own side of the bed.

Excitement had seethed up in a tempestuous greedy burst inside Pippa. Her body was clamouring for the satisfaction that he had taught her to want. She rolled over, and like an iron filing drawn by a magnet, reached for him again. But Andreo dealt her a smouldering look and set her back from him in unashamed rejection. 'I'm still too angry with you…'

'Angry?' she repeated, aghast and in shock from what had just happened.

Andreo settled grim dark golden eyes on her. 'If I ever want someone else, I will tell you up front. That's how I am. I don't lie or sneak around. I don't need to. To date there may have been a fair number of women in my life but none could ever accuse me of dishonesty or infidelity, *cara*.'

'Lili Richards touched you…*that* was infidelity!' Pippa slammed back in a ferocious surge of disagreement. 'One finger on any part of you qualifies as infidelity!'

Andreo screened his amused gaze. 'Is that a fact? I don't like being pawed in public. I think it's tasteless. Presumably you didn't see me push her away and ask her to cool it—'

'No, I didn't. And before you come over all smug and think that you broke my heart and that that's why I left London, think again!' Pippa hauled up the sheet and turned her slim, elegant back on him. 'Our relationship had run its course and it was time for it to end. I decided to go to France right at the *start* of our affair and I never once swerved from that decision!'

During the blistering silence that fell in answer to that declaration, hot stinging tears inched out from below Pippa's lowered eyelids and slid down her cheeks onto the pillow. She knew she would not be able to sleep by his side.

CHAPTER EIGHT

HAVING LAIN AWAKE for half the night, Pippa drifted off around seven and woke with a start an hour later. Her nostrils flared on the rich, aromatic smell of fresh coffee and her stomach instantly rebelled. Eyes flying wide in dismay, she threw herself off the bed, hurtled past Andreo where he stood with a laden breakfast tray and raced at all possible speed into the bathroom. She was sick but, mercifully, it was over quickly and she felt fine in the aftermath.

'Are you OK?' Andreo enquired from the doorway.

Her embarrassment intense, Pippa stalked across the bathroom and slammed shut the door in his face, snapping, 'Can't I even be ill in peace?'

After a lengthy shower, an even slower drying-off of her curls into fluffy childish bangs that infuriated her, she emerged and found the bedroom empty, which, oddly enough, annoyed her even more than a barrage of questions would have done. When she went downstairs, Tabby took her into the dining room for breakfast.

'Andreo said you weren't well. He's worried about you...he's a real hunk too, isn't he?' Tabby lowered her voice to add with an irreverent grin. 'Christien gets on with him like a house on fire.'

'I could have forecast that without a crystal ball,' Pippa confided. 'Where are they?'

'Well, they made a great play about going off to talk business...but I bet you anything that they'll end up either down in the wine cellar or having a spin in Christien's latest new car,' Tabby declared with her warm, contagious laugh.

'What's the fastest way of finding out if you're pregnant?' Pippa asked her friend in a rush.

Tabby blinked and breathed in deep and let the silence linger before saying, 'I could take you to see my doctor. He'll do a test.'

Tabby made the necessary phone call while Pippa sipped at a cup of tea but only shredded a piece of toast for she was too nervous to feel hungry. As they walked out to Tabby's car her friend gave her a rueful appraisal. 'Thanks for trusting me.'

'Terror loves company,' Pippa quipped half under her breath.

An hour later, she knew for sure: she was going to have a baby. No longer could she hide her head in the sand and hope that only nerves were upsetting her system. But she was shattered by that confirmation.

'What are you planning to do?' Tabby asked her friend worriedly during the drive back to the château.

'I don't know,' Pippa confided unevenly, and it was the truth.

She had had such an unhappy childhood and she had only to picture some poor child suffering in a similar way for her heart to sink. Of course, she knew that she would never punish a child for poor academic performance. She would not comment on her child's lack of good looks either. Nor would she ever tell her son or her daughter as her mother had once told her that she was only staying in a bad, destructive relationship for *their* sake.

'Talk it over with Andreo...he *is*... I mean...the baby is his?' Tabby gave her friend an apologetic look.

Pippa nodded in rueful confirmation.

'He's fabulous with kids,' Tabby informed her eagerly. 'Jake and Jolie climbed all over him this morning and he was very good-natured about it. You've just been taken by surprise, Pippa. You'll get used to the idea.'

'I'm sure I will...' The very concept of accepting that new life was growing inside her shook Pippa deeply. It seemed so extraordinary, almost a miracle, something worthy of celebration rather than fear and anxiety.

'I adore babies,' Tabby admitted, bringing her car to a halt outside her huge imposing home and switching off the engine. 'Christien thought we should wait until Jolie was older but I didn't want to. I prefer not to have big age gaps between our children.'

Christien and Andreo strode out through the front entrance to greet them.

One glimpse of Andreo's riveting dark features and Pippa's heart skipped a beat. Casually clad in an aqua short-sleeved shirt and beige chinos, he looked heart-stoppingly handsome She thought of how she had planned to tell him that she was already booked on a train to the Dordogne and abandoned the idea. Now that she knew about the baby, Andreo would have to be told as well. And perhaps, she thought unhappily, it was time she stopped trying to tell herself that she would be able to walk away from him without pain, for that was an outright lie.

'You didn't say you were going out, *ma belle*,' Christien said to his wife, lean strong face reproving.

'You didn't say you were taking Andreo out for a spin round the estate in the McLaren...or did I miss that announcement?' his wife fielded cheekily.

Andreo decided to take advantage of their audience and Pippa's unusually timid aspect, for her bright blue eyes had yet to meet his. 'Your luggage is already on board the helicopter.'

Involuntarily, Pippa experienced a moment of amusement. He had not been able to kidnap her but he had kidnapped her luggage and her diary. Little more than ten minutes later, their farewells exchanged, they were walking towards the helipad.

'How are you feeling?'

'Great…this morning was just one of those things,' she dismissed hurriedly. 'Where's this property of yours in the Dordogne?'

'Near Bourdeilles. The countryside around there reminded me of Tuscany,' he volunteered. 'Unspoilt farmland and woods. You'll like my house. It's very relaxing.'

'I'm sure it is, but I'll be taking a room in Brantome…my mother is buried near there,' she responded brittly. 'This is my first trip back to France since I was seventeen and something of a pilgrimage. There was a car crash that summer and my mother and several of my parents' friends died. If I stayed with you, you wouldn't find me good company.'

Andreo had read about the accident in the investigation report. Having spoken to his pilot, he watched her struggle to do up her seat belt and intervened to do it for her. Her pale, delicate profile was taut, the tension in her slender body as pronounced as that etched in the unusual clumsiness of her hands.

They landed at a private airfield and continued their journey in the Mercedes four-wheel drive that awaited them. The landscape was becoming familiar to her and she was silent. Haunted by painful memories of that fatal summer, she finally closed her eyes and drifted off to sleep.

'We're here…'

When Andreo wakened Pippa, she could not recall ever having slept more heavily. She clambered out of the car in as much of a daze as a sleepwalker. Having simply assumed that Andreo was planning to drop her off in the centre of Brantome, she was disconcerted to find herself standing instead outside a small rural church.

'I remembered the details from the investigation report.' Andreo reached into the car boot and lifted out a beautiful bouquet of fresh flowers. 'I stopped off in a village on the way for these but I should have woken you up so that you could choose—'

'No, they're lovely.' Her voice wobbled, for she was touched by his kindness and suddenly very grateful indeed not to be alone.

Andreo curved a strong arm to her spine because even in the warmth of the sunshine she was trembling. It did not take them long to find what they sought in the beautifully kept graveyard. She knelt down and gently laid the flowers on the springy turf and struggled to maintain control over her unsettled emotions.

'That summer we were staying in a village only a stone's throw from here. It was a disastrous, horrible holiday,' she confided, the words tumbling from her in an enervated torrent. 'Tabby was all tied up with Christien and her ghastly stepmother, Lisa, was flirting like mad with my dad. He loved all the attention. I had a fight with Mum on the day of the accident. I told her we should go home and leave Dad free to flirt with Lisa and Mum was mad with me…and I said I was ashamed of her because she let Dad treat her like dirt!' A sob was wrenched from Pippa. 'We made up but I should never have spoken to her like that.'

Andreo rested level dark golden eyes on her distraught face. 'She was your mother. She would have understood, *cara mia*.'

But Pippa could not stop the tears falling, for she had never come to terms with the terrible costs of that crash or the frightening emotional turmoil into which she had been cast in its aftermath. How could she ever have forgiven herself for wishing even momentarily that it had been her mother and not her father who had survived? For hating her father for insisting that she could not be spared from his bedside to travel to her own mother's funeral? Andreo just held her close and let her cry.

'OK…' Recognising when the storm was over, Andreo assisted her back into the Mercedes.

Pippa felt drained and yet curiously at peace as well. For the first time she noticed that it was a seriously beautiful day, and while Andreo was driving through the town she told him about her infatuation with Pete and subsequent disillusionment. 'Men always did go for Tabby in a big way,' she completed with an accepting shrug of her shoulders.

'She lacks your elegance,' Andreo drawled. 'He had no taste.'

The Mercedes purred through sleepy Gascon villages lined with ancient stone houses. She had forgotten how lovely the lush green landscape was in early summer. The little town of Borde-illes was on the River Dronne and she could remember visiting the tall dignified château that towered over the other buildings.

'Aren't you going the wrong way?' she murmured.

'I'm taking you home with me, *amore*.'

'I should argue but I can't be bothered.' But she knew even as she said it that she was talking nonsense, making excuses sooner than admit that wild horses could not have torn her from his side. She just needed to be with him and she refused to question why that was. A couple of kilometres beyond the town he swung off the road and into a dusty laneway where he paused and lowered the window.

'That's it over there...'

She looked across a field of yellow black-eyed sunflowers to see the building with the tower that sat on the far side of it. Fashioned of the local honey-coloured stone and roofed with warm reddish-brown tiles, the house looked as if it had stood in that precise spot for ever.

'How old is it?' she asked as he drove on down the lane.

'Fourteenth century. It was a priory and it holds a special place in my heart. I bought it when I was eighteen—'

'Eighteen?' she gasped, sitting up out of her slump.

'I ran away from home because my family persisted in treating me like a teenager—'

'You *were* a teenager at eighteen—'

Andreo gave her a mocking glance. 'We'll talk about my misspent youth some other time.'

He drew up in the deep shade of a grove of stately chestnut

trees. At the foot of the hill, a slow-moving river wound through a meadow. There was a stillness that she could literally hear. Drenched in late afternoon sunshine, the house drew her out of the car and the shadows. She roved ahead of him to where the ancient studded wooden door already stood wide in welcome on a hall painted a deep blue as intense as the sky.

'Blue...'

'My favourite colour,' Andreo breathed huskily from behind her. 'Just like your eyes.'

If I didn't already love him, Pippa reflected helplessly, I would love him now for talking nonsense and owning this glorious house. 'Is there someone else here?'

'I asked my housekeeper to air it, stock up for my arrival and then go home again,' Andreo confided. 'She lives only a couple of fields away.'

'You plan everything, don't you?'

'Don't you?'

She was surprised by that comeback, even more surprised to acknowledge that he was right. She did plan virtually everything in her life. Only she hadn't planned on him or the baby. Once more she thought of the baby as the tiny new life force it was: part of him, part of her, an individual created between them and dependent on them both. Her throat thickened. Slowly she turned to face him, blue eyes softening as she let her admiring attention rest on his breathtakingly handsome features. If their baby was a boy, he would be very handsome, and if their baby was a girl, she hoped she inherited her blue eyes and Andreo's gorgeous black hair.

'You'll stay, *cara*?'

With difficulty she shook free of her sentimental little daydream and focused on him. He was temptation personified to her. 'But only—'

Andreo placed a reproachful forefinger briefly against her full pink lower lip. 'No boundaries,' he warned her lazily. 'I don't like boundaries.'

'I need them.'

'You have to trust me.'

She felt like glass he could see through: naked and vulnerable. He had cut through her intended protests to the heart of the matter. An issue of trust. He might as well have asked her to scale Everest barefoot, she thought in dismay. She did not think that she had it in her to truly trust a male of his calibre. He was far too rich and good-looking. *Not* his fault, she conceded painfully. Nature had blessed him with lean, dark, devastating features and an incredibly powerful sexual aura. He had become a target for women and had learnt to appreciate the extent of his own power. But wasn't she going to have to trust him again to tell him about the baby she carried? How could she expect more from him than she was prepared to give herself?

'No boundaries,' Andreo repeated softly, closing a lean strong hand over hers and leading her up the wide stone staircase to the upper floor.

In the bedroom, her attention was stolen by the massive arched window that looked right out over the river valley. The view was spectacular and the light so strong that it hurt her eyes with its brilliance. Coming to a halt behind her, Andreo ran down the zip on her dress and lingered to press his lips to the soft, sensitive spot where her neck met the slope of her shoulder.

The unbearably delicious sensation made her squirm in his hold and with a helpless gasp she let her head fall back. He skimmed the light dress down over her arms and she curved her hands down to ensure the fabric did not catch and linger at her wrists.

'I'm shameless,' she muttered, taken aback by her own collusion.

Andreo uttered a husky laugh. 'I *wish...*'

Pippa tensed, eyes wide and vulnerable. 'Do you?'

'Only teasing, *amore*. I like you just as you are which means that you have to resist every other guy around but be a com-

plete pushover for me,' Andreo confided as he spun her round
in his arms.

Her heart was pounding like crazy. He bent down, swept her
up with an easy masculine strength that was incredibly seductive and tumbled her down onto the cool quilted spread.

Pippa surveyed him with sudden shaken intensity as if she
couldn't quite work out how she had ended up there. 'I shouldn't
be doing this—'

'That's what you like about me... I send you off the rails,
amore.'

'And where do you get that idea?'

'You don't take risks...you're the lady with the colour-coded
wardrobe, the books in alphabetical order, the tidiest desk. But
you took a risk on me.' A vibrant smile that made her heart flip
slashed his lean, powerful face.

'I want my diary back,' she told him unsteadily.

Andreo laughed. 'You know I won't read it. Last night was
payback time and I enjoyed making you dance to my tune. But
don't *ever* walk out on me again without telling me that you're
leaving.'

Something in his intonation chilled her. He wasn't laughing
any more; he was warning her. But I'm not back with you again,
her conscience urged her to tell him. Only how could she tell
him what she was doing with him when she didn't know herself?
She had made a choice without even being aware of it. She was
lying half naked on his bed in his house and, for the first time in
countless days of suffocating unhappiness, she felt alive again.

'Kiss me...' she muttered unevenly.

Smouldering golden eyes raked over her slender figure, lingering on the delicate swell of her breasts above the dainty cups
of her white bra and the lithe shapely length of slender thighs
bisected by white high cut briefs. He pulled his designer shirt
over his head and tossed it aside with unashamed eagerness.
She lay there looking up at him, feeling her straining nipples

pinch tight while a wanton little frisson of heat slivered up from deep within her pelvis.

'You're so beautiful I can't keep my hands off you.' Magnificent torso bronzed and bare, Andreo lifted her up to him. She was already melting like ice-cream in the hot sun from outside in. And then he claimed her mouth with shattering carnality, penetrating between her readily parted lips with the rhythmic erotic timing of an expert lover. Instantly she caught fire, breathing in gasping shallow spurts, coming back to him again and again for more of the same. Deftly, he discarded her bra. One hand at her spine, he crushed her tender rose-tipped breasts against the hard wall of his muscular chest. Rising on her knees, liquid heat thrumming through her, she pushed even closer to find his passionate mouth again for herself.

'I want you now, *amore*,' Andreo growled thickly, pressing her back onto the bed with a sudden masculine mastery that thrilled her and hooking lean, impatient fingers into her panties to peel them off.

She lay there, hot and quivering and aching for him. She was shamelessly aware of her own readiness, of the moist secret heat that had begun gathering even before his first kiss.

He unzipped his chinos, shedding them and his boxers in a careless heap. Her breath caught in her throat at the extent of his bold arousal.

'I don't want to wait,' he murmured raggedly, staring down into her blushing face, drawn by the glow of desire and appreciation she could not hide.

Passion-glazed eyes locked to him, she angled back her hips and parted her thighs in a sudden provocative move that shocked him almost as much as it shocked her. With a ground-out Italian imprecation and his golden eyes ablaze he came down to her, a raw, fierce need stamped on his startlingly handsome face that made her body thrum with wanton anticipation. He sank into her, deep and strong and without ceremony. Like hitching a ride on a rocket, it was the most exciting event of her life. For the first time she sensed that he was no longer in control and that made her own hunger climb even higher.

'Andreo,' she framed, not even aware that she was sobbing out his name.

The sound of that urgent cry drove him on. He plunged into her faster and faster. Lost in the mindless pleasure of his pagan possession, she moved against him, frantic, fevered, abandoned in her encouragement and welcome. Her heart was racing so hard and fast she was convinced she was flying. Raw excitement sent her spiralling into a wild climax. An uncontrollable frenzy of pleasure gripped her in wave after wave of ecstasy and she writhed under him. With an uninhibited shout of satisfaction, he shuddered over her in a white-hot release that surpassed anything he had ever felt and subsided.

Pippa floated back to planet earth to find that she had both arms possessively wound round Andreo in a way that would never qualify as cool. He rolled over, kissed her breathless and kept her clamped to him with a strong arm.

'Sleep, *amore*,' he urged.

She studied him. His black lashes accentuated the tough angles of his hard, smooth cheekbones, wide strong mouth and stubborn jaw-line. He had a classic masculine profile and he was totally, absolutely gorgeous. She pushed her face into a muscular brown shoulder and breathed in the aroma of his skin with an addict's intensity.

'You can have your diary back,' he muttered with a husky sound of amusement. 'You just settled your debt for all time. That was *amazing*...'

She stayed close, for every tiny moment with him felt unbearably precious and she was convinced that telling him that she was pregnant would destroy what they had. Reality would dispel the magic. Instantly she would become the reverse of sexy and fanciable, she thought with pained regret. Instead she would become a problem: a woman with the right to decide whether or not he became a father. It was a choice he got no say in and a situation he could surely only resent. After all, he had not been careless; he had taken all possible precautions to try and ensure that she did not conceive. But fate had decided otherwise.

In truth she was in no hurry to admit that she was carrying his child, for she already knew that she would not seek a termination. She herself had been conceived outside marriage and her mother had acknowledged her right to life, so how could she do less for her own baby?

She loved Andreo and that too had to influence her feelings towards his child. Indeed she had begun to love him within minutes of meeting him. But he was not in love with her and theirs was a casual affair. A fling, frothy and fun, nothing serious, she told herself sternly, suppressing her pain at the threat of the inevitable parting ahead. How long would they have together in France? She feared that the idyll would end the instant she confessed to being pregnant.

'So amazing,' Andreo continued thoughtfully, 'That it is time to come clean—'

She tensed. 'About what?'

'Last night you said that you made plans to come to France after we met and never wavered from that goal,' he reminded her. 'That *must* have been a lie.'

Of course it had been a lie. But in the space of a heartbeat she could picture how trapped he might feel if she were to reveal that she loved him and follow that up with an announcement that she was pregnant. He would feel trapped and she would feel humiliated. Why should she sacrifice her pride to that extent? A baby that was the result of an accident in birth control during a casual affair would be rather less disturbing for him than one conceived with a woman who burdened his conscience with the additional news of her undying devotion.

'You only said it because you weren't ready to admit that all that fierce and very flattering jealousy of yours over Lili was quite unnecessary,' Andreo breathed with lethal conviction. 'I am a straightforward guy in relationships—'

'Perhaps you are, but I was only being honest,' Pippa swore in an uneasy undertone against his shoulder. 'We had a fantastic time in London but these things don't last...'

Long fingers speared into her riotous curls and lifted her head. Burnished golden eyes struck hers in a sparking collision course that made the breath catch in her throat. 'And how would a woman who has never known any other lover *know* that for a fact?' he intoned very soft and low and his accent thick on every syllable.

Her gaze veiled to hide her pain and her colour receded. 'I just knew—'

Andreo tumbled her off him and moved with disconcerting speed and dexterity to pin her under him instead. 'So I give you great sex and nothing else?'

Her face flamed and shamed embarrassment at the depths that pretence had reduced her to made her steal an unwise upward glance. She was ensnared by hot golden eyes as aggressive as an invasion force. 'Well...er—'

Andreo flashed her a scorching smile that was extremely unsettling. 'To think I wasted all that effort on soppy flowers and sentimental cards—'

'No, I really *liked*—'

'No need to pretend, *cara*.' Lithe as a jungle cat, Andreo shifted and settled between her thighs with an erotic expertise that made her heart jump inside her.

He kissed her with passionate force. She quivered, fought to concentrate, knowing she should argue in her own defence. He kissed her again and her thoughts blurred while she burned and she ached all over again for a satisfaction he had given her only minutes earlier. She blushed fierily for her own weakness. 'Andreo—?'

'Want me?' he prompted thickly, an irresistible gleam of sexy challenge in his molten gaze.

And she did, oh, how she wanted him: more than pride or common sense or reason. On every level all that was feminine in her responded to his raw masculinity and she could not fight her own nature. And on that liberating reflection, she surrendered to his passion.

Five glorious days later Pippa woke up to find herself alone, but there was nothing new in that for Andreo always got up first.

Her tummy felt queasy and, with a rueful grimace over the awareness that only Andreo's preference for rising with the dawn had protected her from having her secret exposed, she rolled off the bed and headed into the bathroom. But, as had happened the morning before, that initial nausea slowly receded again. Perhaps the worst of her sickness was already over, she thought cheerfully and, pulling on a light cotton wrap, she went downstairs in search of Andreo. Both he and the Mercedes were nowhere to be found, however, and a note left on the hall table informed her that he had gone out to buy chocolate croissants for her.

An ear to ear smile curved her lips. He was spoiling her again and she had already discovered that she absolutely adored every moment of being spoilt. She had never been a self-indulgent woman or a woman who had ever imagined that any male might put himself out on her behalf. Indeed her father's unfortunate example had persuaded her that all men were instinctively selfish. So for that reason the sheer amount of effort that Andreo was prepared to expend on any gesture likely to please her continually shook her.

'I like surprising you… I enjoy seeing you smile, *amore*,' he had confided with the charismatic grin that made her heart spin inside her.

Eyes dreamy and soft over that memory, Pippa went for a shower and tried to work out without success how five whole days had passed at such speed. Why was it that happy times seemed to shoot past faster than the speed of light and unhappier times dragged? Brow furrowing on that conundrum, she was on far too much of an emotional high to linger on it.

While she was in the act of shampooing her hair, her attention fell on the sunken bath that was set in a glorious multi-coloured mosaic surround and her skin warmed and her smile grew abstracted: when they shared the bath they fooled around like kids. He had taught her how to relax and overcome her innate fear of making a fool of herself. He had made her laugh and, over and over again, he had given her the kind of joy she had never dreamt she might experience in a hundred years.

She loved the long evenings the most. When the shadows had begun to lengthen and the heat of the day had ebbed, they would dine at the stone table overlooking the river and sit talking far into the night. Even the food they were eating was wonderful. Berthe, Andreo's friendly housekeeper, who worked as an occasional chef in her son-in-law's restaurant, performed gastronomic miracles in the kitchen.

Pippa was combing her hair when she thought that she heard the Mercedes return. However, when she ran to the window she could only see Berthe's husband, Guillaume, who farmed Andreo's land, driving a tractor into a field next to the lane. The phone by the bed rang and she answered it.

'It's Tabby,' her friend said cheerfully. 'I've been trying to raise you on your mobile—'

'It's dead,' Pippa admitted apologetically. 'I forgot to charge it—'

'Luckily, Christien asked Andreo for his number,' Tabby explained. 'I was really surprised when you didn't phone me—'

'I know,' Pippa groaned, full of squirming guilt. 'I know I should have phoned you—'

Tabby was not slow to take advantage of her friend's discomfiture. 'So stop holding out on me and tell me what's happening between you two.'

When a noisy click sounded on the line, Pippa assumed they had a bad connection and raised her voice to be heard over the interference. 'There's really nothing to tell—'

'Does that mean that you *still* haven't told him about the baby?' Tabby exclaimed in a tone of disbelief.

'Tabby...' Pippa felt stabbed in the back by that incredulity. After all, what harm was she doing in remaining silent a little longer?

'I wouldn't have asked if I hadn't found you in residence at the end of Andreo's phone line,' Tabby sighed, sounding even more anxious. 'I'm sorry...forget I even mentioned the baby. I really didn't mean to put pressure on you. It's just... I've been *so* worried.'

But Pippa's attention had been stolen from their conversation for she had heard a step on the stone stairs. She spun round just as Andreo appeared in the arched doorway. Sheathed in faded denim jeans and a black designer shirt, he looked darkly handsome and dangerous. When she clashed with the furious challenge in his hard appraisal, she frowned in bewilderment and then gulped at the sight of the cordless phone grasped in his hand. From that phone Tabby's voice could still be clearly heard setting up an echo in concert with the phone that Pippa held herself. Her blood ran cold: Andreo must have lifted the phone downstairs and overheard their dialogue.

'Sorry, I have to go...' Pippa breathed flatly. 'I'll call you later.'

CHAPTER NINE

'I ASSUMED YOU were still in bed. I lifted the hall phone to call Marco. Is it true?' Andreo demanded.

Pippa was very pale but reluctant to accept that he knew her secret. 'Is what true?'

Andreo dealt her a raw look of derision. 'Is it true that you're pregnant?'

Pippa breathed in slow and deep to steady herself and laced her hands together in a nervous motion. 'Yes…'

'And is the baby mine?'

She reddened. 'How can you ask me a question like that?'

'Easily. This is not how I expected to hear that kind of news from you. Since it's clear you're not the very honest woman I thought you were, what else might I have got wrong?' Andreo fielded harshly, lean, strong face rigid with the same tension that was holding her taut.

'Not that anyway…the baby *is* yours,' she stated in driven reproach.

Stunning golden eyes veiling, Andreo swung away from her so that she could not see how he had taken that blunt confirmation of his paternity.

Had he had some wild hope that he might not be the male responsible for impregnating her? Pippa wondered in dismay. She felt demeaned by that suspicion but could not avoid thinking along such lines. He had taken her to bed. At no time had he talked of a future that lay further away than the next day. Those were the facts. Facts that were bare of the taint of her hopes and dreams. Naturally Andreo would have been relieved to hear that the responsibility for the baby she carried was not his.

'This is not the way I wanted you to find out about my...er... condition,' Pippa muttered uncomfortably, shying away from that word, 'baby', lest it increase his shock.

'Don't try to fool me. You had no plans to tell me at all. Why else would you have remained silent this long? Do you think I haven't worked that out for myself?' It was a low, bitter response that sliced through the tense atmosphere like a knife blade.

'I don't know what you're trying to say...' Pippa could hardly think straight because she felt wretched. Last night and every night since her arrival at his idyllic home in the Dordogne she had slept in his arms, but now he was poised on the far side of the room surveying her with grim, shuttered eyes as though she were his mortal enemy. 'Of course I was going to tell you... OK, so I wasn't in a hurry to do it, but I hardly think that's a crime!'

'*Per meraviglia...* I think you were more concerned that I might try to interfere in how you chose to deal with what you no doubt saw as a colossal problem,' Andreo framed in a raw undertone. 'That's why you left London but you weren't prepared to admit that. If I hadn't heard you talking to Christien's wife, I would never have found out that I'd got you pregnant. You intended to keep that fact from me. Why won't you admit that?'

Pippa stared back at him in consternation. 'Because it's not true and I wouldn't behave like that. You've got it all wrong—'

'I don't think so.' Hard dark eyes assailed hers with fierce distrust.

Andreo was playing judge, jury and executioner all at one and the same time and very much in his element, Pippa decided in furious frustration. 'You aren't listening to what I'm saying—'

'Why would I?' Andreo vented a derisive laugh. 'Why would I listen to a woman who has so little regard for either me or our relationship that she leaves the country without even leaving me a note?'

'You *know* why that happened!' Pippa protested, alarmed by that condemnation being recycled. 'I saw you with Lili Richards and assumed the worst—'

'As you chose not to confront me on that score, I only have your word for that. In point of fact, you just vanished—'

'My departure from London had nothing to do with me being pregnant because I only found out that I had fallen pregnant the day after you arrived in France!' Pippa argued vehemently, her bright blue eyes pinned to his lean chiselled features with a concern she could not hide. 'I was planning to tell you, I *was*—'

'I don't think so. Your behaviour speaks for itself—'

'And what's that supposed to mean?'

Implacable golden eyes raked over her with stubborn force. 'I think that the moment you discovered that you were rather more fertile than you wanted to be, you decided to walk out on me and go for an abortion. Perhaps you came to France first in an effort to ensure that you shook me off.'

Pippa's back was so rigid her spine was protesting her stance, but her pallor was now illuminated by angry colour. 'You have no right to talk as if you can get inside my head and somehow know what *I* was planning to do—'

Andreo sent her a fierce look of derision. 'I don't need a fortune-teller, do I? You don't like children—'

'That is untrue and what is more I never said any such thing.'

His wide sensual mouth compressed into an even more intransigent line. 'You don't *want* children—'

'What would you know about what I want?' Pippa flung at

him hotly. 'Maybe I started to feel differently when I realised I was already carrying a baby.'

Andreo's keen gaze narrowed and glittered. His strong bone structure bearing a little less resemblance to a stone wall, he took a sudden fluid step closer. 'Did you?'

'That's none of your business! You should have asked how I felt...*nicely*, not gone straight into attack!' she snapped back at him.

'Don't tell me it's none of my business when you have my baby inside you!' Andreo thundered back at her.

'When you talk like that you sound like a fourteenth-century man,' she told him with a scornfully curled lip.

His sense of humour nowhere in evidence, Andreo jerked a powerful shoulder in dismissal. 'It's my baby too and I made it clear that I would take full responsibility if this happened.'

'Always supposing I wanted you to take responsibility,' Pippa slotted in, if anything more angry than ever that he should dare to imply that she needed him to take care of her and the baby she carried.

'Any decisions you make should be discussed with me,' Andreo delivered grimly.

'All right.' Pippa forced out a facetious laugh. 'Are you any good at changing nappies?'

Andreo gave her an arrested look.

Pippa released an exaggerated sigh of disappointment. 'Obviously you've no experience whatsoever in that line. What about feeds and crying bouts in the middle of the night?'

His level black brows pleated in a bemused frown. 'We'd have a nanny.'

'Oh, would we?'

'Of course...' But for once Andreo was out of his depth and it was showing in the intensity with which he was watching her while he tried to guess what the right answers might be on her terms. He had half a dozen nephews and nieces but he had had precious little to do with them as babies.

'So while you are convinced that you should be involved in any decisions I make, you're not actually willing to do any hands-on parenting—'

'What is this conversation? Are you saying that you *are* prepared to have this baby if I get involved?' Andreo demanded tautly.

'If you had ever taken the time to ask me, I would have told you up front that I had already decided that I was going to have this child.' Pippa was breathing in slowly and carefully because the sheer stress of their confrontation was making her head swim. 'But I don't need you or your money to manage and if a nanny is all you have to offer, I think we might just be better off on our own.'

'That's *not* all I'm prepared to offer,' Andreo breathed with savage clarity, brilliant eyes shimmering over her. 'I'll marry you...obviously.'

Pippa almost flinched from the demeaning form that that proposal took and a great hollowness entered her then, for it hurt her a great deal that he could even think that she would consider allowing him to marry her. Marriage was for people who couldn't bear to live apart and who wanted to make a proper commitment to each other. Occasionally people did enter marriage for more prosaic reasons, but she had too much intelligence and way too much pride to become part of such an unequal union: he didn't love her and that was that. Therefore there was nothing to discuss. As far as she was concerned, how much she loved him did not enter the equation. Nobody knew better than she how disastrous such a marriage could be.

'You need me in bed *and* out of it, *cara mia*,' Andreo asserted with ferocious assurance. 'I want you and I want our child as well.'

Hot tears prickled at the back of Pippa's eyes but she held them back. She would not look at him because she could not bear to betray the utter turmoil of her emotions. Brushing past him before he could even guess her intention, she headed down-stairs and reached for the phone book.

'I'm going to call a cab. What's the address here?' she asked Andreo where he lowered like a dark, threatening storm at the foot of the stone staircase.

'You can't leave—'

'Watch me!' But her defiant glance in his direction fell short for his image was blurring because she was feeling horribly giddy.

'I asked you to marry me,' Andreo ground out with chilling hauteur.

'Gosh, *did* you?' Pippa sniped back in response, fighting off the dizziness assailing her with all her might. 'How did I miss that? I heard you tell me with great condescension that you would marry me and that I needed you. Well, listen well, I don't *need* anybody but myself!'

With feverish haste, she headed back upstairs but on the first step a hand came down over hers where it rested on the balus-trade and effectively arrested her progress. 'This is incredibly childish,' Andreo asserted.

'You said it...' Pippa was desperate to make her escape be-fore she broke down and cried her eyes out.

'I will not chase round France after you,' Andreo breathed in a warning growl.

'I don't want you to chase after me.' Her skin felt horribly clammy and her tummy was rolling with nausea. With a su-preme effort, she dragged her hand free of his restraint and blindly mounted another step.

'I think that you do but this time it's not going to happen. You've done everything you can to undermine our relation-ship and if the proposal didn't come up to scratch, you've only got yourself to thank for it,' Andreo delivered with harsh em-phasis. 'You tell me you don't need anyone. At least admit the truth…you're too much of a coward to give me or what we have a chance!'

For a bare instant, Pippa considered that frightening condemnation but her mind was in a state of flux and by that point she was so giddy that she was swaying where she stood. Still struggling to triumph over her light head, she was sucked down a long, suffocating tunnel into the darkness of unconsciousness.

When she surfaced from her faint she was lying down and no sooner had she attempted to lift her head than the nausea returned with cruel strength. Handling that bout of sickness with infuriating efficiency, Andreo carried her back to the bed and told her not to move while he was downstairs.

He reappeared a few minutes later.

Enraged by her own demeaning bodily weakness, Pippa bit out grittily, 'I'm still leaving.'

'If the doctor agrees…' Andreo murmured in the mildest of tones.

'What doctor?'

'The one I've called out. You were very sick.'

'That was just that stupid morning sickness on my stupid empty stomach!' she hissed at him. 'And until you started arguing with me, I was getting over that!'

Andreo continued to survey her with immense calm and cool.

'Stop looking at me like that!' Pippa launched at him wildly. 'Like I'm a kid having a shocking temper tantrum!'

His glorious golden eyes took immediate cover below the dense flourish of his lush black lashes. He said nothing, nothing at all, and while the silence stretched Pippa squirmed on a torture rack of her own making. He had been exceedingly kind and he had not bolted from a situation that the average male avoided like the plague. He might be drop dead gorgeous but he was also amazingly practical. He very probably *could* handle the less rewarding aspects of baby care, she reflected guiltily. Feeling far too emotional and utterly raging at the maddening tears that came to her eyes all too readily, she flipped over on her side and hid under her bright tumbled hair.

'I don't want you to be upset like this,' Andreo murmured levelly from the foot of the bed, resisting a very powerful urge to offer more physical comfort.

'I'm not upset,' she mumbled.

'I was lying when I said I wouldn't chase round France after you, *carissima*,' Andreo imparted silkily.

'Oh...?' Low though she felt it would be to reach for a proffered olive branch, she discovered that she was eager to mend the breach between them.

'I won't let you go free to get lost again,' he spelt out with the lethally quiet diction of a very confident personality. 'You seem to think that there's something wrong with needing me...but all of us need someone and you don't appear to have anyone else.'

At that unexpected speech, Pippa tried and failed to swallow the thickness in her throat. She felt as though she had hit her lowest ebb: he had taken pity on her. What he was doing for her now, he would have done for any woman carrying his child. Essentially he was an honourable guy. Exactly the sort who could be depended on to accept responsibility for an accidental pregnancy. Hence the marriage proposal. She had been right not to listen and to throw that offer back in his face, she told herself wretchedly.

The middle-aged doctor advised her that pregnant ladies required more rest and that keeping the late hours that were presumably responsible for her shadowed eyes was not to be recommended either. It was all common sense stuff. When he had gone, Andreo brought her a delicious lunch on a tray. Her own keen appetite amazed her: she cleared the plate.

'I didn't hear Berthe's car. She really is a fantastic cook.'

'She hasn't arrived yet. I made it...'

Surprise made Pippa exclaim, '*You*...did?'

'Why not? I once lived here alone for six months. Either I

learned to look after myself or I went hungry,' Andreo said dryly.

She was feeling incredibly tired and she rested her head down on the pillow. Studying his darkly handsome classic profile, she felt the magnetic pull of his charismatic attraction with every sense she possessed and she could have wept over her own susceptibility. 'Was that when you were eighteen? What were you doing here then?'

'Rebelling, what else?' Andreo rested riveting dark golden eyes on her and vented a rueful laugh. 'I fell in love with a model. Her name was Fia and she was five years older. My father was incapable of waiting for the affair to run its course. He demanded that I give her up and he threatened me with disinheritance in time-honoured style. Fia and I came to France to set up home together. *But*...before I could buy the priory, she accepted a lucrative cash offer from my father to ditch me instead.'

Pippa winced and learned that even though she was inexcusably jealous of any woman he had ever been involved with she still could not bear the idea of him being hurt. And she could well imagine how open and trusting he had been as a teenager.

'I stayed on here to lick my wounds. I wasn't destitute. I had a trust fund from my grandparents. It might not have been sufficient to tempt Fia but it was enough to live on.' His handsome mouth quirked.

He was making light of the hurt he had suffered but she knew him well enough to guess how devastated he would have been by that betrayal. In those days he had been a romantic ready to make sacrifices to be with the woman he loved. The cruellest blow of all for a male of his pride and intelligence must have been the reality that the object of his affections should have proved to be so unworthy, not to mention being fonder of money than she was of him.

'Andreo...' she began, feeling ridiculously tearful again.

'Get some sleep.' Six feet five inches of lean muscular masculinity, he vaulted upright.

'You don't *have* to marry me just because I'm pregnant.'

'I do...you may be very clever but you haven't the survival instincts of a flea,' Andreo informed her equably.

Any desire to be tearful evaporated. Colour flying into her cheeks, Pippa thrust herself up against the pillows. 'How can you justify saying that?'

'You turn down a job that's yours and abandon a promising career. You run out on a good relationship,' he enumerated without hesitation. 'You're so stubborn you won't even sit down when you're on the brink of fainting. I think that last says it all, *amore*. You may think you can go it alone, but I'm not impressed.'

'When I get up, I'll be feeling well enough to leave,' Pippa asserted tightly, refusing to listen to him. 'I'd be grateful if you'd book a taxi to pick me up here at three.'

Andreo had gone very still. 'No.'

'I intend to have this baby. Right now, that is all you need to know. If I need your help in any way, I'll contact you.' Turning her head away, Pippa hunched under the sheet.

Leaving was the right thing to do, she reminded herself with stubborn determination. If he wanted to take an interest in their baby after the birth, she would allow him to do so. He did not know how lucky he was that she had turned him down. She might have been a gold-digger willing to marry him just to take advantage of his wealth! He was gorgeous, wonderful company and fantastic in bed. Whether he appreciated it or not, her refusal to be impressed by his attack of gallantry was evidence of just how much she loved him. If only they had had another few days together before he had found out that she was pregnant, she reflected miserably.

Andreo tossed something on the bed and her eyes flew open

and lodged on her fluffy pink diary. 'I haven't read a word of it,' he assured her.

Pippa flushed and bent her head. 'I know that.'

'I'm supposed to be meeting with my *notaire* this afternoon to discuss the purchase of some land but I'll cancel.'

Pippa did not trust herself to look near him. 'Don't be daft,' she told him with fake casualness. 'All I intend to do is catch up on my sleep while you're out.'

Andreo dropped down into an athletic crouch to establish the visual connection that she was denying him. 'I'll ask Berthe to keep an eye on you…'

'Don't embarrass me like that,' Pippa urged unevenly, bright blue eyes clinging involuntarily to his lean, powerful face.

Andreo reached for her hand. 'OK, but you have to promise to be sensible and sit down at the very first sign of dizziness—'

'OK…'

He bent his arrogant dark head and let his tongue delve provocatively between her lips. He set up a quivering, delicious tightness low in her pelvis. 'You also have to promise to eat everything Berthe puts in front of you—'

'No problem,' she mumbled, tipping up her mouth to the sexy onslaught of his again with all the self-discipline of a rag doll.

'And if you're really good, you get chocolate croissants as an afternoon snack. Get loads and loads of sleep so that I can make passionate love to you when I get back,' he husked between teasing expert kisses that left her literally begging for more, her fingers biting into his forearms. 'But if I still think you're tired, I *won't*…'

Detaching himself from her hold, he strode across the room to pull the shutters closed on the bright morning sunlight. She stared at him and then recalled in sudden dismay that she had not taken a single photo of him since her arrival. 'Hold on…' she urged, panicking at the threat of having to get by in the future without any photos of him.

Andreo watched in astonishment while she scrambled out of bed and dug a camera he had never seen before out of her bag.

'Smile...' she instructed in a slightly wobbly voice and fiddled with the shutters to let in more light.

'You're supposed to be in bed,' Andreo censured.

She caught his smouldering frown for posterity. 'Smile... look normal,' she pleaded.

She managed a handful of shots before she heard Berthe's noisy little car arriving and she got back into bed to rest to please Andreo. As soon as he had gone downstairs, she got up again and furtively packed her case. Conscious that he would probably look in on her before he left to keep his business appointment, she lay down again and was asleep before she knew it.

When she woke up, the bedroom door was just closing and it was almost two in the afternoon. She had slept for almost two hours. Minutes later, she heard the Mercedes engine fire. Andreo was going out and she would not be here when he returned. Like a child she wanted to leap out of bed and watch him drive off and she found it tough to resist that temptation. She stared into space with strained eyes and reminded herself of why, regardless of her love for Andreo, she could not even consider marrying him...

As a teenager, Pippa had learned that her parents' marriage had been a shotgun affair that would never have taken place but for her own unplanned advent into the world. Her father had been a newly qualified teacher when he'd first met the French student working as a language assistant in the same school. For Pippa's mother it had been love at first sight and in later years she had been painfully honest with her daughter in her efforts to excuse her husband's infidelity.

'We only went out together a few times. By the time I realised that I was going to have a child, your father was already dating someone else. He was very popular with the girls and

I was too quiet for him, but when I told him that I was pregnant he immediately said that he would marry me,' the older woman had confided. 'It was a huge sacrifice for him and I was grateful.'

But then her mother had had the attitudes of a different generation and had had pitifully few expectations in life. Pippa's mother had clung to the father of her unborn baby and had meekly accepted that he should neither be kind to her nor faithful. Having married a man who did not love her and who indeed resented her, she had paid a heavy price.

That awareness strengthening Pippa's own conviction that she had to leave Andreo before she was tempted into yielding to the strength of her own feelings for him, Pippa pulled on a pale green shift dress and teamed it with a gold linen jacket. The housekeeper, the plump and attractive Berthe, emerged from the kitchen to greet her. The ensuing exchange of pleasantries, voluble on Berthe's side and more strained on Pippa's, was interrupted when the older woman noticed Pippa's suitcase and the conversation took another tack.

Learning that Pippa intended to call a taxi to ferry her into Bourdeilles, Berthe frowned in surprise and then insisted on giving her a lift into the town, explaining that she herself had some shopping to do.

The elderly little Citroën lurched and bounced down the rough lane at alarming speed. Too late did Pippa recall that Andreo had told her that his housekeeper drove as if she were a bat out of hell in a demolition derby. Reminding herself that the minor road beyond was usually very quiet, Pippa only betrayed her state of nerves with a faint gasp when her companion raked her car straight into a left turn.

The lorry thundering towards them seemed to come round the corner at them out of nowhere. A high-pitched squawk of alarm broke from Berthe as she hauled the steering wheel round in a frantic effort to get out of its path.

I should have married him...was the only thought that animated Pippa's mind and it was a thought that pierced her with literal anguish in the instant that the little car crashed.

CHAPTER TEN

PIPPA OPENED SHAKEN EYES.

The Citroën was nose down in a ditch. Berthe was sobbing in shock. But neither of them appeared to be hurt and there was no sign of the lorry, which had apparently speeded on past without deigning to notice the car that had almost come to grief below its enormous wheels.

Pippa reached across with an unsteady hand and switched off the car engine. Checking that the older woman was indeed uninjured, she persuaded her that it would be safer to get out of the car. As Pippa clambered out into the dusty ditch the sleeve of her jacket snagged on the wire attached to the fence post that had been torn down by the crash. The fabric ripped and Pippa gritted her teeth as she attempted to free herself without success. Exasperated, she shrugged out of her jacket and, leaving it where it fell, moved with some difficulty over the rough ground to the driver's side to help Berthe.

By the time she had assisted the heavy older woman to climb out of the Citroën, a battered truck containing Berthe's husband, Guillaume, and her strapping son had pulled up beside them. Her relatives had seen the accident from the field across the road where they had been working. Berthe lamented the reality that she had not had a chance to see the registration of the lorry.

Her husband ignored that remark and tucked his wife into his truck as tenderly as if she had been a queen. 'You are safe,' he pointed out, urging Pippa to join the older woman.

'Travel back home with us and I will take you into town in my car instead,' Berthe's son promised Pippa.

'Thank you but I've changed my mind. I don't think I'll go anywhere today.' Pippa's voice emerged a little unevenly but she lifted her head high with an air of decision.

It was amazing how a near brush with mortality could focus the mind, Pippa acknowledged once she had been dropped back to the priory and had managed to convince Berthe and her menfolk that she felt perfectly fine and could safely be left there alone. In fact the sky had never seemed more blue, the sun more golden or the myriad colours of nature's bounty more intense.

How could she have even considered running out on Andreo a second time? She was ashamed of herself and yet curiously excited too by her own daring in choosing to return and lay herself open to the type of hurt that she had always protected herself from. At the same time she was still able to cringe when she remembered Andreo telling her that she was too scared to give him a chance. It was true. Right from the start, she had foreseen the end of their relationship and had sought to make a self-fulfilling prophecy out of her low expectations. At every turn she had undervalued him and what they shared.

Why had it taken her so long to appreciate that Andreo bore not the faintest resemblance to her late father in character? Judging Andreo in the bitter shadow of her parent's infidelity, she had denied the younger man a fair hearing and she had refused to concede him the smallest trust. She had to be more honest with him and the very last thing he deserved was for her to walk out on him again while so much was still unresolved between them.

Twenty minutes later, Andreo drove back from the meeting, which he had cut short, and the first thing he saw was the Citroën upended in the ditch and a woman's jacket lying by the side of the road. Braking to an emergency stop, for his recognition of that garment was instantaneous, he leapt out to check that the car was unoccupied. For an instant he was frozen there and then he flung himself back into the Mercedes and accelerated down the lane.

Waiting to greet him, Pippa hovered in the doorway of the airy salon. The light flooding through the tall, elegant windows behind her burnished her hair with fiery highlights and threw into prominence her taut pallor.

Andreo strode into the hall. Lean, strong face stamped with savage tension, his gaze alight with ferocious strain roved over her in wondering disbelief and shock. *'Per meraviglia!* You're here? Safe and unhurt? When I saw your jacket beside Berthe's car I thought you had been injured...perhaps seriously...and I assumed you had been taken to hospital, only I did not know which one...' At that point, his dark deep drawl thickened and came to a halt.

'We were almost run down by a l-lorry.' Blue eyes welded to his extravagantly handsome features, Pippa was embarrassed by the nervous catch that had crept into her voice. Her heart seemed to pound so frantically inside her chest she could hardly breathe and she found herself gabbling in an almost inaudible rush, 'My mother would have said that an angel must have been in the car with us for Berthe is all in one piece as well...'

Venting a roughened phrase in his own language to best express his disordered emotions, Andreo overcame his paralysis and strode forward to close his arms round her. *'Porca miseria*...if you only knew what I have been thinking!'

Almost immediately he drew back from her again. Pippa watched him swallow hard and stood without complaint while he ran lean hands down from her shoulders to her hips and studied her with intense concern as though he was not yet able to accept the evidence of his own eyes and credit that she too had escaped injury.

'I got a shock too... Berthe just drove out without looking—'

'You will never, ever get into a car with her again, *amore*,' Andreo intoned harshly, long fingers closing into her shoulders and giving her the tiniest, barely definable shake in emphasis of that embargo.

'She got a terrible fright and I'm sure she'll be much more cautious in the future. I gather the road is usually very quiet—'

He closed one hand into her vibrant mane of curls to tip her head back and scorching golden eyes assailed hers. 'I think if you had died, I would have wanted to die too,' he breathed in a raw, driven undertone. 'You are so much like a part of me now and when you are not with me, I don't feel right. Had I lost you, I should never have felt complete again, *bella mia*.'

Stunned at the extraordinary emotional intensity of that passionate declaration, Pippa stared up at him with parted lips, her amazement palpable. He cared about her, he really, really cared about her. Some of the hard, hurting tension with which she had braced herself to face him began to yield inside her. 'I suppose you've already guessed but I was a-about to take off on you again—'

Dark colour accentuated the sculpted perfection of his masculine cheekbones. '*Sì*...but I was asking for it. I wasn't honest with you. I was still trying to play it cool and of course you needed my reassurance and I had too much pride to let you see how I felt about you...'

Brooding golden eyes veiling below lush black lashes, Andreo fell frustratingly silent at that point when Pippa was hanging on his every word with superhuman concentration and attention. 'How you feel about...er...me?' she prompted shamelessly.

'I'm working on that,' Andreo assured her between compressed lips, graceful brown hands curving briefly to her cheekbones while he continued to study her and then dropping from her again.

'Oh...' Just for an instant there she had thought he might be about to say he loved her or something crazy like that, and she was really mortified by the fantasy element able to bloom within her own imagination. For the merest instant she wanted to kick him for saying that insane thing about thinking he would have wanted to die had she died. On that score he had undoubtedly led her up the garden path but she was quite sure he had not meant to do so. He had been very much shocked by the sight of that crashed car and he felt very protective towards the baby she carried, and at least she now knew where the Latin reputation for romantic and dramatic exaggeration came from...

'I had backed into your corner and challenged you. I suspected that you were ready to take flight again and I cut short my time with the *notaire*,' Andreo volunteered, his hands dropping from her to accompany the speech.

At the stark look of reproach in his gaze, Pippa reddened with guilt. 'My thinking was all skewed and—you know? I was trying to save face too but I wasn't being fair to either of us in running away from things just because I couldn't handle them—'

'You need me to keep on proving myself to you. That's all and for what it's worth, I would have chased after you again, *carissima*,' Andreo confided huskily. 'And I would have done it again...and again until I won your trust.'

'Is that what I was doing?' That was when Pippa saw her own behaviour in a different light. On a subconscious level, she had been testing him out, hoping that he would make the effort to follow her and convince her that he was a guy she could rely on. 'Well, it won't be happening again. I haven't been fair to you. Apart from that misunderstanding we had about Lili Richards, you had been very honest with me—'

'What I had with Lili was strictly casual. I should have called Lili and told her I'd met you but ditching her by phone would have been tacky. It would also have felt like overkill when Lili and I had agreed that we were free agents before she left. I also...' his strong jaw-line squared and he forged on grimly, 'I also think that I was reluctant at that point to accept how important you had become in my life, *cara*.'

He was firing that fantasy element in her imagination again. 'Important? Was I?'

Andreo frowned. 'I haven't been serious about a woman since Fia.'

'My goodness...you don't get serious much.' Pippa heard herself make that inane comment in a distinctly squeaky voice.

'I made such an ass of myself over her that I had no wish to allow any woman that much power over me again,' Andreo confided with a grimace.

Pippa smoothed her hand in a soothing gesture across one broad shoulder and her fingers lingered to maintain a physical connection between them. 'You were very young. You shouldn't be so hard on yourself.'

'I lost face in my own eyes. My family were very forgiving but I was deeply ashamed of my own lack of judgement,' Andreo admitted curtly. 'I fell in love with an imaginary image of Fia rather than with the woman she really was—'

'I made the same mistake with that student Pete when I was seventeen,' Pippa rushed to tell him. 'I saw him as Mr Perfect but I haven't done that with you...'

Andreo tensed and gazed down at her with rather touching wariness.

'I mean, I know you're not perfect! No human being is perfect,' Pippa hurried to add, recognising too late that he really, really wanted her to think he was the most perfect guy imaginable. 'But I swear you're the closest thing ever—'

'No... I've made too many mistakes. If anything had happened to you or to our baby today, I would never have forgiven myself for not telling you how I feel about you,' Andreo proclaimed.

'I felt the same way,' Pippa whispered tenderly.

'I've been a lost cause from the first night I saw you, *cara*,' Andreo interposed. 'Why do you think I was so hot for you? I've never felt anything that powerful before.'

Cheeks burning, and suspecting that he was referring to lust alone, Pippa mumbled, 'I hadn't either—'

Andreo looked down at her with glittering golden eyes and, closing his hands round hers in a sudden movement, breathed, 'Being with you feels wonderful but at the beginning that unnerved me—'

'Feeling wonderful unnerved you?'

His hands tightened on hers and she flinched, soon appreciating that he was so deep in serious thought that he had not a clue that he was crushing her fingers. 'Falling in love when you're not expecting it can be...' Andreo hesitated in search of the right word '...traumatic.'

'Traumatic?' Pippa parroted as he released her hands to execute a restive movement towards the window.

Andreo swung back to her again. 'You didn't feel the same way...of course it was traumatic!' he pointed out. 'You were about one degree warmer than a freezer the next day, and the minute you found out who I was you wanted nothing to do with me!'

'But I did... I did feel the same way.' Her thoughts had only slowly reached the awareness that he had to be talking about having fallen for her. Pippa blinked rapidly. Andreo *loved* her? He loved her?

'Are you saying that you love me?' Andreo shot at her incredulously.

'To death...love you just so much,' she stressed, suffering from emotional overload and very near to tears in her overexcitement.

Andreo focused on her with dazed dark golden eyes. 'But you were leaving me again...'

Pippa nodded and compressed tremulous lips.

'For the *second* time,' Andreo emphasised.

Pippa nodded again, tears of regret clogging up her vocal cords.

'Even though I'd asked you to marry me...'

The tears overflowed and streamed in a silent river down her cheeks.

'But all that is *absolutely* OK!' Andreo insisted in panic at the sight of those tears. 'Honestly, I have no idea why I'm so full of complaints. I'm crazy about you and I'll be crazy about our baby too. I can forgive you for anything. Please don't cry, *amore*.'

'I can't help it...my emotions are all over the place and you only have to touch my heart a little at the minute and I could flood the sea with tears. I think it's my hormones, something to do with being pregnant.' Pippa loosed an embarrassed laugh. 'But I'm just so happy!'

Andreo caught her to him with two possessive hands and claimed her ripe mouth with hungry, demanding urgency and it was the best cure for tears imaginable.

'Happy...happy...happy,' she repeated, wicked, wanton excitement sending tiny little shivers through her as she stayed melded to his lean, powerful frame.

'And I think you need to lie down,' Andreo informed her huskily, vibrant amusement lighting his keen appraisal as he swept her up into his arms and began to mount the stairs to the master bedroom. 'I know *I* do...'

Pippa felt incredibly warm and safe: he loved her. All her fears had been empty fears born of her insecurity.

'Am I allowed to ask what changed your mind about babies?' Andreo prompted, lowering her down onto the bed with immense care.

'I think I was most scared of the responsibility. My parents had a bad marriage and my childhood suffered because of it,' Pippa confided awkwardly. 'I was afraid that if I had a child I would make him or her unhappy too.'

'I can understand that, *amore*. But if you valued yourself as

I do, you would already know that you are far too sensitive to behave as your parents did.'

At that vote of confidence, her discomfiture melted. 'I felt different once I knew I was pregnant,' she admitted softly. 'I realised the baby would be part of both of us and all of a sudden our baby was this fascinating little person in his own right. I still worried about how I would measure up as a parent but I felt excited too.'

'You're such a perfectionist and so hard on yourself. I promise that I will never let you down,' Andreo swore with tender force. 'I was too impatient with you. In time, you will learn to trust me.'

'I trust you now but I'll still watch you like a hawk,' Pippa warned him cheerfully. 'There are desperate women out there.'

An appreciative grin slanted his wide, sensual mouth. 'Will you marry me now?'

'I'll think it over,' she dared, confident enough to tease him while still marvelling that he could have fallen in love with someone as ordinary as she believed herself to be.

Halfway out of his shirt, a virile wedge of bronzed muscular chest revealed, Andreo froze and groaned, 'If you want me in your bed again, you *have* to marry me.'

With a sense of joy and freedom entirely new to her, Pippa burst out laughing and feasted her eyes on his lean, darkly handsome features. 'If I agree to marry you as soon as it can be arranged, can I have something on account?'

All male provocation at that request, Andreo let his shirt drop to the floor with a flourish. 'So you want to marry me?'

Pippa arched her toes so that her sandals fell off and heaved a blissful sigh of agreement. 'Definitely…do you mind if I ask you how *much* you love me?' she muttered more shyly.

Andreo rested adoring eyes on her. 'Head over heels and crazy about you. Enough to last two lifetimes at least, *amore*.'

Reassured, Pippa stretched up her arms and linked them

round him to draw him down to her, all the while maintaining her loving connection with his appreciative gaze. 'I love you every bit as much...'

Four weeks later, Pippa married her Italian boss.

The run-up to the wedding was an incredibly busy time for her. She spent almost two weeks flitting about Italy getting to know Andreo's family: his fashionable and friendly mother, Giulietta, his six-foot-two-inch teenage brother, Marco, and his three older sisters and their respective husbands and children. The D'Alessio clan made an enormous fuss of Pippa and she went from feeling rather intimidated by the sheer number of Andreo's gregarious relatives to feeling warmed by their affectionate acceptance of her as Andreo's chosen bride.

Giulietta D'Alessio persuaded Pippa to allow her to organise the wedding and having little taste for that kind of thing, Pippa was delighted to hand over the responsibility for what was already promising to be a major social event.

Andreo and Pippa were married in Rome. Tabby and Hilary had gone shopping with Pippa to help her choose her wedding outfit. She selected a sleeveless bodice made of duchess satin and a long swirling skirt of Thai silk and a detachable embroidered train. Wearing it on the day with the superb diamond tiara that was a gift from her bridegroom and a short delicate veil, she was much admired as a stunningly elegant bride.

Tabby acted as matron of honour and Hilary was to be a bridesmaid but had to surrender the honour to Andreo's eldest niece a week before the ceremony when her little sister, Emma, was rushed into hospital for emergency surgery. Andreo's boyhood friend, Sal Rissone, was best man. In his speech the best man confessed that he had first suspected that Andreo was in love the minute he'd begun clock-watching at the office and seeking privacy to make his phone calls.

'You look so beautiful you take my breath away, *bella mia*,'

Andreo told his bride when they finally got a moment alone together on the dance floor at their reception.

Pippa's heart had not stopped racing since she'd seen Andreo waiting for her at the altar. As befitted the occasion, his lean, dark, devastating features were serious but his proud, possessive gaze had remained welded to her with intoxicating intensity. Over the past frantic month, Andreo's need to catch up with work and clear the space in his busy schedule for a honeymoon had ensured that they had had little time together. When he drew her close, she shivered at the contact with his lean, powerful body, ultra sensitive to his raw, virile masculinity and the wicked promise of the sensual smile curving his beautiful mouth.

'I want to be alone with you so badly I *ache*,' Andreo admitted with such feeling force that she blushed to the roots of her hair and struggled to damp down her own wanton response to his unashamed hunger for her.

Only a minute later, Marco cut in on Andreo to dance with her. His youthful features held all the promise of the same good looks that distinguished her bridegroom. Having cheerfully ignored his older brother's protests, he sighed with mock reproach, 'It's not cool to cling to each other the way you two do.'

Pippa laughed. 'We don't,' she said and angled her head round to try and spot where Andreo had gone.

'Don't worry…he hasn't gone far.' It was Marco's turn to laugh for his older brother was poised on the edge of the floor, his attention exclusively pinned to his beautiful bride. 'I can see I'm going to get a lot of mileage out of teasing you.'

For their honeymoon, Andreo took Pippa to his birthplace on the island of Ischia in the Gulf of Naples. There she was carried over the threshold of the magnificent villa that Andreo regarded as his home. He and his siblings had been born on Ischia but his widowed mother had moved her family to Rome after her husband's death.

After breakfast the next morning, Pippa walked out of their

bedroom onto the sun-drenched marble terrace. She was enchanted by the glorious views. The chalk white houses were set against a landscape of old stone walls, silvery olive groves and lush green vineyards and backed by the deep sparkling blue of the sea.

'So this is where we're going to live,' she murmured, resting back against Andreo with the perfect trust of a woman who knew she was loved. 'Have you always spent most of your time here?'

Andreo closed gentle arms round her and spread lean fingers in a tender speaking gesture across the faint protuberance of her tummy. 'No, but now that I'm to become a father I shall need to cut down on my trips abroad, *cara*. Off the tourist track, the pace of life is slower here. It's a wonderful place to raise a child.'

Contentment filled Pippa to overflowing. Turning within his embrace, she gazed up into his darkly handsome features with her heart in her eyes, but there was still one tiny nagging concern to be faced. Breathing in deep, she worried at her lower lip before saying shyly, 'I'm probably being very silly, but are you going to end up getting bored with me?'

'*Dio mio!* What are you talking about?' Andreo demanded in frowning disconcertion. 'I could never become bored with you or what we have together. It is more than I ever hoped to have with any woman—'

'Even though I'll never be in the diamond-studded handcuffs line?' Pippa prompted in an effort to be more specific about what he might or might not miss in the future.

Andreo tensed and wondered which he was going to put first: his rampant reputation as a living legend in the bedroom or his bride's peace of mind? The only diamond-studded handcuffs he had ever purchased had been of the miniaturised variety, quite literally a gold charm for a bracelet, the most casual of gifts. A kiss-and-tell story sold by the same lady who had briefly shared his bed had first employed the outrageous lie presumably to make her revelations seem more newsworthy.

'All that's behind me...' But as he looked down into Pippa's anxious blue eyes Andreo's conscience stirred and he released his breath in a sudden hiss. He confessed the truth about the diamond-studded handcuffs.

Pippa looked up at him for a long, timeless moment and then she just crumpled into helpless giggles. Every time she tried to stop laughing, she would recall the rueful look on his face as he chose to make that lowering admission and it would set her off into whoops again.

'But now that I've found the woman of my dreams, I can at last live out my every sexual fantasy,' Andreo drawled in a super-fast recovery, bending down and scooping her up to carry her back into the bedroom.

Hot-cheeked, eyes startled, Pippa gazed up at him. 'Are you serious?'

He came down on the bed with her and covered her soft pink mouth with the passionate demand of his. Erotic heat sizzled along her every nerve ending and she quivered.

'How serious would you like me to be, *amore*?' Andreo teased and then he told her all over again how much he loved her and she smiled, buoyant with joy and trust.

Seven months later, Pippa gave birth to their first child. She enjoyed an easy pregnancy and delivery. They called their infant daughter Lucia. She was an exceptionally pretty baby with her father's eyes and her mother's cinnamon curls and both her parents were besotted with her.

They took Lucia to France with them when they attended the christening of Tabby and Christien's second son, Fabien. The two couples had become fast friends and distance did not get in the way of their socialising. Andreo even asked Tabby to paint a miniature portrait of Lucia to mark the occasion of the first anniversary of his marriage.

The week in which their wedding anniversary fell, Andreo and Pippa left their beloved daughter in the care of her grandmother, Giulietta, and went to stay at the idyllic priory in the Dordogne, which held a special place in both their hearts.

'Would you marry me again if you had a choice?' Pippa asked daringly the night they arrived.

'Faster than the speed of the light, *bella mia*. I love you and I love having you and Lucia in my life,' Andreo intoned huskily.

Pippa looked up into his stunning golden eyes and linked both arms round him tight. 'I love you too,' she whispered, her heartbeat racing as he claimed her mouth with his.

* * * * *

The Banker's Convenient Wife

CHAPTER ONE

'NATURALLY YOU WILL not renew his contract. The Sabatino Bank has no place for inadequate fund managers.' Lean, dark, handsome face stern, Roel Sabatino was frowning. An international banker and a very busy man, he considered this conversation a waste of his valuable time.

His HR director, Stefan, cleared his throat. 'I thought…perhaps a little chat might put Rawlinson back on track—'

'I don't believe in little chats and I don't give second chances,' Roel incised with glacial effect. 'Neither—you should note—do our clients. The bank's reputation rests on profit performance.'

Stefan Weber reflected that Roel's own world-class renown as an expert in the global economy and the field of wealth preservation carried even greater impact. A Swiss billionaire, Roel Sabatino was the descendant of nine unbroken generations of private bankers and acknowledged by all as the most brilliant. Strikingly intelligent and hugely successful as he was, however, Roel was not known for his compassion towards employees with personal problems. In fact he was as much feared as he was admired for his ruthless lack of sentimentality.

Even so, Stefan made one last effort to intervene on the unfortunate member of staff's behalf. 'Last month, Rawlinson's wife walked out on him…'

'I am his employer, not his counsellor,' Roel countered in brusque dismissal. 'His private life is not my concern.'

That point clarified for the benefit of his HR director, Roel left his palatial office by his private lift to travel down to the underground car park. As he swung into his Ferrari his shapely masculine mouth was still set in a grim line of disdain. What kind of a man allowed the loss of a woman to interfere with his work performance to the extent of destroying a once promising career? A weak character guilty of a shameful lack of self-discipline, Roel decided with a contemptuous shake of his proud dark head.

A male who whined about his personal problems and expected special treatment on that basis was complete anathema to Roel. After all, by its very nature life was challenging and, thanks to a childhood of austere joylessness, Roel knew that better than most. His mother had walked out on her son and her marriage when he was a toddler and any suspicion of tender loving care had vanished overnight from his upbringing. Placed in a boarding-school at the age of five, he had been allowed home visits only when his academic results had matched his father's high expectations. Raised to be tough and unemotional, Roel had learnt when he was very young neither to ask for nor hope for favours in any form.

His car phone rang while he was stuck in Geneva's lunch-time traffic jam and regretting his decision not to utilise his chauffeur-driven limo. The call was from his lawyer, Paul Correro. When it came to more confidential matters, he preferred to utilise Paul's discreet services rather than those of the family legal firm.

'I think it's my duty as your legal representative to point out that the time has arrived for a certain connection to be quietly terminated.' Paul's tone was almost playful.

Roel had gone to university with Paul and he usually enjoyed the other man's lively sense of humour for nobody else would have dared that level of familiarity with him. However, he was not in the mood to engage in a guessing game.

'Cut to the chase, Paul,' he urged.

'I've been thinking of mentioning this for a while...' Unusually, Paul hesitated. 'But I was waiting for you to raise the topic first. It's almost four years now. Isn't it time to have your marriage of convenience dissolved?'

Taken aback by that reminder, and just when the traffic flow was finally beginning to move again, Roel lifted his foot off the clutch of his car. The Ferrari lurched to a sudden choking halt as the engine cut out and provoked a hail of impatient car horns that outraged Roel's masculine pride. But he did not utter a single one of the vituperative curses on the tip of his tongue.

From the car speakers Paul's well-modulated speaking voice continued in happy ignorance of the effect he had induced. 'I was hoping we could set up an appointment some time this week because I'll be on vacation from the following Monday.'

'This week is impossible for me,' Roel heard himself counter instantaneously.

'I hope I haven't overreached my remit in raising the issue,' Paul remarked with a hint of discomfiture.

'*Dio mio!* I had forgotten about the matter. You took me by surprise!' Roel proclaimed with a dismissive laugh.

'I didn't think it was possible to do that,' Paul commented.

'I'll have to call you back...the traffic's unbelievable,' Roel asserted and he concluded the dialogue without engaging in the usual chit-chat.

His handsome mouth was set in a taut line. Paul had been right to bring up the subject of the marriage, which Roel had felt he had little choice but to enter into almost four years earlier. How could he possibly have overlooked the necessity of breaking that slender link again with a divorce? He reminded himself that he led an incredibly busy life and thought back instead to the ridiculous situation that had persuaded him to circumvent the terms of his late grandfather's will with a fake wife.

His grandfather, Clemente, had been a rigid workaholic well into his sixties, in every way a chip off the rock like Sabatino banker block. But after his retirement Clemente had fallen in love with a woman less than half his age and had suffered a rebellious sea change in outlook. Throwing off all restraint, he had embraced New Age philosophies and had even briefly married the youthful gold-digger. His undignified behaviour had led to years of estrangement between Clemente and his son, Roel's conservative father. Roel himself, however, had retained his fondness for the older man and maintained contact with him.

Four years ago, Clemente had died and Roel had been incredulous when the terms of his grandfather's will had been spelt out to him. In that most eccentric document, Clemente had stated that in the event of his grandson failing to marry within a specified time frame, Castello Sabatino, the family's ancestral home, should devolve to the state rather than to his own flesh and blood. Certainly, Roel had lived to regret telling his grandfather that, as the chances of a happy marriage were in his own considered opinion slim to none, he would not be addressing the need to wed and father an heir until he was, at the very least, in late middle age.

Although Roel had been raised to scorn sentimentality, he had nonetheless still cherished dim childish memories of warm and happy visits to the Castello Sabatino. Although he was wealthy enough to buy a hundred ancient castles, he had learnt the hard way that the *castello* had an especially strong hold on his affections. Sabatinos had inhabited the castle, which stood high above a remote valley, for centuries and Roel had been appalled by the genuine threat of the property going out of the family, perhaps for ever.

A couple of months later, while he'd been in London on business, he had been using his mobile phone to discuss with Paul the almost insurmountable problems created by his grandfather's will. Even though he had been in a public place at the time, indeed he had been getting a haircut, he had assumed that the very fact that the conversation was taking place in Italian had meant that it was almost as private as it might have been in his office. He had learnt that he was mistaken when his little hair-stylist had leapt headlong into his private conversation to first commiserate with him over his grandfather's 'weirder than weird' will and, second, to offer up herself as a 'pretend' wife so that he could keep Castello Sabatino in the family.

Ultimately, Hilary Ross had sold her hand in marriage to him in a straight business deal. What age would she be now? Roel mused. Twenty-three years old last St Valentine's Day, his memory supplied without hesitation. He was willing to bet that she still didn't look much older than a teenager. She was very small but wonderfully curvaceous and back then at least her dress sense had rested on the extreme gothic edge of fashion. Black from head to foot, clumpy boots and vampire make-up, he recalled with a frowning smile rather than a shudder. It was strange how very sexy a vampire could look, he reflected abstractedly. Before the traffic lights could change, he dug out his wallet and with long, deft fingers extracted the snapshot Hilary had pressed on him. A snapshot adorned with a teasing signature, 'Your wife, Hilary,' and backed by her phone number.

'Something to remember me by,' she had said, babbling like a brook in flood because he had known and she had somehow sensed that, aside of any necessary legal need to keep tabs on her whereabouts, he would not seek any further personal contact with her.

'Kiss me,' those huge eyes of hers had pleaded in a silent invitation.

Resolute to the last, he had withstood temptation. They had had a business arrangement that had to remain unsullied by sex: Paul had made it clear to him that if he'd consummated what had essentially been only a marriage on paper he would have made himself liable for a substantial maintenance claim.

He must have imagined being tempted by her, Roel told himself in exasperation. What possible appeal could she have had for him? She had left school at sixteen. She was an uneducated girl from a poor working-class background. *Dio mio*...a hairdresser! A giggly little hairdresser, only five feet plus in height and wholly without cultural interests or sophistication! They had had only their humanity in common. Finally he allowed himself to glance down at the photograph. She wasn't beautiful, he reminded himself, exasperated by his own disturbing absorption in such thoughts. He drew his own attention to the fact that her brows were too straight and heavy, her nose a little too large. But regardless of her flaws his brilliant dark gaze still locked to the impish look of fun in her eyes and the wide, bright smile curving her lush mulberry-painted mouth.

'When I worked as a junior on Saturdays, I used to blow every penny I earned on shoes,' she had once confided unasked and in much the same way he had picked up other titbits and glimpses of a lifestyle as far removed from his own as that of an alien.

'When my grandma met my grandpa, she said she knew he was the love of her life before they even spoke...anyway, they *couldn't* speak. She didn't know a word of English and he didn't know a word of Italian. Don't you think that's romantic?'

He had considered it beneath his dignity to respond. In fact he had stonewalled all her attempts to flirt with him. So he was a snob, socially and intellectually, but she had not been from his world. Furthermore he was all too well acquainted with the Sabatino male habit of marrying gold-diggers and far too clever to risk following in his father's and his grandfather's footsteps to make the same crucial mistake. He had suppressed what he had recognised as an inappropriate and dangerous attraction to an unsuitable woman.

Yet he still couldn't forget the last time that he had seen his fake wife: her jaunty wave in spite of the suspicious glisten in her eyes, the gritty, defiant smile that had told him that she was going to find a guy who *did* believe in romance...had she found that mythical male? Discovered his feet of clay? Was that why she had yet to request a divorce on her own behalf?

In the act of wondering that while rounding a notorious bend, Roel only had a split second to react when a child ran off the pavement into the road in pursuit of a dog. Braking hard, he wrenched at the steering wheel in a ferocious attempt to avoid hitting the little girl. The Ferrari smashed nose first into the wall on the other side of the street with a bone-numbing jolt, but he would still have walked unhurt from the wreckage had he had the chance to get out of his car before another vehicle crashed into it. As that second collision followed a blinding pain burst at the base of Roel's skull and plunged him into darkness.

The photograph still curled within fingers that refused to relinquish their grip, he was rushed into hospital. His late father's sister, Bautista, was called to the emergency room. With haughty scorn, Bautista watched two young nurses react to Roel's extravagant dark good looks with hungry eyes of awe.

A spoilt and imperious brunette dressed in a style that the less charitable might have judged inappropriate for a woman of sixty, Bautista was furious at the interruption to her day. Roel would be fine! Roel was indestructible; all the Sabatino men were. Aside of the blow to his head, his other injuries were minor. The following day, Bautista was due to fly to Milan to attend a gallery opening with her fiancé, Dieter, and she was determined not to change her plans.

Only ten days earlier, Roel had infuriated her with the information that the handsome young sculptor whom she was planning to marry had a history of chasing wealthy older women. How horribly insulting Roel had been! Why shouldn't Dieter want her for herself? Bautista was confident that she was still a remarkably good-looking woman, possessed of a most engaging personality. Four staggeringly expensive divorces had failed to diminish her shining faith in love and matrimony.

When a consultant finally came to Bautista to tell her that, although Roel had recovered consciousness, he appeared to be suffering from some degree of temporary amnesia, her annoyance and subsequent frustration were intense.

'Is Mr Sabatino's wife on her way?' Bautista was then asked.

'He's not married.'

With a look of surprise the older man extended a somewhat crumpled photograph to her. 'Then who is this?'

In astonishment, Bautista studied the photo and its revealing inscription. Roel had married an Englishwoman? My goodness, how secretive he had been! But then was he not *famed* for his cold reserve and reticence? His extreme dislike of publicity? His marriage would indeed excite the kind of headlines that he would consider to be distasteful and intrusive, Bautista conceded. Exactly when had he been planning to inform his relatives that he had taken a wife? But at that point happily appreciating that Roel's possession of a wife freed her from all further responsibility for him while he lay in his hospital bed, Bautista rushed off to phone her nephew's mystery bride.

The instant Hilary walked into her tiny flat and saw her sister Emma's troubled face, a cold shiver trickled down her spine.

'What's wrong?' Hilary asked, hastily setting down the evening paper she had gone out to buy.

'While you were out, a woman phoned... I want you to sit down before I pass on her news.' Emma was a tall slender blonde with a steady look in her grey eyes that hinted at an unusual degree of maturity for a girl of seventeen.

Hilary frowned. 'Don't be daft. You're here and all in one piece and the only family I've got. Who phoned...and with what news?'

'I'm not the only family you've got,' her sister said in a strained undertone. 'Roel... Roel Sabatino has been involved in a car accident.'

The blood slowly draining from her cheeks, Hilary stared

back at the younger woman with stricken eyes. Her legs wobbled beneath her and she swayed. 'He's—?'

'Alive...*yes*!' A supportive arm curving to Hilary's slight shoulders, Emma urged her smaller sister down onto the small sofa in the kitchen that also had to serve as a sitting and dining area. 'Roel's aunt phoned. She spoke very little English and she only called for about two minutes max—'

'How badly has he been hurt?' Hilary was trembling and feeling sick. Her mind was a blank and then suddenly a frightening sea of disturbing images. Even as she strained to hear Emma's response she was praying that that response would offer some hope.

'He has some kind of head injury. I got the impression that it might be serious. He's being transferred to another hospital and I did make sure that I got the details.' Emma squeezed her sister's hand in a bracing gesture. 'Take a slow deep breath, Hilly. Concentrate on the fact that Roel's alive. You're in shock but you can be with him by tomorrow morning.'

Bowing her swimming head, Hilary was half in a world of her own. Roel, the precious secret love of her life—even if she had not been anything more than a useful means to an end for him. It was strange and terrifying how love could strike like that, Hilary reflected, gripped by a momentary agony of regret. Roel, the husband of her heart, whom she had never even kissed. Roel, so tall and dark and vitally strong, who right this minute might be fighting for his life in a hospital bed. Her skin clammy with fear for him, she prayed that he would recover but it was a big challenge for Hilary to be optimistic on such a score. Almost seven years earlier, the car crash that had killed both her mother and their father had shattered her and Emma's lives. On that occasion, the long nerve-racking wait at the hospital concerned had not resulted in any last-minute miracle survivals.

'Be with him?' Hilary echoed belatedly. '*Be*...with Roel?'

Could she be with him...dared she try? Wild hope leapt up inside Hilary. She might be his wife in name only but that did not mean that she could not be concerned about his well-being. Hadn't his aunt called to tell her about his accident? Obviously their marriage was not the secret she had assumed it would be within his family circle. It seemed evident too that his relative believed that theirs was something more than a marriage on paper.

'I knew that every minute counted and I knew exactly what you'd want to do,' Emma hastened to assure her. 'This is an emergency. So, I went straight on to the Internet and booked a flight to Geneva for you. It leaves first thing tomorrow—'

With an effort, Hilary parted dry lips and strove to temper her desperate desire to rush to Roel's side with a little common sense. 'Of course I want to go to him but—'

'No buts...' Her dismay palpable and her voice betraying a sharp edge of strain, Emma leapt upright. 'Don't be too proud to rush over there to be with Roel. You're his wife and I bet that what you once had together could still be mended. I'm old enough now to appreciate just how much trouble my bad attitude must've caused between the two of you!'

Hilary was very much taken aback by that explosive speech. Until that moment, she had had no idea that Emma might have blamed herself for the apparent breakdown of her sister's marriage. 'My relationship with Roel just didn't work out. You mustn't think that you had the *slightest* thing to do with that,' she stressed in awkward protest.

'Stop trying to protect me.' Emma groaned. 'I was a selfish little madam. We'd lost Mum and Dad and I was so possessive of you that you were afraid to even let me meet Roel!'

Registering with a sinking heart that every lie, even one that had once seemed like a little white harmless lie, would eventually exact its punishment, Hilary could no longer look the younger woman in the eye. 'It wasn't like that between Roel and me,' she began uncomfortably.

'Yes, it was. You put me first and let me spoil your wedding day and ruin your marriage before it even got off the ground. I was horribly rude to Roel and I threatened to run away if you tried to make me live abroad. I came between the two of you... of course I did!' Emma sucked in a steadying breath. 'You were so much in love with him. I still can't believe how cruel I was to you...'

Hilary had to struggle to concentrate on the unexpected angle the dialogue had taken, for the greater percentage of her thoughts was anxiously lodged on the state of Roel's health. Resolving to sort out her sister's unfortunate misapprehensions at a more suitable time, she prompted, 'What exactly did Roel's aunt say?'

'That he was asking for you,' Emma lied, crossing two sets of fingers behind her back as though to apologise for a fib that she hoped would make her sister feel more confident about flying out to be with her estranged husband.

Roel was asking for her? Surprise that was overwhelmed by a surge of pure joy washed over Hilary and, suddenly, she felt equal to any challenge. She would walk on fire for him, swim lakes, climb the very mountains to reach his side. Roel *needed* her! That knowledge cut through every barrier like a knife through butter. If a male of Roel's intimidating self-sufficiency could express a wish for her presence, however, he had to be very weak or seriously ill, Hilary decided worriedly. She hurried into her bedroom to pack.

'But the salon,' she groaned, rifling the wardrobe for essential clothes and barely able to think straight. 'Who'll look after it?'

'Sally,' her sister suggested, referring to Hilary's second-in-command at the hair salon, Sally Witherspoon. 'You said she was brilliant when you had the flu.'

In the dimly lit hall, Hilary snatched up the phone, eyes an abstracted but luminous grey. The silky hair that framed her oval face shone bright as a beacon. It was that gleaming shade of silvery fairness most often achieved by artificial means. Times without number, Hilary had been forced to explain to disbelieving customers that her hair was natural. Perhaps as an apology for not having had to resort to the permanents and the bleach so beloved of her clientele, she occasionally added a faint hint of another colour to the tips of her hair and this particular month she had employed a pale and delicate hue of pink.

She arranged for Sally to collect the salon keys and phoned another stylist who occasionally came in when things were busy to offer the woman full-time work during her own absence. Those practicalities dealt with, she refused to even think about how all such extra costs would eat into her already tight profit margins. She focused on her sister, Emma, and winced. 'How can I leave you here alone in the flat?'

'My half-term break is over tomorrow and I'll be catching the train back to school anyway,' her sister pointed out. 'I hope I can manage that for myself. I'm seventeen, Hilly.'

Embarrassed by that reminder, Hilary gave the sister she adored an emotional hug.

With hindsight, she could only marvel at the difference that time and Roel's financial rescue package had made to both their lives. She owed Roel so much. In truth, she owed him a debt she could never repay!

Four years ago, the sisters had been living in a dingy flat on a crime-ridden council estate and life had been bleak. Emma had always been clever and Hilary had been determined to ensure that the tragic early death of their parents did not prevent the younger girl from achieving her full academic potential. Hilary had been devastated by a guilty sense of failure when her kid sister had fallen in with the wrong company and started playing truant from school. At the time, Hilary had been working long hours as a junior stylist. She had been in no position to afford either a move to a better area or to spend more time supervising a rebellious teenager.

Roel's generosity had turned their lives around. She hadn't wanted to accept his money but she had realised that that money would give her the best possible chance of setting her little sister back on the straight and narrow path again. She had spent only what it took to set up her own hairdressing business in the far from fashionable London suburb of Hounslow. Taking into account Emma's needs at the time, Hilary believed that she had made the right decision. Only, sometimes, she would still find herself wondering if Roel would have lowered his guard, respected her more and even retained contact with her had she *stuck* to her original intention of simply marrying him and refusing any reward whatsoever.

After all, she had meant to marry him in the same guise as that of a friend doing him a favour. Besotted beyond belief as she had been with Roel, a guy who had hardly seemed to know that she was alive, she would have done almost anything to please or impress him. But sadly, once she had succumbed to the lure of allowing his wealth to solve her problems, once she had taken his money, she had changed everything between them, she conceded unhappily.

'I prefer to pay for services rendered,' Roel had drawled and he had made her feel horribly like a hooker. 'That way there's no misunderstanding.'

Mid-morning the following day, Dr Lerther strove to conceal his surprise when his secretary ushered in Roel Sabatino's wife, Hilary. The tiny blonde woman whose anxiety was writ large in her bright grey eyes was in no way what he had expected.

'I did try to phone before I left the UK but the operator couldn't find the number for this place,' Hilary confided in an explanatory rush.

She was very nervous. The last word in opulence, the hospital was like no other she had ever entered and she had had to advance considerable evidence of her identity before she'd even been allowed in. Her increasingly desperate requests just for word of Roel's condition had been repeatedly met with polite but steely blankness. Baulked of her expectation that Roel's aunt, Bautista, would be waiting to greet her and smooth her passage, she had been forced to introduce herself as Roel Sabatino's wife. Having done so, she felt horribly dishonest but she was convinced that were she to tell the truth about their marriage, she would not even be allowed to visit Roel.

'This is a private clinic and as our patients demand discretion and security, the number is not freely available.' The grey-haired older man extended his hand. 'I'm relieved that you were able to get here so quickly—'

Reading dire meaning into that assurance, Hilary turned pale as milk and gasped, 'Roel?'

'I'm sorry; I didn't mean to worry you. Physically, aside of a severe headache, your husband is suffering from nothing more than a few bruises.' With a soothing smile the consultant swept her across his luxurious office into a seat. 'However, his memory has not been so fortunate.'

The worst of her apprehension set to rest and weak with relief, Hilary sank down into the armchair and then looked puzzled. 'His...er...memory?'

'Mr Sabatino suffered a blow to the head and he was unconscious for some hours. A degree of disorientation is not unusual after such an episode...unfortunately, in this case, there seems to be some temporary impairment of the memory system.'

Alerted by the older man's air of gravity, Hilary had become very still. 'Meaning?' she pressed, dry-mouthed.

'A standard examination after he first recovered consciousness at the hospital revealed a discrepancy in his perception of dates—'

'Dates?' Hilary queried again.

'Roel's memory has misplaced what I estimate to be the past five years of his life. He himself was unaware that there was a problem until it was pointed out to him. He is fully in control of every aspect of his past as it was *then*, but all events since that time are a closed book to him.'

Hilary stared back at the older man in shaken disbelief. 'Five whole...*years*? Are you certain of this?'

'Of course. Mr Sabatino has no memory of the car crash either.'

'But why has this happened to him?' Hilary asked worriedly.

'It is not that unusual for there to be a degree of memory loss as a result of a head injury but as a rule only very small spaces of time are involved. It is called retrograde amnesia. Occasionally emotional trauma or even stress may lead to such an episode but I think we may discount that possibility in this particular case,' Dr Lerther opined with confidence. 'It is almost certainly a temporary condition and within hours or even days what has been forgotten will be recalled either in parts or, indeed, all at once.'

'How is Roel taking this?' Hilary asked weakly.

'Once your husband realised how much time his mind has effectively omitted from his recollection he was very shocked.'

'I bet...' Hilary was struggling to imagine how Roel, who took for granted that he should be one hundred per cent in control of himself and everything around him, would cope with a huge big spanner being thrown in the works.

'Prior to that revelation, Mr Sabatino was on the brink of ignoring all medical advice and returning to his office,' Dr Lerther admitted ruefully. 'For a man of such strong character and intellect, indeed a man accustomed to wielding considerable power, an inexplicable event may be a very frustrating challenge to accept.'

An expression of profound dismay had set Hilary's mobile features as she worked out the ramifications of the five years that the older man had chosen to describe as being simply, 'misplaced'. 'For goodness' sake... Roel won't even remember me!'

'I was leading up to that point,' the consultant asserted in a bracing tone. 'But I'm most relieved that you're here to give Mr Sabatino the support he needs to deal with this situation—'

Her brow had pleated. 'Isn't Roel's aunt Bautista here too?'

'I understand that the lady left the country this morning to attend a pressing social engagement,' Dr Lerther advanced.

Astonished by that information, Hilary swallowed hard on an exclamation. So much for Auntie Bautista! Evidently there was little family affection to hope for from that quarter. Her own head was swimming with a mess of conflicting promptings. At first reassured by the news that Roel was not seriously hurt, she had been thrown right out of her depth when informed of his loss of memory. She tried to picture waking up to her own world as it had been five years earlier rather than as it was now. Even in trying to take fleeting account of all the many changes that had taken place since then in her life, she reached a more disturbing appreciation of just how disorientating Roel's condition would be for him.

She was disgusted by his aunt's uncaring attitude but not that surprised for she and her sister had once endured similar indifference from a close relative. She thought of the debt that she still felt she owed Roel and of how much she wanted to see him. In a purely disinterested and friendly way, she could be of help and support to him. It was an innately tantalising and seductive idea. But wouldn't it be dishonest to pose as his *real* wife? She was his wedded wife in name but in no other way.

A quiver of shamed distaste at the concept of letting such a lie stand slivered through Hilary's slight frame. However, she had promised Roel that she would never, ever reveal the true terms of their marriage to anybody and, to ease her conscience, she decided to tell a half-truth instead. 'I should admit that Roel and I have been...er...estranged,' she said awkwardly.

'I thank you for your confidence and I assure you that what you have told me will go no further. But I must also ask you not to reveal *any* potentially distressing facts to my patient if you can avoid doing so,' the older man emphasised with considerable gravity. 'Although your husband will not acknowledge it, he is already under great stress and adding to that burden could endanger his full recovery.'

As that hard reality was spelt out to her Hilary lost colour and nodded in earnest understanding. From her lips, Roel would learn nothing that might upset him.

'As Mr Sabatino's wife, you are his next of kin and you may do what others may not for his benefit. He has countless employees; those he pays to do his bidding but mercifully you are in a much stronger position,' Dr Lerther opined cheerfully. 'Your husband needs to feel that he has someone close whom he can trust. Make no mistake. His present state makes him vulnerable.'

'I can't imagine Roel being vulnerable.' Hilary's throat was thick with tears and she could no longer meet the consultant's kindly gaze. She was all too painfully aware that she too fell into the demeaning category of being someone whom Roel had once paid to carry out his wishes. But she was also devastated by the obvious fact that he should have nobody other than her available to take on such a role.

'Nonetheless, if I may speak freely…it will be your responsibility to stand between him and all those business personnel who will seek access to him. His own needs must be put first,' Dr Lerther advised her. 'The Sabatino Bank must survive without him at present. He requires rest and relaxation. I am also sufficiently acquainted with the world financial markets to be conscious that no hint of Mr Sabatino's current condition should go beyond this room.'

Hilary's brow had furrowed for she had not even a passing acquaintance with the state of the world financial markets. She had no grasp whatsoever of that aspect of Roel's existence and very little interest in the matter either. Instead, with innate practicality she had homed in on what would plainly be her own role. It would be her duty to look after Roel until such time as he regained his memory.

'May I see him now?'

The consultant recalled his patient's initially appalled reaction to the discovery that he was a married man and hastily suppressed the image of a loving little Christian being thrown to the lions. Hilary Sabatino could well be more resilient than she appeared. She might even be capable of standing firm against the glacial freeze of her billionaire husband's despotic and wholly intimidating character...but even if Dr Lerther had been a gambling man, he would not have risked a bet on that outcome.

Hilary breathed in deep and followed in the nurse's wake. In just minutes she would see the only male who had ever managed to make her cry...

CHAPTER TWO

A WIFE, Roel thought morosely.

Was it any wonder his memory had chosen to betray him by overlooking the most unprofitable acquisition in a man's life since the advent of disease? Although he was only in his thirtieth year, it seemed that he had already sacrificed his freedom. Just as his father had done and his father before him: marry young, repent in millions. Yet he had sworn to himself that he would not make the same error.

He had steered clear of messy personal entanglements and kept mistresses who excelled between the sheets instead. He had a high sex drive, so he took care of it. Lust could not control him. Nor had he ever believed in love. So, love could thankfully have had nothing to do with his evident change of heart on the matrimonial front.

Certain things, however, he did not require memory to know. Indeed certain things he knew by instinct. The wife, whom his undisciplined mind had chosen to forget, would be a tall, elegant brunette because that was the type of woman who attracted him. She would be from a wealthy background and possessed of impeccable society lineage. She might be a career woman—

a banker or even an economist, a possibility that was of some small comfort to him. Perhaps while discussing risk management and investment strategy he had recognised a working soul mate. An unemotional and otherwise quiet woman, who would respect the demands of his schedule when he was too busy to see her.

A knock sounded on the door. He swung round from the window, a male who stood six feet four inches, broad of shoulder and lean of hip, his tall, well-built frame sheathed in an Armani business suit of faultless cut.

'Will you close your eyes before I come in?' a low-pitched British voice asked. 'Cos if you don't I'm likely to feel really silly introducing myself to you as a wife.'

Shock one...he had married a foreigner with a definable regional accent rather than the clear flattened vowel sounds of the English upper class. Shock two...she used teenage slang and made childish requests.

'Roel?' Hilary prompted in the taut silence.

Raw impatience clenched Roel's even white teeth together. He recognised that there were two ways of playing the scene. Either he could blast her out before she even came through the door or he could play along until such time as he had worked out exactly who and what he was dealing with. 'OK...'

'I suppose you're really nervous about this too but, now that I'm here, you don't need to worry about anything any more.'

His back turned to the door, his dark deep-set eyes alight with intense disbelief, Roel actually found himself snatching in a sustaining breath. Shock three...he had married a woman who, in the space of a mere sixty seconds, could contrive to antagonise and offend him by treating him with disrespect.

'I was just so touched that you were asking for me at the hospital...' Hilary gabbled, hastening in and closing the door behind her and only then daring to open her own eyes.

'I *asked* for you?' Roel questioned with incredulity. 'How could I have asked for you when I don't remember you?'

'My goodness, what are you doing out of bed?' Hilary demanded in astonishment, losing all track of what they had been talking about.

'Tell me, do you work using a list of stupid comments or do they come to mind without effort?' Roel shot back with sardonic bite as he swung round to face her.

Standing upright and only three feet from her, Roel's sheer size was menacing. She had to tilt her head back to get a proper look at him and then, even though she had flinched at that cutting comeback, she could not take her attention from him. Her mouth ran dry and her heartbeat speeded up for before her stood the living, breathing male embodiment of her every desire and dream.

The stark male beauty of his lean dark features hit her with explosive force. He was incredibly good-looking and shockingly sexy. But he also had a magnetic presence of command and icy authority that she could feel right down to the marrow of her bones. He did not smile and she wasn't surprised. His charismatic smile was rare and the chill in the room was pronounced. And she understood, she understood even his aggressive attack on her, and her heart twisted inside her with loving forgiveness. Torture could not have dragged the truth from him but she knew that he was as close to scared as he was ever likely to be. She was well aware that the sudden onslaught of a forgotten wife was probably his worst nightmare come true.

'I don't like sarcasm,' she told him, tilting up her chin.

'I don't like stupid questions.' Roel discovered that he had to lower the angle of his gaze even to bring his wife into his field of vision. She was tiny but not remotely doll-like, very much an individual and only in her early twenties at most, he noted, succumbing to grudging fascination. Her grey eyes were the colour of stormy seas. Her hair was a shimmering silvery blonde worn in a short spiky cut and tipped with pink. *Pink?* It had to be a trick of the light, he decided. She had a smatter-

ing of freckles across her nose and luscious cherry-red lips that
would have tempted a saint.

The distinct tightening in his groin caught Roel by surprise
for he was long past the teenage years when his body had last
cast off his disciplined control. But as his attention roamed
down over his wife's glorious hourglass shape his arousal only
became more pronounced. Full, rounded breasts were moulded
by a blue cotton tee shirt while low-slung hipster jeans accentuated her tiny waist and the pronounced curve of her highly
feminine hips. While his rational mind struggled to name shock
four in his encounter with his wife as her total lack of exclusive designer elegance, his appreciative hormones were win-
ning hands down. He might not remember her but the dynamite
sexual charge she ignited in him spoke a great deal louder than
memory or words. Roel always had to explain the inexplicable
and he was now satisfied as to why he must have married her.

'I think you should still be resting.' Involuntarily, Hilary
connected with smouldering dark golden eyes and what little
grasp she had on the muted dialogue vanished.

'Are you in the habit of telling me what to do?' Roel enquired,
striving for a warning note that ended up unaccountably husky.

'What do you think?' As she met his stunning gaze her mouth
ran dry and her tummy flipped. The atmosphere sizzled and
her whole body leapt with energised awareness. No matter how
hard she tried she couldn't drag in enough oxygen to fill her
lungs. Her bra felt too tight, her breasts full and sensitive. Her
nipples pinched tight and stung, reacting to the same sensual
heat that was flaring into wicked being deep within her pelvis.
She knew exactly what was happening to her and, worse, that
she was powerless to stop it. This was, after all, the guy who
had almost sunk her to the degrading level of offering up her
virginity for a no-strings-attached one-night stand. She had
craved Roel that much and that bad and, had he displayed any
interest in that direction, pride would not have held her back.

Exercising the fierce strength of will that was the backbone of his character, Roel removed his intent gaze from his wife. So at least he understood why he had married a youthful sex kitten with no dress sense: lust, mindless, rampant lust, he labelled, his handsome masculine mouth hardening. He was appalled that he could have been that predictable but not one to beat himself up over a sin of the flesh.

'The woman who tried to tell me what to do would be a fool,' Roel murmured with smooth, cutting cool. 'I'm sure you don't fall in that category.'

'I don't squash easy either,' Hilary told him doggedly, her colour high but her spine rigid as she utilised every scrap of dignity she possessed to rise above the humiliating weakness of her own body. 'After what you've been through, you should still be in bed.'

His beautifully shaped ebony brows drew together in a fleeting frown line. 'I have no further need for medical attention. I'm sorry if you have been concerned but I'm heading back into the office.'

Her eyes widened to their fullest extent. 'You can't be serious.'

'As I am rarely anything else, I cannot imagine why you should suggest otherwise. Or believe that I'm likely to be in need of your opinion on the issue,' Roel sliced back in glacial dismissal.

'Well, for what it's worth, I'm going to give you my opinion unasked,' Hilary slammed back at him angrily. 'Maybe you think it's dead macho to act like there's nothing wrong with you but I just think that that's plain stupid!'

Dark golden eyes flared, incandescent with anger. 'I—'

'You're suffering from a very worrying loss of memory and you are not thinking through what you are doing—'

Roel flung his proud dark head high. 'I never act without thought—'

'By going back to work, you would be denying that there's even a problem. I can't let you do that—'

'Tell me one thing,' Roel countered with sardonic clarity. 'Before the car smash, were we in the process of divorce?'

'Not that I know of!' Hilary tossed back, small hands spreading on her hips to maintain a firmer grip, her grey eyes bright with resolve. 'You may be a very clever guy but you can also be very stubborn and extremely impractical. Right now, it's my job to make sure that you don't do *anything* that you'll later regret, so get back in that bed and take it easy!'

Brilliant eyes enhanced by black spiky lashes, Raul surveyed her as though she were a madwoman in need of restraint. 'Nobody tells me what to do. I'm astonished that you should think that you have the right to impose your views on me.'

'Yeah, marriage is a toughie for a control freak,' Hilary slammed back unimpressed. 'I'm not about to apologise for trying to protect you from yourself. If you go back into the bank, your employees will realise that there's something wrong with you—'

'There is nothing wrong with me, only a temporary phase of *slight* disorientation—'

'During which you forgot about a great fat chunk of your past life!' Hilary slotted in heatedly. 'I think that's very relevant and a lot more dangerous than you're prepared to admit. There'll be employees and clients you won't even recognise, situations you don't understand and which you may screw up. You're also five flipping years out of date with your precious work. Who are you planning to take into your confidence in an effort to avoid making embarrassing mistakes? Because one thing I *do* know about you, Roel…just about the only person alive whom you trust is yourself!'

Out of breath and trembling with the force of her feelings, for she was aghast at the very idea of him attempting an immediate return to work, Hilary glared at Roel in challenge. Just as quickly her expression changed to one of anxiety as she saw him frown as though with pain. Only then did she register the

ashen cast of his complexion and the slight tremor in his hand
as he raised it to his head.

'Sit down...' Closing both hands over his, Hilary urged him
back towards the armchair behind him.

Roel was swaying but he still fought her attempt to help him.
'But I don't need—'

'Shut up and sit down!' Hilary launched at him fiercely and
she used his uneven balance to topple him down into the chair
like a felled tree.

'Per meraviglia...' Roel groaned in frustration. 'It's only a
headache.'

But Hilary had already hit the call button to bring a nurse
and the presence of that third party, soon followed by the entry
of Dr Lerther, prevented Roel from expressing his fury at her
interfering and taking charge in such a way.

In any case, Roel had recognised that his wife had panic written all over her. He decided that there was something to be said
for a woman with a face that seemed to wear her every passing thought. Her eyes were dark with stress and worry and she
stood humbly at the back of the room, demonstrating what he
considered to be exaggerated respect for the medical personnel
while nibbling anxiously at a nail.

He couldn't take his attention off his nail-biting wife. She
looked so scared on his behalf and she was trembling. Concern
for his health must have made her shout at him. She seemed to
be fond of him. She might well be fonder still of his immense
wealth and all that it could buy her, Roel conceded cynically
but, indisputably, she seemed to cherish some degree of genuine
fondness for him. He knew all women were terrific actresses but
any single one of the previous lovers he could recall would have
withstood torture sooner than succumb to cannibalising a nail.

In addition his wife was neither as uncomplicated nor as
predictable as he had initially assumed. A startling amount of
fire and defiance lurked behind that cute and curvaceous feminine exterior. He was accustomed to women who said yes to

his every request and worked hard at meeting his expectations before he could even be put to the trouble of voicing a request. He had never met a woman who had the nerve to shout at him or one who would go toe to toe with him in a fight. In actuality, he did not argue with people *ever*. He had never had to argue. Arguments just didn't happen to him.

Hilary was feeling hugely, *horribly* guilty and shaken up. Roel was still suffering from the physical after-effects of a serious accident and she had lost her temper with him. How could she have done that? As a rule she had an even temper and a sunny easygoing nature. What had come over her? Instead of being calm and coaxing and patient, she had been strident and emotional and accusing. He had looked taken aback. She didn't think he was used to being shouted at and she could not believe that she had done so.

Sucking in a deep steadying breath, she studied him. Her heart jumped as though it were on a trampoline. His luxuriant black hair was tousled, bold profile taut, his dense black lashes cut crescent-shaped shadows over his proud olive cheekbones. Extravagantly handsome, he had a raw masculine appeal that turned female heads wherever he went. He still took her breath away. Just as he had the very first time she'd seen him and the recollection of that particular day nearly four years ago swept her back in time…

Talking on a mobile phone, Roel had walked through the door of the busy salon where she'd worked as a junior stylist. There he had stilled, ebony brows elevating with a faint air of well-bred surprise as he'd taken in his surroundings. She had immediately understood that, like others before him, he had mistaken the salon for the much more exclusive place a few doors further along the street. In that split second when he had been on the brink of wheeling round to leave again something had propelled her forward. Something? The fact that he was so outrageously good-looking she would have gone without food for a week just to own a photo of him? How could she explain her own unbelievably powerful need to prevent him walking back out of her life again as casually as he had wandered into it?

'Just you stay on the phone and I'll take care of your hair,' Hilary suggested, planting herself between him and the door, relying on his essential male instinct to avoid acknowledging that he had made a mistake to guide him.

He flicked her a perplexed glance, the sort that told her he did not really see her and was much more interested in his phone conversation. She expected that to change when she wielded the styling scissors around him. In her admittedly slender experience handsome men were well aware of being handsome and as keen as any woman to ensure that their hair was cut only to their own exact specification.

'Do what needs to be done,' Roel told her impatiently.

Asked for guidance a second time, he gave her an unbelieving appraisal. 'But it's only a haircut, nothing important.'

So she just copied the existing conservative style. Even the feel of his luxuriant black hair thrilled her fingertips. As he paid she urged him to make sure that he came back. He had just walked out when she noticed the large denomination banknote that she assumed he had accidentally dropped on the desk. Ever eager, she rushed out into the street after him.

'It's a tip,' Roel said in a pained tone when she attempted to return the money. He stared down at her from his great height while a limousine the length of a train drew up behind him and a uniformed chauffeur leapt out to throw open the passenger door for his entry.

'But it's too much...' she mumbled, staggered by the sight of that limo and the concept of a tip that size.

With a shrug of imperious dismissal, Roel swung away into his opulent car.

Hilary drifted back to the present to discover that while she had been lost in her thoughts Roel had contrived to regain his natural colour and was upright again.

'Should you be standing?' Hilary queried, watching him set down the phone he had been using.

'We're going home,' Roel imparted, ignoring the question.

In search of support, Hilary looked in dismay at the consultant. 'Dr Lerther?'

The older man aimed a stiff smile at her. 'There is no physical reason why your husband should remain at the clinic.'

'*Naturalmente*...the other problem will vanish,' Roel pronounced with supreme confidence.

We're going home. Home? For goodness' sake, where was home? Caught totally unprepared for the development, Hilary followed Roel out to the lift, which swept them down to the ground floor. There she learned that the case she had left at reception had already been stowed in the transport awaiting them.

'So where were you when I crashed my car yesterday?' Roel enquired a tinge drily.

'In London...er... I have a business there,' Hilary answered in an undertone while she frantically wondered what she was supposed to do or say next for she had no script on which to act. Nothing was as she had assumed it would be. He was walking wounded, conscious, but by no stretch of the imagination was he himself.

A limousine with tinted windows sat outside the clinic. A chauffeur doffed his cap. She climbed in and sank into a seat upholstered in rich hide leather. She struggled not to gawp at the astonishing luxury of the car interior.

'How long have we been married?' Roel drawled softly.

Without looking at him, Hilary breathed in deep. 'I think it'll be more relaxing if I don't force-feed you facts—'

Roel reached out a lean brown hand and closed long, sure fingers over hers. 'I want to know everything—'

Startled by the ease with which he had touched her, Hilary could not prevent her fingers from trembling within the hold of his. 'Dr Lerther said that telling you things that you didn't really need to know would just complicate matters—'

'Let me decide what I need to know,' Roel incised without hesitation.

'I think Dr Lerther has your best interests at heart and I don't want to risk your recovery by going against his advice,' Hilary confided unevenly, for that physically close to him for the first time ever she was a bundle of nerves.

'That's nonsense.'

'In a few days you'll have remembered it all for yourself,' Hilary pointed out in urgent consolation, appreciating how much more that scenario was likely to appeal to him. 'It would be better that way...much better.'

In her eagerness to convince him that patience was his best option, Hilary finally dared to glance up. She met his dark golden gaze in a head-on collision. Her mouth dried and her heart pounded like crazy.

'And in the short term?' Roel prompted in his dark, deep drawl.

His delicious growling accent seemed to shimmy down her sensitive spine and set up a chain reaction through her tense body. She was welded to the spot by the electrifying gold of his appraisal; her mind was a blank. 'The short term...?' she parroted like someone who had never heard the expression before.

'You and I,' Roel specified with a low-pitched laugh that sent the colour flying up into her cheeks while she stared up at him with eyes the same shade as winter skies. 'What do I do with a wife I've forgotten?'

'You don't need to do anything. You just trust her to l-look out for you,' Hilary stammered, fighting with every fibre of her being to suppress her embarrassing lack of self-control around him. Why was she hanging on his every word like a lovelorn schoolgirl and gaping at him like a star struck fan? She was infuriated by her own weakness. Her role was to be a supportive friend, nothing more, nothing less. But the sheer thrill level of just being alone with Roel seemed to have stolen her wits.

'Look out for me?' Roel studied her from below black spiky

lashes. She was planning to look out for him? In all his life he did not think that he had ever heard anything more naive or ridiculous. Yet he said nothing because she shone with sincerity and good intentions.

'That's what I'm here for...' Hilary extended, but she could hardly find her voice to make that added assurance for her vocal cords were threatening to let her down. His proximity and the casual confidence with which he touched her were sending her brain into freefall.

Even as she spoke Roel raised a hand to let his forefinger trace the luscious fullness of her soft pink lower lip and that did nothing to cool her temperature. Indeed, where he touched her skin seemed to tighten with an awareness so acute it almost hurt to experience it. Leaning closer without even being aware of it, Hilary gave an almost imperceptible gasp as her nipples hardened into stiff straining points below her tee shirt.

'You're trembling...' Roel murmured huskily. 'But then why not? This is a stimulating situation.'

'I beg your pardon...?' Hilary whispered, convinced she had misheard him.

'A wife I've forgotten,' Roel quipped, watching her with eyes as bright and tough as metallic bronze. 'A woman with whom I must have shared many intimacies but who appears to me at this moment in the guise of a complete stranger. It's a sexually intriguing concept, *cara mia*. How could it be anything else?'

CHAPTER THREE

A RIVER OF BRIGHT guilty colour washed up Hilary's throat and surged as high as her hairline.

Sexually intriguing? Hilary shifted on her seat. *A woman with whom he had shared many intimacies?* Naturally Roel would make that assumption. It would not occur to him that she could be anything other than a normal wife. After all their arrangement nearly four years back had been highly unusual in its terms.

'You have a novel way of viewing things,' she muttered awkwardly, fighting not to betray how uncomfortable she was.

'You blush like an adolescent,' Roel noted with husky amusement.

'Absolutely *only* with you!' Hilary shot back at him, infuriated by the suspicion that her face was hot enough to fry eggs on. As a teenager her habit of flushing to the roots of her hair when she got embarrassed had made her the butt of many jokes at school. Mercifully she had grown out of the affliction but *not*, it seemed, around Roel.

'We can't have been married long,' Roel commented, his

rich dark drawl roughening and slowing as he reached out and tugged her into his arms.

'*Don't!*' Hilary yelped as though he had pushed a panic button.

An involuntary grin crossed Roel's lean, darkly handsome face because, although she wasn't much bigger than a doll, she had an extremely bossy streak. 'Don't worry...kissing my wife is unlikely to put me back into hospital—'

'How do you know that?' Hilary demanded jerkily, angling her blonde head back a little more out of reach. Yet her every physical prompting urged her just to throw herself at him and make hay while the sun, as it were, shone. 'I just don't think there should be any kissing...yet—'

'*Non c'e problema,*' Roel teased, in his element, reading the look of concern that his wife wore and more amused than ever by her fear that sexual activity might somehow be detrimental to his health. 'Think of it as a useful experiment. It might even awaken lost memories, *bella mia.*'

'Roel...'

But anticipation was rising at wicked speed inside Hilary: she didn't want to stop him; she didn't have the will-power to stop him; she couldn't wait to experience what she had once been denied. And when his wide, sensual mouth tasted hers the pathways between every erogenous zone she possessed turned to liquid fire and blazed. Her heart thumped with mad, crazy excitement.

Long fingers sliding into her hair, he tilted her head back the better to gain access to her mouth. She leant back into the strong arm, bending her spine in the most encouraging way imaginable. He dipped his tongue between her readily parted lips and plundered the inner sweetness with a driving male hunger that took her by storm. Her body leapt into almost agonising life, pulses racing and nerve-endings quivering. Forbidden heat surged at the very heart of her. Defenceless against her own desire, she moaned low in her throat in response.

Dragging in a ragged breath of restraint, Roel released her. Ebony lashes veiling his gaze to a reserved flash of gold, he murmured without expression, 'We're home.'

Breathless and dazed by that unfamiliar explosion of passion, Hilary lowered her head and tried to get a grip on herself. Deep down inside her body in a private place that she wasn't even used to thinking about, she was conscious of a wicked ache of disappointment. She had got carried away: he could have made love to her on the back seat of his limo and he probably knew it. Hilary was so ashamed of herself for encouraging him that she wondered how she would ever look him in the face again. She had behaved like a sex-starved groupie let loose on her idol. What on earth was she playing at? He had accepted her on trust and, to be worthy of that trust, she needed to keep a proper distance between them! When the chauffeur opened the door beside her, she scrambled out of the limo in haste and only then took a good look at her surroundings.

Home? Roel appeared to live in a vast stone mansion set within the seclusion of high screening walls. A middle-aged manservant was stationed beside the imposing entrance. The huge hall was adorned with classical statues, gilded furniture and a marble floor. She was intimidated by such grandeur, and her steps faltered.

'Santo cielo...'

Roel's roughened exclamation made Hilary spin round. Wearing a stark frown of disconcertion, he seemed to be staring at the handsome marble fireplace. Swift understanding gripped her. Something had surprised Roel. Something was different or at least not as he had expected. As he evidently had no memory of the change taking place, he would naturally feel disorientated, and when that happened within his own home it had to be that much more disturbing.

Aware of the manservant's covert scrutiny, Hilary hurried over to Roel, tucked a confiding hand into his arm and stretched up to whisper, 'Let's go upstairs...'

In the very act of wondering why one of his grandfather's favourite paintings should be hanging in his grandson's town house, Roel reacted to that breathy little feminine invitation as red-blooded males had done for centuries. The conundrum of the painting momentarily forgotten, he was startled by a desire to scoop his diminutive wife up and kiss her breathless for reading his mind with such accuracy. Was that how he usually acted around her? It shook him to acknowledge that he had no idea.

'I just remembered something...you go on ahead,' Hilary said when they reached the marble landing above. Pulling free, she then hurried back downstairs to speak to the manservant before he could disappear from view.

'I'm sure you're wondering who I am,' Hilary began uncomfortably. 'You are...?'

'Umberto, *signorina*. I run the household and you are Mr Sabatino's guest,' the older man responded smoothly.

'I'm not...actually, I'm Roel's...er...wife, Hilary,' she explained in an apologetic undertone.

Well-trained though Umberto was, he could not conceal his surprise.

'Please ensure that no personal or business phone calls are put through to my husband.'

Umberto stiffened, his lips parting in an anxious way.

'Don't ignore my instructions,' Hilary added, tilting her chin.

When she drew level with Roel again, he dealt her a keen appraisal and then, strong mouth quirking, he bent down and swept her up into his arms.

'Roel?' Hilary squawked, utterly taken aback by his behaviour. 'What on earth are you doing?'

Striding across the elegant landing, Roel vented a husky, sexy laugh and deftly shouldered open the door of the master bedroom suite. 'Ensuring that last-minute instructions to Umberto concerning dinner or whatever...won't interrupt us again!'

'Please put me down...' Hilary pressed in an enervated rush. 'You're supposed to be resting, Roel.'

Roel lowered her down onto a massive bed with exagger-ated care. 'I have every intention of doing so...but only if I have company to do it with, *cara*.'

Hilary rolled over and off the other side of the bed. Her face was pink with embarrassment. 'That wouldn't be restful—'

Lean fingers jerked loose his silk tie, pulled it free and dis-carded it. Glinting golden eyes flared back at her in blatant chal-lenge. 'I don't need to recall the last five years to know that I'm not a restful individual or given to lazing about doing nothing. If I'm not working, I require occupation—'

'But not this,' Hilary slotted in breathlessly. 'You only think that you want to sleep with me but you don't...not really, you don't. You just want to make me feel more familiar—'

'I can't believe I married a woman who makes a three-act major production out of sex,' Roel incised with biting derision.

'I'm trying to think of you, that's all.' Hilary twisted her hands together in an unwittingly revealing gesture of stress. 'This isn't what you need right now—'

'Allow me to decide that.' But Roel had fallen still and his brilliant eyes no longer appeared to be focused on her. His wide sensual mouth twisted and then set into a grim line.

'What is it?' Hilary asked worriedly.

Roel glanced back at her, his stunning dark gaze bleak and bitter, hard cheekbones prominent below his olive skin. 'Cle-mente, my grandfather, is dead...*that's* why the Matisse paint-ing is here in our home instead of at the *castello*. Am I right?'

As he spoke Hilary lost colour.

'On this score, you don't withhold information,' Roel warned her icily.

Eyes stinging with tears of sympathy, Hilary nodded con-firmation with pained reluctance. 'Yes, I'm sorry. Your grand-father died four years ago—'

'How did he die?' Roel demanded.

'A heart attack. I believe it was very sudden,' Hilary proffered, grateful that she at least knew that much and praying that he would ask for no other details.

Roel swung away from her and strode over to the tall windows. His powerful shoulders were rigid with tension below the expensive cloth of his jacket. He was closing her out and she knew it. He had mentally dismissed her from his presence as surely as if he had slammed a door in her face.

'Roel...' she murmured, aching with a compassion she was afraid to show for fear of offending.

'Go check the dinner menu,' he advised very drily.

Hilary's troubled gaze sparked and she stood taller. 'I couldn't care less about stuff like that. Don't push me away. I was very close to my gran and I was devastated when she passed away—'

'Some of us choose not to parade private emotions,' Roel whipped back.

'OK... OK!' Hilary threw up both hands in a peacemaking gesture, expressive brows raised at his vehemence.

Face pale and tight with discomfiture, for he could not have rejected her attempt to offer comfort more clearly, she spun round and walked out of the room.

So what do you do for an encore? a snide little voice asked inside Roel's head. Kick puppies? Do a Scrooge for the festive season?

Umberto was in the corridor. With him was another man, who was carrying her case. Hilary came to an abrupt halt.

'Signora.' With a smooth inclination of his head, the man-servant thrust open the door of the next room and stood back so that she could enter it first.

His and hers bedrooms, Hilary registered, blinking at the magnificence of the furniture and the awesome amount of space. Just as well it didn't seem to be the thing for wealthy husbands and wives to share the same room. My goodness, that could have got really embarrassing, she told herself. But that attempt to give her thoughts a different direction didn't work. Nor did pursing her lips so hard they went numb. When she got an unwelcome glimpse of her reflection in a fancy dressing mirror, she could see that her eyes were still overbright with the threat of stupid, weak, impressionable tears! How could one hard word from Roel turn her to weepy mush?

Why did she have to recall that Roel had once acted more relaxed around her? Yeah, much as if she were the equivalent of hair-trimming wallpaper, she jeered inwardly. But it was true. One day when she had confided how much she still missed her gran he had started telling her about how his grandfather, Clemente, had gone to Nepal to 'find himself' when he was sixty-five years old. Better late than never, she had teased and Roel had groaned.

Snatching in a stark breath, Hilary made herself concentrate and she followed Umberto from the room. 'I'd appreciate a quick tour of the house,' she told him with a friendly smile, knowing that the request was a necessity. She could hardly pretend that she had been living below Roel's roof if she didn't even know her way round it.

Even so the amount of deception involved in the pretence she had taken on with such little forethought was beginning to unnerve Hilary. In just a couple of days, she reflected, Roel would surely regain his memory and he would have no further need for her then. Would he appreciate that she had been trying to help him out? That in fact she had only acted like a good mate?

Umberto was very precise. He would have been happy to show her the interior of every cupboard. Hilary speeded him up by darting from one room to the next, amazed at the sheer size of the house, daunted by the extreme formality of the furniture and all the staff but enchanted by the many paintings. In the basement kitchen she made the acquaintance of the chef but demonstrated dismay rather than approbation when she learned that the exact same menus were rotated on a seasonal basis every year. Scenting the likelihood of greater gastronomic freedom, the French chef kissed her hand, rushed out to the back garden, plucked a vibrant yellow rosebud and raced after her to bestow it on her. Laughing, she slid the bloom into her hair and went back upstairs to freshen up before dinner.

The slender contents of her suitcase had already been tidied away into the dressing room. She had to open every drawer and wardrobe door to find a change of clothes. The shower in the *en suite* was a multi-jet delight. Smiling at such unfamiliar luxury and wrapped in a giant fleecy towel, she padded barefoot out of the bathroom again.

Roel was in the bedroom waiting for her. She jerked to a halt, her bemused gaze taking in the open door that evidently connected with his room.

'*Dio mio*... I like the rose,' Roel murmured softly.

Hilary semi-raised a self-conscious hand to the bud that she had threaded back into her hair again. 'Your chef gave it to me...'

Roel had shed his business suit for black designer chinos of faultless cut and a blue casual shirt. He looked so downright gorgeous that she couldn't stop staring. His smouldering dark sexual attraction hit her like a tidal wave and swept her straight out of her depth and under.

Her admission made Roel quirk an ebony brow. He was not amused by his chef's impertinence. Yet he could see what had inspired the gesture. His wife had flawless skin, grey eyes as deep as a northern glacier lake and a mouth as provocatively ripe as a cherry. He felt his body harden with almost scientific interest. Every time he saw her, did he always want to have her again? Was he always *this* hungry to sink into that slim, shapely body of hers?

The awareness of her own naked skin below the towel gripped Hilary with painful shyness. She was mortified by the generous swell of her full breasts above the fleecy fabric but when she collided with Roel's burning golden gaze her embarrassment was blotted out by the strength of her own response to his overwhelming masculinity. The tingle in her pelvis expanded into a burst of shameless heat and her legs shook. She couldn't move, couldn't even think of anything to say.

The atmosphere was electric.

'I want you, *cara*,' Roel breathed.

That confession sent pleasure and pain rushing through Hilary in equal parts. Once she had nurtured secret fantasies of such a magical moment. The moment when Roel would miraculously cast aside all formality and see her as a desirable woman. What had once been her most fervent dream was actually happening. Roel was saying he wanted her and in every one of her dreams she had always thrown herself at him in joyful reward. Only in the present circumstance that was not an indulgence that she could allow herself.

Roel didn't really want *her*, Hilary reminded herself with pained reluctance. He was expressing a natural desire for a woman who was in fact an illusion: his wife, the woman he believed he had a normal marriage with and whom he understandably believed he could trust. But she was not that mythical wife. She was just someone he had once paid to go through a wedding ceremony with him, someone whom he cared nothing about on a personal basis. And as if all that were not enough, she was also way beneath his touch in terms of status and success.

Interpreting the forlorn air of desperation that her expressive face wore, Roel was frowning with incomprehension when he reached for her. 'Hilary—?'

'We don't have this sort of relationship,' Hilary protested half under her breath.

Ignoring her evasive step back from him, Roel closed long fingers round her wrist to halt her steady retreat. 'I don't understand—'

Tears clogged her throat, for doing what she accepted was right was the hardest thing she had ever had to do in her life. 'Look, it's not important and certainly nothing for you to worry about. But just take it from me, I'm really not a big deal in your life and when you get your memory back you'll remember that and be glad I put you on your guard—'

Roel had stilled. Brilliant eyes shimmering down at her, his questioning gaze narrowed with suspicion. 'What have you done that I should treat you in such a way?'

Taken aback by his reaction, Hilary paled in consternation. 'I haven't *done* anything!'

Roel appeared to have forgotten his own strength, for his fierce grip was threatening to crush the narrow bones of her wrist and she was provoked into a gasp of discomfort. 'You're hurting me...'

Instantly he released her and his concern and his apology were immediate but his next words made it clear that the issue under discussion was not to be so easily set aside. 'Explain what you meant by describing yourself as not being a big deal in my life.'

'All I meant was that you're so busy working you hardly notice I'm around,' Hilary mumbled weakly.

'If you've been unfaithful don't make a mystery of it,' Roel drawled with stinging softness. 'Just pack and get out of my life again.'

Hilary realised that she had stirred up a hornet's nest. Instead of prompting Roel to exercise greater reserve around her she had made the mistake of rousing more stressful concerns. Dismayed, she spluttered, 'Don't be ridiculous...of course I haven't been unfaithful to you!'

'Sabatino men have a habit of marrying flighty women,' Roel derided with a brooding roughness of pitch that was entirely new to her, but which carried an impressive note of foreboding. 'But we waste no time in divorcing them.'

'I'll consider myself warned,' Hilary told him, striving in vain to come up with a light-hearted smile before she vanished back into the bathroom.

In bewilderment, Roel fell back a step. His keen mind was seething with fast and furious questions.

We don't have *this* sort of relationship.

I'm not a big deal in your life.

You're so busy working you hardly notice I'm around.

What kind of a marriage was it where, young though they both were, they were already occupying separate bedrooms? Had that been his choice? She had implied that their relationship was as *he* wanted it to be. He was angry at the conclusions he was being forced to draw. Failure was anathema to him. Instinct had always made him strive for perfection in every facet of his life. Yet it seemed his marriage was in trouble. Without any apparent desire to rebuke or challenge him, his wife had given him a picture of himself as a workaholic husband indifferent to her needs. He could barely bring himself to credit that he rarely slept with her either. But what else was he to think? Now he could look back and recognise that her initial response to being kissed in the limo had been shock and surprise. Shock and surprise followed by an undeniably eager and encouraging response, he reminded himself. So what was wrong could be fixed...*easily*!

Hilary got dressed. She put on a stretchy black skirt that ended four inches above the knee and teamed it with a fitted green top that had ribbon ties. Having checked the time, she called her sister's mobile phone.

'I've been thinking about you all day...how's Roel doing?' Emma demanded anxiously.

'Basically he's all right but that head injury is still causing him some problems. He's not quite himself yet.'

'Meaning?' her sister probed.

'That, right now, I can make myself useful over here...purely as a friend,' Hilary hastened to add.

Almost four years ago, she had not told her sister the truth about her marriage of convenience. She had been afraid that if she did Emma would lose respect both for her and for the institution of marriage. What had then seemed to be a harmless fib couched for the sensitive ears of a girl of thirteen, however, now seemed rather more dishonest and less forgivable. When the emergency with Roel was over, Hilary knew that it would only be fair if she told Emma the whole story. She wasn't looking forward to the challenge but she knew she could not allow the younger woman to go on believing that she herself might have contributed in some way to the demise of her big sister's marriage.

'Exactly what is wrong with him?'

Hilary took a deep breath and explained in a few words.

'You know what all this means?' Emma exclaimed. 'This is going to give you and Roel the chance to make a completely fresh start!'

'There's no question of anything like that.' Hilary sighed, her face clouding with unease. 'I just want to help him out... that's all.'

When she went downstairs, Umberto ushered her into the candle-lit dining room where the table glittered with crystal, gleaming china and heavy silver cutlery. Fresh lilies with petals as pale and perfect as snow ornamented the polished wood.

'This is just *so* beautiful,' Hilary was telling the older man when Roel entered.

Roel almost groaned out loud when he saw the embellished table arrangements. *Inferno!* What was the special occasion? Was it her birthday or their anniversary?

'Are we celebrating something?' he enquired.

Hilary went pink and picked up her glass of wine with a nervous hand. 'Your release from hospital, I expect.'

'I've come up with a safe conversational topic,' Roel informed her. 'Tell me about your family.'

Truth to tell, Hilary could not see a problem with discussing her own background with him. 'There's not much in the way of family to talk about—'

'Your parents?' Having repeated that demand for information, Roel lounged back in his chair with a daunting air of expectancy.

'They're dead…in a car crash in France when I was sixteen,' Hilary explained heavily. 'My sister, Emma, was eleven.'

Roel frowned. 'Who took charge of you?'

'We lived with my father's cousin.' Hilary saw no reason to burden him with the reality of what an unhappy and short-lived arrangement that had turned out to be. 'Emma's at boarding-school now.'

'Here in Switzerland?'

Hilary stiffened. 'No. In England.'

'No other relatives?'

'None. My gran mostly raised me,' she volunteered. 'She was Italian and when I was a child she lived with us and that was how I communicated with her.'

'Yet you don't speak Italian now with me?' Roel censured in the same language but his incisive dark eyes were forgiving because she had established a link between their backgrounds that he respected.

She winced. 'No way. I understand much more than I can speak—'

'Time that that changed,' Roel decreed without hesitation.

'No.' Hilary continued to answer him in English, her chin at a stubborn angle, remembered humiliation in her gaze. 'You once laughed yourself sick at my Italian!' she condemned. 'You said I sounded like a hill-billy because some of the words I used were out of date.'

'I was teasing you, *cara*.' Amusement and satisfaction combined in Roel's response for she had forgotten her embargo on talking about the past.

Her face shadowed. No, he had not been teasing her; he had been annoyed with her for having sufficient grasp of Italian to follow what he had arrogantly deemed to be a confidential conversation. 'We had a bit of an argument,' she admitted stiffly, 'but I don't want to discuss it.'

It was better to stay silent than risk giving him the wrong impression, Hilary decided uneasily. She concentrated on eating instead and the food was delicious. Umberto refreshed her wineglass on at least three occasions. She refused coffee and announced that she was going to bed early because she was tired.

'It is barely eight o'clock,' Roel pointed out gently.

'I never stay up late,' Hilary told him woodenly and stood up.

Roel thrust back his chair and rose. As she passed by he closed a hand over hers. 'One question you *must* answer—'

'No...don't say that to me,' Hilary muttered in alarm.

Diamond-hard dark eyes sought hers and brooked no denial. 'Whose idea was it that we use separate bedrooms?'

Her mouth ran dry. 'Yours...' she told him, recognising that that was the only sensible reply that she could give.

A scorching smile slashed Roel's handsome mouth. Her heart hammered in response like a bird trapped inside a cage. He released his hold and she stepped back from him on knees that felt wobbly.

'Goodnight,' she muttered hurriedly and fled.

Ten minutes later, her teeth brushed and her face bare of cosmetics, she switched out the light and leapt into her comfortable bed with an appreciative sigh. But her adrenalin was still on too high a charge to allow her to relax into sleep and her restless thoughts strayed back to the past and her initial meetings with Roel.

She had fallen in love with a guy who never even took her out on a date. About once a month he had returned to the salon where she worked. In the aftermath of his first visit, for his limo and the size of that tip had been noticed, the most senior stylist had insisted on taking Hilary's place. To Hilary's surprise and delight, Roel himself had objected to the change of personnel and had asked specifically for her.

'Did you remember my name?' Hilary questioned.

'I described you.'

'How?' she prompted with unhidden eagerness.

'Do you always talk this much?'

'If you tell me how you described me, I'll shut up,' she promised.

'Very small, purple lips, workman's boots.'

She was less than thrilled by that portrayal but after five minutes she forgot her promise to give him peace and soon became engaged in finding out what age he was and whether or not he was single. In the appointments that followed, it would have been an untruth to say that he chatted to her but he didn't object to her chatting to him. She tried to get to know him by letting him get to know her. She asked him what he did for a living.

'I work in a bank.' A long time afterwards, she quite accidentally noticed the Sabatino name heading an article in the business section of a Sunday newspaper. That article revealed that, far from merely working in a bank, Roel pretty much *owned* a bank.

The day she heard him lamenting his grandfather's will and the potential loss of the family home he so clearly loved, she leapt into his dialogue on pure impulse and offered to become his 'fake' wife. Breaking off from his phone call, he surveyed her in disbelief.

'Well, why not?' she continued, face burning at her own nerve in making such a suggestion, but even so she was desperate to grab at the chance to do something for him. Something, *anything*, that would make him more liable to take notice of her and maybe even like her.

'I can think of a thousand reasons why not,' Roel fielded in an icy putdown.

'Probably because you're a very cautious guy and you complicate things,' she pointed out gently. 'But you have a simple problem. You need a fake wife so that you can hang onto your home and I would help out—'

'I refuse to discuss this with you. You eavesdropped on a personal conversation.'

'Maybe you should ask one of your friends to help you out and stop being so proud,' Hilary advised in addition.

'Where did you learn to speak Italian like a hill-billy?'

'Like a *what*? What's wrong with my Italian?' she flamed back at him, distracted as he had no doubt intended by the insult.

Roel started to laugh. 'You use archaic words and expressions—'

'Sometimes,' Hilary seethed, 'you're incredibly rude!'

'You interrupted a confidential dialogue and slung an outrageous proposition at me. What did you expect?'

'I was offering to *help* you—'

'Why? We're strangers,' Roel derided.

Cut to the bone, she just jerked her chin down in a nod and shrugged her stiff shoulders. 'Sorry I spoke—'

'Sulking is not attractive.'

Hilary perked up at amazing speed. 'What *do* you find attractive about me?' she pressed hopefully, less than subtle at the age of nineteen years.

'Nothing,' Roel imparted drily.

'Come on...you don't mean it...there's got to be something reasonable about some part of me,' she cajoled.

Watching him in the mirror, she saw him smile. That rare, wildly charismatic smile that made her palms damp and her tummy flip. But he still refused to be drawn. Three weeks later, he phoned her at work and asked her to meet him for lunch at a hotel.

'Business,' he specified lest she get the wrong idea.

'I'm not fussy,' she admitted cheerfully. 'Don't be surprised if I dress up.'

While Roel spelt out the terms of the marriage of convenience that she herself had originally suggested might meet his requirements, he was terrifyingly businesslike. He killed her appetite and she ate nothing. He said he would have to compensate her for doing him a favour. She said no, she didn't want to be paid and she meant it. Then he mentioned a sum of money that bereft her of breath.

'Think it over and we'll discuss it next time I see you—'

'Look, if I had wanted money, I wouldn't have offered to do this. It wouldn't be right to take money for going through a marriage ceremony. I mean, all you want to do is hang onto the home that's been in your family for generations and there's no way you should have to pay me or anyone else to do that!'

Roel dealt her a cool, measuring scrutiny. 'I have no wish to become too personal but you live on the poverty line and you have little hope of improving your own prospects—'

'That's a matter of opinion—'

'A financial injection would give you choices you've never had before. You could go back to school—'

Hilary gave him an aghast look. 'No, thanks. It was bad enough the first time round. I didn't just end up doing what I do, you know... I always wanted to be a hairdresser and I love it!'

'You should continue your education,' Roel completed as though she hadn't spoken. 'Expand your horizons. You should be more ambitious.'

'Would you go out with me if I went to college?' Hilary asked in sudden hope. 'I suppose you wouldn't want to wait that long.'

'Don't be flippant. I was merely trying to offer you some advice.'

'And tempt me with your money.'

And he had tempted her successfully because in the days that followed she worked out that she could turn her life and her sister's life around with just a fraction of the vast sum of cash he had mentioned. If she found them a flat in a nicer area, she would be able to separate her sibling from the bunch of trouble-makers that the younger girl was hanging around with. If she opened up a small hair salon of her own, she would be able to choose her own working hours and spend more time at home with Emma. In the end she agreed to accept a tithe of the amount he had wanted to give her. She was seduced by the idea of what she could do with that money and only after she accepted Roel's cheque did she realise how much of his respect she had lost.

As she suppressed a sigh for a past that could not be altered

Hilary's mind roved back to the present. She was rudely sprung from her drowsiness by the sound of a door opening. A second later, lights illuminated the room. Startled and blinking furiously, she focused on Roel and tried to persuade her brain back into activity.

Before she could achieve that goal, however, an imperious hand closed over the edge of the bedding and flung it back from her prone body. She let out a yelp of mingled astonishment and mortification. He bent down and scooped her up like a parcel he had come to retrieve.

'What are you doing?' she squealed.

'From now on, we share the same bed, *cara*,' Roel delivered, striding back into his own room with both arms firmly wrapped round her.

'I don't think that's a good idea,' Hilary mumbled.

CHAPTER FOUR

ROEL SETTLED HILARY down on his bed.

Feverish heat lit her cheeks. The short blue nightdress she wore had not been chosen for modesty. In the privacy of her own bedroom, Hilary loved to wear highly feminine lingerie that made her feel glamorous but she had never had an audience before. Thrusting herself up into sitting position, she yanked in desperation at the sheet, keen to cover her bare legs.

He unbuttoned his shirt and embarked on removing his shoes. She stopped breathing. She told herself to look away but she knew she wouldn't. She was twenty-three years old and she had never seen a man undress. She had never even been alone in a bedroom with a man. Why? She was still a virgin. In many ways she thought that she was still a virgin because she had met Roel first and learnt to want what she could not have.

At nineteen she had discovered that physical desire could cut like a knife through every thought and all pride. Roel might not have reacted to her in the same way but she had never forgotten the sheer exhilarating strength of her response to him. Every guy who came into her life after him had been measured up against the same yardstick. She had wanted to feel again what she had felt for Roel and it had made her picky.

'I'm going for a shower, *bella mia...*'

Face hot, she dredged her attention from the vibrant slice of muscular brown chest showing between the parted edges of his shirt. 'I'm not beautiful...don't call me that,' she muttered.

Roel came down on the bed on one knee. Laughing dark golden eyes assailed hers. 'If I tell you that you're beautiful, I mean it—'

'But—'

'You have a heavenly shape—'

'I'm not very tall—'

'But what there is of you is of exceptional quality. I keep on getting an irresistible urge to snatch you off your feet and flatten you to the nearest bed...so here you are.'

Roel vaulted off the bed and unzipped his well-cut trousers.

'You're supposed to be resting...' Hilary fought a valiant battle with her conscience and averted her eyes in chagrin at her own longing to spy on his every move. 'I should be in my own room.'

'Go to sleep and stop fussing.' Roel laughed.

He was laughing, smiling. He seemed happy in a way that was unfamiliar to her. She turned over and told herself that there was no harm in sharing the same bed. It was a gigantic bed. It would be silly of her to make a fuss about such a small thing. But suppose he rolled over in the middle of the night and...and became amorous. Yes, just suppose. Would she be able to resist him? She knew she wouldn't want to. Tears of self-loathing stung her eyes and she blinked them back furiously.

On the other hand, another inner voice reasoned, he would soon get his memory back and if something physical had happened between them before that point, how would she feel about it? He was a sophisticated single guy and sex was unlikely to be something he regarded in a serious way. If she acted casual, he would think it had not meant anything more to her. Hilary pressed cool fingers of restraint hard to her hot cheeks and strove to kill her own seditious thoughts stone-dead. She was mortified to appreciate that she was trying to talk herself into the conviction that it would be all right to let Roel do whatever he wanted to do with her.

'Still awake, *cara*?'

At the sound of his deep, dark drawl Hilary pulled her head out from under the pillow and peered at him over the top of the sheet.

Only a towel knotted round his sleek brown midriff, crystalline drops of water still glittering in the cluster of dark curling hair hazing his powerful pectoral muscles, Roel studied her with slumberous cool. Slowly she nodded. He sank down on her side of the bed and her heart started thumping so hard she thought she might be about to suffer a panic attack. He eased back the sheet degree by degree while she held her breath.

'I want to see you,' he told her almost roughly.

Her mouth tingled at the mere thought of his on hers.

'I want to see *all* of you...' he completed huskily.

She was going to say no, she really was just a whisper's breadth from mustering all her defences and saying no to herself and then disaster occurred: she met smouldering dark golden eyes and her conscience drowned there. 'Roel...'

'I like the way you say my name.' He leant down and tasted her pink mouth with devastating expertise. His tongue pried apart her lips. He delved deep and sure in an exploratory foray. As she made a low sound of driven response her hands flew up to sink into his luxuriant hair and hold him close.

'You have the most incredible mouth,' he growled, hauling her up into his arms and across his spread thighs.

Dazed grey eyes roved up to his darkly handsome features. 'We can't do this...' she warned him shakily. 'We just can't.'

'Watch me...' Roel invited thickly, deft fingers releasing the tiny provocative pearl buttons on the bodice of her nightdress.

He thrust back the fabric to expose her full breasts. '*Santo cielo*...you're gorgeous...'

She was blushing fierily. He toyed with the straining raspberry pink crests that crowned the ripe mounds. Her heart was racing so fast it felt as if it were in her throat. All at one and the same time she was shy and embarrassed and thrilled by his touch. With a groan of appreciation he lowered his proud dark head and captured a taut nipple with his mouth, teasing the tender bud with his teeth and his tongue.

'Oh...' Sensual shock engulfed her unprepared body. As a delicious sensation of pleasure-pain darted from the sensitive tip of her breast to the secret place between her thighs she jerked and dragged in an audible breath. Her neck extended and her head stretched back over his arm in surrender.

'Ever since I laid eyes on you at the clinic I've been thinking about spreading you across my bed. Instant lust,' Roel confided, spectacular golden eyes raking over her with raw masculine heat. 'Was it like that the first time I saw you?'

'You never said,' she muttered, pushing her face into his shoulder and hiding it there.

'So I don't share my every waking thought with you?'

'No...'

He pushed her back onto the pillows so that he could study her and he kissed her again long and hard. The kernel of heat in the pit of her tummy swelled and made her hips shift restively against the mattress.

'You're hot for me, *bella mia*,' Roel pronounced with satisfaction.

There was no denying that. Her body felt tight and tense and terrifyingly sensitive on the outside. She had never felt more aware of it. She had never, ever felt anything as strongly as the sensations he was introducing her to and that very intensity was the most complete seduction. She couldn't think, she could only feel. Burning with a dulled frustrating ache, she reached up to him with a need she could not control.

'Don't be in such a hurry,' he teased in a sexy undertone and he skimmed sure hands down over her hips to remove her night-dress. Hungry golden eyes scanned her ripe curves and centred on the tangle of silvery blonde curls at the apex of her thighs.

'Roel...' Hilary gasped for she was too conscious of her own imperfections to withstand that audacious appraisal, and with a stifled moan of embarrassment she rolled over and dragged the sheet over herself.

Vaulting upright, he shed the damp towel and her eyes flew wide and her mouth ran dry for he was boldly aroused. He also had the lithe sun-darkened magnificence and sleek muscular power of a born athlete. Unconcerned by his nudity, he pad-ded back to the bed to join her. Anticipation gripped her like a shower of sparks lighting her up from within but she still couldn't meet his smouldering gaze.

'I want you,' he growled, repossessing her swollen mouth with the driving demand of his own. The erotic invasion of his tongue left her weak, submissive to the storm of his hot sexu-ality. 'But I also want to torment you with pleasure...'

She rejoiced in the weight of his hard naked body against her, linked her arms round his neck when he crushed her softer curves beneath his powerful torso. She couldn't get enough of his devastating mouth. Every kiss was in itself even more than she had once dreamt of and she was lost in a dark world of sen-suality that was utterly new to her. She breathed in short little gasps. The expert attention he paid to her tender-tipped breasts was almost more stimulating than she could bear for she twisted and turned, little cries breaking low in her throat.

'I like watching you,' Roel confided.

The tight sensation of aching fullness between her thighs made her squirm. He touched her where she had never been touched before. He discovered the moist secret heart of her, traced the swollen entrance, forcing a pleading moan from her parted lips. She was on fire for him and writhing, enslaved by the fierce hunger he had unleashed in her.

'Roel...please,' she sobbed.

He drove her wild. In the grip of that fevered seduction, she was helpless and out of control. Waves of throbbing heat were washing over her. He tipped her back and plunged into her slick, damp core.

'You're so tight, *cara mia*,' he groaned with ragged pleasure while she was still in shock from that unfamiliar invasion.

He thrust again, overcoming her resisting flesh and driving home to the very centre of her. She cried out in pain, startled tears pooling in her eyes.

Stilling, Roel stared down at her with incredulous force. 'You were still a virgin...or am I imagining things?'

Already her body was adjusting to the bold incursion of his and the sharp edge of pain had faded. Emotions and responses running at storm-force strength, she stretched up to give him a forgiving kiss. That Roel should be her first lover was what she had always dreamt of and she had no room for regret. 'I didn't know I could feel like this...don't stop—'

'My wife...a twenty-two-carat virgin,' Roel commented again, rich dark accented drawl not quite level.

Hilary wrapped her arms round him and angled up to him in frantic invitation. 'Please...'

As she made that instinctive movement of encouragement he succumbed and sank into her again. The racing excitement that had momentarily gone into abeyance claimed her afresh. With every fluid shift of his powerful body he mastered her and she surrendered to his primal rhythm with helpless abandon. The excitement built and built until she could have screamed with frustration and only then did he send her spiralling out of control into a convulsive climax of explosive pleasure. Bereft of all breath and voice in the aftermath of that revelation, she fell back against the pillows and lay shell-shocked for long moments afterwards.

Roel had made love to her and it had transcended her every naive expectation. However, not only was she already becoming guiltily, uneasily aware that she should not have succumbed to temptation, it was also dawning on her that in becoming intimate with Roel she had trapped herself into a tight corner. She had been too inexperienced to appreciate that Roel might realise that he was the very first lover she had ever had. She was supposed to be a married woman, not a virgin.

At that precise moment, Roel released her from his weight and curved a strong arm round her to carry her over into a cooler patch in the bed. Tawny eyes framed by dense black lashes inspected her hectically flushed face. He dropped a kiss on her brow. 'So…amazing virginal wife…is it possible that you are still almost a bride?'

Hilary paled and lowered her head. Of course he was now wondering if they were a newly married couple. If he had not been holding onto her, she would have taken refuge under the bed and refused to come out again. She was so ashamed of herself that she couldn't look at him and even less did she want to examine her own behaviour. Had she gone clean crazy?

'You're very quiet…' Roel remarked.

'Gosh, I'm dying for a shower!' Hilary exclaimed and practically threw herself out of the bed.

Escape having been the only thing on her mind, she was then aghast to appreciate that she was naked as the day she was born. Flopping down on her knees on the floor with more haste than grace, she scrabbled madly round the side of the bed to find her nightdress and put it on again with frantic hands. Decently covered again, cheeks fiery red, she endeavoured to stand up again and vacate the room in a more normal way.

Lounging back against the tumbled white pillows, Roel was frowning at her with complete incomprehension. *'Che cosa hai?'* he asked incredulously. 'What's the matter with you?'

Hilary forced a smile and aimed it in his general direction. 'What the heck could be the matter?' she fielded and, backing into her own bedroom, took to her heels the minute she knew she was out of view to lock herself into the adjoining bathroom.

What was Roel going to think of her when he recovered his memory? Fierce shame assailed her. He was going to think she was a pretty sad individual to have slept with him in such circumstances. Or was he more likely to recognise that only a truly besotted woman would have seized on the one chance she had had to get close to him? He would guess that she had fallen head over heels in love with him almost four years ago and still found him absolutely irresistible and he would think that she was totally pathetic. She cringed and died a thousand mental deaths at that threat.

In the bedroom next door the internal household phone buzzed and Roel answered it. Umberto informed him in an almost covert tone that a visitor had arrived.

'Who?' Roel queried even as he began to reach for his clothes.

The older man demonstrated a great reluctance to name the arrival but managed to get over the concept that that identity was a matter of immense necessary confidentiality.

Minutes later, Roel descended the stairs. 'Why all the mystery?' he asked his manservant, his tone dry in the extreme.

'The lady is Celine Duroux.'

Roel's strong facial bones clenched, for the name meant nothing to him and he was infuriated and frustrated by that reality.

'Did I do wrong in allowing her into the house?' Umberto quavered.

Rebelling against the galling sense of being at a loss, which his amnesia had induced, Roel refused to lower himself to the level of taking the older man into his confidence. He would very much have liked to know why his employee should believe that the woman might reasonably have been refused entrance to his home. But ferocious pride kept Roel silent.

He entered the rarely used rear reception room where Umberto had stashed the unexpected guest. A beautiful green-eyed brunette surged towards him. Almost six feet in height with perfect features and the chic of a fashion model, she threw herself into his arms exclaiming, 'Have you any idea how frantic I've been? When you didn't show up yesterday, I simply assumed you were too busy. But when I heard a rumour that there'd been an accident, I just *had* to come here!'

Disconcerted by the intimacy of her greeting, Roel set her back from him. His piercing dark eyes were glacier-cool with caution.

'As you can see, your concern was unnecessary. I am in good health.'

Celine Duroux gave an exaggerated shiver. 'Don't be so cold with me,' she complained.

'Am I being cold?' Roel was playing for time.

The brunette pouted and sent him a provocative look through her eyelashes. The calculated artificiality that seemed to accompany her every word and gesture grated on him.

'OK...' she sighed. 'I know I shouldn't have come here because you think your mistress should be ultra-ultra discreet. But it isn't the nineteenth century any more.'

Not by so much as a flicker of expression did Roel reveal the shock she had just dealt him. A four-letter exclamation that was a curse and a word he never utilised lit up like neon inside his brain. Finally he understood what had rocked Umberto's fabled nerves of steel. Celine Duroux was his mistress and sufficiently confident to visit his home even though she had to be aware that he was a married man.

Unhappily his mistress's attitude said a lot about what had to have been his own attitude towards his wife. It crossed Roel's mind that that four-letter word he had mentally applied to the situation might also be reasonably applied to his own character prior to the car crash. It did not take great genius to work out why his marriage appeared to have been under strain or why his wife had informed him that he paid her little attention: he was having an affair.

'I still think that it would have been wiser if you had resisted the urge to call here,' Roel countered. 'As you have, however, it's only fair to tell you that I believe our relationship has run its course and must now end.'

While Celine surveyed him in angry surprise, Roel concluded that speech with conventional regrets. He knew he did not sound convincing, but then his sole motivation at that point was to get Celine out of the house before Hilary was slapped in the face by the sight of her. He was not accustomed to finding himself in the wrong and he was furious at the revelation that his personal life was a mess. Celine had referred to his failure to show up for an appointment with her only yesterday. So, there was no doubt about it: he had been unfaithful to his wife. No wonder he had sensed so much tension in their relationship!

Did Hilary know about Celine? Of course she knew there was another woman! That had to be why their marriage had not been consummated. Had Hilary refused to sleep with him while he was still keeping a mistress? Doubtless warned by Dr Lerther not to give her husband any disturbing information, Hilary had told him nothing that might trouble him. Had it not been for her inability to hide her distress and confusion after they had shared a bed, he would undoubtedly have concluded that she was still a virgin only because they were newly married.

Instead he had been confronted by a far less pleasant explanation and guilt was a new experience for Roel. In fact as a Sabatino male he was used to holding the moral high ground. Sabatino men prided themselves on their sense of honour. It was their undeserving wives who had in recent generations proven their unworthiness with greed, promiscuity and moral weakness. But Hilary already seemed rather an improvement on the women chosen by his forebears, he acknowledged, his wide sensual mouth compressing.

He remained silent while Celine endeavoured to tease him into changing his mind before sharply accusing him of being cruelly insensitive. He said nothing. She would be richly compensated for the sudden termination of their arrangement. Without his encouragement the scene could not escalate and, outraged by her failure to have a discernible effect on him, Celine finally stalked past him and out into the hall.

Having gathered her courage to go off in search of Roel because she was worried that he had vanished from his bedroom when everything she had ever heard about men had led her to expect him to fall asleep after sex, Hilary was just in time to see Celine Duroux crossing the hall below. Hilary fell still on the upper landing and stared at the stranger with her tumbling mane of chestnut hair, dazzlingly lovely face and legs that looked as long to Hilary as her own entire body.

She watched the brunette depart and wondered who on earth she was. Had she been visiting Roel? Could she have been a girlfriend? For goodness' sake, why had it not occurred to her that Roel might be involved with someone? Overtaken by anxiety and unease, she hurried back to her own room and went to bed. Her last waking thought before exhaustion claimed her was that if Roel had had another woman in his life, his aunt would scarcely have contacted her in London.

Ten minutes later, Roel gazed down at his sleeping wife. Her lashes were clogged together as though she had been crying. The conscience he had not known he had until that moment slashed at him. He was such a bastard. There was nothing new in his awareness of that fact. Even as a teenager he had not wasted much time or thought on women. He had never loved and he had always left them. But *this* woman was in a class of her own because he had married her and made her unhappy. Her bitten nails spoke for her and she deserved better. She had not mentioned Celine. That was sensible; he would not raise that issue either. Some things were better left buried. In any case, as of tonight his wife was very much his wife and they would proceed from that point...

As Hilary wakened she stretched and the unfamiliar intimate ache between her thighs shot her back to full awareness faster than anything else could have done.

She looked at her watch in dismay for it was afternoon. Uneasy dreams had given her a disturbed night and she had slept late. Scrambling out of bed, she flung herself into the activity of getting up but all the time her mind was betraying her. She was remembering how Roel had looked while he was making love to her: his black hair damp, beautiful dark knowing eyes savage in their intensity. She quivered. Just thinking about Roel made her go weak at the knees. His outer shield of ruthless cool concealed a hot and passionate temperament.

But her biggest thrill had been the simple joy of being able to pretend that Roel was *her* guy. Ridiculous as it was, that had been her dream come true. The night before she had been overwhelmed by guilt at having slept with Roel. She had always been a very honest and straightforward person. Unfortunately circumstances had made it impossible for her to be honest with Roel. But now as she flung back the curtains on the clear bright light of day she decided that she had been over-tired and too hard on herself.

So…she had made love with Roel. While that had been a very big deal on her terms she doubted very much that he attached similar importance to the act of sex. He was very rich and very good-looking and whether she liked it or not he had to be very experienced with women. She might be his wife but he had had no memory of her whatsoever. Yet he had still taken her into his bed and had wasted no time in satisfying his high sex drive with her. To be frank, though, she had no complaints on that score. In fact, she reflected with guilty amusement, she might even be at risk of fawning on him like a willing slave girl in the hope that he would feel free to repeat what for her had been an extraordinarily pleasurable event.

Did she have the soul of a slut? No, she was still madly in love with him and she could not imagine ever sharing something so personal and intimate with anyone other than Roel. Why shouldn't she build up a few harmless memories for the future? Long after he had again forgotten that she even existed, she would be living alone and sleeping alone because she would always prefer that to settling for second-best. And next to Roel, who was fiercely handsome and sexy, not to mention intelligent and strong, other men just shrank in stature. That was why she had never managed to fall back out of love again. A sound came from the bedroom and she turned away from the bathroom vanity with a lipstick still clutched in her hand.

'Oh...it's you,' she muttered unsteadily when she saw her husband lodged in the doorway.

'*Dormiglione*...sleepy-head,' Roel said huskily.

Her attention glued to his lean powerful face and her heart-beat went haywire.

'You don't need this stuff.' Roel bestowed a frowning look of reproof on the sizeable collection of cosmetics scattered on the counter. 'Get rid of it.'

His domineering streak had come to her rescue. Turning back to the mirror, Hilary tilted back her head to paint her lips with a defiant hand. 'I like make-up.'

'But you must know that I don't,' Roel informed her in a tone that hinted at his amazement that she should be wielding a cosmetic wand in his vicinity.

'Well, it's good that you have a free choice *not* to wear make-up,' she pointed out.

'Don't be facetious. I dislike anything false.'

Hilary glossed her lips with a raspberry tint and gave him a forgiving grin. 'You're an amazing guy...you're just so controlling and spoilt—'

'*Spoilt?*' Roel repeated with an edge of disconcerted rawness.

'Every place you go you're surrounded by people you can order around. Servants, employees. I should think you'd get tired of being incredibly bossy but instead you seem to thrive on handing out orders—'

'Expressing a preference is not handing out an order,' Roel delivered icily.

'When you express a preference, it's the same thing as a command. But I'm not going to bin all my make-up just because you don't approve of it. You're wearing a pretty boring suit…are you about to throw it away because I think it's deeply untrendy?'

'I don't do trendy at the bank,' Roel told her drily.

'But you're not at the bank now,' she heard herself say, her voice husky from lack of oxygen and the disturbing little bubble of excitement flaring up inside her.

Without warning Roel snaked out his hands and caught her to him. 'You're very…feisty—'

With every sense leaping with wicked anticipation, Hilary sparkled up at him. He dragged her even closer. Adoring his hard, muscular strength, she melted into his overwhelmingly masculine frame. 'You mean cheeky?' she whispered.

Roel raised lean brown hands to her face and framed her cheekbones. Her grey eyes were mirrored pools of encouragement. His scorching golden gaze locked to her triangular features with hungry force. 'All I know is that you make me hot for you. If the maids weren't next door packing for you, I would take you up against the wall. I'd like to do it hard and fast and I think you'd like it too, *bella mia.*'

A wave of burning heat rose up under Hilary's skin in the mother of all blushes. She could barely credit that he had said such a thing to her but the sensual intensity of his appraisal underscored how serious he was. Her legs trembled. She felt wildly out of her depth but feverishly excited by his boldness. Her nipples had swollen into stiff peaks below her tee shirt and the forbidden tingle in her pelvis made her feel unbearably weak.

'And I believe I could do it without messing your make-up,' Roel continued in the same considering tone.

'Probably…' Her voice emerged a little squeakily.

Looked down at her passion-glazed face, Roel laughed with very male satisfaction. 'But I think I'll resist the urge until you take it off again!'

'You'll be waiting a very long time!' Mortified by his mockery, Hilary yanked herself back from him and then hesitated.

Whether she wanted to or not, she knew that she really ought to ask him who his female visitor the night before had been. 'I saw the woman who called here to see you last night and I wondered who she was...'

As Roel stilled his stunning eyes veiled. 'What woman?'

Hilary reddened. 'She had long dark hair...she was very attractive...'

'Oh, that one...' Roel shrugged with magnificent cool, not a muscle moving on his lean, intelligent face. 'She works for me.'

The current of relief that passed through Hilary left her feeling a little light-headed. It had been silly of her to take fright at the sight of the beautiful brunette. She heard someone in the bedroom next door ask Roel a question.

'Hilary?' Roel requested her attention. 'The maids say they can only find a handful of garments. Where is the rest of your wardrobe?'

Wrenched from abstraction with a vengeance, Hilary froze in strong dismay. Naturally Roel would expect her to have an extensive collection of clothes. Weren't all rich men's wives supposed to be mad about fashion? That dressing room ought to be lined with wall-to-wall designer stuff. How on earth was she to explain all those empty cupboards and drawers?

Frantically striving to come up with a good reason for her lack of clothing, Hilary drew level with Roel and shrugged. 'I decided to have a good old clean out,' she announced.

His ebony brows pleated. 'But according to our staff you have only two outfits here, *cara*.'

Hilary worried at her lower lip with her teeth and dropped her eyes. Her mind was a total blank. 'I got a bit carried away...?'

The silence stretched and she threw a nervous glance in his direction.

His lean, darkly handsome features were unreadable. He looked levelly back at her.

'I really must go shopping,' she mumbled.

'If I didn't know better, I would think you had been living somewhere else,' Roel commented.

'For goodness' sake…' Hilary exclaimed tautly.

'So explain the empty closets in a way I can believe.'

Taut as a bowstring, Hilary breathed in deep and, mercifully, inspiration grabbed her. 'We had a stupid row because you don't like my taste in clothes…and I was so annoyed with you, I dumped them all!'

Roel treated her to an appreciative appraisal. 'Now that, with your quick temper, I *can* picture.'

Some of her fierce tension ebbed. 'Why are the maids packing for me? Are we going somewhere?'

'The Castello Sabatino.'

CHAPTER FIVE

THE CASTELLO SABATINO was a medieval castle that stood guard over a remote wooded valley that lay close to the Italian border. A still lake of crystal-clear water lapped the foot of the massive stone walls, acting like a mirror for the bright blue vault of the sky and the snow-capped majesty of the alpine peaks. Both the setting and the building were breathtakingly beautiful and Hilary was not at all surprised that Roel had been prepared to marry her to ensure that he kept his ancestral home.

The helicopter that they had boarded in Geneva landed on a purpose-built heli-pad. Having lifted her out with easy strength, Roel engulfed her hand in his to walk the last few yards. She watched him frowning into the sun and lowering his proud dark head as though the bright light were a knife.

'Are you feeling all right?' she asked worriedly.

'I'm a little tired, nothing more.' His dark, deep drawl was brusque, dismissive and laced with all the annoyance of a male unaccustomed to anything less than a full quota of buoyant energy. 'I went into my office at five this morning—'

Hilary stopped dead. 'You did...*what*?'

'I *am* the Sabatino Bank. It cannot easily manage without

me,' Roel countered drily. 'I had to familiarise myself with current events, ensure that business could continue without me and deal with what I did not understand.'

'I can't believe that less than twenty-four hours after your doctor told you to rest you went into that wretched bank at the crack of dawn!' Hilary fired at him in shaken reproof.

'I did what had to be done.'

She studied his hard jaw line. It might as well have been etched in stone. He was so stubborn she could have screamed. In the unforgiving strong light his olive complexion had an ashen quality. He looked exhausted.

'You really don't have any respect for your own health.'

As Roel strode beneath the ancient arched entrance to the Castello Sabatino he shot her a hard-edged impatient glance. 'Did you imagine that I could simply stage a vanishing act? Were I to absent myself from the bank without an explanation, it could cause a panic that would ultimately damage business.'

'So what was your explanation?' Hilary prompted, watching what she was quite certain were lines of pain settle between his pleated ebony brows.

'I said that the impact of the accident had left me suffering from double vision and that I must rest my eyesight. In that way I was able to access useful information from my executive assistants without creating comment.'

'Really, really sneaky,' Hilary conceded in grudging admiration.

'I added that I would take advantage of the enforced break from work to enjoy a vacation with my wife.'

'My goodness…were people surprised?' Hilary asked, dry-mouthed, for Umberto's dumbfounded response to the news that Roel had a wife had given her the impression that with the exception of his aunt, Bautista, he had indeed kept their marriage a closely guarded secret. So any seemingly casual reference to his suddenly having acquired a wife would certainly have startled his staff at the bank.

'Their surprise was understandable,' Roel fielded. 'I am not in the habit of taking time off. By the way, you should have discussed barring all my phone calls with me.'

Hilary went pink. 'You would've insisted that you could handle them.'

'In the short term, it was good thinking.' Acknowledging the respectful greeting of a middle-aged housekeeper whom he addressed as Florenza, Roel stilled at the foot of a mellow stone staircase. 'But don't take action again on my behalf *without* prior consultation,' he concluded with measured censure.

Stung by that reproof, Hilary opened her mouth on heated words.

Roel pressed a taunting forefinger against her parted lips and she shivered, suddenly achingly conscious of the size and power of his lean, hard physique that close to her own. 'You know I'm right—'

'No, I *don't* know that you're right...what's wrong?'

Roel was staring down at her with brooding concentration. For perhaps a tenth of a second, his lush black lashes swept down and he frowned before lifting them again to focus on her with dazed and questioning force. 'You ran out into the street after me...'

In the wake of that strange statement, Hilary regarded him with incomprehension. But when he pressed an uncertain hand to his damp brow, she reacted. 'Roel? For goodness' sake, come and sit down—'

'No...' Roel incised almost roughly and he closed an imprisoning arm round her narrow waist instead. 'We'll go upstairs and talk about this in private.'

'Talk about what?' she whispered, her nerves leaping about like jumping beans.

And then the proverbial coin dropped and she understood: *you ran out into the street after me.*

'You've just remembered something from the past...' Hilary

framed, her tummy lurching with fierce tension. 'And you've remembered something about me...'

'It was as though someone had flashed an old photograph in front of me...' In an impatient movement, Roel thrust open a door into an elegant reception room. Although that brief flare of lost recollection had disconcerted him, he had gained visible strength from it. 'You were trying to return the tip I'd left...'

'Yeah...' Her hands wound together and then parted and then laced back together again to flex.

Roel gazed at her in bewildered disbelief. 'Why would I have been tipping you? Was that a joke or something?'

Hilary turned pale as death and hurt as much as if he had slapped her. She could already see the chasm opening up between them. She was not what he had expected her to be. She was not and could never be a part of his privileged world. 'I'd just cut your hair...'

'My hair?' Roel stared at her much as if she had suddenly started performing back flips for his amusement.

Hilary compressed her lips and gave a tight nod of confirmation. 'I'm... I'm a hairdresser. That business with the tip you left happened the very first time we met—'

'*Inferno!* I can recall everything I was feeling and thinking in that one tiny moment in the street! You had me as hard as a rock,' Roel admitted with shattering frankness, his fierce gaze wholly pinned to her. 'I wanted to haul you into the limo, check into a hotel and have a lost weekend.'

Hot pink flooded her triangular face and then slowly and painfully receded again. Well, at least he wasn't throwing her any false sentimental lines. She should be grateful to learn that he had found her attractive even though he had been far too aloof to show the fact. But she wasn't grateful. She was hurt and furious. A lost weekend? Was that all she had seemed good for? A right little tart likely to go to a hotel with a guy she barely knew for casual sex? Anguish arrested her feverish thoughts at that point. She would have gone. Maybe not that first day but later, if he had asked, she would have gone because by that stage she had been so besotted she would have settled for anything she could get. Even if that did encompass just the physical side of things, she conceded, her throat closing over with angry tears.

'*Scusate!* I should not have said that.' Roel lounged back against the wall, visibly struggling to master the total exhaustion weighting him.

'Oh, don't let it worry you. I'm not thin-skinned,' Hilary told him in an artificially bright voice. 'Please lie down for a while. You look ill.'

Shedding his tie and unbuttoning his shirt where he stood, he strode heavily through to the connecting bedroom.

'I think I should call the doctor,' Hilary remarked from the doorway.

'*Dannazione*…there's nothing the matter with me!' Roel slashed back at the speed of a cracking whiplash. 'Stop fussing.'

Hilary watched him sink down onto the bed and then tumble back against the pillows. He had not even removed his shoes. She pulled the blinds at the windows. Eyes semi-closed, he extended a lean hand in a graceful conciliatory gesture.

'You should know by now that I make my own decisions, *cara mia.*'

'That's not a problem,' Hilary assured him tenderly, strolling back and sitting down on the bed to let her small fingers curl into the warm clasp of his. No, his desire to make his own decisions was not a problem as long as his decisions agreed with her own conclusions.

'What I said…that flash of memory caught me off guard and I was crude.'

'Not crude,' Hilary responded in a quiet voice as sweet as honey, for she was determined to get her own back for the hurt he had caused her. 'A bit basic, but I can forgive you this once because the rest of the time you are the most romantic guy I've ever known.'

Roel's grip on her hand loosened and his spiky black lashes lifted on stunned dark golden eyes. 'Romantic...?' he parroted.

Even in the shattered state he was in, his wide sensual mouth was ready to curl with extreme scorn at such a suggestion. 'You're teasing me...'

'No, I'm not,' Hilary asserted.

Roel tugged her below a powerful arm and muttered sleepily. 'You can stay until I fall asleep.'

She almost made the mistake of asking him if his mother had done that, but mercifully recalled that no such cosy events could have figured in his childhood. He had only been a year old when his mother had taken off with her lover and never come back even for a visit. Unable to avoid answering her nosy questions, he had once told her that in a single derisive sentence that had pierced her tender heart.

When he was asleep, she went downstairs. She ate a beautiful meal in a superb dining room filled with enormous furniture. Her heart was too full to allow her thoughts to settle on anything other than Roel. It seemed obvious that before very long she would be going home again and instead of being happy at that possibility she felt unbearably sad because it meant that she was going to lose Roel again. He had already remembered something from those missing five years in his memory bank and it had happened even sooner than she had expected.

She had suspected that Dr Lerther was being rather too optimistic when he had repeatedly stated that Roel's amnesia would be of a very temporary nature. Now she could see that the consultant had been right on target with his forecast. Soon Roel would recall everything about the five years he had forgotten. He wouldn't need her any more. Had he ever really needed her? Or had that just been her own wishful thinking?

She curled up in a chair by the bed to watch over Roel while he slept. From now on, she told herself that she would ensure that their relationship remained strictly platonic. When he had remembered the truth about their supposed marriage how would he look at her? Would he think it strange that she had slept with him? Would he even care? He was a guy, a little inner voice protested soothingly. He was not going to waste loads of time agonising about *why* she might have done certain things. No, he would only want to get back into his real life. He would probably be very relieved to learn that, in strictly conventional terms, he did not really need to think of himself as a married man. In fact when he had regained his full memory he would most likely laugh at how events had developed.

When Hilary wakened she was lying in bed. Daylight was striking through a slender gap in the curtains and gleaming over Roel's proud dark head as he looked down at her. At some stage of the night he had stripped. His bare bronzed chest was just inches away from her and she was incredibly conscious of the hair-roughened masculine thigh lying against her own.

'What time is it?' she mumbled, taken aback by the fact that they were in the same bed again.

Brilliant dark golden eyes rested on her. 'Five after seven. I slept the clock round. I feel *amazing...*'

'I don't remember coming to bed—'

'You didn't. You were sleeping in the chair. You shouldn't worry so much about me, *cara*,' Roel reproved. 'I'm brilliant at looking after myself.'

The dark, husky timbre of his accented drawl shimmied down her taut spinal cord. Without responding to any conscious prompting, she found herself shifting even closer to him. It was like being possessed, she thought in panic at her own behaviour. There was to be no more intimacy, she reminded herself wretchedly, and in a sudden movement she made herself sit up.

Without hesitation, Roel tipped her right back again, lean, strong face intent, smouldering dark golden eyes full of unashamed sexual hunger. 'You're not going anywhere, Signora Sabatino.'

If anything his use of that form of address made Hilary's conscience hurt even more. 'But—'

'You're very restless this morning.' Laughing, Roel slid a thigh between hers to anchor her in place beneath him. 'But you're not allowed out of bed until I say so.'

As she gazed up into his darkly handsome features her heart jumped and she felt weak with lust and longing. In the interim he brought his intoxicatingly sensual mouth down on hers. His hungry urgency sent her temperature rocketing.

Golden eyes bright with male appreciation, Roel bared her creamy rose-tipped breasts. Something pulled tight low in her pelvis and made her squirm up her hips. He cupped her swollen flesh, let knowing fingers play over her distended nipples and excited a low cry from her throat.

'You want me, *bella mia*,' Roel stated with satisfaction.

'Yes...' Hilary could not believe how fast it had become impossible to think, never mind fight what she was feeling. She craved his mouth and the erotic mastery of his touch. Her body was burning with impatience, eager and hot. That craving made it all the easier for her to suppress the little voice at the back of her mind that warned that she was doing wrong.

Eager for the hard demand of his mouth on her own, she rejoiced in his passion. She luxuriated in the right to shape his proud dark head, sink her fingers into the springy depths of his black hair and stroke her palms over the satin-smooth skin covering his muscular shoulders. She licked his skin there and thought he tasted sublime. Tingles of eager response shock-waved through her slender length and drove her to a fever pitch.

'You make me so hungry for you,' Roel growled and he flipped her over and into a position she didn't expect before he plunged into her with one driving thrust.

The wave of wicked pleasure took her in a stormy tide that made her whimper in shock at the delight of such sensation. The damp, sensitive place at the heart of her had become a fiery furnace. Ecstasy had her in its hold and there was no room for pride or shame in her passionate response. When the rush of sweet pleasure became unbearable, she surged into a shattering release with an abandoned cry, her excitement only heightened by the shudders of climax racking him in concert.

Still engulfed in the after shocks of rapture and with her eyes misted with happy tears, Hilary tumbled back against the pillows and held Roel's big powerful body close. He kissed her long and slow and deep and she struggled to catch her breath again.

She looked up at him, marvelling at his hard male beauty. A giant wave of love and appreciation was engulfing her. His slumberous dark golden eyes withstood her tender inspection and her fair skin warmed with self-conscious colour, but still she could not stop revelling in the very right to stare at him. High cheekbones slashed his bold dark features into proud planes and hollows. He was stunningly handsome even with dark stubble roughening his hard jaw line.

'You take my breath away...' she whispered shakily, laying her fingers against his wide, sensual mouth.

He caught her hand in his and then gazed down at her bare fingers with palpable surprise. 'Where's your wedding ring?'

Hilary froze in consternation. That a husband might reasonably expect his wife to be wearing a ring should have occurred to her, but it had not. 'I...er... I didn't want to wear one—'

Resting back against the pillows, Roel surveyed her with brooding intensity. 'Why not?'

Beneath that grim scrutiny, Hilary went scarlet and stammered, 'I—I just thought rings were a bit old-fashioned and didn't see why I should bother.'

'I don't like it,' Roel decreed without hesitation. 'I married you and I expect you to wear a wedding ring.'

Feeling horrible that she was allowing herself to tell more lies to protect her own masquerade, Hilary could no longer meet his gaze. 'I'll think that over.'

'No. You won't think anything over. I'll buy a wedding ring. You'll wear it. *End* of discussion,' Roel delivered with derisive force and sprang out of bed to pull on a pair of black silk boxer shorts.

Halfway across the room his long forceful stride came to a halt and he swung back to her. His lean dark face was impassive, his brilliant eyes decidedly challenging. 'You know, you never did tell me why my wife was still a virgin...?'

'And I'm not going to when you speak to me in that tone,' Hilary fielded, tautly defensive, sitting bolt upright in the vast bed, clutching the sheet round her as though it were her only sanctuary in the storm.

'You'll have to do better than that, *cara mia*,' Roel drawled.

Her eyes flashed and she stormed back at him in Italian. 'No, I don't! When you get your memory back you'll realise that there's no big mystery on the score of my lack of experience—'

'Is that a fact?'

'*And* you're not going to think it's remotely important either!' Hilary completed.

'Tell me just one thing,' Roel fired at her. 'Why did I marry you?'

Hilary stilled and finally muttered indistinctly, 'You married me for all the usual reasons...'

'Are you saying that I fell in love with you?' Roel demanded.

'I'm not saying anything...' Colliding unwarily with his shimmering dark golden eyes, she decided that she might as well tell him what he expected to hear so that the issue could be laid to rest. 'OK...you fell in love with me.'

Roel paced back a step towards her, his tension palpable. 'So I bought into the whole fairy tale?'

'Why not?' Hilary asked, her voice rising a little with strain.

'No reason.' Roel bent down and scooped her off the mattress. 'But if I went for the whole fairy tale, it means you'll definitely be the kind of woman who wants to share the shower with me,' he teased.

'Is that blackmail?' she dared unevenly.

Over breakfast in a charming sunlit courtyard ornamented with lush flowering climbers and pots overflowing with greenery,

Hilary asked Roel about the history of the castle. That he loved every time-worn stone was obvious to her. She tried not to think about the lies she had told him earlier. He had stopped asking awkward questions and he was no longer concerned about their relationship. Since Dr Lerther had advised her to give Roel nothing to worry about, didn't that mean that she had done the right thing? A couple of soothing little fibs was not going to cause any lasting damage, she reasoned.

'I organised a surprise for you yesterday,' Roel revealed as he walked through the grand hall.

'What kind of a surprise?'

'I thought it was time to take care of the clothing problem,' he told her softly and cast open the door on a huge and crowded reception room.

Roel had issued invitations to several designer salons to visit the *castello* with a selection of garments. Hilary was whisked into the room next door to have her vital measurements taken and her attention fully claimed. She was in a panic. How could she allow Roel to go the expense of buying her an entire wardrobe? But how could she persuade him that she didn't need anything new when he himself had seen how seriously short of clothing she seemed to be?

Only minutes later she was paraded back into Roel's presence. She was wearing a skirt suit that was at the cutting edge of the latest fashion trends.

Roel studied her. The aqua shade flattered her fair skin and bright silvery blonde hair while the short fitted jacket and flirty skirt emphasised her stunning hourglass figure and shapely legs. His keen gaze glinted with masculine approval. 'Delectable,' he murmured huskily for her ears alone.

And for the first time in her life Hilary felt worthy of special attention. Her own imperfections seemed to vanish beneath the balm of Roel's unashamed appreciation. She was blushing like mad and feeling hugely self-conscious but at the same time she held her head high and she felt proud. When Roel was admiring her, she could no longer lament her imperfect features, lack of height and too generous curves.

From that point on, Hilary was enjoying herself and existing in a realm in which Roel was her only focus. She tried on outfit after outfit. The expensive fabrics felt wonderfully luxurious against her skin. The tall gilded mirrors on the walls reflected her in a myriad unrecognisable guises. She saw herself twirl in a magnificent evening gown, a stunning trouser suit and a series of incredibly flattering little dresses, every one of which Roel seemed to signal a special liking for. Shoes and bags were produced to match. It was like a glorious dream in which everyone conspired to encourage her to play her favourite game of dressing-up just as she had when she was a little girl.

In the space of hours she acquired more clothes than she had ever owned in her whole life. She knew that she would never wear most of them and told herself that Roel would be able to return them once she had gone home again. She did, however, succumb to selecting several bra-and-pants sets as well as night-wear for she had packed nowhere near enough for her Swiss sojourn. Breathless and still on the crest of an excited wave, she kept on a cream skirt and a sleeveless draped top.

'I'm never going to wear all this stuff,' she warned Roel.

'You're my wife. You should have everything you want.'

Something twisted in the region of her heart and her eyes shone overbright because she was so painfully aware of the pretence she was maintaining.

'Hilary?' Roel queried.

'You're being too generous to me,' she said tightly.

'Don't you know how to be generous in return?' Dazzling golden eyes flicked hers with sensual provocation and a scorching smile of devilment slanted his beautiful mouth.

Her heart hammered like a road drill and her mouth ran dry. He was so gorgeous he made her tremble. His power over her was terrifyingly strong but for a young woman who all her life had followed only her own counsel there was something deeply, disturbingly thrilling about his innately forceful temperament.

'And if you don't know... I can certainly give you hints, *bella mia*,' Roel purred with sensual huskiness.

She pressed her slender thighs together on the tingling responsive heat forming an ache of emptiness at the heart of her. Shocked at the strength of her own reactions, she lowered her eyes, fighting her own weakness as hard as she could.

But Roel drew her up against him. As she felt the taut power of his male arousal her face burned and yet she wanted to melt into him with every fibre of her being. Blazing golden eyes held hers. 'You look incredible, but what I want more than anything else in this world is for you to take those new clothes off again,' he confided raggedly.

Hilary moved back from him. She did something she'd thought she would never do. With unsteady hands she closed her fingers to the hem of her top and peeled it off. Then she unzipped her skirt, let it fall and stepped out of it.

'I suspect I married you because you keep on surprising me,' Roel commented rawly as he hauled her back to him with impatient hands and captured her mouth with devastating passion.

'It's out of this world.' Hilary's voice wavered. 'I just don't know what to say... I wasn't expecting this.'

She stroked a wondering finger over the delicate platinum band on her ring finger and gazed at Roel with dreamy gratitude. A wedding ring. She was touched to the heart that he should have wanted to see her wearing the symbol that signified marital commitment.

His brilliant dark golden eyes were level. 'I will not fail at anything, *cara*,' he admitted. 'I intend our marriage to be a success.'

A stab of discomfiture pierced the veil of fantasy behind which Hilary had buried all her misgivings about the role she was playing. For four whole days she had refused to think further than one minute into the future. She had revelled in every moment she had spent with Roel and if it was possible she had fallen even more deeply in love with him. He was bitterly frustrated by the reality that he had yet to recover his memory. The return of that one tiny recollection had only increased his impatience. But he had demonstrated extraordinary strength of character in the way he dealt with his amnesia and made her more than ever aware of his rock-solid assurance and self-discipline.

Now, made uneasy by his grave sincerity on the topic of their supposed marriage and wounded too by the wretched awareness of what she could not have, Hilary dragged her attention from his lean, extravagantly handsome features and made herself study her surroundings instead. After all, it was a gorgeous day and the landscape was spectacularly beautiful. They were sitting on the stone terrace of an exclusive restaurant set high above the lake at Lucerne. The sky was a dense bright blue and the picturesque medieval city was spread out below them.

'Hilary...?'

Roel reclaimed her attention with a frown just as a broadly built man with earnest features and blonde hair came to a halt several feet away and said, *'Roel?'* in a tone of pleased surprise.

His rare smile forming, Roel immediately vaulted upright to greet him. Hilary was aghast to recognise the man as Paul Correro, who had acted as a witness at their wedding. Sheer panic filled her and she was paralysed to the spot by the lawyer's intent scrutiny. This was someone who knew that she was a fake wife, who had been paid to perform a service. He had to be astonished to see her in Switzerland in Roel's actual company!

CHAPTER SIX

HEART THUMPING OUT her state of alarm like a manic road drill, Hilary decided that she had no choice but to attempt to brazen the situation out.

'Anya and I are staying with friends,' Paul Correro was telling Roel, who was kissing the cheek of the pretty pregnant redhead standing by his lawyer's side.

Arrogant dark head turning, Roel cast Hilary a glance that queried her lack of participation. Perspiration beading her upper lip and a fixed smile on her tense mouth, Hilary got up from the table and moved forward on legs that felt as clumsy as solid wood.

'Hilary...' Paul Correro dealt her a smooth smile that somehow contrived to send a shiver of foreboding down her rigid spine. 'London's loss is our gain!'

At that gibe, Hilary almost flinched and she stood like a criminal waiting for the executioner's axe to fall. But Roel mercifully removed his lawyer's attention from her by engaging him in a low-pitched dialogue. As the two men lounged back against the stone balustrade several feet away, Paul's companion approached her.

'I'm Paul's wife, Anya,' she announced, her gaze coldly assessing.

'Yes.' Nervous as a cat on hot bricks and quite unable to think of anything to say in the face of that hostile appraisal, Hilary stole a strained glance over at Roel and Paul and wondered frantically what they were talking about. An urgent desire for escape overcame her and, with a muttered excuse, Hilary headed for the cloakroom.

How dared Paul and Anya Correro look at her as though she were some sort of criminal? She was hot and bothered and her tummy was churning. She ran cooling water over her hands while she fought to get a grip on her seething emotions. Everything she had done she had done for Roel's sake and, for a guy of his temperament still frustrated by a five-year gap in his memory, Roel was managing very well! But was Paul Correro telling Roel right now that Hilary and their apparent marriage were twin giant fakes?

Hilary emerged from the cloakroom only to find Paul Correro waiting to corner her. Already pale, she turned the colour of bleached bone.

'What's your game?' the blonde man demanded. 'Roel has just explained *why* he has barely been seen since the accident.'

'I'm glad he's taken someone else into his confidence,' Hilary mumbled, wondering if Roel had already been told that she was not quite the wife she had allowed him to believe she was. Her heart sank like a stone.

'Don't treat me like an idiot,' Paul Correro condemned in a harsh undertone. 'The head of Roel's security team called me yesterday to ask for my advice. Imagine how astonished I was to learn that *you* had shown up at the clinic claiming to be Signora Sabatino! This meeting is no coincidence. I interrupted my vacation to come here. How could you think that you could pull a scam like this off?'

Beneath the lash of his scorn, Hilary was trembling. A security team worked for Roel? They had been so discreet she had

had no idea of their existence. 'There hasn't been any scam. Have you told Roel the truth about our marriage?'

'In a restaurant?' the blonde man derided. 'I intend to call at the *Castello* this afternoon—'

Her eyes raw with appeal, Hilary closed a desperate hand over his sleeve. 'Let *me* tell Roel. Give me until tomorrow to sort all this out—'

'No. I'll give you until this evening. That's long enough, and if you don't keep your word I'll take care of it for you,' Paul Correro warned her, his distrust unconcealed.

It took enormous courage for Hilary to meet his accusing scrutiny. 'I'm not what you think I am. I love him. I've always loved him—'

The lawyer winced. 'Whatever,' he cut in dismissively. 'He'll never forgive this level of betrayal.'

In a daze, Hilary walked back to Roel's side. Anya was begging him to give a speech at some charity event. Paul joined his wife. Mentioning that they were running late for an appointment, Roel cut the dialogue short and swept Hilary back out to the limousine.

'Paul was in a weird mood.' A frown had hardened Roel's lean, strong face. 'Why was he so uncomfortable with you?'

'Oh, you know Paul,' she muttered weakly.

'I do. I know him well and he has never learned the art of deception. I sensed a certain disrespect in his attitude towards you,' Roel admitted. 'I found that offensive.'

Guilt pierced Hilary deep. She said nothing, saw that in the circumstances there was nothing she could say. Roel was an acute observer and he had noticed his lawyer's hostility. However, Roel would soon know and understand why Paul Correro had been unable to conceal his scorn. A heady combination of fear and despair overwhelmed Hilary. How could she face telling Roel that their marriage was not a real marriage? How could she possibly face doing that?

Only when the limo came to a halt outside an exclusive

beauty salon did Hilary recall that the day before she had booked an appointment there. An appointment to get the pink tips removed from her hair because she had decided that her bi-coloured locks looked a little juvenile. Why not be honest with yourself? a little inner voice asked. She was ditching the pink tips in an effort to achieve a more elegant appearance for Roel. But what was the point now? What was the point when the bottom had just fallen out of her fantasy world?

'Hilary?' Roel prompted.

'Could we just drive round for a minute or two?' she gabbled without daring to look at him, for she was so confused she could hardly think straight. But she was aware of how reluctant she was to get out of the car and leave him.

The truth *hurt*. Who had first said that? She had no idea. She only knew that for the past week she had been foolish enough to try and live her dream. She had buried her every scruple and surrendered to the fairy tale of pretending to be Roel's wife. And she had been incredibly happy, happier than she had ever known she could be because the guy she loved had treated her as though she was the woman he had married. But the point was that she was not what he believed her to be and all the wishing in the world could not change that fact.

Paul Correro had destroyed her pathetic pretences. He had also made her painfully aware that her actions could be judged in a harsh and self-serving light. But she had never intended to hurt or worry anyone. Even less would she have wished to cause the smallest harm to the guy she adored! However, just remembering how Paul Correro had looked at her brought Hilary out in a cold sweat. The cosy fantasy that had featured only Roel and her had been invaded and she had been plunged into terrible confusion.

'Do you want to skip this appointment?' Roel questioned with an edge of impatience.

He was so decisive. He could answer the average question before she had finished asking it. How would he feel about her when he realised that she had encouraged him to live a lie with her? Would he, as Paul Correro had implied, despise her for her behaviour? She was unbearably hurt by that idea but minute by minute an awareness that her masquerade had gone too far was bearing down on her. Perhaps her masquerade had gone too far the very instant she had lain in Roel's bed and allowed their relationship to become intimate.

'What—?'

'It's OK... I've made my mind up and I'm going to get my hair done!' Hilary proclaimed with a forced laugh as she turned to look at him.

Brilliant dark golden eyes telegraphed a mixture of impatience and wonderment over the strange way that her brain seemed to work when compared with his. Getting out of the car wasn't made any easier by the fact that he looked absolutely devastatingly gorgeous. In a sudden movement she skimmed across the seat and kissed him with bitter-sweet fervour.

'It's been such a wonderful few days...' she mumbled unsteadily, snatching up her bag and hurtling out of the limo before she could embarrass herself and him any further.

In the hairdressing salon she felt as though a glass wall separated her from the buzz of familiar activity. Dully she recognised that she was in shock. She also finally understood what her mind was so reluctant to confront and accept: it was time for her to bow back out of Roel's life again. She needed to leave quickly as well. What would be the point of returning to the *castello* to tell Roel what she had done? That would only plunge them both into an unpleasant confrontation and how was that likely to profit either of them?

She decided that it would be wiser to fly straight back home to London instead. Fortunately, she had kept her passport in her bag and once her hair was done she could head for the airport at Lugano. She had only brought a few clothes with her to Switzerland and what she was leaving behind would not be missed. She would leave a letter of explanation for Roel in the limousine. Wouldn't that be the most sensible choice? When he appreciated the truth of what she had done, he would be astonished and furious and probably consider himself very well rid of her. Any good opinion he had had of her would be utterly destroyed.

Her tight throat convulsed on the tears she was struggling to hold back. How on earth had things gone so very wrong? She had set out only to help Roel and had somehow got sucked in so deep that she had closed her eyes and ears to the promptings of her own conscience. She had allowed herself to get carried away with her own fantasy. Only now when she was forced to wonder how Roel would judge her behaviour did she appreciate that she had crossed the boundary line of what was honest and acceptable. That acknowledgement hit her very hard for Hilary never hid from her own mistakes. But on her terms the toughest punishment of all had to be the hard reality that she would never, ever see Roel again...

'Haven't you taken your break yet?' Sally Witherspoon asked Hilary.

Hilary set a pile of freshly laundered faded towels on the shelf behind the washbasins. 'I'm not hungry—'

'Well, you ought to be.' Her senior stylist's homely face was concerned. 'You can't work the hours you're working on an empty stomach. You look so tired.'

'Stop worrying about me. I'm fine.' Her silvery blonde head bent, Hilary got on with topping up the shampoo bottles as if her life depended on it. And in a sense her life did depend on activity because, the busier she kept herself, the less opportunity she had to brood. She knew that she had shadows under her eyes and that she was looking less than her best. She wasn't sleeping well and her appetite had vanished. She was horribly unhappy but she despised self-pity and was doing her utmost to behave normally and regain her spirits.

What was done was done. It was two weeks since she had

flown back from Switzerland. For seven days Roel had been the centre of her world and now he wasn't there any more and he never would be again and she had to learn to live with that. But what she also needed to accept was that what she had shared with Roel had been unreal and false and that was the hardest lesson of all for her to bear.

'Your eleven o'clock appointment's here...' Sally hissed. 'He's a right good-looking bloke too...aren't you the lucky one?'

Hilary lifted her head. Roel was poised in the centre of the room. Her hand jerked the giant bottle of shampoo she was holding and the liquid began to pour down the sink instead of into the dispenser.

She was so shattered by the sight of him standing there that she gasped out loud. Her grey eyes locked to him with helplessly hungry intensity and she felt dizzy. Sheathed in a dark blue designer suit that outlined every lean, powerful line of his magnificent stature, his proud dark head at an angle, Roel was subjecting his surroundings to a keen scrutiny. He swung back, entrapping her mesmerised gaze. His dark-as-night eyes flared brilliant gold and glittered over her and he strolled fluid as a big cat towards her.

'Are you my eleven o'clock appointment?' she whispered.

Roel nodded in confirmation and subjected her rigid figure to a raking appraisal that drummed hot pink up into her cheeks. Clad in a white tee shirt and black cropped combat pants that hung low on her hips teamed with three-inch-high stiletto boots, Hilary discovered that she was suddenly alarmingly conscious of her every flaw. That sardonic inspection made her feverishly aware of her own body and of his deeply intimate acquaintance with it. Yet he had never looked at her before in quite that way. She realised that there was something different about him but did not know what it was. All she grasped was that she felt shamed.

'We need to go somewhere we can talk,' Roel murmured

smooth and soft and for no reason at all that she could imagine her blood ran cold inside her veins.

'I'm… I'm…er…working,' she mumbled, a coward to the backbone at that instant.

'*Bene*…then I assume that you don't have a problem with your staff and your clientele hearing what I have to say to you.' Hard, handsome face merciless, Roel switched with fluid ease from his native Italian to English. 'I'll begin by admitting that I'm not impressed with the business I recall you set up with my money.'

Hilary almost cringed where she stood. But a split second later she was rocked by the ramifications of what he had just said. If Roel recalled their arrangement, he could no longer be suffering from amnesia. Since she had left Switzerland, Roel had evidently recovered his memory of those five lost years. Although his consultant had forecast exactly that conclusion, Hilary was severely shaken by the knowledge that Roel now remembered everything that had ever happened between them.

Her stomach churning with nervous tension, she turned aside to Sally and asked the other woman if she could cover her appointments until lunchtime.

'We can talk upstairs,' she told Roel tautly. 'When did you get your memory back?'

'After you disappeared. That probably helped. After all, you had me living a life that wasn't mine,' Roel pointed out sardonically.

Hilary paled at that unfeeling jibe and unlocked the door of her flat. 'I'm surprised you're here. I didn't think you'd want to see me again.'

The silence seethed. Roel sent the door flipping shut behind him. The hall was very narrow and dark and Hilary backed out of it into the kitchen/living room. Roel surveyed the worn furniture and general shabbiness and distaste flashed across his lean dark features.

'You're even poorer than I imagined. This place is a dump,'

Roel pronounced in a grim undertone. 'When my foolish aunt, Bautista, contacted you when I was in hospital, the temptation to profit from my misfortune must have been overwhelming for you—'

'It was nothing of the sort!' Hilary was shattered by that accusation. 'How can you say such a thing? All I was worried about was you. For goodness' sake, I thought you were dying!'

Roel had lifted a letter lying on the table and he was reading it. He winced. 'You're in debt—'

Embarrassed to realise that he was looking at a communication from her bank urging her to settle the overdraft she had recently run up on her account, Hilary snatched it out of his hand again. 'Mind your own business!'

'Everything about you is my business. Knowing that gives me a good feeling,' Roel informed her with stinging softness.

Hilary had no idea what he was getting at and in any case was more keen to defend herself against the charge that she had gone to Switzerland in the hope of somehow enriching herself at his expense. 'Let me explain *why* I'm in debt. I spent a fortune on two very expensive last-minute flights to and from Switzerland and on paying extra wages to staff to cover for me while I was away. My budget doesn't run to extravagances like that.'

Unimpressed, Roel elevated a scathing ebony brow. 'Is poverty your only excuse for jumping at the opportunity to leap straight into my bed?'

Her hands balled into fists. 'You *put* me in that bed—'

'Oh, you really fought me off, didn't you?' Roel derided with a honeyed scorn that cut her like a knife blade. 'You're a conniving little con artist and you knew exactly what you were doing. Only by consummating our marriage could you ensure that you could claim a substantial divorce settlement from me.'

Hilary was bone-white. She felt horribly humiliated by his suspicions. 'I won't be claiming anything from you now or at any other time. I don't understand why you're thinking like this about me. Was it such a crime for me to want to see you when I heard you'd been injured? I told you I was sorry in my letter—'

Roel vented a sardonic laugh that made her flinch. 'All four lines of it? Even then you couldn't tell me the truth or admit the extent of your deception. You staged a vanishing act and you left me no explanation—'

'When it got down to it, I just didn't know what to say,' Hilary muttered tightly.

'You didn't want to warn me that I had been sharing my bed with a lying, cheating little whore?'

'Don't call me that!' Hilary launched back at him on a wave of angry hurt.

'You were a class act, *bella mia.*' Unforgiving golden eyes clashed with her anguished scrutiny and remained resolute. 'You knew the way to my heart…for an entire week you screwed my brains out every time I asked an awkward question!'

In a wild tempest of mortified pain at that wounding crack, Hilary snatched up the mug sitting on the table and threw it at him. 'That's not how it was; that *isn't* how I behaved!'

Offensively still, as though it was beneath his dignity to duck, Roel underlined his point by raising a speaking brow as the item hit the wall several feet to the left of him. 'When you're cornered you're very childish but that doesn't cut any ice with me. Neither do tears—'

'I'm not going to cry over you!' Hilary yelled at him full volume. 'You'd have to torture me to get tears!'

'Tears irritate me as do emotional scenes and flying pottery. But you should get it all out of your system now,' Roel advised grimly. 'If you make an ass of yourself in public again, I will be very angry with you.'

Growing stress was making Hilary's brow pound with a painful pulse-beat of tension. 'Make an ass of myself? *Again?* What are you talking about?'

Roel removed something from the inside pocket of his well-cut jacket and tossed it down on the table for her perusal. It was a magazine clipping and she was aghast to recognise the woman in the photo, who was clearly dashing tears from her unhappy face, as being herself. It had been taken that last day in Switzerland when she was walking into the airport at Lugano and she had not even noticed the photographer. Beneath ran several lines of French.

'What does it say?' Hilary finally prompted.

'"All that money and still miserable,"' Roel translated grittily.

Hilary folded her arms. 'Well, I'm sorry if I embarrassed you but it does prove that I was upset about the situation we'd got into—'

Roel dealt her a chilling glance. '*We?* Who created that situation? Who claimed to be my wife? Who lied her way into my home and my trust?'

Hilary unfolded her arms again with a jerk. Her eyes were bright with appeal and discomfiture. 'Look, try to understand that I just got in too deep. When I arrived in Switzerland I genuinely did think you were seriously hurt and I did really want to see you. I also believed you'd been asking for me—'

'Why the hell would I have been asking for a woman I had not seen in almost four years? A woman who meant nothing to me?' Roel demanded. 'And how could I have been asking for anyone while I was unconscious?'

Absorbing that salient fact for herself, Hilary's troubled face tightened with chagrin. Yes, it did indeed sound highly unlikely that he would have been asking for her. Had her sister, Emma, told her a little white lie? Had Emma made up that touching assurance in a naive attempt to encourage her elder sister to rush over to Geneva to be with her husband?

But before Hilary could fully consider that possibility Roel's own words sounded afresh inside her head in the cruellest of echoes. *A woman who meant nothing to me?* That was what he had said. That was how he thought of her. As nothing and nobody. Well, what had she expected? Tender affection? For the brief space of a week her pretences had led him to believe that he must have some feelings for her and he had behaved accordingly. But that comforting time was now at an end.

Determined not to betray how terribly hurt she was, Hilary struggled to get back to the point she had been intending to make before his casually cruel honesty had hit her like a punch in the stomach. 'Dr Lerther warned me not to tell you anything that might disturb you—'

'So you let me think I was married? Didn't that strike you as *very* disturbing news to give a man who revelled in being single?' Roel slammed back at her.

'I expect you really appreciate your freedom now that you know you never lost it—'

'I did not lose my freedom. You stole it from me.' His stunning golden eyes were full of contempt. 'You claimed to be my wife and now rumours abound that I am a married man. As, strictly speaking, I *am* a married man, I cannot deny those rumours and the paparazzi have already managed to print a photograph of you.'

Guilty tears lashed the back of Hilary's eyes. 'I suppose that has to be embarrassing for you—'

'I don't embarrass easily,' Roel cut in drily.

'I don't think you understand just how sorry I am,' Hilary mumbled wretchedly.

'Sorry is not enough to satisfy me. You really wanted to be my wife.'

Hilary's pallor became laced by feverish, embarrassed colour.

Roel sent her a sizzling look of scorn. 'You wanted to be my wife so badly that you lied and you cheated your way into the position.'

Shame and anger at the humiliation he was inflicting roared through Hilary. 'I know it looks bad but—'

'I won't listen to your excuses. It looks bad because it *was* bad,' Roel incised. 'You took my beautifully organised life and trashed it. I dumped my mistress for you—'

'You did…what?' Eyes widening, Hilary glanced up at him.

'The gorgeous brunette...she was my mistress and I ditched her because you made me believe that I was a married man.'

Hilary just closed her eyes. *The gorgeous brunette.* How could she ever have allowed herself to believe that a male like Roel Sabatino had no other woman in his life and his bed? She hadn't wanted to accept that there might be a woman because accepting that would have made her own position untenable. Wasn't that why she had chosen to assume that Roel was free of any entanglement? How could she have been so naive when it came to her own motives and so selfish? She really had messed up his life. Guilt and shame tore at her and made her throat thicken.

'So there is a current vacancy in my bed and you are about to fill it again.'

'I beg your pardon...?' A frown of incomprehension had formed on Hilary's strained face.

'You're coming back to Switzerland with me—'

Hilary was bemused. 'Why would I do that?'

'I'm not giving you a choice. Did you give me one when you told me that I was living in a fairy-tale marriage?' Roel shot at her with cold condemnation.

Hilary paled as if she had been struck and evaded his harsh gaze. 'I can't think of one good reason why you'd want me to come back to Switzerland—'

'I want to use you as you used me and then throw you away again when I get bored. Does that clarify the issue?' Lean, strong face hard, Roel met her shocked stare levelly.

Hilary released a dazed little laugh. 'You don't mean that...'

'I've arranged for us to lunch with your sister, so you should start packing.'

Hilary froze. 'How could we be meeting Emma for lunch? She's at a school miles out of London—'

'As we speak she's being driven down for the occasion.'

'But how... I mean why would you make such an arrangement?'

'I had excellent reasons. Did you think you were the only one of us who could pull a dirty trick? I'm a master at manipulation, *bella mia*.' Roel dealt her a look of pity. 'Emma thinks we're enjoying a reconciliation and she is ecstatic at the news, so you'll have to come up with loads of smiles and lots of that bouncy chatter at which you excel to keep her happy—'

Hilary's skin had turned clammy with shock. 'How the heck could you have even got in touch with my sister?'

'She phoned me at the town house this week and very touchingly apologised for her hostile attitude when we first got married.'

'Oh, no...' Hilary groaned in guilty dismay because she realised that it was her own fault that Emma had contacted Roel. Since her return from Switzerland, Hilary had only spoken to her sister on the phone and she had ducked all the younger woman's questions about the state of her relationship with Roel. Unable to tell the truth, she had not been able to bring herself to tell lies. 'I never did get round to admitting to her *why* we got married because I was scared...well scared—'

'That she might be less respectful of a sister who marries a man for money?' Roel slotted in with cruel accuracy. 'You'll be relieved to know that I left all her illusions intact. She told me how upset she was that we appeared to be living apart again and asked if that was her fault.'

'And what did you say...that we were having a reconciliation?' Hilary recalled with a visible effort to overcome her disbelief. 'Was that what you said a moment ago?'

'We *are* having a reconciliation...on my terms, and if they turn out to be on the punitive side of vengeful you only have yourself to thank for that.'

'You think I'm a lying, cheating, horrible person... I'd have to be out of my mind to go anywhere with you!' Hilary flung at him.

'*Non c'e problema*...don't worry about it,' Roel urged. 'I'll take your sister out to lunch on her own and tell her the entire unlovely story of our relationship from start to finish—'

'That would be a rotten, nasty thing to do!' Hilary broke in, her horror unconcealed.

'Unlike you, I would only be telling the truth as it happened. I'm relieved that you appreciate just how inexcusable your conduct has been,' Roel spelt out grimly as he left the room.

Hilary raced out into the hall in his wake. 'If you want me to grovel, I will, but don't drag Emma into this—'

Roel gave her a sardonic glance. 'Grovelling is for peasants and you should know me well enough by now to know that when I want something, I take it. You're going to learn how to be a Sabatino wife and you'll save me the time and effort of picking out another mistress by taking on the role personally—'

'No way!' Hilary yelled at him.

'But you worked so hard to get yourself into that position. Not indispensable, you understand,' Roel asserted drily, striding back to the front door and pulling it open, 'but certainly worth a return visit.'

'You wouldn't dare tell Emma what I did,' Hilary told him. 'I *would...*'

A chill of apprehension enclosed her. 'But doing that wouldn't profit you in any way. Why would you be so cruel?'

'It's what you deserve.' Roel studied her with brooding dark intensity. 'You conned me into giving you a wedding ring and, before I kick you back out of my life again, I intend to level the score.'

'I didn't con you... I *didn't*—'

Roel did not appear to be listening. 'A limo will collect you in an hour and a half and deliver you to the hotel where we're lunching with Emma. I'll meet you there. I'm calling into my London office first.'

Hilary was panicking. 'If I leave my business again, I'll be risking bankruptcy and I can't do that because—'

Roel gave her a withering look. 'I'll settle your debts—'

Hilary bridled. 'It's a two-hundred-and-fifty-pound over-draft run up on air fares...all right, it's money I owe, but stop talking like it's—'

'I'm a banker. An unauthorised overdraft is a debt—'

'You can't *do* this to me, Roel.' In her desperation, Hilary followed him out onto the landing. 'If I leave London, who's going to take my place while I'm away?'

'You hire a manager. I'll cover the expense—'

In furious frustration and lingering disbelief, Hilary watched Roel start down the stairs. 'If you use my relationship with my sister as a threat, I will never forgive you,' she warned him.

Lean, intelligent face cold and impassive in cast, Roel cast her a darkling glance. 'You think I'd care about that?'

Chilled, she slumped back against the wall and slowly breathed in deep in an effort to calm herself. He might even be glad of the excuse to punish her by revealing all to Emma. It was not a risk she could afford to run. She thought her sister might understand why she had signed up for such a marriage almost four years back when their lives had been so bleak, but she would be very hurt that Hilary had allowed her to believe that their marriage was a genuine one. To that injury would be added the facts of Hilary's more recent behaviour and how would Emma view that? Dear heaven, would Roel let Emma realise that Hilary had actually slept with him this time around? Hilary literally writhed with horror at the idea of having her own failings paraded for her kid sister's benefit. She was supposed to set standards for her younger sibling, not break them.

Roel had, with merciless precision, chosen the one threat capable of making Hilary dance to his tune...

CHAPTER SEVEN

'I'M JUST SO happy for you!' Emma hugged Hilary with bubbling enthusiasm between the first and second courses of their meal. 'When I start university after the summer, you'll see even less of me and I was worried you'd get lonely. Does that sound selfish?'

'Of course it doesn't,' Hilary reassured her with as bright a smile as she could manage. Living away from home had made her sister independent and, although it hurt a little sometimes that Emma relied more on her own judgement, Hilary was very proud of her.

'Hilary needs to have some fun,' Emma informed Roel earnestly. 'She's given up so much for me. My scholarship only ever covered part of my school fees and Hilary's been paying the rest. That's why she's always so broke. When I realised how much my education was costing, I tried to persuade her to move me—'

'You were doing really well where you were and that was the most important thing,' Hilary slotted into that embarrassing flood of personal information being freely proffered to Roel. 'Emma wants to be an international lawyer. She's really good at languages.'

Roel spoke to her sister in French and Emma responded with impeccable cool. They both had that confident sharp edge that Hilary had always rather envied in others. After the meal, Roel took a call on his mobile and Hilary and her sister had a few minutes alone. Emma was returning to school to revise for her A-level exams. Once they were over, she was flying straight out to Spain to stay with a friend at her family's holiday villa. Having waved off her sister, Hilary climbed into the limo with Roel.

'I haven't finished sorting things out yet, so I'll have to go back to my flat.'

Roel sent her a hard glance. 'We don't have time.'

Hilary lifted her chin. 'You don't but I do. Fly me out economy tomorrow.'

'I'll reschedule our flight for later this evening—'

'That's not necessary,' Hilary said woodenly. 'I need more time to organise things. I'd prefer to travel tomorrow.'

Roel surveyed her mutinous profile. 'I'm not leaving London without you.'

'I don't want to go to Switzerland—'

'Liar,' Roel murmured huskily.

Hilary bristled. 'What's that supposed to mean?'

Roel ran a taunting forefinger along the generous curve of her lower lip. Her sensitive skin tingled and her breath caught in her throat.

'Show me how much you hate what I do to you, *bella mia*,' Roel suggested in a silken invitation.

Even though she was trying to fight the impulse, she found herself leaning forward. He drew her like a fire when she was freezing cold. Her nostrils flared on the achingly familiar scent of him: masculine overlaid with a trace of some expensive lotion, incredibly sexy. Her breasts stirred inside her bra cups, tender crests straining into stiff points.

'You're not trying hard enough,' Roel censured.

'Trying what?' Her mind was a total blank, her voice hoarse with the effort required to speak.

He raised a lean brown hand and stroked a provocative fingertip over the taut prominence of an engorged nipple outlined by the thin fabric of her top.

When he touched that sensitive peak a soft whimper of sound broke from her. Her heart was pounding like a drum. Her head felt too heavy for her neck and she let it tip back. Between her slender thighs the heat of wanting rose to a bitter-sweet peak of craving that burned.

Roel let the tip of his tongue flick the delicate hollow at the base of her collar-bone where a tiny pulse was going crazy and she moaned and pushed forward. She wanted him to kiss her so badly that she could taste it. He lifted his dark head and she looked up at him. Framed by impenetrable black lashes, the hard sexual glitter of his brilliant gaze was the equivalent of an electrical charge.

'Do it...' she was finally reduced to pleading.

'No. I'm not into sex in the back of limos.' Roel withdrew from her with a pronounced air of derision.

Her cheeks burned like beetroot on the boil. Her hands balled into fierce fists. She wanted to hit him. She wanted to say very rude things to him. But just in time she restrained herself from a revealing outburst. She was mortified by her own vulnerability. How could she have been so weak? *Show me how much you hate what I do to you!* If she continued to offer herself up on the equivalent of a plate to Roel, he would soon guess that she was head over heels in love with him. And, in Hilary's opinion, nothing would be worse than that development and nothing would be more humiliating. Given a choice, she decided that she much preferred to be thought of as a cunning gold-digger.

The limo pulled up outside the hairdressing salon and Hilary fled. While Sally grabbed a much-needed break, Hilary worked. Just before closing time, the older woman agreed to manage the salon as long as there was enough cash in the kitty to hire another full-time stylist to work alongside her. Relieved that she would be leaving her business in reliable hands, Hilary locked up, went over the account books with Sally and then went up to her flat to finish her packing.

At seven o'clock the doorbell sounded. Although she had assumed it was Roel, it wasn't. Her visitor was Gareth, an engineer, whom she had dated a couple of times the previous year and who had become a friend.

'*Love* the hair!' Gareth laughed and ruffled the glossy black tips that provided such a contrast to her silvery fair hair. 'Very gothic.'

'You like it?' Hilary grinned for Roel had not even seemed to notice and in truth it hardly mattered as the black highlights would wash straight back out of her hair again the next time she was under the shower.

'Fancy going out tonight?'

Lean, dark features grim, Roel strode across the landing. 'Hilary has other plans.'

'Are you her social secretary…or something?' Gareth sniped.

'Her husband,' Roel drawled with cold finality.

As Gareth clattered red-faced downstairs Hilary knew he would never darken her doorstep again and she slung Roel a furious look of reproach for his interference. 'That was quite unnecessary—'

From the benefit of his commanding height, Roel dealt her a strong glance of disagreement. 'You were flirting—'

'I wasn't flirting…and even if I was, what's it got to do with you?' With difficulty Hilary controlled her temper because Roel's chauffeur had appeared round the bend in the stairs. Her cases were removed from the hall and she locked up with a flourish.

'You were expecting that guy tonight. That was why you didn't want to leave until tomorrow,' Roel condemned in a harsh undertone.

Hilary tossed her head on her passage down the first flight of stairs. But he was making her feel as irresistible as Helen of Troy and she glowed. 'I'm a real hot chick. You'll have to watch me night and day in Switzerland. Are you sure I'm worth the effort?'

Without the smallest warning, Roel closed his hands to her slight shoulders and backed her up against the wall of the landing. It happened so fast and so disconcerted her that she gasped. Volcanic golden eyes obdurate as bronze raked over her startled face in stormy warning. 'Have you noticed something? I'm not laughing,' Roel derided with raw-edged softness. 'Be careful. If I catch you flirting with other men, I won't be amused.'

Her mouth had run dry and, taken aback though she was by his vehemence, a dark and dangerous excitement was licking through her slight figure. 'I was just joking—'

'That wasn't funny,' Roel delivered darkly.

Her lively sense of humour sparked. 'At least Gareth noticed I'd put black tips into my hair—'

'Only he was too much of an oil slick to tell you that you look like a hedgehog.' Releasing her, Roel took a fluid step back to let her go on down the stairs.

Hilary drew in a shattered breath. *'A...?'*

A hedgehog? She was mortified. Passing through the airport, she could not help stealing glances at her reflection in shop windows. At the same time she could not help noticing how short and dumpy she looked alongside his tall, lean physique. While they waited to board Roel's private jet, Hilary's mobile phone buzzed. When she heard her friend Pippa's voice, she moved away from Roel to keep the conversation private.

Pippa and her husband, Andreo D'Alessio, lived in Italy and, as luck would have it, Pippa was calling to tell Hilary that she would be over in London for the weekend and was looking forward to meeting up with her.

'As we speak, I'm waiting to board a flight to Switzerland,' Hilary admitted ruefully. 'You're also going to have every excuse to get annoyed with me. I've been keeping a secret from you. I'm married—'

'Married? I don't believe you!' Pippa exclaimed in shock.

'He's standing right by me listening in on my phone call so I don't find it quite so hard to disbelieve,' Hilary confided tartly, slinging Roel a challenging glance. 'But the story of our marriage is—'

Roel filched the phone from her in a move so fast it left her with a dropped jaw. 'A total fairy tale,' Roel dropped in faster than the speed of light as he took over the dialogue without skipping a beat. 'I'm Hilary's husband...and you are—?'

Outraged, Hilary hovered while Roel engaged in smooth chit-chat with her friend and then deftly concluded the dialogue by announcing that their flight had been called.

'How *dare* you?' Hilary bit out in a tremulous voice, so mad she was shaking with fury as Roel escorted her across the tarmac towards the jet.

'*Dannazione!* You left me with no choice.' Scornful golden eyes skimmed over her angry face. 'You were on the brink of blabbing everything—'

'I don't "blab",' Hilary forced out between gritted teeth.

'You could blab for England. You have the discretion of a public address system,' Roel contradicted icily.

On board the jet, Hilary stalked down the aisle of the luxurious cabin and picked a seat as far away from him as she could get. She was furious that he had interfered with her call and accused her of being a gossip. How dared he?

'Just who do you think you are?' she heard herself demand when they were airborne and the steward had left them alone again.

Darkly handsome face unapologetic, Roel held her accusing gaze with level cool. 'I am a very private individual. What happens between us should be equally private. Girlie chatterbox sessions are out.'

Hilary turned her head away and curled up in her comfortable seat. Tears were not her style but all of a sudden she felt as though she could weep a river dry. Perhaps that was because she was feeling so tired that it was an effort to keep her heavy eyes open. The steward tried to interest her in a meal and she shook her head, her tummy reacting with a queasy roll at the prospect of food. She wanted to fight with Roel but for once she had to acknowledge that she did not have the energy.

The following morning, Hilary slept late. When she woke up she was eager to confront Roel with all the arguments she had been too enervated to employ when lunching with her sister, Emma, had been on the agenda. Over breakfast Umberto informed her that Roel had long since departed for the Sabatino Bank.

Her recollection of how she had got to bed the night before was dim but embarrassing. Having dozed through the flight, she had stumbled like a zombie through the airport, drifted off again in the limo and had allowed Roel to cart her up to bed when they had finally arrived at the town house. Never before had she suffered from such overpowering fatigue and it was a relief to feel the restored spark of her usual energy.

She had thought that she was really really hungry but when the cooked breakfast that she had ordered arrived her appetite suffered a sudden mysterious disappearance. Pushing away the plate, she nibbled at a fresh roll and savoured a hot chocolate drink, which was sinfully rich and satisfying. Having decided that a visit to that holy of holies, the Sabatino Bank, required a special effort in the grooming department, she was relieved to discover all the designer clothes that Roel had bought for her stowed away in the dressing room. She donned a burgundy lace slip dress, which took on a much more conservative aspect when teamed with a short floral cotton coat.

The Sabatino Bank in Geneva was hugely intimidating in size and very contemporary in design. Her nervous tension began to increase. Explaining that she was Roel's wife created a decided stir of discreet interest at the reception desk. A young man in a smart suit escorted her up to the executive floor. He showed her through double doors into a very large office.

Roel was lounging back with tigerish grace against the edge

of a sleek light wood desk. Garbed in a dark blue tailored suit, grey shirt and stylish silk tie, he looked nothing short of spectacular. 'Fill me in,' he invited softly. 'It's not anyone's birthday. To what do I owe this interruption? What is the special occasion?'

'I just wanted to speak to you—'

'Then you should get out of bed earlier,' Raul spelt out drily. 'This is the middle of my working day and I am not available for personal visits.'

'That's good...cos this is a business call,' Hilary informed him, hoping to really grab his attention with that declaration.

Role vaulted upright and extended an authoritative lean brown hand. 'Come here. I want to show you something.'

Disconcerted, Hilary moved forward. He closed a hand over hers and proceeded to urge her towards a door on the other side of his office. 'Where are you taking me?' It was a washroom. Stepping behind her, Roel posed her in front of the vanity unit, so that she could see their reflections twinned in the mirror above the basin. Her grey eyes focused on his lean bronzed face. Pulses quickening and heart racing, she sucked in an audible breath.

'What do you see?' Roel asked as he tipped the light coat off her taut shoulders and slowly removed it.

Hilary was mesmerised. 'Us?'

As though to draw attention to them, Roel flicked the narrow beaded straps of her dress, which bared her slender shoulders. Then his long fingers glided from her tiny waist up over her narrow ribcage to rest just below the burgeoning thrust of lush breasts enhanced by the flattering fit of the stretchy lace fabric. Hilary stopped breathing altogether. At that precise moment the reason why she had come to Roel's office was a complete blank to her. His big powerful body was touching hers and she was infinitely more aware of his bold masculine arousal.

'Is this how a woman dresses for a business appointment, *cara*?' Roel enquired silkily.

'I know the dress is a bit flirty but I love it, so I put the coat on top of it so that I would look more conservative,' Hilary told him breathlessly.

'That's not the point I was making. Just for the record, put a dress like that over a shape like yours and the result could not be described by any stretch of the imagination as...*conservative*.'

Hilary leant back into him and gave him a huge dreamy smile. 'You like it?'

'Isn't that what you wanted?'

'I didn't think about it but you're probably right.'

A superior gleam in his brilliant golden eyes, Roel set her back from him with gentle but firm hands. 'So this scene belongs in the bedroom, not inside my bank.'

Absorbing that speech, Hilary blinked on the sizzle of pure rage that lit up like a neon sign inside her. He actually thought that she had come to his precious bank to try and seduce him away from a working ethic set in ancient stone!

'I came here to have a serious discussion,' Hilary snapped and, stooping to pick up her coat, she stalked back into his office. 'And I intend to have that discussion. Sorry if you can't keep your mind on business just because a woman's wearing an attractive dress.'

Dark colour girding his proud high cheekbones, Roel sent her a slashing glance. 'Try me...'

'Almost four years ago, I signed a contract to become your wife. In return I accepted a certain sum of money. I returned two thirds of that sum when I discovered I didn't need it and—'

Roel had raised a silencing hand. 'Stop there. You *returned* part of that cash settlement? How?'

'I paid it back into the account you had set up and sent you a letter through your lawyer, that suspicious Paul guy—'

'Who had great foresight,' Roel sliced in with satiric bite. 'Thanks to your antics, I broke his nose last week—'

Eyes rounded, Hilary stared at him in consternation. 'You did what...you broke his nose? But why?'

'He had the misfortune to suggest that my wife might not be all that I believed her to be...*before* I recovered my memory.'

Hilary turned bright pink with mortification. 'Oh... I was talking about that money.'

Roel looked unimpressed. 'I'm not aware that you returned any part of that settlement.'

Hilary folded her arms with a jerk. 'Well, the point is that I did. I realised that I didn't need to buy a property when renting one would do just as well. I only kept what I needed to rent the flat and set up the salon in the empty shop beneath it. Fitting out the salon was expensive enough. You didn't think my business was much of a paying proposition but it pays my rent and covers the bills, so I've never had any complaints—'

'Would you tell me where this dialogue is heading?'

'Once Emma finishes school, I can sell the business as a going concern and repay everything you gave me. So if I put that promise on the table, we'll be quits and you can let me go home again.'

'Did you really put on your sexiest outfit to come and make that offer to me?'

Infuriated by a putdown of a response that made it clear that he did not even deem her offer worthy of consideration, Hilary breathed in very deep. Meanwhile, Roel lounged back against his desk, watching the rise and fall of her full breasts below the lace and then whipping up again to rest on her luscious pink mouth.

'As far as I'm concerned, this isn't about money. It never has been. Surely you've grasped that by now?' Roel murmured softly.

'I understand that you believe I owe you a debt. I understand that you have rather unforgiving principles—'

'You're doing really well on the understanding front,' Roel dropped in with deflating amusement.

'But I can't think of one good reason why you'd want to force me to be here—'

Roel sent her a sardonic smile. 'But I've got *more* than one good reason. The power kick. I am receiving very real satisfaction from making you do what I want you to do.'

'That's disgusting...you should be ashamed of yourself!' Hilary was outraged that he could admit that without hesitation.

His stunning eyes narrowed intently. 'But didn't *you* receive a similar satisfaction when you took advantage of my amnesia to lull me into a false sense of security?'

'I'm not like you... I didn't take advantage either!' Hilary flung at him, hurt by that unpleasant suggestion. 'I was only trying to keep you calm and happy.'

His handsome mouth quirked with amusement. *'Per meraviglia*...you certainly put a smile on my face in the bedroom. As for forcing you to be here, isn't it time you faced facts?'

'What facts?'

'That you didn't exactly have to be dragged kicking and screaming back to my lair? You want me too.'

'Not enough to allow you to think you can use me,' Hilary stated hotly.

Roel let his forefinger slowly glance down between her breasts to pause at her navel. 'What would be enough?'

Where he stroked, her body became stingingly alive and tender. It was as if her every skin cell lit up.

She set her teeth together and trembled. 'Sex isn't enough for me.'

'I could make it enough,' Roel informed her huskily.

'I value myself more.'

'Yet you didn't four years ago. If I'd snapped my fingers then you would have come running.'

She was devastated by that crack. For an instant she was torn from the present and plunged back into the past. She had been so desperately in love with him and without hope. She had been young and foolish and she would have done just about anything to get a chance with him. To be forced to accept that he had known exactly how she felt then and yet still walked away from her was unbearably painful.

'You bastard…' she framed jaggedly. 'You were attracted to me too but you wouldn't do anything about it—'

'I was too sensible—'

'Too much of a snob,' Hilary contradicted with wounded and angry blue eyes. 'I bet if I'd been some spoilt little debutante you would have given me a spin!'

'I'm not a snob. I have expectations in certain fields and I don't apologise for them—'

'You're the guy who was born with an entire silver service in his mouth. All your life you have had the best and you looked at me and you felt the same attraction I did… I *know* you did!' Hilary stressed in a mixture of furious and hurt accusation. 'Because you admitted that to me while you had amnesia—'

'I walked away because you couldn't have handled me. You were too young—'

'You walked away because you have a brain that functions like a deep freeze—'

'Is that your definition of common sense?' Roel drawled silkily.

'—and because I didn't fit the right image—'

'You still don't…yet here you are.' Dark drawl razor-edged, Roel curved controlling hands to the shapely curve of her hips and drew her to him.

'You think kissing me is somehow going to make me less furious with you?' Hilary threw at him tempestuously.

He did it anyway. He crushed her soft mouth under his and then lingered to demand a greater response. He teased at the full curve of her lower lip and she shivered, abruptly leaning forward to brace her hands on his hard, muscular shoulders. He stopped teasing, hauled her close and plundered the tender interior of her mouth with driving explicit strokes that made the blood drum through her veins at an insane rate.

'I can't wait until seven tonight,' Roel growled thickly, pausing to nip at the lobe of her ear with his teeth before burying his carnal mouth in the hollow of her neck.

'Oh...' In reaction to that contact, an incredibly erotic sensation darted through her and she snatched in a startled breath. He wasn't supposed to be kissing her, she reminded herself. She was angry with him, she reminded herself. But she curled her nails like talons into the expensive fabric of his suit jacket and found his tempting masculine mouth again for herself.

Roel released the back zip on her dress and cool air washed her spine. She fought to catch her breath while the lace fabric shimmied down over her hips into a pool at her feet. 'No...you can't do that!' Hilary gasped in shock.

'Too late...' Roel framed thickly.

Hilary whipped up her hands in a genuine effort to cover herself. She was in a panic. 'We're in a bank...any minute now someone might come through that door!'

'It's locked...we're safe.' With single-minded purpose, Roel tugged her hands back down to her side. He tipped back his handsome dark head to better appreciate the sight of her luxuriant curves embellished by a frivolous bra and panties. 'But you're *not*...'

As Hilary began to stoop to reach for her dress Roel lifted her up into his arms with easy strength. He brought her down on the desk and flipped loose the catch on her bra. 'Roel!'

'Irresistible...' Roel surveyed the pouting perfection of her pink-tipped breasts and groaned out loud.

Smouldering golden eyes met hers and the raw hunger she saw there shook her. His uninhibited desire lit a fire inside her. He might not love her but his passion was very real. Emboldened, she angled up on one elbow and tugged him down to her by his silk tie.

Lean, strong face hard with male need, he vented a roughened Italian imprecation. '*Inferno!* You're in my blood like a fever.'

He curved his hands to the ripe swell of her breasts, making her moan soft and low. He rubbed her tightly beaded nipples and she gasped in helpless response. Liquid heat started to gather at the apex of her thighs. He let his expert mouth wander at will across her sensitised flesh and all thought was suspended. Her hips gave a restive upward surge and he sank his hands beneath them to bring her even closer.

A phone began buzzing. He swore, reached behind her and the noise stopped. He laced long fingers into her hair, holding her to him while he drove her lips apart with the demanding force of his passion.

'I want you,' she muttered, snatching in a frantic shallow breath, her whole body thrumming with passionate need.

'Not as much as I want you, *bella mia*,' Roel ground out, ripping off her last garment with more haste than care. 'You've taught me that two weeks can feel like two lifetimes.'

He spread her thighs and discovered the hot, damp ache of her most secret flesh. As he explored her slick, wet heat a sobbing sound of frustration was wrenched from her and she arched in a frenzy of helpless impatience. Positioning her with strong hands, he plunged into her in one powerful movement. It was intolerably exciting. A surging wave of pleasure splintered through her. All control was gone. He was taking her to the outer limits of an exquisite peak of sensation. When it claimed her in a wild climax of shattering intensity, he smothered her cries with the cloaking heat of his mouth.

In the aftermath she was shell-shocked by her own abandonment.

Withdrawing from her, Roel stared down at her with stunned golden eyes. 'I can't believe we just did this... I can't believe you're lying naked across my desk.'

It needed only that one reminder for Hilary to recall both her surroundings and her unclothed state. She leapt off his desk like a scalded cat. She wanted to crawl under it and hide but not before she got herself decently covered again. Fighting hands that were all fingers and uncoordinated thumbs, she struggled back into her bra and pants. All around her the silence seethed.

'You're banned from my office,' Roel drawled coolly.

'Sorry...s-say that again,' she stammered weakly, engaged in hauling up her dress with frantic hands.

'I think you staged a deliberate power play. You came here dressed to kill with a purpose,' Roel condemned with outrageous cool.

Hilary almost flung herself at him sobbing with raging hysteria. He thought she had planned her own downfall? He thought she was proud of having been spread-eagled across his desk? Was he out of his mind? Face bright red with shame, she wriggled in an agitated effort to pull up her zip for herself.

'From the minute I came through that door, you had only one thought in your mind. Don't you dare blame me...thanks,' she muttered in absent aside as, noticing her acrobatic twists, he flipped her round and took care of her zip. 'Who locked the door? Who ignored me when I tried to remind you of where we were? Who told me two weeks without sex is like two lifetimes?'

'Hilary—'

'And the same second you get what you want, you start acting like I threw myself at you,' she ranted at him feverishly, because while she was still shouting and simultaneously heading in the direction of the door she could pretty much avoid looking at him. 'Who flattened me on that desk with lustful intentions? Believe me, wild horses wouldn't get me back inside this bank!'

Roel swept up her coat and extended it.

'You've got lipstick on your shirt,' she told him with considerable satisfaction.

Glittering golden eyes ensnared hers with bold determination. 'Can we do this again soon?'

Hilary stared at him in mortified disbelief. 'After you virtually accused me of setting this up?'

'I'd like to set you up for a repeat visit, *cara mia*.'

'Dream on!' Hilary flung at him.

'I'm a connoisseur,' Roel murmured smoothly. 'And sex that good is rare.'

Paling, Hilary veiled her eyes and dropped her head. He was so unemotional. With only a handful of words he could virtually flay the skin from her bones. *Sex that good is rare.* Just when had she forgotten how he felt about her? Just when had she forgotten that he thought of her as a gold-digging, lying cheat, who had taken advantage of him when he was vulnerable? Vulnerable. She studied Roel: a superb male animal in peak physical condition. A guy who looked at her with lust and cool mingled. A guy quite capable of having sex with her and then forgetting she existed. In short, someone likely to hurt her a good deal if she didn't watch out…

'This isn't going to happen ever again,' Hilary swore, spinning on her heel and heading for the door in a blind need to escape the scene of her own downfall.

'Not for the next twenty-four hours at least,' Roel conceded with velvet-smooth precision. 'I leave for Zurich this evening. I'll see you tomorrow evening.'

Hilary considered several counter-attacks of the don't-hurry-home variety before deciding that any such response would be less than impressive after the mortifying way she had behaved with him. In chagrined silence she left his office. A knot of executive types wearing perplexed expressions was waiting outside. Everybody backed away to let her pass. Convinced that what she had been doing was somehow written on her pink-cheeked face, she walked to the lift at speed.

He had somehow discovered the magic combination that transformed her into a woman who acted like a slut. For that alone, she should hate him, she told herself. But at that point she recalled Roel's own initial reactions in the aftermath of their intimacy. He had been knocked off balance by the passion that had betrayed them both. He had also informed her that she was banned from his office. Banned as though she was possessed of such overpowering appeal that only a complete embargo on her presence could keep him on the sexual straight and narrow.

She tossed her head back. A very slight swing assailed her hips while a cheeky grin of one-upmanship dared to tug at the tight line of her compressed lips.

CHAPTER EIGHT

THE NEXT DAY one-upmanship was not in Hilary's thoughts when she contemplated her breakfast with an appetite that had once again chosen to disappear. She was actually feeling quite nauseous. Not for the first time in recent days either, she reflected. Had she picked up some virus? But it was not as though she felt truly ill, more as though something was not quite right.

Only while she was considering that conundrum did it dawn on her that her body was behaving oddly in other ways as well. A quick calculation on her fingers suggested that her period was a few days overdue. She recounted, but accurate dates evaded her because she had never bothered to keep a record of her cycle. She was getting her dates mixed up, she told herself. About there she froze on a very much belated acknowledgement that, from that very first night she had spent with Roel, she had done nothing whatsoever to protect herself from becoming pregnant. And nor had he.

Everything that had happened with Roel had happened so fast. Their intimacy had not been a pre-planned event. At no stage had she even thought of the risk that she might conceive a child. Had Roel been as thoughtless as she had been? Or had he assumed that she was taking the contraceptive pill? For goodness' sake, why was she working herself up into such a state?

The previous month she had only shared Roel's bed for a week. How likely was it that she could have conceived in so short a space of time? Hadn't she read a newspaper article about falling fertility rates? Most probably stress had upset her menstrual cycle and that very disruption was throwing her whole system out of sync and making her feel unwell. She would wait a few days and if she were still concerned she would have a pregnancy test. In the meantime it would be madness for her to start fretting herself into a panic over something that might never happen.

Umberto brought her a phone. It was Roel.

'I meant to call you last night but the meeting went on too late,' he asserted.

His dark, deep drawl sounded wonderful on the phone line and she was furious with herself for noticing that. 'Don't worry about it. I wasn't expecting to hear from you.'

'We're attending a party tonight, *cara.*'

'Oh, so I get a night out for good behaviour,' she sniped.

'And a night in for bad. No prizes for guessing which I would prefer,' he incised smoothly. 'I'm no party animal.'

While she dressed that evening she waited with bated breath for the communicating door between their bedrooms to open. Sheathed in a green evening dress that bared her shoulders and accentuated the creamy perfection of her pale skin, she finally descended the stairs.

Roel strolled out into the hall below her. Heavily lidded dark-as-night eyes scanned her and glittered gold with appreciation. 'You look good.'

Madly conscious of his scrutiny, she turned pink. 'No need to sound so surprised.'

'It crossed my mind that you might try to score points by opting to wear something totally inappropriate,' Roel admitted.

'I wouldn't be that childish.' She cleared her throat. 'I put the wedding ring back on...by the way.'

'Why not? You worked hard enough for it,' Roel derided with silken cool.

Her face flamed as though he had slapped her. 'When you speak to me like that I hate you!'

Roel vented a jeering laugh. 'It's traditional for hatred to blossom between married couples in my family.'

'Your mother fell for someone else. That didn't mean she hated your father—'

'Didn't it? She was in love with that same man when she married my father. My father's love turned to hate when he re-alised the truth.'

Hilary winced. 'Why on earth did she marry him?'

'Money,' Roel said succinctly, tucking her into the limousine waiting outside the house. 'My grandmother was equally rapa-cious but more moral. She gave my grandfather, Clemente, one child and then informed him that her duty was done. Although they remained below the same roof until her death, they never lived as man and wife again.'

'It seems wrong that your mother married your father when she loved another man. But maybe there were pressures on her that you don't know about or maybe she even believed that she was doing the *right* thing and would learn to love your father,' Hilary contended, keen to encourage him to be less judgemental when it came to other people's mistakes.

'That possibility had never occurred to me,' Roel said very drily. 'Do you suppose that she gave birth to me in the hope that she might learn to love me too?'

Hilary blenched at the cutting note of ridicule in that sug-gestion. 'I was only trying to say that there are two sides to any unhappy marriage and there might have been extenuating cir-cumstances... I was trying to comfort you.'

'But I don't need comfort.' Bold, bronzed face taut, Roel

spoke with acid clarity. 'I don't even remember my mother. She died before I was four years old.'

'How?'

Roel shrugged. 'She drowned.'

'I'm sorry you never had the chance to know her. Yes, I know you think I'm very sentimental,' she conceded. 'But if you only knew how *much* I would give to have my mother back to talk to for just five minutes... I would do just about anything for that chance—'

'If you can't persuade your heart to bleed in silence,' Roel interrupted with icy derision, 'I'll attend the party on my own.'

'I think that would be the best idea,' Hilary retorted a little unevenly because her eyes were glimmering with tears and her throat was closing over. 'I don't think I want to spend one more second in the company of someone as unfeeling as you are!'

'We're almost at the airport. Calm down. You're too emotional—'

'Not an affliction likely to attack you, is it?' Hilary slashed back at him shakily. 'I'm not ashamed of my emotions.'

'I am not asking you to be ashamed, merely to keep them in check,' Roel decreed with immoveable cool.

But Hilary was finding it quite impossible to control the number of powerful emotions swilling about inside her. 'I loved my parents very much and I still miss them terribly. They taught me to think the best of everybody and even though I soon learned that the world isn't always that nice a place—'

'Who taught you that lesson?'

'My father's cousin, Mandy. The minute she knew our parents were dead she went into action. She convinced Social Services that she was a fit and proper person to take responsibility for raising Emma. I was considered too young and I was terrified that my sister and I would be parted. Mandy moved us all into a big rented house...' Hilary recalled painfully.

'*And?*' Roel prompted.

'Mandy and her boyfriend then fleeced us out of every penny

they could lay their hands on. She got control of the money my
parents had left. There wasn't a lot but there would've been
enough to keep Emma and I comfortable for a few years. When
there was nothing more left to steal or sell, she just walked out
one day and never came back.'

'I assume you called in the police. Misuse of funds in a situation of that nature is a crime.'

'The money was gone and nothing was going to bring it
back. I had more important things to worry about—like finding
somewhere cheaper to live and looking after my sister,' Hilary
countered defensively.

In an unexpected gesture of sympathy, Roel closed his hand
over her clenched fingers. 'You trusted Mandy because she
was related to you. Her betrayal must have come as a considerable shock.'

'Yeah...' She was dismayed to realise that, far from reced-
ing, that dangerous and unfamiliar urge to burst into floods of
tears was merely growing stronger.

'When I had amnesia, I had no choice but to trust you,' Roel
murmured with husky bite, dark golden eyes resting on her with
punitive force. 'I believed you were my wife—'

Hilary yanked her hand free of his grip with positive violence. 'You don't need to say any more... I've got the message.
But all I did was try and act like your wife. I did not go to bed
with you with any ulterior motive, nor do I have any intention
of trying to make money out of our marriage!'

'Only time will prove the truth of that claim.'

'Look, what's your problem? You're an incredibly good-looking, sexy bloke yet you seem to find it impossible to accept that
any woman could want you just for yourself!' Hilary slammed
back at him chokily.

'Or for my body,' Roel countered in a tone smoother than silk.

With a suddenness that shook her, Hilary lost her head in
an explosion of rage she could not control. 'You see, that's just
one of those things I can't stand about you. You always have to

have the last word and it's always a smart-ass remark. You're so convinced that you never do anything wrong that you blame me for everything. If the sky fell down on us right this minute, you'd say it was my fault!'

'*Sì*...' Roel responded, impervious to attack, a bright glitter in his intent scrutiny. 'Screaming has been known to cause avalanches.'

Hilary breathed in so deep in an effort to restrain herself that she was honestly afraid she might burst. But she was seeing his extravagantly handsome features through a mist of red. In that brief interim in hostilities, the chauffeur swept open the door.

'I just want you to know that I *hate* you!' Hilary was reduced to hissing shrewishly at him as he settled into the seat beside hers on the helicopter.

He meshed long brown fingers into her hair and held her still for the descending force of his mouth. She fell into that kiss much as if she had charged full tilt off a precipice. Down and down and down she went into the hot, wild, honeyed excitement of it. The stinging electrical charge of his seething sensuality took her prisoner and she revelled in every moment of his unleashed passion.

He drew back an inch, fierce golden eyes blazing over her. 'We'll stay only forty minutes at the party.'

She was out of breath and stunned by the frightening intensity of her own emotions. She saw inside herself, understood why she had been fighting with him and struggling to hold him at a distance. He had so much power to hurt her and hurt her he would while she still loved him. 'Roel...'

'You make me burn for you... I barely slept a night through while you were in London. But now you're mine again and you will *stay* mine until I decide otherwise, *bella mia*.'

The helicopter delivered them to a huge, opulent yacht where they were greeted by their hosts like visiting royalty. Hilary was in a daze. All she was really conscious of was Roel, his big powerful frame taut and restless by her side, the possessive masculine arm anchored to her spine. Good manners took him from her when his host urged him over to meet an old friend.

Hilary clutched her untouched glass of wine. The music and the chattering voices seemed to be crowding in on her. Her hostess introduced a constant procession of strange faces to her. The bright dresses of the women and the glitter of their fabulous jewellery blurred in her gaze and she blinked. The slight motion of the yacht beneath her did not help. Clammy heat assailed her and she felt horribly sick and dizzy. Even as she turned in desperation to look for a seat it was too late and she slid down on the deck in a dead faint.

When she recovered consciousness, Roel was staring down at her with cloaked dark eyes. 'Take it easy, *cara*. I'm taking you home.'

Lashes fluttering down again, she offered up a silent prayer that the nausea would evaporate. He lifted her up into his arms, exchanged a brief dialogue with their concerned hosts and carried her back up to the upper deck to board the helicopter again.

'I don't think I've ever seen a more immediate or magical performance,' Roel informed her with mocking appreciation once the craft was airborne.

Belatedly she recalled his assertion that he was prepared to spend less than an hour at the party and only then appreciated that he honestly believed she had staged a fake collapse to please him and achieve an even earlier departure. The wheels and dips of the flight did nothing to settle her uneasy tummy and conversation was beyond her. At the back of her mind lurked worrying questions that increased her tension. Why had she fainted? She had never fainted in her life before, but she remembered Pippa telling her that dizzy spells were common in early pregnancy.

Vaulting off the helicopter as soon as it had landed, Roel swung back to assist her. 'That was a most impressive faint.' A wickedly sensual smile illuminated his lean dark features. 'For a moment, even I thought it was for real.'

'It was... I think I got seasick,' Hilary mumbled, leaning against him because her legs still felt distinctly untrustworthy in the support department.

'Seasick?' Roel exclaimed.

'I still don't feel so great,' Hilary added apologetically.

Roel groaned and bent down to lift her again. 'Seasick,' he breathed in wonderment. 'You were only on board fifteen minutes.'

An hour later she was lying in bed, circumspectly clad in a nightdress. Roel was poised by the foot of the bed and surveying her with keen attention. 'I don't want to lie here like a corpse,' she was protesting by then. 'I feel great now.'

'Healthy people don't faint,' Roel drawled in a censorious tone as if it were something she could have helped. 'If the doctor says it's OK, you can get up again.'

'Doctor...what doctor?' she gasped.

A knock sounded on the door. 'That should be her now. I called her from the limo to request a home visit.'

In sheer fright, Hilary sat up. 'I don't want to see a doctor... for goodness' sake, I don't need to!'

'Let me be the judge of that—'

'What's it got to do with you?'

'I'm your husband. I'm responsible for your well-being,' Roel imparted grittily. 'Even if you are ungrateful for my concern.'

Shame and embarrassment silenced Hilary. He opened the door to an older woman with greying dark hair swept up in a no-nonsense style.

'I'd like to see the doctor alone,' Hilary announced when Roel betrayed a nerve-racking reluctance to leave the bedroom.

She answered the doctor's questions honestly and submitted to an examination. Afterwards, the woman smiled. 'I think you already suspect the cause. You're pregnant.'

Hilary lost colour because all she could think of at that instant was how unwelcome such an announcement would be to Roel. 'Are you sure?'

The older woman nodded. 'Certain signs are unmistakable.'

'I don't want to tell my husband yet,' Hilary confided.

Her body had shocked her. She was going to have Roel's baby. Maybe a little boy with black hair and an irresistible smile or a minx of a little girl with glorious tigerish eyes and a belief that she ruled the world. Yes, she was going to have Roel's baby and, unless she was very much mistaken, he would hate her for it.

When Roel entered the room she couldn't look at him and she scrambled out of bed. 'What are you doing?' he demanded.

'I was a little bit seasick and now I'm fine and I'm getting dressed.'

Roel scooped her up mid-step and deposited her back on the bed. 'No. The doctor said you needed a sensible meal and plenty of sleep and I intend to ensure that you follow her advice.'

'Benevolence doesn't suit you,' she told him waspishly while he stood over her to watch her eat the delicious food, which had been brought to her on a tray embellished with flowers.

Roel sent her a languorous smile that made her heartbeat quicken and her tummy flip. 'I'm only thinking of my own needs.'

'Oh, really?'

'You'll have to be one hundred per cent fit to meet my expectations over the next few days. I've decided to take a break—'

'But you don't take breaks—'

'Give me you and a bed…and a PC connection and I can take a break.'

Hilary went pink to the roots of her hair.

'I shall get you out from under my skin or die in the attempt, *cara*,' Roel murmured huskily.

'Then what?'

In the silence that fell she was too enervated even to take the breath she needed lest it somehow obscured his answer.

'I fly you home and return to my free and uncomplicated former life as a single male.'

It took immense courage but she did not flinch at that come-back. 'So why wait? Why not do that now?'

'Right now I'm still enjoying you. You're different from my usual lovers.'

'Does how I feel come into this in any way?' Hilary snapped.

'I make you feel *incredible* and you know it,' Roel reminded her with merciless cool and the cruel intimacy of a lover, well aware of his own ability to turn her inside out and upside down with sheer longing.

Hilary subsided back into the pillows and closed her morti-fied eyes. Sometimes forbearance was the better part of valour, she reminded herself. Sometimes there was nothing wrong with just going with the flow. He might never need to know that she had conceived his child. Did she really *have* to tell him? When they parted, she would never see him again. She wanted their baby so much and she had loads of love to give. She was pre-pared to work incredibly hard to give their child a decent home. How could she be such a coward that she was already trying to excuse herself for not immediately telling Roel that she had fallen pregnant?

'I told you I didn't want anything,' Hilary whispered urgently under her breath the instant the unctuous salesman moved out of hearing. 'What are we doing in here?'

Roel dealt her a look of warm amusement. 'You have no jew-ellery. It's time I bought you some.'

Hilary stretched up on tiptoe to murmur with forced amuse-ment, 'It's not wise to take the mistress idea out of the bed-room…the joke wears thin—'

'This time the joke's on me. No decent gold-digger would miss out on an opportunity of this magnitude.' As Hilary flinched in surprise and pain her eyes flew wide and darted up to lodge on his lean dark chiselled features. He curved an imprisoning arm round her slight, taut figure to prevent her from pulling back from him. 'Think about what I just said,' he urged in a husky tone of intimacy. 'In fact maybe you should be capturing this on film. I'm admitting that I misjudged your motives four years ago...'

Hilary snatched in a stark breath. 'Are you serious?'

'Never more so.' Taking advantage of her shock, Roel manoeuvred her down onto the elegant stool by the counter. 'Some sad individuals say sorry with flowers—'

'Is that a fact?' she said breathlessly, hardly able to think straight because he had plunged her from hurt straight into a disconcerted state of relief and happiness.

'Some never say sorry at all and some will even buy you diamonds in the hope that you will not expect any action that could be interpreted as grovelling.'

Her easy smile broke out like the sun at dawn and she almost laughed out loud, for she had never forgotten him saying that grovelling was only for peasants.

An hour later, when they had returned to the villa, she wandered out onto the terrace where he was enjoying a drink. A giant ancient fig tree provided shelter from the sultry heat of the Sardinian sun. Even late afternoon, it was very hot. Lush planted terraces and steps ran down the steep hillside to the private beach below.

'It obviously pays to catch you out,' she teased Roel, angling up her wrist so that the platinum watch glittered in the arrow of light breaking through the leafy canopy above her. And all the while she was doing that she was still watching Roel, luxuriating in his proximity, his bold, uncompromising masculinity and even that fierce will of his, which she had dared to cross in that exclusive jewellery store.

As always attuned to her scrutiny, Roel elevated an ebony brow, his brilliant dark eyes full of reproof for she had been adamant about accepting only that one gift. 'I wanted to cover you in diamonds.'

'I'd have looked downright silly,' she quipped.

'Naked you would have looked like a pagan goddess, *bella mia.*'

Her tummy flipped. It took Roel to imagine her as nobody else ever would. Self-conscious beneath his molten appraisal, she muttered unevenly, 'You still haven't explained why you changed your mind about me being greedy for money?'

His lean, strong face tensed. 'When you claimed in London that you'd paid most of the cash settlement I gave you back into the account from which you originally received it, I didn't believe you. But I had it checked out. That money has been lying unacknowledged in that account for well over three years—'

'But what happened to the letter I wrote to Paul Correro?'

'It never arrived. Around that time he moved into new legal offices. Your letter would have been sent to his old address and it must have gone astray. Paul is very upset about all this.' His handsome mouth compressed in acknowledgement. 'He knows he is the broken link in a chain, which has led to much misunderstanding between us.'

Hilary was grateful that the subject of that cash settlement could finally be freely discussed. 'I never meant to take money from you but I did, so you can hardly blame him for having a low opinion of me—'

'He had no right to make that judgement—'

A pained light had entered Hilary's unguarded gaze for she was tempted to point out that Paul Correro had simply taken his lofty air of disapproval from Roel himself. 'I'd like to explain a couple of things. When we first met, Emma and I were living in a rough area and her friends were kids who thought it was fun to shoplift. She was skipping school and I was having trouble controlling her.'

Roel was listening with grave attention. 'I had no idea your home life was that grim. You always seemed so cheerful.'

'A long face doesn't change anything for the better. Your money gave us a new start. I rented the flat, opened up the salon and got Emma into another school. All the problems we were having vanished one by one,' Hilary explained. 'I didn't have to work evenings any more, so she had to stay home and she studied. The next year she won her scholarship and she has never looked back since.'

'You should be proud of yourself. I wish you had been more frank with me at the time—'

As she connected with his stunning golden gaze Hilary's mouth ran dry and she looked away. 'In those days, you didn't want to know.'

'I wouldn't allow myself to get to know you and you paid the price for that. But that was then and this is now...' Enclosing her hand in his, Roel pressed a slow, burning, sensual kiss to her palm.

She quivered, legs trembling, heat surging between her slender thighs. At a leisurely pace he undid her wrap top and flicked loose the clasp on the silk bra she wore beneath.

'It's broad daylight...' she muttered.

'You shock so easily,' Roel savoured, pressing her back against the sun-warmed wall and peeling off her sarong skirt. 'Relax... I will do everything.'

And, shamelessly, she let him. There against the worn stone wall he stripped her naked. She was boneless, ready for him even before he scored expert fingers through the silvery blonde curls crowning her feminine mound to tease the swollen, sensitive, secret flesh below. He probed her passion-moistened depths with a carnal skill that made her sob out loud against her own fierce and unbearable longing.

'Don't stop...' she cried hoarsely.

'I love it when you're out of control. It makes me want to drive you even wilder.' Roel flipped her round and bent her over the wall, lifting her up to penetrate her with his hard male heat. Shock and overwhelming delight made her dizzy. He filled her to the hilt. She couldn't breathe for excitement. Sensation made her forget everything but the fierce, desperately rousing surge of his demanding body into hers. His animal passion sent her flying into glorious frenzy of release.

In the aftermath, he gathered her limp body up into his arms and carried her into the shuttered cool of the bedroom. He discarded his own clothes. All rippling muscle and damp bronzed skin, he was magnificent. Coming down on the bed, he drew her back into his arms and smiled with slumberous satisfaction and approval down at her. She wanted to cry with love for him. She wanted that sweet moment of silent intimacy to last for ever. He smoothed her hair out of her eyes, kissed her, held her close and she felt as frantic as though she were trying to live her whole life out in those minutes when she was at her happiest.

'I adore your breasts,' Roel confided lazily, lifting her up to arrange her astride him and reaching up to cup the pert, firm mounds with unashamed masculine appreciation. 'I swear they've got fuller since the first time we made love.'

Hilary lowered her lashes to hide the panic in her eyes.

'Not that I'm complaining, you understand,' Roel breathed huskily. 'I've noticed what a pushover you are for Swiss chocolate...'

He thought she was putting on the beef because she was stuffing herself with chocolate drinks! She rolled off him in haste.

Roel groaned out loud and tugged her back to him by dint of his greatly superior strength. 'Don't be so touchy. You have a to-die-for shape. Angels in heaven would fight over you and I shall revel in keeping you stocked up with chocolate,' he imparted. 'It's very refreshing to be with a woman who eats whatever she feels like.'

So not only did he think she was overweight, but also a greedy pig into the bargain, Hilary thought crazily. If only that were true...if only an over-indulgence in chocolate *were* responsible for the fact that her bosom had already jumped an entire cup size!

'I'm going for a shower,' she muttered, yanking herself free of his loosened hold and scrambling off the bed.

'How the hell can you suffer from such low self-esteem?' Roel sat up to demand with very male frustration.

'I saw Celine...beside her, I'd probably look as heavenly in shape as Humpty Dumpty!' Hilary fielded chokily.

Anger brightening his spectacular gaze, Roel sprang out of bed. '*Che idea!* Celine answered my needs...but you arouse them. I can't keep my hands off you for longer than an hour. I've even taken time out from the bank to be with you.'

Her eyelids were gritty with unshed tears. 'That's just sex,' she accused.

A ferocious silence fell and she waited and she prayed for him to break that silence with even a single word of disagreement.

Roel stared back at her with stony, stubborn intensity, black-lashed brilliant dark eyes unreadable, his long, lean, powerful frame still as a predator ready to fend off attack.

Her throat ached so much with disappointment that it really hurt. He had not contradicted her. She should have known better than to hope that he would. With a brittle throwaway smile designed to persuade him that a purely physical relationship was fine by her, she disappeared into the bathroom and locked the door behind her.

She switched on the shower. Tears were rolling down her cheeks. She choked back her sobs. Sex was all she had ever had to offer him and nobody could say he had not taken full advantage of her willingness. Or that she had any grounds for complaint. It was a week since he had brought her to Sardinia, to this fantastic coastal villa where they enjoyed complete seclusion and sheer, unvarnished luxury.

For seven days they had been inseparable. There had been picnics on the beach, moonlight swims, late-night romantic dinners, languorous siestas in the heat of the day and long discussions about all sorts of subjects on which they rarely ever agreed. He was incredibly stimulating company and wonderfully entertaining. When he needed to work for an hour or two, she had taken to curling up nearby with a magazine and keeping him company. For her it had been a time of idyllic happiness but also a challenging time while she'd slowly struggled to come to terms with the reality that she was carrying his baby.

Physically she was feeling terrific. But then she had been careful about what she ate and now rested whenever she felt tired. Roel had teased her about her slothful ways but her body had rewarded her newly learnt caution. The nausea had been less of a problem and she had only once felt light-headed when she stood up too fast. Yet already her body was changing to a degree where even Roel had noticed that her breasts were bigger. In fact her bras were becoming uncomfortably tight. Keeping her condition a secret would not be an option for much longer. Nevertheless she was filled with sick dread at the prospect of having to tell Roel that she had conceived.

This time around with him she had been determined not to build fantasy castles in the air. She had faced everything in their relationship as it was and not as she would have liked it to be. Every morning, before she got around to kissing him awake in the variety of imaginative ways that he most liked, she had duly reminded herself of certain hard facts...

He was not in love with her. He was in lust and it was lust that made him an insatiable lover. That he could spend hours just talking to her, that he could also be amazingly tender and amusing and caring, was irrelevant. After all, he was a hugely sophisticated guy and it was impossible to imagine him being guilty of coarse or ignorant behaviour. She was not his wife in the truest sense of the word because he had once given her a fee to go through that wedding ceremony with him. She was the wife he had bought, not the wife he might have chosen.

Furthermore she would never fit the mould of the perfect partner whom he would eventually pick. She matched none of his instinctive preferences...yes, one by one, she had weaselled those preferences out of him without him even realising just how much information he was revealing. He liked leggy brunettes and his last mistress had also been terrifyingly beautiful. He thought background and breeding were important. He believed a university education was crucial. She failed on every count. She was not and never could be a wife whom he might want to keep.

On those grounds, the news that she was expecting his baby was likely to strike Roel as a total disaster. That was why she had been so reluctant to tell him. That was why she had prevaricated for seven entire days and lived every precious moment as though it might be the last she ever spent with him. But, in all fairness to him, it was time she spoke up.

She donned peacock-blue silk trousers with an artfully simple embroidered matching top. The shade accentuated the colour of her eyes. Only a month earlier she had worn a lot more make-up but now she applied cosmetics with a much lighter hand. Roel had introduced her to a different world and she had naturally studied the women within those exclusive circles. Always observant and quick to learn, she had soon recognised how more subtle effects could enhance her appearance. But she was growing out her short, spiky hairstyle purely for Roel's benefit...

'It's the most fantastic colour,' he had intoned with flattering appreciation, 'but I want more of it, *lots* more of it! I want to see your hair rippling down your back like a fantastic sheet of silver, *bella mia.*'

'But it would take for ever even for it to grow down to my shoulders,' Hilary had complained.

'I'll wait... I can be very patient when I want something.'

And, solely to please him, she had promised not to cut her hair short again. She had not allowed herself to wonder how many inches her spiky tresses might get to grow before how she wore them became a matter of the most complete indifference to him.

The table was set for dinner on the terrace. It was very beautiful. Coloured glass lanterns hung in the branches of the fig tree and candles glittered in the midst of crystal glasses and gilded bone china. At a lower level and screened by vegetation she could just see a reflective glimmer of the swimming pool in the moonlight.

It was Roel's villa. Sometimes he only visited it once a year and some years not even that. He owned an enormous amount of property round the world. He did not like hotels. Even here, in one of the more remote locations on the island, Roel received only the best service and a chef was still on hand to produce the most superb meals. Within the cocoon of Roel's almost unimaginable wealth he took for granted a level of freedom and comfort that other people could only dream about and envy. He had complete control. How was he likely to react to what she had to tell him? To a situation that she could not allow him to control? Her soft mouth quivered with the tempestuous emotion she was fighting to repress.

Roel strode out to join her. 'Turn round,' he invited her huskily.

A little stiffly, she obliged.

'You look delectable... I could devour you like an animal,' he confessed with a frankness that sent a piercing shard of shameful excitement flaring through her taut figure. 'Think yourself lucky if I can restrain myself to the end of our meal.'

In strained silence she moistened her bone-dry mouth with a hasty sip of mineral water.

Keen dark golden eyes rested on her and his beautiful mouth took on a humorous quirk. 'Humpty Dumpty... I don't think so,' he pronounced.

A miserable flush lit her fair skin. She wanted to seal her lips closed, rush into his arms and hug him tight, hold onto the happiness he had given her.

'You've been very moody the past few days,' Roel continued. Disconcerted, she shot him a glance. 'Er... I—'

'One minute you're smiling like mad and the next you're

way down deep in the doldrums and all weepy,' Roel slotted in. 'That's not your nature, so I assume it's PMT.'

Hilary flinched and then braced herself to stand as rigid as a stick of rock. 'I have something to tell you,' she said starkly.

CHAPTER NINE

A SUDDEN IRREVERENT smile slashed Roel's extraordinarily handsome features. 'Don't take this as a criticism. As a pragmatic male, I find your natural flair for drama fascinating,' he assured her in his dark deep drawl. 'But may we eat first? I have to confess that I'm very hungry.'

Nervous as a cat on hot bricks, Hilary nibbled at the soft underside of her lower lip. His raw charisma, his vast confidence that she could have nothing of any great import to confide, knocked her off balance. She sank down at the table. By the time the main course had been served, her contribution to the conversation had sunk to the level of monosyllabic responses.

'When you go this quiet, it worries me,' Roel commented.

'Sometimes I talk too much,' she said uncomfortably.

'But I'm so accustomed to it now that I like it, *cara mia*.'

Roel stroked a blunt forefinger down over her clenched fingers where they rested on the pristine table cloth. 'Obviously I miscalculated when I implied that you couldn't have anything that couldn't stand a rain check to tell me.'

'Yes…' Hilary swallowed hard. 'But it's not something you could have guessed and I—'

His intent gaze flashed a sudden stormy gold. 'Did you sleep with that guy I surprised on your doorstep in London?'

That icy demand shook her. 'Gareth? No...no, of course not!'

'Just checking out my worst case scenario,' Roel told her, deadpan.

'Will you hear me out before you say anything?' Hilary pressed unevenly.

'I'm not in the habit of shouting people down.'

'Don't be angry with me... I know that's going to be hard but don't be angry with me,' she heard herself plead and she despised her own weakness. 'In one sense, we're both responsible.'

Hard jaw line clenching at that statement, Roel surveyed her with narrowed eyes. 'The point being? My patience has limits...'

'I'm...' She fiddled with the fork in her hand and put it down, her insides hollow with fear and lack of food for she had been unable to bring herself to eat a morsel. 'I've fallen pregnant... it happened the first week we were together.'

His natural colour ebbed from below his healthy olive skin, accentuating the slashing prominence of his superb bone structure.

'I know you've got to be shocked. I was shocked too,' she admitted tightly.

Shimmering golden eyes executed a search and destroy mission over her shrinking figure. In one powerfully revealing motion, Roel thrust back his chair and sprang upright. He strode over to the wall like a tiger on the prowl and stood looking out into the night. In the terrible silence, the surge of the surf on the beach sounded eerily loud.

Awkwardly she cleared her throat. 'I never dreamt that I would end up in bed with you and, when it happened, I didn't even think about contraception. There was so much else going on and I *knew* I shouldn't have let you make love to me and I felt so guilty...all those things got in the way.'

His back was still turned to her. She longed for him to turn round. His broad shoulders were rigid with tension, corded muscle visible beneath the thin, expensive fabric of his black short-sleeved shirt.

'I know you're annoyed about this.' She pleated her fingers together in a strained gesture. 'That's OK...that's understandable. You weren't expecting this situation to develop. But I wasn't either. I couldn't cope with a termination though, so let's not discuss that...'

In receipt of that hoarse plea for his understanding on that score, Roel swung round and directed a bleak look at her from impassive eyes so dark they chilled her to the marrow.

'I know... I know. Maybe you didn't even *want* to discuss that option. But it's easier if I say now that this may not be a planned baby but I-I'll make it welcome all the same,' she stammered. 'Although, right now, I just feel scared and overwhelmed by all this.'

Roel helped himself to a very stiff whisky and tossed it back in one unappreciative gulp.

Her taut face stamped with apprehension, Hilary rose from behind the table and moved on stiff legs to the middle of the terrace. 'Please say something...'

'You're now the future mother of my child.' The insolent edge to his intonation somehow made the label sound like a freezingly polite term of abuse and she stiffened and paled. 'I have to be very careful what I say to you. A pregnant wife has many rights and not the least is civilised consideration for her condition. How long have you known?'

'Since you called in that nice doctor after I fainted.'

Roel bit out a harsh laugh. '*That* long? How did you manage to keep your promising announcement under wraps all of this week?'

'Easily...if I could have run away from it, I would've,' she confided half under her breath. 'I didn't...*don't* want to lose you—'

Hard dark eyes assailed hers with merciless force. 'You never had me...except in the most basic way.'

'I know,' she whispered jaggedly. 'But this is still about to wreck what we have.'

'Don't presume to know what I think or I feel. Or what I intend to do next,' Roel advised her grimly.

'You're free to tell me what you're thinking. I won't take offence.' She was desperate to bridge the chasm that had opened up between them and if the truth hurt, so be it.

His lean, intelligent face hardened. '*Bene*...very well. Why should I be surprised by your achievement? The babies in the Sabatino family have always come with a very large price label attached.'

'Not our baby...' Hilary told him with fierce conviction.

Ruthless cynicism laced the derisive light in his keen gaze. He strode past her as if she weren't there and went indoors. After a disconcerted pause she chased after him and caught up with him in the main hall as he was leaving the villa.

'Not our baby,' she said again and her voice might have quivered but her eyes were resolute and she frowned. 'Are you going out?'

Roel dealt her a hard mocking look. 'What do you think?'

'Where are you going?'

'That's my business.'

Long after his departure, she was still hovering in the hall hugging herself as if she were cold. Eventually she pulled herself together and walked back out to the terrace. The staff had already cleared the table. She thought of the tiny life in her womb and wondered if it was suffering because she hadn't eaten and her eyes stung like mad. She ordered toast and a chocolate drink for supper.

And all the time she was trying not to dwell on how Roel had behaved. As if he utterly despised her. As if she was beneath contempt. As if she had got pregnant deliberately and planned to sell her baby to him for the highest possible price. He had hurt her but she still felt that it was better that he had voiced what he was feeling. But she wished he had not gone out. An hour after his departure, she called him on his mobile phone.

'Are you coming home soon?' she asked with fake cheer.

'I'm not coming *home* at all,' Roel breathed icily.

'Before you make your mind up about that,' Hilary muttered anxiously, 'I should warn you that if you stay out all night I'll be very unhappy about it. I don't think I could just sit here waiting either. I'd be so worried I'd have to come and look for you—'

'We are not having this conversation.' He killed the call.

Half an hour later, bolstered by her toast, she called him back. When he answered she heard a soft feminine giggle somewhere close by and her heart sank to her toes. 'Are you with a woman?' she demanded sickly.

'If you phone again, I won't answer.'

'I think we're worth fighting for but I couldn't forgive infidelity...' she warned him shakily, her throat thick with tears.

'Emotional blackmail doesn't work with me.'

'What about hysterics? Look, I know I sound like a maniac but all I want is for you to come back here and talk.'

'But I don't want to and you will not make me do what I don't want to do.'

It was one in the morning when Roel appeared in the bedroom doorway. She was lying awake in the moonlight and she had left the door wide so that she could listen out for his return. Sitting up with a jerk, she switched on the bedside lamps. Black hair tousled, dark stubble outlining his obdurate jaw line, Roel stared across the depth of the room at her. Without hesitation, she scrambled off the bed and raced over to hurl herself at him. He had come back. That was all she cared about at that instant.

'No...' That single word was very decisive, very, very unyielding. He set her back from him with cool hands.

She fell back a step, horribly crushed by that rejection, suddenly conscious that with her mussed hair and red swollen eyes she had to look like hell. She was also fearfully aware of the weak part of her willing to do or say anything to hold onto him.

But she knew that wouldn't work. If she crawled, Roel would walk right over the top of her and despise her even more.

'I've reached certain decisions,' Roel delivered.

'It takes two people to make a decision in a marriage,' Hilary dared.

'Not when only *one* of them is in the wrong,' Roel splintered back at her without hesitation.

Hilary sucked in a slow deep breath. If she fought with him, he would only get angrier. It wouldn't hurt her to stand a little humble pie while emotions got the chance to simmer down.

'I want you to have a medical examination so that the relevant dates can be checked. Before the baby is born I want to be as certain as I can be that it's mine,' Roel drawled with no expression at all.

Her face pinching tight with pained mortification, she backed away from him. 'You have doubts?' she whispered and she was appalled that he could even suspect that someone else might have fathered the child she carried.

'Some women would kill for a tiny percentage cut of what that baby will be worth to you in financial terms,' Roel contended.

'Oh… I don't think any woman would kill to be me just at this moment,' Hilary mumbled unevenly because, instead of returning to talk, he had returned to annihilate her hopes.

'Naturally I'll have DNA testing carried out as a final check after the birth,' Roel continued as if she hadn't spoken. 'I'm aware that you could have conceived during those two weeks you spent back in London. I think it's unlikely but I'd be foolish not to seek full confirmation.'

'Yeah…' A shadowy attempt at a smile briefly skimmed her tense mouth. 'Why hesitate when you've got yet another golden opportunity to humiliate me?'

'What did you expect? Approval? I refuse to believe that this pregnancy is an accidental development.' Scornful golden eyes settled on her. 'After all, conceiving my child ensures that you will live in luxury for the rest of your life.'

'You're not being fair to me. If you don't have any faith at all in me, how can I ever hope to prove that you've got me wrong?' Hilary slung at him in growing distress.

'But I *haven't* got you wrong—'

'Only today you were telling me that you accepted that I was never a gold-digger—'

'Before the latest revelation persuaded me otherwise—'

'How could I possibly have known that I would fall pregnant after one week with you?' she argued passionately. 'This is not how I would have chosen to have my first child. Why would I want to curse my baby with a reluctant father who hates me?'

'I'm not reluctant and I don't hate you—'

Hilary threw up her hands in frustration. 'All your anger stems back to the fact that when you had amnesia I kept you in the dark about our marriage—'

'You lied to me over and over again—'

'I didn't think I was doing any harm…so I got a bit carried away, so I was living my dream—'

'Now you're *finally* telling me the truth,' Roel sliced in with derisive satisfaction. 'You were so seduced by my lifestyle you didn't care how low you had to sink to enjoy the benefits—'

Hilary vented a bitter little laugh. 'For your information my dream was a fairy-tale marriage with a guy who treated me like an equal…yeah, how pathetic of me to put you into a scenario like that! The guy who wouldn't even give me a date when I was begging for it! But then it was *my* fantasy and not yours, so I—'

'*Santo cielo!* You made me *live* your stupid fantasy,' Roel grated with raw accusation.

Hilary lifted her head high and her eyes shone bright as jewels. 'Oddly enough, you seemed perfectly happy living in my fantasy…'

Roel went as rigid as if she had hit him. She paled, defiance leaking from her. The silence simmered like poison on the boil. Black fury glittered in his ferocious gaze.

'Let's concentrate on the baby,' Roel said glacially.

With difficulty Hilary focused her weary mind back to the all-important task of dissuading Roel from his conviction that she had set out to become pregnant. 'Please listen to me. When I slept with you, I didn't consider consequences. I've never had to worry about birth control before. I was heedless and foolish but nothing worse.' She sent him a look of appeal. 'You didn't think either.'

His lean, strong face clenched in disagreement. 'That first night, I checked the cabinet by the bed for condoms,' he revealed drily. 'I have always visited my lovers in their homes to retain my privacy. But you were my wife. Understandably the absence of contraception in my bedroom encouraged me to assume that you were taking care of that requirement.'

'The idea of precautions didn't cross your mind after that?'

Roel elevated a sardonic ebony brow. 'Contraception was scarcely in the forefront of my concerns. I had amnesia and a wife who was a total stranger.'

'As I recall...you found that angle more of a turn-on than a problem,' Hilary dared to remind him, desperate to break through his polished shield of self-command and penetrate his reserve.

'I chose to trust you. That was a mistake and, like all my mistakes, I expect to pay for it,' Roel spelt out with brutal cool. 'But you have to live with me knowing you for exactly what you are. A little schemer who got into my bed to turn a substantial profit!'

'If you don't get out...' Hilary framed unsteadily, rage and self-loathing and pain combining into a combustible flame of wretchedness inside her, 'I'm going to scream at you like a fishwife and physically attack you!'

Treating her to a sizzling appraisal, Roel scooped her up into his arms before she could even guess his intention. 'Stop dra-matising yourself—'

'Put me down!' she launched at him furiously.

'No. It's late. You look exhausted and you *should* be asleep—'

'I'll go to bed when I—'

'Why do you think I came back tonight?' Roel demanded with an icy clarity that made her stop struggling and go limp in his arms.

'I don't know...'

'You're my wife and you're carrying my child. I hope that, no matter how angry I am, I know better than to risk your health.'

Superior bastard...she hated him! She shut her wounded eyes tight. She wanted to scream at him but knew he would read loads and loads of clever things out of being screamed at. Quiet as a mouse, she let him settle her back into bed. He handled her as if she were a pane of glass with a hairline crack running through it. She remembered his wild, explosive desire out on the terrace only hours earlier and she almost wept: he had just covered her up as though she were his great-great-great-grand-mother. For the first time he slept away from her and she felt that rejection like a knife in her breast. He wasn't just spelling out the reality that she had no emotional hold on him, he was putting her at a physical distance as well.

The next morning they flew back to Switzerland. An hour into the flight, she abandoned her proud attempt to pretend that she watching the film she had selected. Roel was working. She hovered within a couple of feet of him and he ignored her.

'OK... I've got the message,' she proclaimed shakily. 'You just wish I'd vanish like the evil fairy!'

Lean, dark face grim and impatient, Roel lodged unim-pressed dark golden eyes on her.

Hilary planted her hands on her hips. 'Don't look at me like I'm an attention-seeking child,' she told him hotly. 'If I'm get-ting on your nerves to that extent, go ahead and divorce me!'

Roel rose upright, graceful as a prowling jungle predator,

and towered over her in the most intimidating fashion. Dense black lashes lowered over his hard, glittering gaze. 'I was wondering how long it would take you to make that demand. Sorry to disappoint you, but you don't qualify for the get-out-of-gaol-free card yet, *cara*.'

'What's that supposed to mean?'

'No separation, no divorce. You're staying in Switzerland where I can watch over you.'

Hilary thought it was interesting that, no matter how greedy and wicked he was determined to believe she was, he could think of no greater punishment than keeping her in Switzerland with him. The ache in her heart subsided a little and a tiny charge of hope flared. Perhaps she had been guilty of expecting too much too soon from him.

'How do you really feel about the baby?' she plucked up the courage to finally ask.

'I was planning on one eventually,' Roel conceded grudgingly with the same amount of emotion as he might have expended when voicing a desire to acquire a new set of cuff-links. 'Now it's coming sooner rather than later. I'll adjust... I have no choice but to do so.'

Her delicate features tightened and her nails bit sharp crescents into her palms. She returned to her seat. She would give him time. He was very stubborn, very cynical in his suspicions. He needed more time. He needed her understanding. She loved him so much. He would come round, wouldn't he?

But to what extent would Roel ever come round to accepting Hilary Ross, hairdresser, as his wife? And how long would her tenure last? He seemed to think it was his bounden duty to keep an eye on her while she was carrying his baby but he could well be planning on divorcing her straight after the birth. For all she knew he had already worked out the legal ins and outs of such timing.

He had never accepted her as his wife. Could she blame him for that? He had never asked her to be his wife and live with him and he had certainly not invited her to conceive his baby! It was important that she faced facts and the facts were painful, she conceded miserably. Roel felt trapped. Roel preferred his freedom.

If she sunk her pride all over again and was truly humble until things settled down, what was the most she could hope to receive from the guy she adored? That he would bed her again when he felt like sex? Throw her the odd piece of very expensive jewellery when she performed really well between the sheets? And would he always be rubbing her nose in her mistakes? Making her feel small and cheap and like nothing? Was she really prepared to let that happen?

CHAPTER TEN

THE FOLLOWING MORNING, Roel took Hilary to see a consultant gynaecologist.

Roel disconcerted Hilary by asking loads of complex questions. The gynaecologist was delighted to answer him with a great deal of scientific detail. Hilary felt like a womb on legs. She was hurt that Roel felt able to reveal his first show of interest in their baby to a third party but not to her. Then she wondered dismally if he had simply been putting on an act for the sake of appearances.

In the three endless days that followed, Hilary became more and more unhappy. Roel was heading in to the Sabatino Bank practically before the sun came up and returning late in the evening. He did not eat a single meal with her, nor was he making the smallest effort to ease the tension between them. But he phoned her twice a day to ask how she was. That seemed to be about as intimate as he was prepared to get for the communicating door between their bedrooms remained rigidly closed. His frigid politeness chilled her.

On the fourth morning she got up at the crack of dawn. After a sleepy shower and a hurried effort to make herself presentable without either looking suspiciously overdressed or unsuitably sexy, she hurried downstairs to the dining room to join Roel for breakfast.

Lean, strong face taut, Roel studied her with frowning force. 'What are you doing up at this hour?'

'I wanted to see you. It was either breakfast…or a forbidden interruption to your working day.' A determined smile on her soft tense mouth as she attempted to make that weak joke, she looked at him hopefully.

Stunning dark golden eyes rested on her kimono-style dressing gown and his wide, sensual mouth took on an almost infinitesimal curl. Made of the finest silk, the garment covered her from throat to toe with a modesty that he considered highly deceptive. Her tiny waist was defined not just by the wide sash but also by the glorious contrast of the burgeoning swell of her lush breasts above and the ripe sweet curve of her hips below. He set down his coffee cup with a jarring rattle. Hilary helped herself to toast from the buffet table, her heart pounding like a drum. She was tormentingly aware of his intent scrutiny and of the sizzling tension in the atmosphere.

'I…' The tip of her tongue snaked out in a nervous flicker to moisten her lips as she turned back to face him and mustered the courage to rise above her pride and not count the cost. 'I'll miss you—'

'*Dannazione!* I don't want to hear it!' Tossing aside his morning paper, Roel sprang upright. Scorching angry derision fired his scrutiny and she gazed back at him wide-eyed, her lips parted in complete disconcertion.

'I'm not falling for it. Not even if you clamber on the table and dance like Salome! Been there, done that, don't require the postcard as a reminder when we'll be inundated with christening mugs in a few months' time!' Roel launched at her with withering bite. 'When I want you, I'll let you know.'

Tears of angry humiliation prickled at the back of her eyes. She listened to the limo drive off. Right, well that was that, then. He could get stuffed, she thought in an agony of swelling emotion. He needn't think he could get away with treating her like some slut who would do anything to get him back into bed! She should never have accompanied him back from Sardinia. That had been a crucial miscalculation. He had made his contempt clear and she had been too much of a drip to accept that their marriage, such as it had been, was over.

But before she left Switzerland pride demanded that she clear her own name and made Roel see just how wrong he had been about her. Pacing up and down her bedroom, she decided that there was really only one way of achieving that end. She would have a proper legal agreement drawn up that would prove once and for all that she had no mercenary intentions. Furthermore she knew just the guy to approach. Paul Correro would be overjoyed to see her sign away all right to the Sabatino billions and she would leave Switzerland with her dignity intact.

When she arrived at the lawyer's smart offices later that morning, she was ushered straight in to his presence. She was surprised that Paul was able to see her immediately and initially taken aback when he greeted her with an anxious look and actually thanked her very much for coming.

'Anya wanted to visit you and Roel and apologise but I fouled up to such an extent with you that I thought it would be wiser to let the dust settle first,' the blonde man confessed heavily. 'I threatened you and I frightened you. Believe me, that is not how I usually treat women—'

'I'm sure it's not,' Hilary said soothingly.

'When Roel realised that it was my fault that you had disappeared into thin air, he hit the roof and I don't blame him—'

'That wasn't your fault—'

'Don't try to make me feel better,' Paul groaned. 'I interfered in something that I should have stayed well back from. In retrospect it was obvious that there was a whole dimension to your relationship with Roel that I knew nothing about. But I went galloping in arrogantly convinced I was coming to his rescue. Roel needing rescue?' He loosed an embarrassed laugh. *'As if...'*

'Wires got crossed. That's all. It's all over and done with now. Actually I came to see you today about something entirely different,' Hilary confided, striving to mask her unhappiness with a façade of calm. 'I need a lawyer to write up some legal stuff for me and to do it fairly quickly.'

When she gave a brief outline of her requirements, Paul could not conceal his dismay. 'A document of that nature would present me with a conflict of interests. I can't represent you and Roel. You need independent legal advice.'

Stiff with discomfiture, Hilary got up from her chair. 'OK.'

'Off the record...' Paul Correro hesitated and then pressed on with open concern. 'As a friend, and I would hope that some day you will be able to regard me in that light, I would advise you against following this route. I'm very much afraid that Roel might misunderstand your motives and be hurt.'

On the drive back to the town house, Hilary conceded that Paul was a very nice bloke. He was the polar opposite of Roel and therefore totally incapable of appreciating how a male of Roel's ice-cold intellect and emotional reserve operated. No matter how hard she tried she could not think of Roel and the concept of hurt in the same statement. In her opinion, Roel had shown himself inviolable. She was the one who kept on getting hurt.

Now she was asking herself why she had decided to go to such elaborate lengths to disprove Roel's conviction that she was a gold-digger in the first place. Why did she still care? He didn't love her. He thought the very worst of her. Even the sight of her at his breakfast table offended him. It was hard to believe that just a few days ago she had been so happy with him. Even harder to accept that she had believed this was a rough patch that they could survive.

The trouble was that, when it came to Roel Sabatino, she had always been willing to settle for too little. And, deservedly, too little was what she had received. There came a time, though, when she had to be mature enough to stand up for herself, take account of her own needs and bow out of a destructive relationship.

Roel would never tell Emma the truth about their marriage. Indeed, she marvelled that she had ever swallowed that outrageous threat whole. Although he did his utmost to hide it, Roel was very honourable, but he would never parade that reality because he saw it as a weakness. Perhaps she had seized on that threat as an excuse to be with Roel when she'd been desperate to have that excuse. But now it was over and she was lifting her pride back out of the closet where she had hidden it. He was an unhealthy addiction and it was time she got over him.

The car phone buzzed. It was Roel and the very sound of his rich, dark, accented drawl was sufficient to tip her teeming emotions over the edge. 'Please don't ask me how I'm feeling because I know you don't really care,' she heard herself condemn. 'I'm leaving you and I hope that you and your precious money live happily ever after!'

She sent the phone crashing down and trembled, shaken by what had erupted from her own lips. But it was the truth and he had deserved to hear it. He had flung her love back in her teeth for the last time. She was going to pour all her love over their child instead. The phone buzzed. She ignored it. Her mobile phone sounded out its tune and she switched it off. There was nothing more to say.

Half an hour later she was in her bedroom packing when the door crashed back on its hinges and framed Roel. 'You *can't* leave... I can't go through that again!' he swore with vehement force.

Caught unprepared by that turbulent entrance that was so uncharacteristic of the calm, controlled male she knew, Hilary stared at him. He was ashen, his proud cheekbones tight with tension. Fierce dark eyes locked to her. 'Have you any idea what it was like for me the last time?' he demanded. 'Don't you know what I went through?'

Numb in the face of a display of more emotion than he had ever shown her he possessed, Hilary shook her head slowly in dumb negative.

'*Santo cielo!* That first week before I regained my memories just about killed me. One minute you were there and the next you were gone and I hadn't a clue why. You walked out on our marriage and left me a four-line-long apology like you'd cancelled a dinner date,' he breathed in raw wonderment. 'It was unreal. I didn't even know where to find you. I almost went out of my mind with worry!'

Hilary was aghast at what he was telling her. 'I never thought… I didn't even suspect that you would feel like that—'

'It *should* have been you who told me the truth about our marriage.'

Recognising the justness of that censure, she hung her head. She had been a coward and she had made excuses for herself. But what all those excuses came down to in the end was the simple fact that she had chosen to save face at his expense. How too could she have been so insensitive that she had not foreseen how her disappearance would affect him?

'I had complete trust in you.' Roel ensnared her troubled gaze when she would have evaded his scrutiny. 'Admittedly that was my only option at first. But our relationship developed fast and I let my guard down with you. I believed we were a couple. I learned to think of you as my wife. Then it all blew up in my face.'

Hilary's throat ached. Ever since he had brought her back from London she had refused to consider how much her own behaviour must have contributed to his angry and cynical distrust. She was ashamed. 'I must have seemed very selfish to you…but I honestly didn't think you'd miss me that much—'

Roel released a humourless shout of laughter. '*Inferno!* What do you think I am? A block of wood?'

'Ice,' she countered unevenly. 'Very self-contained and disciplined and proud of it too.'

His beautiful mouth twisted. 'I was brought up to be strong
and well warned never to make myself vulnerable with a
woman. Their failed marriages embittered my father and my
grandfather. By the time Clemente changed his tune, it was
too late for him to influence me. That was why he made that
insane will. It was his last-ditch attempt to persuade me that if
I would only make the effort and take the risk I could rewrite
family history and end up in a happy marriage.'

'Well...' her nose wrinkled as she fought back the awful
tickle of threatening tears '...so much for that hope but at least
the *castello* is still in the family.'

'I want you to know that I was already on my way home to
see you when Paul contacted me—'

A mortified flush lit her creamy complexion. 'Why do guys
always stick together?'

'Mutual terror?' Roel quipped in a roughened undertone,
level dark golden eyes welded to her. 'When I understood what
sort of agreement you were seeking, I was ashamed. I knew instantly that I had driven you to it.'

Hilary surveyed him with wide, bewildered eyes. 'What is
it with you? Why weren't you pleased? Why would you be
ashamed? I was willing to sign a declaration saying I would
never make a claim on your wealth or anything else you owned!'

'But that would have been wrong because you have every
right to share what I have—'

'It would have shown you once and for all that I don't want
or need anything from you!'

Roel drew in a ragged breath and squared his broad shoulders. 'I accused you of being a gold-digger because that way I
could avoid dealing with how I really felt about you.'

Her brow indented. 'I don't understand.'

'When I had amnesia, I got used to having you around. After

I got my memory back, I was furious with you because you had made one hell of a fool of me!'

That frank condemnation leeched colour from below Hilary's skin. 'That wasn't my intention and it isn't how I see what happened between us,' she protested.

'But it changed everything. You'd fooled me successfully and I had no confidence in my own ability to read you after that.' Savage tension emanating from his lithe, powerful frame, Roel swung away from her. 'But no matter how great my distrust of you was, I still wanted you back and *not* only because the sex was dynamite.'

Hilary perked up at that promising confession. 'But you were quite happy for me to think that it was just that.'

His bold bronzed profile clenched as she put him on the spot yet again. 'I was covering up... I was—' He bit off whatever he had been about to say and raised and dropped a broad shoulder in visible frustration. 'I was...'

'You were...what?' she prompted.

'Scared! *OK?*' He shot that reluctant admission at her as if she had turned a gun on him. 'I was scared. I was feeling stuff I'd never felt before and it spooked me. But even by the time we arrived in Sardinia I had simmered down. I was relaxing and beginning to trust you again...'

Hilary opened dry lips. 'Then I admitted I was pregnant—'

'Once again you'd been secretive. If only you had shared that news with me immediately. All that week we had been together and we had been closer than I had ever been with any woman but, throughout it, you'd been hiding the fact that you were carrying our child. That hit me hard, made me wonder what else you might be hiding,' he confessed heavily.

'I was afraid of how you'd react.' But her attempt to defend herself was half-hearted for she could now see that keeping Roel in the dark about her pregnancy had damaged his view of her all over again.

His stunning dark golden eyes held her strained gaze levelly.

'I needed you to be honest. You weren't and I had lost faith in my own judgement. From that point on, everything went haywire—'

'*You*...went haywire,' Hilary slotted in unhappily. 'But I'm not holding that against you. It's not a hanging offence if you don't want a baby you didn't plan to have with me—'

'I *do* want our baby very much. But I was afraid that you were taking me for another ride,' Roel breathed with suppressed savagery. 'I've been at war with myself ever since. Although I was determined to hang onto both of you I hated the idea that you might stay with me solely because you were expecting my child. Does that sound crazy to you?'

'No... I felt the same way,' she muttered ruefully.

'I was trying so hard to stay in control that I went off the rails...' Roel spread lean brown hands in a gesture that denoted honest remorse, dark colour accentuating his hard, handsome features. 'I ended up accusing you of things I didn't even believe. I *knew* the baby was mine but I didn't want you to suspect that you had hurt me again, so I decided to hurt first.'

In receipt of that surprising admission, Hilary listened with even greater concentration. She had hurt him? Had he really said those words?

'I've been fighting what I feel for you ever since and I can't do it any more,' Roel confided hoarsely. 'I've been trying to work up a resistance to you—'

'I'm not a disease...' Hilary whispered.

'Not seeing you was the only thing that worked. Then you came down in that kimono thing for breakfast *and*... I realised I was failing badly in the resistance stakes—'

'You were offensive—'

'I'm sorry. I was angry with myself, not with you. I was furious that I could not control my desire for you. I took refuge in sarcasm. It's an unfortunate defence mechanism.'

'It was the last straw—'

'It won't happen again,' Roel intoned urgently. 'I'm new at

all this and it's not easy. Do you think you could give me another chance?'

Her eyes misted over and she shook her head, too worked up to manage a verbal negative.

Roel reached for her clenched hands. *'Please...'*

Again she shook her head. 'I don't want a guy who's just making the best of things with me,' she confided on the back of a sob. 'Or a husband who thinks I'm so much of a second-class citizen he has to fight even fancying me—'

'It's not like that. If it were only sex, I wouldn't have messed up to this extent. I'm at home with sex...it's all this other stuff I'm useless with. Don't you realise how much you mean to me?' Roel held fast to her hands, brilliant dark eyes pinned to her with fierce appeal. 'You said it in Sardinia. You said I was perfectly happy living in your fantasy fairy-tale marriage. You were right...in fact I have never been happier.'

Hilary was so shaken by that admission she gaped at him.

'So possibly you can imagine how I felt when the fairy tale turned out to be a fantasy. I had thought you loved me. I had learned to like that idea—'

'Really?' Her voice came out all squeaky.

'I fell in love with you. But I've never been in love before and, unfortunately, I didn't recognise what was wrong with me—'

'What was *right* with you,' Hilary corrected with helpless stress, hanging eagerly on his every word.

'Well, it didn't feel right at the start,' Roel asserted feelingly. 'You were coming between me and work...'

'Oh, dear...' she said chokily. 'Do I really?'

Roel looked very grave. 'Sometimes my mind wanders to you even in important meetings.'

'That's more than I ever hoped for.' Unashamed tears in her eyes, Hilary slid her arms up round his neck. 'I love you too. I love you so much and I'm going to make you very, very happy.'

He crushed her into an emotional embrace that spoke far louder than any words could have done. For a long time they just stood there wrapped tight in each other's arms, each of them savouring that closeness that they had both feared was gone for ever.

'You make me feel good, *amata mia*,' he muttered a shade gruffly.

'You see—loving me is not all bad news,' she said warmly.

'It is when you keep on disappearing and threatening to leave me,' Roel disagreed.

'I won't ever disappear again and I will never—no matter *how* mad you make me—threaten to leave you again,' she promised solemnly.

He bent his handsome dark head and stole a single, almost unbearably tender kiss that made her entire being light up with loving feelings. His lustrous golden eyes clung to her upturned face. 'I think on some level I knew four years ago that you could be very dangerous to the single lifestyle I cherished, *cara mia*.'

'I was a bit immature for you then. But I did fall for you the first time I saw you.'

'I never admitted it even to myself but I was very strongly attracted to you. That's why I kept on coming back to the salon where you worked.' He kissed her again and her eyes slid dreamily shut. 'Once we'd been through that wedding ceremony, though, I couldn't trust myself anywhere near you—'

'Seriously?'

'Seriously. Marrying you put you off limits but I've been carrying your photograph in my wallet for four years,' Roel murmured ruefully.

Big grey eyes opened wide to take full appreciative note of his discomfiture. She glowed with pleasure.

His lean, intelligent face tender, he looked down at her with immense appreciation. 'I'd love to see you wearing a wedding dress for me. We need to make more of the occasion. We should renew our vows and have our marriage blessed.'

'I'd love that…' she muttered, touched to the heart. 'But you'll have to wait until after the baby's born.'

'Nonsense,' Roel contradicted without hesitation.

Eleven months later, Hilary and Roel renewed their vows in the atmospheric little chapel only a mile from the Castello Sabatino.

Hilary carried yellow roses and wore a beautiful boned brocade bodice teamed with a frothy skirt. The happy couple only had eyes for each other. A superb meal and a lively party followed the ceremony. Her two closest friends, Pippa and Tabby, attended with their husbands, Andreo and Christien. Paul and Anya Correro shared the top table, for over the past year Anya and Hilary had forged as good a friendship as their respective husbands now enjoyed. Her sister, Emma, was also present. The guest of honour was indisputably Pietro, the smallest and newest member of the Sabatino family. But being barely three months old and quite unimpressed by the festivities, he slept through most of the day.

Later that evening, Hilary settled her baby into his cot in the beautiful nursery, which she had had great fun furnishing for his occupation. Her son had his father's black hair and an adorable smile that ensured he got loads of attention. In that she reckoned he was rather like his father as well.

She found it hard to credit that she and Roel had almost reached their first unofficial anniversary and she smiled to herself, relishing her own sense of security and contentment. They spent a lot of time at the *castello* where the slower pace of life was more relaxing. Roel had started travelling less during her pregnancy and he spoilt her like mad.

'Gorgeous…' Roel pronounced huskily from several feet away.

Hilary bestowed a proud look upon their sleeping son. 'I know he's ours but he really is a good-looking baby, isn't he?'

Roel closed his arms slowly round his wife and turned her to face him. 'It wasn't Pietro I was referring to, *amata mia.*'

'No?' Looking up into his darkly handsome features and the sensual appreciation in his golden eyes, she felt her heartbeat quicken and her mouth ran dry.

'You looked incredibly beautiful today. I was so proud that you are my wife.' His dark, deep drawl exuded unashamed satisfaction. 'Do you realise that this is the equivalent of the wedding night we never had?'

Her knees felt weak and she leant up against him, shamelessly angling for the intoxicating heat of his mouth on hers. With a sexy groan of masculine compliance he kissed her before he carried her down the corridor into their bedroom.

'Still love me?' she whispered, breathless with excitement.

His charismatic smile flashed over her with the special warmth that was hers alone. 'I love you more every day.'

Joy in her heart, she matched those loving words and, lacing her arms round him, she drew him down to her.

* * * * *

Keep reading for an excerpt of
The Lawman's Romance Lesson
by Marie Ferrarella.
Find it in the
Autumn Blockbuster 2024 anthology,
out now!

PROLOGUE

THE EVENINGS WERE the hardest for Shania. Somehow, the darkness outside seemed to intensify the silence and the feeling of being alone within the small house she used to occupy with her cousin.

Before she and Wynona had returned to Forever, Texas, the little town located just outside of the Navajo reservation where they had both been born, noise had been a constant part of their lives.

Joyful noise.

Noise that signified activity.

The kind of noise that could be associated with living in a college dorm. And before that, when they had lived in their great-aunt Naomi's house, there had still been noise, the kind of noise that came from being totally involved with life. Their great-aunt was a skilled surgeon and physician who was completely devoted to her work.

Because Naomi volunteered at a free clinic at least a couple of days a week as well as being associated with one of the local hospitals, patients would turn up on their doorstep at all sorts of hours. When she and Wynona grew older, Aunt Naomi thought nothing of having both of them pitch in and help out with her patients. She wanted them to learn how to provide proper care.

Between the volunteer work and their schooling, there was never any sort of downtime, never any time to sit back, much less be bored.

She and Wynona had welcomed being useful and mentally stimulated because that was such a contrast to the lives they had initially been born into. Born on the Navajo reservation to mothers who were sisters, Shania and Wynona spent their childhoods together. They were closer than actual sisters, especially after Wynona lost her mother. She'd never known her father. Shania's parents took her in to live with them without any hesitation.

Shania herself had been thrilled to share her parents with her cousin, but unfortunately, that situation didn't last very long. Nine months after Wynona had come to live with them, Shania's father was killed in an auto accident. And then less than six months later, her mother died of pneumonia.

At the ages of ten and eleven, Wynona and Shania found themselves both orphaned.

The girls were facing foster care, which ultimately meant being swallowed up by the social services system. Just before they were to be shipped off, their great-aunt Naomi, who had been notified by an anonymous party, suddenly swooped into town. In the blink of an eye, the strong-willed woman managed to cut through all manner of red tape and whisked them back to her home in Houston.

And after that, everything changed.

Shania and her cousin were no longer dealing with an uncertain future. Aunt Naomi gave them a home and she gave them responsibilities as well, never wanting them to take anything for granted. They quickly discovered that their great-aunt was a great believer in helping those in need. Naomi made sure to instill a desire to "pay it forward" within them.

They had found that their great-aunt was a stern woman, but there had never been a question that the woman loved them and would be there for them if they should ever need her.

Shania sighed and pushed aside her plate, leaving the food all but untouched. Having taken leftovers out of the refrigerator, she hadn't bothered to warm them up before she'd brought them over to the table. She could almost hear Aunt Naomi's voice telling her, *If you're going to eat leftovers, do it properly. Warm them up first.*

Shania frowned at the plate. She really wasn't hungry.

What she was hungry for wasn't food but the discussions they used to have around the dinner table when Aunt Naomi, Wynona and she would all talk about their day. Aunt Naomi never made it seem as if hers was more important even though they all knew that she made such a huge difference in the lives she touched. Each person, each life, Aunt Naomi had maintained, was important in its own way.

When she and Wynona had moved back to Forever, armed with their teaching degrees and determined to give back to the community, for the most part those discussions continued. She and her cousin had been excited about the difference they were going to make, especially since both the local elementary school and high school, for practicality purposes, were now comprised of students who came not only from the town but also from the reservation. The aim was to improve the quality of education rendered to all the students.

But there were times, like tonight, when the effects of that excitement slipped into the shadows and allowed the loneliness to rear its head and take over. Part of the reason for that was because she now lived alone here. Wynona had gotten married recently and while Shania was thrilled beyond words for her cousin, she had no one to talk to, no one to carry on any sort of a dialogue with.

At least, not anyone human.

There was, of course, still Belle.

Just as she got up to go into her den to work on tomorrow's lesson plan, Belle seemed to materialize and stepped into her path. The German shepherd looked up at her with her big, soulful brown eyes.

"You miss her too, don't you, Belle?" Shania murmured to the dog that she and Wynona had found foraging through a garbage pail behind the Murphy brothers' saloon the first week they moved back. After determining that the dog had no owner, they immediately rescued the rail-thin shepherd and took her in.

Belle thrived under their care. When Wynona got married, Shania had told her cousin to take the dog with her. But Wynona had declined, saying that she felt better about leaving if Belle stayed with her.

Belle rubbed her head against Shania's thigh now, then stopped for a moment and looked up.

"Message received," Shania told the German shepherd with a smile. "You're right. I'm not alone. You're here. But there are times that I really wish you could talk."

As if on cue, Belle barked, something, as a rule, she rarely did. It was as if Belle didn't like to call attention to herself unless absolutely necessary.

"You're right. I shouldn't be feeling sorry for myself, I should be feeling happy for Wyn." Dropping down beside the German shepherd, Shania ran her hands along the dog's head and back, petting the animal. "You really are brighter than most people, girl," she laughed.

As if in agreement, Belle began licking her face.

And just like that, the loneliness Shania had been wrestling with slipped away.

NEW RELEASES!

**Four sisters. One surprise will.
One year to wed.**

Don't miss these two volumes of
Wed In The Outback!

When Holt Waverly leaves his flourishing outback estate
to his four daughters, it comes to pass that without an
eldest son to inherit, the farm will be entailed to someone
else…unless all his daughters are married within the year!

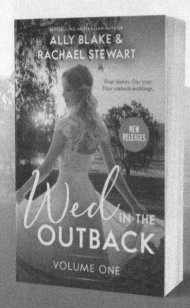

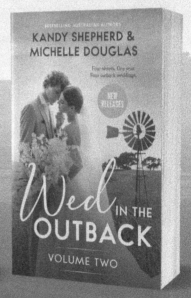

May 2024

July 2024

Subscribe and fall in love with a Mills & Boon series today!

You'll be among the first to read stories delivered to your door monthly and enjoy great savings.

WE
SIMPLY
LOVE
ROMANCE